CAST UP BY THE SEA !

CAST UP BY THE SEA

BY

VICTOR HUGO

Fredonia Books
Amsterdam, The Netherlands

Cast Up by the Sea

by
Victor Hugo

ISBN: 1-58963-235-4

Reprinted from the original edition

Fredonia Books
Amsterdam, The Netherlands
http://www.fredoniabooks.com

In order to make original editions of historical works available to scholars at an economical price, this facsimile of the original edition is reproduced from the best available copy and has been digitally enhanced to improve legibility, but the text remains unaltered to retain historical authenticity.

DEDICATION.

Since the publication of " Albert N'yanza " and the " Nile Tributaries of Abyssinia," 1 have received numerous letters from boys to whom I was entirely unknown, and who are at this moment unknown to me except through their spontaneous correspondence. Their letters were written in the youthful enthusiasm of the moment, when, having shared in the excitement of our African journeys, they had closed the book, and, full of sympathy, they wrote to me effusions which I prize as the outburst of boyish admiration for a successful struggle with difficulties.

As a proof of the value that I attach to these warm expressions of interest taken by the young in our past adventures, I now dedicate to all boys (from eight years old to eighty) a story of fiction, combined with certain facts, that will, I trust, relieve the dreariness of a long Christmas evening.

At the same time that I have endeavored to avoid all improbabilities, I must apologize for having taken an astronomical liberty in producing an eclipse of the sun which is not in the almanac.

S. W. BAKER.

LIST OF ILLUSTRATIONS.

CAST UP BY THE SEA

CAST UP BY THE SEA.

CHAPTER I.

SANDY COVE.

ON the rugged coast of Cornwall, where the waves of the Atlantic break in their rudest force against the inhospitable cliffs, there stood in the year 1791 a small fishing village.

This hamlet was hardly worthy of the name, as it consisted of merely two or three clusters of huts, chiefly formed of decayed vessels which, no longer sea-worthy, had been sawed in halves and inverted; thus their well-tarred bottoms became the roofs to protect the occupants, who in former days had navigated their dwellings in the double capacity of fishermen and smugglers.

The spot was well chosen. In the rough wall of precipices which rose from the water's edge to the height of several hundred feet there was a sudden break, and a narrow cleft in the face of the cliff of about fifty yards width opened into an inclosed bay so completely land-locked as to form a natural harbor of exceedingly small dimensions, the entire diameter of the horseshoe form being within two hundred yards in width.

This bay, surrounded by lofty, precipitous cliffs, formed an amphitheater excluded from the rest of the world, as its very existence would be unknown to a stranger until he suddenly approached the verge, and observed the calm basin below, with the sea horizon beyond the narrow gap that formed the entrance to the bay. At low tide the sand was exposed for a considerable extent, while at high water the waves rippled upon the shingly beach, upon which were arranged the boats belonging to the villagers, while fishing-nets with crab and lobster-pots were stretched upon the stones to dry.

Strewed upon the beach in all directions was an ominous amount of ship timber, the fragments of wrecks that had been washed into the bay; while staves of casks, wooden hoops, and remains of broken cases attested the loss of ship and cargo that had been driven on this fatal shore. Among the numerous casualties upon that portion of the Cornish coast few shipwrecked persons survived to tell their tale. There was no landing-place for many miles along the shore but Sandy Cove, except at low water during calm weather, when certain exposed points that had been worn away by the waves afforded a rough beach of broken crags that had fallen from the cliffs above. These slippery rocks, covered with long sea-weed, were often the hopeless refuge of the strong swimmer, who had struggled with the storm only to be dashed to pieces against the cruel shore that refused him shelter. It was reported vaguely that the inhabitants of this pitiless coast were equally inhospitable, and that the fishermen of Sandy Cove combined the professions of smugglers and wreckers with their more honorable occupation.

The huts or cabins that composed the village might have amounted to twenty. These were erected in various localities, without any regard to arrangement, in such positions as were most favorable—generally about fifty feet above high-water mark—upon the level plateaus that had been formed by the detachment of portions of the cliff. Upon these narrow terraces the boat cabins were built directly against the abrupt face of the wall-like rock that rose for several hundred feet above them, while the tiny gardens that faced each hut were fenced with the remnants of ship timber that was the principal feature of the locality. Many of these gardens showed the care and taste of the owners; and the bright flowers that bloomed in that warm and sheltered nook contrasted strangely with the plain black cabins of inverted boats that formed the rude dwellings of the fishermen.

Before these huts were high forked sticks whitened by long use, upon which were stretched the drying lines, whence dangled in the breeze the dark-blue Guernsey frocks, checked shirts, and gray stockings of the men, with blue petticoats distended by the wind, and square, queer-shaped shifts that evidently belonged to the females of the establishment.

So completely were the dwellers sheltered and concealed

by the high cliffs above that a stone might have been dropped perpendicularly upon the roofs, and the only approach from the higher ground was by zigzag paths winding down the rocks to the beach below.

Only one exception to the rule of general concealment showed that the coast was inhabited. About two hundred feet above the bay, but sheltered by the still higher cliff at the back, there stood upon a natural terrace a neat cottage formed of clay, built up with portions of wreck, the whole whitewashed, excepting the timber-work that was carefully blackened with a coating of pitch. The garden which fronted the dwelling was luxuriant in dense bushes of myrtle, while sweet verbena ornamented the walls of the cottage, at the back of which the red marble cliffs rose about a hundred feet to the summit. There was no approach from the higher ground, but it was necessary to ascend from the village below by a winding path hewn out from the rough face of the cliff.

From this lofty point the sea view overlooked the entrance to the bay with an unbroken line of horizon, while from the low wall of stone that bordered the narrow garden was a bird's-eye view of the little harbor beneath, in which were lying at anchor several small fishing-boats, but above all a smart-looking lugger of about forty tons. This vessel was said to be a trawler, and was called the " Polly."

It was a sultry night in August. The day had been oppressive; it was a dead calm upon the sea, and, as the sun had sunk, a yellowish glare of haze had obscured the horizon, while long thin streaks of fleecy clouds, tinged with vermilion with the sun's last rays, turned ominously black when the bright light faded. The swallows had been flying so low as to merely skim the ground, and the sea-gulls had been screaming in a wild manner as they followed the shoals of porpoises that chased the mackerel at the entrance of the bay. For some weeks no rain had fallen, and unusual heat had parched the country. Such was the sunset of the 19th of August, 1791: the sea and atmosphere were so mingled together that, in the dull twilight, nothing could be distinguished on the surface; but an unnatural stillness pervaded the darkening scene.

At this time a strange figure sat upon the low garden-wall that overlooked the sea, and, apparently motionless, strove to pierce the mysterious haze that shrouded the horizon. At the first sight it would have been difficult to determine the sex, but a closer examination showed it to be a female. She sat at that giddy height crouched and balanced upon the unstable wall, with her knees close to her thin and scantily bearded chin, while, to steady her position, she tightly clutched her ankles with her long and wiry hands. She wore neither shoes nor stockings. A ragged petticoat of blue serge, with a long jacket of the same coarse material, formed the whole of her clothing, while an old sailor's oilskin cap, known as a " sou'-wester," covered her head, and descended to her gaunt shoulders. It would have been impossible to have guessed her age—she might have been seventy or ninety; her hair was white, and fell in long grizzled locks that had been uncombed for years; her face was weather-beaten and brown, but so wrinkled and cadaverous as to resemble nothing earthly, and a long, sharp, hooked nose descended to a level with her thin, compressed lips. In the dead stillness of the evening this ill-omened figure gazed intently upon the dark sea. Presently she muttered: " Sou'-west! sou'-west! luck comes from the sou'-west—fog on the sea, and fire on the cliff! Ha, ha! ha, ha! The storm's a-coming."

The darkness increased until the figure of the old hag first dwindled to a shadow and was soon utterly obscured, her presence in the same spot being only revealed by a low, guttural rattle or chuckle at every increased moan of the wind, which now rose at intervals, although the air was still death-like calm.

At this moment a light shone from the window of the cottage about twenty paces distant.

The interior of this cottage was a combination of neatness and disorder; fishing-nets were hung from beams in the ceiling, spare corks and leads for nets were strung upon ropes and hung in festoons upon various hooks upon the walls, while oars and boat-hooks were arranged across the beams, upon which planks were fitted to form a loft: upon these were piled a variety of objects in great confusion. The floor was paved with red brick strewn with white sand; the lattice windows were ornamented with geraniums in pots brightened with red lead, and the mantel-piece was arranged with shells: in the center stood a large wooden clock, above which hung a print in a black frame of King George the Third. There were several prints of vessels hanging on the walls; but there was one that was in a superior frame, as though of more importance: this was a lugger in full sail with a spanking breeze, beneath which was written in gold letters, " The Polly—forty tons." On either side of this were hung a brace of ship pistols and a cutlass, while half a dozen muskets were ranged above the fire-place.

The cottage consisted of a bedroom and sitting-room, with a small back kitchen, one wall of which was formed by the cliff against which the dwelling was erected. The clock struck.

" What o'clock's that?" inquired the man from the inner room; " nine or ten?"

" I hardly listened," said a sweet woman's voice; " for I am too sad to think of time, but I see it is already ten."

At this moment a fine-looking seaman entered the room, and, approaching the table at which the last speaker was sitting, he drew his chair to her side.

" Don't be cast down, Polly, my girl," he exclaimed, in a rough but sympathizing tone; " it's a bad job, but it can't be helped. Cheer up! Sobbing won't bring him back again; we must bear the loss and wait for better luck; he's saved from many a rough night, poor child!"

This attempt at comfort, far from giving consolation, produced a burst of tears, and the lovely girl to whom the words were addressed buried her face in her hands, and gave way to unrestrained emotion as she bowed her head upon a much-worn old family Bible that lay open before her.

Mary, or, as she was commonly called, Polly Grey, was the young wife of the manly specimen of a British sailor who now, sitting by her side, vainly sought to soothe her affliction. She was the only daughter of a respectable farmer in the neighborhood, and she had been nearly a year married to Paul Grey, the happy and much-envied husband whose frank, straightforward manner and handsome person had won the prize that had been sought by many of greater wealth and position.

Polly Grey was a fair sample of an English rustic beauty; of middle height, finely, but vigorously formed, a lovely complexion, with large, deep-blue eyes, and rich blonde hair that, when released from the simple but neatly twisted coil, fell in heavy masses far below her waist. She was now in her twenty-first year; she had been the happiest of the happy since her wedding-day. Two months ago she had first known the joy that a mother alone can feel, when she pressed a lovely child to her heart. The scene had changed; she was now in black; hardly a week had passed since her first hope was shattered, and the child upon which all her joys had centered had ceased to live. That first grief pressed heavily upon her. Till now her life had been all sunshine; a husband that she loved, her infant boy in the image of his father; but hardly had he learned to smile upon her when he died. "Why was he born if only to die? Why was he given if only to be taken away? Why was she a mother if only to be a mourner?" These were the thoughts that added to her sorrow, and vainly the young mother turned to her Bible for consolation. She could not unravel the mystery, she could only feel her loss.

Paul Grey, although a warm-hearted man, had been too much accustomed to the rude chances of his life to allow this domestic sorrow to oppress him. Two days ago he had carried the little coffin to the grave, and as the father's tears fell upon the spot, so they were the last he shed, and with a sailor's curt philosophy he had consoled himself and strove to console his wife with the idea of "better luck next time."

At this time Paul was about twenty-eight years of age, but the rough life of a sailor had so bronzed his features that he appeared somewhat older; he was remarkably handsome, and considerably above the middle height, but his herculean width of shoulders reduced his appearance to that of a man of five feet ten. When the heart of Mary Dale was won, and she became Polly Grey, Paul had not only put his cottage in order to receive his young bride, but he had also invested the whole of his ready cash, and had even borrowed money, to complete the new lugger which now lay anchored in the bay. This vessel was the darling of his heart, and next to his wife it shared his affection; therefore the new boat had been christened the "Polly," under which beloved name it formed a member of the family. There was no smarter craft on the Cornish coast; neither was there a better or more lovely wife than Polly Grey.

Now, although the "Polly" had been afloat no longer than a year, she had already gained a great reputation;

but mingled with the reports of her good qualities as a sea-boat there were vague rumors that were connected with her mysterious disappearance and rapid return voyages which raised the suspicions of the coast-guard; and in the public-houses of the neighboring village, about five miles distant, it was more than insinuated by jealous fishermen that the "Polly" was a smuggler, and no trawler. At the time I describe, the occupation of wrecking or of plundering the cargo of vessels that had perished on the coast was by no means considered unworthy of the Cornish fishermen; and in those days smuggling was regarded in no unfavorable light by the amphibious inhabitants of the southern shore, but the profession was considered more honorable than otherwise, provided that it could be prosecuted without discovery; even should the smuggler be apprehended by the authorities, the sympathy of the coast inhabitants sided with the offender. Certainly the fishermen of Sandy Cove deserved the reputation that had been earned by successful enterprise both in wrecking and in contraband adventures, but how far Paul Grey was connected personally with such acts was a matter of simple suspicion. The "Polly" belonged to him, but the crew of the vessel were natives of Sandy Cove; and such was his influence, and the general respect in which he was held, that few of the revenue officers would have ventured to insult his dwelling by a visit of search. It was currently reported that even among the coast-guard Paul had friends who closed their eyes to the voyages of the "Polly." The station was about six miles distant, and the detachment was commanded by an old school-fellow of Paul's, a lieutenant in the navy, who had lost his left arm in an action with a French frigate. This man, who was known as Captain Smart, had been an unsuccessful admirer of Mary Dale, now Polly Grey; but as an old and honorable friend of his more fortunate rival, he had advanced Paul the sum required for the completion of the "Polly," with no other security than his note of hand for two hundred pounds. This was a private affair, only known to the parties concerned, and the visits of Captain Smart to the neat white cottage of Sandy Cove were equivalent to a certificate of Paul Grey's character. In fact, Captain Smart, or Joe Smart, as Paul familiarly called his old school-fellow, was a true friend; and although his honest heart had, as he described it, "struck hard and well-nigh gone to pieces" when Mary Dale refused him he consoled himself with the fact that she loved his old friend Paul, who had two arms, while he had only one. Joe Smart was well-to-do in the world; he had a permanent appointment in addition to a comfortable independence left him by his father; but he had made up his mind since his first disappointment never to love again. He was an active, resolute-looking sailor, with a peculiarly open expression. He was about two years older than Paul, and on the day that had just closed he had been down to Sandy Cove to ask after the "little sailor," as he termed Paul's child, to whom he was to have been godfather. He had then heard the mournful news, and, seeing the distress of the young mother, he had simply pressed her hand in sympathy, and had hurried back to the coast-guard station, feeling almost as much as though the loss were his own.

The old wooden clock had just struck ten when Paul's rough attempt at comfort was addressed to Polly Grey. They were now sitting at the table, his arm around her waist, while, as her head rested upon his shoulder, he tenderly wiped the tears from her large blue eyes, and warmly kissed her forehead. At this moment there was a hurried tap at the window.

"What's that?" said Polly.

"Only a bird that has flown against the glass attracted by the light," said Paul; but several taps in quick succession drew their attention to the window, against which was pressing the hideous face of the old hag who had been seated as sentry upon the terrace wall; her thin nose was flattened against the glass, and an expression of fierce excitement increased the horror of her appearance.

"Come out," cried the old woman; "there's work to-night. D'ye hear the bell?"

"What is it, mother?" said Paul. "It's coming on to blow, I know, but the 'Polly's" all snug; she's got two anchors down, and she won't hurt in the cove."

In another instant the face disappeared from the window, and the door opening from without, the old woman hobbled into the room.

"Such a night I never saw," said she; "it's black as pitch, and thick fog on the sea, and not a breath of wind except above, where it's moaning like a dying man. It's

the last night for many, but a good night for some. I
heard the bell!"

"What bell, Mother Lee?" inquired Polly Grey; "you
couldn't hear the church-bell under the cliff."

"Ha, ha! the church-bell!" replied the old woman;
"very good, very good! The church-bell! It's tolling
for the dead before they die—the church is at sea, and the
bell's tolling in the fog—the fog-bell's tolling, and the
ship's coming on the shore. It's a good night for some;
the tide's running in. Out with yer, Paul, and get the
first pickings!"

Mother Lee, as the old hag was called, was the widow of
a certain Stephen Lee, who had been hanged about fifty
years before for piracy. Report said that the old woman
had deserved the same fate; but it was certain that as long
as the oldest inhabitant could remember Sandy Cove she
had been the evil genius of the spot. Half-prophetess and
fortune-teller, always promoting evil, she had so worked
upon the superstitions of the people that she was considered to possess more than human power, and to be capable
of producing mischief and calamities through spiritual
agency. Thus Mother Lee subsisted upon charity; she
lived in an old inverted boat, and gathered fuel for the
winter from the pieces of wreck upon the shore. Clothes
she had none, except those cast off by both sexes; those she
adopted without choice, and she usually appeared in a
hybrid attire of male and female. From long practice she
had become so thoroughly acquainted with the tide, cur-
rents, weather, and other local phenomena, that the superstitious fishermen of Sandy Cove thoroughly believed in
her prophecies, and even accredited her with the power of
raising a storm and of drawing a vessel upon the coast. As
the wreck of a ship was considered a blessing to the neighborhood, Mother Lee was an important person in Sandy
Cove, and although feared, and certainly not loved, she
was never refused a request. The only person who disbe-
lieved in Mother Lee was Polly Grey. This had reached
the old woman's ears, and curses that she had muttered in
the village against the young mother were quickly succeeded by the fading away and death of the child. This fact
was generally accepted as a proof of witchcraft.

As has been already mentioned, Paul Grey's garden was
the best spot for a lookout, as commanding the entire sea

view; thus, to the intense dislike of Polly Grey, old Mother
Lee would take her seat like a vulture for hours together
upon the terrace wall, undismayed by the precipice of two
hundred feet that sunk sheer below her to the beach.

There was something horrible in the delight that the old
hag exhibited in the approaching calamity. Paul knew
that she was to be trusted; and, rising from his seat, he
whispered to his wife, who clung to his arm as though
spell-bound by the fixed look of the old woman, and, accompanied by Mother Lee, he opened the door to look at
the night. In the same moment a sudden puff of wind
extinguished the candle, and Polly Grey, left in the dark,
felt chilled to the bone as she heard the coarse chuckle of
the old woman, as she muttered on the threshold, "There's
luck from the sou'-west. There's the bell in the fog!"

Mother Lee was right. Hardly had Paul quitted the
house than the puff of wind that had extinguished the light
was succeeded by a momentary but violent gust. Almost
at the same instant a distant flash of lightning shone hazily
through the foggy darkness. The old woman had vanished. Presently a low roll of thunder was heard, and
again a violent gust of cold air swept along the cliffs
direct from the sea. This was succeeded by a few moments of dead-calm, in which Paul started as the distant
sound of a bell struck distinctly upon his ear. The bell
was on the sea. There could be no doubt that some vessel, obscured in the fog, had been carried out of her course
by the strong current that set toward a rocky point within
half a mile of Sandy Cove, which, stretching far into the
sea, formed a bluff cliff, against which many a good ship
had gone to pieces. The fog-bell was repeatedly sounded,
and, as the breeze came directly toward the land, it could
be heard from a great distance. Paul had concluded that
the vessel was a mile and a half from the shore; in which
case her position was one of great danger, as there could
be no doubt that a severe tempest was about to commence
from the south-west, which would infallibly drive her upon
this dangerous coast. There was not much time for consideration, for the few heavy gusts, that had been succeeded at intervals by unnatural calms, were suddenly followed
by a terrific squall that blew the sand and small pebbles
clattering against the windows, which were now once more
illumined by Polly Grey's rekindled light. A long roll of

thunder sounded like heavy artillery in the distance, but the roar of the wind, and the angry rumble of the waves upon the rocky beach, had so much increased that all other sounds were deadened.

Paul entered his cottage, and quickly closed the door. His wife had been anxiously awaiting his return.

"Where is that dreadful old woman?" asked Polly. "Although I believe in nothing but her wickedness, and despise the superstitions connected with her, I can not help my blood freezing when she glares upon me as she did to-night."

"She's gone," said Paul. "I don't know where, if she's not gone over the cliff by the squall that nearly took me off my legs. But the old woman's right, Polly. There's a vessel in the fog not far from shore, and nothing but a miracle can save her in the gale that's now driving dead upon the coast."

"How dreadful!" replied the kind-hearted wife. "What can we do to save her, Paul? Think of the poor creatures, if wrecked upon this horrible shore! What if we light a fire upon the cliff to give them warning? There may yet be hope!"

Polly Grey had never been at Sandy Cove on the happy occasion of a shipwreck, and she little knew the feelings of the villagers in a moment of such excitement; even Paul, from long experience, had ceased to regard a wreck with the sympathy that such a calamity should awaken, but he accepted it as a natural consequence of bad seamanship that ought to have been avoided.

"You can't save her, Polly; and the people of the cove wouldn't thank you if you could. It isn't often that they get a good turn, and they count a wreck as good luck to the cove if it's bad luck to the ship. But there's no harm in lighting a fire," continued Paul; "it may give her a chance. So help me while I roll out an old tar barrel that lies in the shed. You get an armful of shavings, Polly, and we'll soon have a blaze."

In a few minutes Paul had rolled a large tar barrel to the front of the cottage, and with his wife's assistance he had crammed it full of straw and shavings. "Don't go too near the cliff, Polly," said Paul, as the tremendous force of the gale nearly lifted her off her feet. "Sit down

on that stone by the window, while I get some fire;" and
he quickly returned from the cottage kitchen with a couple
of blazing sticks that he had taken from the hearth. These
he thrust into the interior of the barrel, and in an instant
the strong breeze ignited the inflammable material, and the
flames wrapped around the mouth. In a few minutes the
fire flared to a great height, and brightly illumined the
white cottage and the high cliff behind. Paul brought
fresh fuel in the shape of old staves and pieces of broken
boats, which, being thickly coated with pitch, created an
intense light.

"They'll see that, anyhow," said Paul; "if the fog will
only lift. It can't last long in this gale."

These words were hardly uttered when a bright flash at
sea was shortly followed by the heavy boom of a cannon.

"They've seen the fire," said Polly. "Please God,
they are safe!"

Another gun now sounded from the same quarter.

"They are driving on the rocks," said Paul; "those
guns are signals of distress. Our fire has given them the
warning of the coast. There's no hope except in their
cables and anchors!"

At that moment the fog rose like a curtain, and the moon
that had been obscured shone brightly between the dark
clouds that hurried rapidly across her. The scene was at
once changed, and, the mist having dissolved, there was no
longer any doubt of the position. A fine full-rigged ship
was close-hauled to the wind with double-reefed topsails,
and was endeavoring to clear the coast. No sooner, however, had the fog lifted than those on board at once perceived their hopeless situation as the bright fire showed
them their true distance from the shore; accordingly with
great alacrity two anchors were let drop, and, the ship
swinging head to wind, the sails were quickly taken in,
and the cables were veered out to their full extent. During this time the storm had frightfully increased; the sea
was white with the crests of angry breakers, which dashed
with such violence against the rocks that the roar of water
and rolling shingle almost equaled the thunder that rever-
berated overhead. The ship was now the plaything of the
waves. Tremendous rollers came surging toward the bay,
threatening to beat down the noble vessel beneath their falling crests; but she gallantly rose to each breaker, and,

although the seas swept across her decks, she always recovered herself in time to withstand the shock of the suc-
ceeding wave.

The gale had increased to a hurricane, and, as the
enormous waves dashed against the perpendicular cliffs,
the spray flew a hundred feet above the sea level. The
night was wearing away; it was about two A. M.; and Paul
and his wife had been watching the exciting scene, and
keeping up the fire until the fuel was well·nigh exhausted.

"Go to bed, Polly!" he exclaimed. "Nothing can be
done. If she can hold on till morning the storm may
moderate, or perhaps the wind may change, and if so there
may be a chance of safety."

The fire had burned low, and, as Paul spoke, a shadow
flitted upon the cottage wall, and the low chuckle of Mother
Lee was heard, as she approached the fire, and warmed her
skinny hands.

"Ha, ha!" she muttered; "the luck comes from the
sou'-west. There's no hempen cable that'll stand a Cornish rock. She'll cut before the morning. Get to bed with
yer!" cried the old hag; "and wake fresh for the pickings.
There'll be work for all hands before sunrise."

Horror-struck at the cold-blooded prophecy of Mother
Lee, and glad to escape from her presence, Polly retired to
the cottage, and throwing herself, without undressing, upon
the bed, in spite of her anxiety she fell into a sound sleep,
thoroughly tired out with watching. Paul would not sleep,
but busied himself with preparing ropes for the expected
emergency. In the meantime Mother Lee scraped together
the hot embers, and arranged the few unburned pieces that
remained to restore the fire, over which the old woman
crouched, apparently without heeding the hurricane, which
at every gust swept showers of sparks against the cottage-
wall.

There were many watchers that night in Sandy Cove
who had been aroused by Mother Lee, who had gone her
rounds to the various cottages and prophesied "luck from
the sou'-west."

It was about five o'clock in the morning, and Paul, having first completed his coils of lines, had slept for an hour,
when he was awakened by a sharp knocking at the door.
In another instant it opened, and Mother Lee entered the

room. "Get up with you! get up!" she cried; "one
cable's cut, and a mast has just gone overboard; she won't
last long!"

Paul hurried out, accompanied by his wife, who had hastily thrown her cloak across her shoulders, for the morning
was cold and raw.   "God help them!" exclaimed the kind-
hearted Polly as she first looked upon the terrible scene.
The storm was, if possible, more intense than before; the
ship had changed her position during the night, and had
apparently dragged her anchors; she was now lying about
half a mile from the coast, exactly opposite the entrance to
the little bay of Sandy Cove, which, not being above fifty
yards in width, was unseen and unknown by the crew of
the vessel.   As Mother Lee had already made known, the
rocks had chafed through one of the hempen cables, the
slack end of which now hung loosely in the water, while
the remaining cable was as tight as an iron bar whenever a
tremendous wave struck the bows of the ship.   In those
days chain cables were very rare, and many a vessel and
crew would have been saved from destruction had they been
provided as now with the faithful metal.   When anchored
among sharp-edged rocks it was next to impossible that a
hempen rope should escape the friction.   One rope, as we
have seen, had just parted, therefore the ship swung by a
single cable in a storm that rendered her position hopeless.
She appeared to be an Indiaman of about twelve hundred
tons.   The mizzen-mast had been carried away a few feet
above the deck, and the crew were actively employed in
cutting away the mainmast to lighten the ship, and to
lessen the strain upon the anchor.

The natural feeling of the sailor now burst from Paul.
"Fools!" he exclaimed, as he stamped his foot upon the
ground, and gesticulated vainly to the fated vessel.   "Up
with the jib! Slip the cable, and bring her head to the
shore! Loose the foresail, and run for the mouth of the
bay!"   Alas! they knew nothing of the coast, neither could
they distinguish the narrow entrance in the midst of spray
and white-headed breakers that burst upon the rocks.
Even the little bay, usually so calm, was now a heavy sea,
as every wave, although broken in its force, swept through
the gap and rolled heavily upon the beach.   The " Polly "
rode safely at anchor, with a long cable, and although every
now and then the surf broke over the forecastle, her hatch-

ways were secured, and there was nothing to fear in Sandy Cove for so good a vessel.

The Indiaman was, as usual with that fine class of vessel, exceedingly well-manned; and had the crew been aware of the little harbor that lay concealed so near them, there would have been no difficulty, with good seamanship, in running in and beaching the ship upon Sandy Cove. However, there was no means of communicating with the doomed vessel; and although a harbor of refuge was actually at hand, the axes were plied at both the remaining masts, which presently fell by the board.

Paul was watching these operations with a telescope, and explaining to his eager wife all that passed upon the deck. "They are making a raft with spars," said he; "but it will be of little use among those breakers." After a little pause he continued, "Poor things! There are women and children on board, all clinging to each other on the poop-deck."

"Oh, Paul, dear Paul, can we do nothing to help them?" cried his wife, in intense excitement. "How dreadful for the poor children and mothers!" At this moment her own recent loss awakened in her heart a deep sympathy for those who were shortly to part forever, even before her eyes.

Suddenly Paul lowered the telescope. "The cable's parted!" he shouted; "they're lost!"

At that moment the ship, that had hitherto been lying with her stern toward the shore and her head direct to the wind, leaping over the opposing waves, although almost buried in surf and spray, suddenly altered her position, and her head turning slowly away from the gale she fell into the trough of the sea with her broadside to the wind. A tremendous wave with curling crest came towering toward her, and, hardly rising to meet the shock, the ship merely heeled over, and the terrific wave swept clean across her decks. For an instant nothing was visible but a confused mass of foam and spray, with a dark object in the center; but in a few seconds the hull again appeared. The decks that had been thronged with people were nearly empty; only a few of the strongest men remained hanging on to any rope that offered a secure hold. Another sea struck her, and once more the powerless hulk lay buried. Again she righted, and still fewer people remained upon her decks; she now rolled helplessly on, buried by every sea, and nearly turning bottom upward as each successive wave struck her. The current set rather away from the entrance to Sandy Cove, but the wind being dead on shore she would evidently strike a little on the left of the mouth.

" She'll strike on the Iron Rock before she reaches the shore," said Paul.

This was a black mass that only now and then reared its threatening form above the surface, about three hundred yards from the entrance to the bay, over which the breakers dashed in a tremendous surf. As Paul foretold, the vessel was evidently being driven directly against this rock.

Again Paul searched the wreck with his telescope; she was now within a short distance of the fatal rock. "They're lowering a boat," said Paul; " some women have just come on deck from the cabin. Well done! the boat's lowered, and they are getting the women down. Off she goes! That's right; now pull hard for the mouth of the cove! Keep her straight!—here comes a breaker!—its close together in the stern! Ha! what's that? the tiller broken? My God! she's over!"

A raging breaker burst directly over the boat, and after rolling over several times she disappeared. Polly sobbed aloud.

In the meanwhile the once noble ship, sometimes lifted upon a wave, sometimes half buried in the surf, rolled heavily toward the Iron Rock. At length a wave higher than the rest bore her forward with resistless power, and raising her far above the general level, it appeared to drop her bodily upon the rock, the crash of the collision being distinctly heard on shore. She remained fast, lying athwartships, and in another instant a wave burst against her as though she had been a portion of the cliff, and the spray flew high in the air, while the sea rolled completely across her decks.

" She can't stand that for half an hour," said Paul. " Stay here, Polly; or, better, go in-doors; she'll break up directly, and there's no soul living on her now."

But Polly could not quit the dreadful scene, and as Paul now descended from the cottage to the beach below by a zigzag path, she accompanied him to the bottom of Sandy Cove. Here all the fishermen had congregated with their wives and children, intent upon the plunder that the cargo would afford whenever the wreck should break up and the prize should be washed on shore. In such a storm it was impossible to descend the cliffs, as the waves beat against the face; when the storm should abate, at low tide, there would be a narrow beach at the base of the precipice, upon which the cargo would be washed on shore, if not previously destroyed by being beaten against the rocks; but they now all waited in expectation that some portion of the spoil might be washed upon the shelving beach in Sandy Cove by the narrow entrance, especially as the vessel had grounded at no great distance from the mouth of the bay, where she now lay within view of the village.

For about an hour the hull of the vessel withstood the fury of the sea, which dashed against her with irresistible force; but as each wave retired large volumes of water poured in cascades from her opened timbers, showing that she could not much longer hold together. At length the entire deck floated off the poop as a heavy wave broke full upon her; a short time afterward the stern rose bodily to an advancing breaker, and as the sea rushed over her it separated and disappeared, leaving only the fore part of the vessel fixed upon the rocks. From that moment the waves became enriched with the cargo, which was to be seen floating in the surf in all directions in the shape of bales, cases, tea-chests, barrels, and packages of all descriptions. This was the signal for a general cheer from the wreckers and their families who now thronged the shore. A few minutes later a couple of large casks were seen at the entrance of the cove, which, lifted by a rolling wave, were driven directly into the harbor; they were apparently lashed together. There was a general rush forward on the part of the people who lined the beach in their eagerness to secure the prize. Among the men who dashed into the surf were some of the most desperate wreckers of the coast; but the force of the breakers was so great that they were not only beaten down by the curl of the waves, but they were dragged back by the under-tow, and only regained the shore by the assistance of the crowd who, with joined hands, formed a line, and were thus enabled to resist the rush of water. There was only one man who had been able to force his way through the breakers and swim out to the floating barrels; this was Paul Grey, who had thrown off his coat and boots, and, with a coil of thin line across his broad shoulders, now struck out manfully through the rough sea; sometimes he was for the moment buried in the broken waves, at others he would dive through the advancing wall of water just as it curled above his head and threatened to beat him down. "Bravo, Paul!" shouted many voices, especially those of women, who were standing on the beach; "he'll have it now!" "There's good spirits in those casks, or they wouldn't swim so light!" said a grim-looking ruffian, who had just failed in his attempt to swim through the surf. "Paul's the cat's-paw, but we'll cry halves when it comes ashore." "He can't drag the casks ashore," said another fellow; "we must all give a hand and share the profit." "He's got it now!" shouted many voices, as Paul, having reached the barrels, dexterously fastened a hook that was attached to his line, and turning toward the shore, having thrown off the coil while he held the end of the rope in his teeth, he swam vigorously for the beach.

There was one heart that beat with pride as the powerful form of Paul Grey struggled bravely with the surf that had beaten back all others, and Polly clapped her hands with enthusiasm, and headed the crowd to dash into the water to help her husband when he gained his footing on the rolling shingles. Her hair had blown from its fastening, and now flowed in long waves driven by the wind in wild confusion, while the excitement of the moment had flushed her cheek, and added a fire to her large eyes that rendered her perfectly beautiful, and as Paul pressed her hand when he landed dripping from the sea, he thought he had never seen his Polly look so lovely.

"It shall belong to you, Polly, whatever it may be!" said Paul. "It's my prize, and you shall have it."

"Halves!" cried the surly ruffian who had already spoken in the crowd; and one and all, seizing the line, began to haul the barrels toward the beach.

"Avast hauling!" cried Paul, as he pushed two or three men on one side as though they were children. "The line is mine, and you sha'n't break it when I've had the trouble of the job." He then carefully drew in the rope, hand over hand, until the barrels approached the surf; in an instant, as a broken wave hurried them toward the beach, a dozen men rushed into the water and dragged them to the shore.

Hardly had they pulled the barrels high and dry than they surveyed them with an air of disappointment. "They're empty!" was the general exclamation.

This was evident. Two empty rum puncheons that would contain ninety gallons each were firmly lashed parallel together by means of broken oars that formed a frame-work, in which the casks were beautifully secured. At one end was a strong rope that had apparently been arranged for the support of some person who should have clung to the raft; to this rope some long fair hair was attached as though it had become entangled with the hands that had vainly attempted to keep their hold. On the top of the buoyant raft, and well secured in the center between the two casks, was a box covered with a piece of tarpaulin that had been fastened down with nails to the side in order to preserve the contents dry. Some treasure of importance was evidently well secured.

"Halves again!" shouted the first ruffian, as he rudely pushed Polly on one side and grasped the box with both hands; at the same time he staggered and rolled upon the shingle as Paul's fist descended full upon the side of his head.

"Now, my lads, fair play," said Paul. "The prize belongs to me, and I don't mind sharing a portion after I know what it is. But hands off till Polly takes her share!"

Paul was a match for any two men in the village; and as none could contest in the present case either his strength or his argument, the crowd immediately agreed, and standing around the mysterious prize they watched with much curiosity the opening of the box. It was an old wine-case, and as Paul broke off the nail-heads with a stone, and removed the tarpaulin, a few bars of wood beneath, that had supported the water-proof cover, were easily withdrawn. A rich cashmere shawl was loosely arranged above some object; beneath this was a wrapper of pink flannel. With extreme curiosity Polly now removed this covering, and started back with an exclamation of surprise that was echoed by the crowd as the mystery of the box was suddenly revealed. Apparently asleep or dead lay the body of an infant about two months old; around its neck was a locket suspended by a thin gold chain. Was it possible? Could a miracle restore the child that she had buried but a few days since? It was the facsimile of her own boy, but pale as alabaster.

"Is it dead?" asked Polly, trembling with emotion as she regarded the motionless figure that lay before her like an apparition of her own child.

"I fear it is," said Paul, who was himself not unmoved at the wonderful resemblance; "but there's no water in the box; the clothes are damp, but not absolutely wet. It has died for want of air. I said the prize should be yours, Polly; so I'll carry box and all up to the cottage, and we'll see what can be done."

"Luck comes from the sou'-west, ha, ha!" muttered a hoarse voice succeeded by a chuckle, and Polly saw the wrinkled face of old Mother Lee peering into the box; and laying her skinny fingers upon the chest of the infant, she once more muttered, "Luck comes from the sou'-west; yer'll get no other, Polly Grey, except what's cast up by the sea—ha, ha!"

"Go, wretched old woman," replied Polly, stung by the taunt; "frighten fools who are worthy of you, but leave me and mine alone."

The old woman's face changed to something devilish, and scowling upon Polly she spat upon the ground, and hoarsely croaked, "We'll see, we'll see."

"Come along, Polly," said Paul, who had uncorded the fastenings of the box, and raised it upon his head; "don't quarrel with Mother Lee; and look you, mother, if you're going to bring bad luck on my Polly, I'll heave you over the cliff to feed the crabs the next time you come up the hill; d'ye hear?"

Paul now left the crowd, and followed by his wife he ascended the zigzag path with his burden, and quickly reached his cottage on the cliff. Having placed the box gently on the floor, Polly took away the damp shawl and wrappers; and covering the child with a warm flannel she held it close to her breast, and briskly rubbed its back and spine. It was very cold, but the limbs were not stiff; she had therefore hope; and with the door and window opened to give fresh air, which blew violently from the sea, she anxiously watched for some sign of returning animation. In a few minutes it gasped faintly; and to her intense delight after an hour's careful attention she was rewarded by hearing it cry lustily. She now dressed it in some clothes that had belonged to her own child, and pressing it gently to her bosom, she felt a mother's happiness as it clung eagerly to her breast, as though she had been its proper parent. As she watched the lovely infant now peacefully resting in her arms she could hardly believe in her recent loss. It appeared as a dream. Her boy had been replaced by another that she might have mistaken for her own. She felt bewildered; so many scenes had changed in rapid succession within the last few hours; her loss, the storm, the wreck, the infant now her child, that had been thus mysteriously cast up by the sea.

CHAPTER II.

A BODY FROM THE WRECK.

THE day following the storm was a harvest for the people of Sandy Cove. The wreck had entirely broken up, and not a vestige of the ship remained except the fragments that, together with the cargo, strewed the coast for miles on either side the bay.

Paul Grey had been out at day-break, and when he returned to breakfast he found his wife happier than he had seen her for many days. The table was spread. The newly arrived baby was snugly asleep in its cradle, looking as blooming as though nothing extraordinary had happened; and as the storm had passed and the day was fine, the sun was shining gayly through the open window.

When breakfast was finished Paul took his telescope and sat upon the terrace wall above the sea. He had not been long seated before his attention was attracted to some object floating in the water beneath, at no great distance from the shore; as the waves gave it motion sometimes it was completely submerged, while at others a portion appeared upon the surface.

"Polly," he said, "can you make out what that is? Sometimes it looks like a long mass of sea-weed, but it is too white."

Neither could distinguish the object clearly; therefore, descending to the beach, Paul, accompanied by his wife, launched a small skiff and rowed out of the harbor toward the spot. Rounding the point that formed a natural break-water to the small bay, they at once discovered the cause. Upon nearer approach there could be no doubt that it was the body of some unfortunate who had perished in the wreck of yesterday. A few more strokes brought them close to it.

"It is a woman," said Polly, who was steering the boat. "Look, Paul, your oar will now touch her. Help me to lift her from the water."

It was the body of a beautiful woman of about two-and-twenty, which the united exertions of Paul and his wife soon placed on board the boat; her long blonde hair he had mistaken in the distance for sea-weed. Although they knew that she was dead, they arranged her in a reclining position, with her back resting against the seat of the boat.

"Poor creature! she is a lady," said Polly; "and so beautiful!"

She had no other clothes than a night-dress; several valuable rings of diamonds and rubies were on her fingers, in addition to her wedding-ring, and a necklace of large brilliants was hung round her neck. Some of her long hair was twisted among her delicate fingers; the button of the collar of her night-gown had burst, and her beautiful snow-white bosom was exposed.

"She had a baby," sighed Polly; "poor woman, how sad! Who knows whether she is the mother of the child we have saved?"

"Very likely," said Paul; "for the hair that we found upon the rope handle attached to the barrels is exactly the same as that now twisted in her fingers. See! the inside of her soft hands is chafed with holding on to the hard rope. Her long hair must have become entangled while struggling in the water, and she had no strength to keep her hold."

The expression of this beautiful but unfortunate mother was one of calm serenity; and as Polly Grey straightened her gracefully formed limbs, and covered her breast with her long flaxen hair, she kissed her pale cheek, and vowed inwardly never to forsake her orphan child. She then took off her cloak, and spread it gently over the body.

"Take off the rings, Polly, before we get to the cove," said Paul. "We must take care of them, as some day they may be wanted if the child should live. It wouldn't do to let the people at the cove see the gold and stones." Accordingly Polly, not without some difficulty, drew the rings from her taper fingers, and unfastened the snap of the necklace.

It was well that this had been done, for on their arrival at the cove they found a great influx of people; the news of the wreck had spread rapidly throughout the neighborhood, and people from all quarters had flocked to the spot. Among others was the good clergyman of the neighboring village, Dr. Jones, who with his excellent wife had driven down to the cove with a good supply of warm clothing and restoratives in case they should be required by the survivors from the shipwreck. Alas! there were none; the little child was the only soul living of all those who but a few hours before were happy in their near approach to their native land and homes after a long and tedious voyage from China.

"What have we here?" cried Dr. Jones, as Paul approached the shore. "Ah's me! ah's me! here's a disaster," exclaimed the good man. "No hope, Mr. Grey; no hope, I'm afraid? No, no hope," he mournfully and slowly repeated, as he looked at the figure covered with Polly's cloak. The boat struck the beach, and Polly uncovered the face of the drowned mother. "Ah's me! ah's me! Poor thing! so young, so lovely! And did you say a mother?" asked Dr. Jones, in a tone of despair. In a few minutes Paul had explained the incident and his suspicions, which touching story at once enlisted the sympathy of the good doctor; but Paul said nothing about the trinkets, and merely stated that his wife had determined to nurse and to adopt the child.

A few days after this event a simple funeral entered the church-yard of Stoke; the coffin was carried by some of the fishermen of Sandy Cove, foremost of whom was Paul Grey. Many women and children followed as mourners one whom they had never known, but whose fate had engaged their sympathies; and Polly Grey carried the infant smiling unconsciously in her arms as it followed its dead mother to the grave. The good Dr. Jones not only paid the expenses of the funeral, but some weeks afterward he erected a stone in the form of a cross upon the spot, with this short inscription: "A lady unknown, aged about twenty-two. Cast up by the sea at Sandy Cove, 21st August, 1791."

Paul and his wife had returned to their cottage after the

2

funeral, when a sudden thought struck him. "What was in the box with the child? Was there nothing except the Indian shawl and the wrapper?" he asked Polly.

"Only some thick cotton wool at the bottom for the child to lie upon," said Polly, "which I did not remove; but if you like I will fetch the box and empty it."

In a few minutes she brought the box. "There is nothing here, you see, except the wool that makes a kind of bed at the bottom." As she spoke she quickly emptied the contents in double handfuls. "What is this?" she exclaimed, as something heavy in a canvas bag suddenly arrested her hand. Paul lifted it up from a mass of cotton wool in which it was securely packed.

"It is gold!" said Paul. Marked in ink upon the bag was " 200 guineas."

" Oh, Paul," said Polly, "this is dreadful! We have no right to this money, and its possession will bring some trouble; what can we do? Is there no paper in the box— no writing to give some clew to the name of the owner?"

"Nothing," answered Paul, "nothing, except this bag of two hundred guineas, which no doubt the poor lady packed with the child. We must stow it away with the trinkets in some safe place, until perhaps some day we may learn something more about it. It's lucky that we found it, and still more lucky that we didn't unpack the box in the crowd at the cove; there would have been a pretty scramble for the gold."

At this moment a knock at the door disturbed the conversation. Paul quickly concealed the bag of gold in the wool within the box from which he had taken it, while Polly, blushing deeply at the act of caution, hesitated until the knock was repeated before she gave a reply. The door opened: Dr. Jones entered.

"Good-morning, Mrs. Grey. I feared you were not at home, which would have disappointed me much, as I wished to have some conversation with you about your new charge. How is the poor little castaway?"

"Doing very nicely, sir," replied Polly, "thank you. It is a lovely child, and as strong and healthy as could be wished. It does not miss its mother, and there is no fear that it will not thrive."

"It is a strange thing," said Dr. Jones, "that we can find no clew to the name beyond the letters ' K. N.' upon the night-dress. Was there no paper inclosed in any portion of the clothes or wrappers that were contained in the case that held the child?"

Polly could not help a slight confusion in manner. It was true that no paper had been found; but her natural honesty felt repugnant to the idea of concealment, and she would gladly have intrusted the good Dr. Jones with the secret had not a warning glance from her husband suggested caution. She could only reply, "There was nothing that could give the slightest clew to a discovery; and strangely enough, no portion of the wreck bears a name. No boat has been washed on shore, but everything appears to have been dashed to pieces against the rocks; thus we have no idea of the vessel, except that portions of the cargo, such as bales of silk, suggest that she must have sailed from India. Many parts of the beach are strewn with tea leaves, as every chest has been entirely destroyed."

"Well," said Dr. Jones, "we must remember carefully every circumstance connected with the disaster, as the time may arrive when it will be necessary to prove the identity of the child. There can be no doubt, from the appearance of the poor mother's body, that she was a person in a high position. Poor thing! so young and so beautiful!—so very beautiful!"

"I have cut off a quantity of her long hair," said Polly, "which I have carefully packed with the—the—the Indian shawl and night-dress."

Polly had very nearly said "the diamond necklace," and, once more annoyed at herself for the necessary concealment, she looked imploringly at her husband for permission to relieve herself of the secret. A look from Paul closed her lips.

"Well," said Dr. Jones, "the hair may some day be of service; it was a good thought, Mrs. Grey—a very good thought. Then so the matter rests. The child has fallen into kind hands, thank God; and when you have done your portion of the good work, and he grows to the proper age, I must begin my share, and he must come to school."

Dr. Jones was the clergyman, and also the school-master, of the village of Stoke; he was much beloved, and being a man of considerable fortune combined with a generous disposition, he was looked upon as the father of the poor in his neighborhood. He kept a school simply be-

cause he loved to bring up boys according to his own ideas
of morality; therefore, without considering pecuniary
profit, he received the pupils of the wealthy as boarders,
while he gratuitously admitted as daily scholars many of
the poorer classes, but judiciously arranged them in separate forms; in fact, Parson Jones, as he was generally
called, was a thoroughly good specimen of a Christian minister, and he had the rare qualities of good common sense
and judgment combined with other virtues.   The case of
the drowned lady and the infant child that was supposed
to belong to her had struck deeply upon his imagination,
and Parson Jones had resolved to keep an eye upon the
child throughout his career; he had known Polly Grey
from her infancy, as her parents, who were now both dead,
had been his parishioners, and he had almost regretted that
she had married Paul, who followed the hazardous occupation of a fisherman, while so many well-to-do farmers had
striven for her hand.   However, it was he who had himself married them; therefore he took an additional interest
in their welfare, and he felt perfectly satisfied because the
child had fallen into the kind hands of Polly Grey.

CHAPTER III.

TWELVE YEARS AFTER.

TWELVE years had passed away since the storm of 1791.
There had been few changes in Sandy Cove, except that
boys had grown to manhood, and those who were girls
were now mothers of families; but among the adult population there had been little alteration, with the exception
of a few deaths among the older people.   The cottage stood
upon the cliff as neatly whitewashed as before; the myrtles
in the little garden had grown larger, but otherwise there
was no change; and Polly Grey, almost as charming as
ever, but rather saddened in expression, sat before her cottage door knitting a woolen comforter, and anxiously watching the sea.

It was about an hour before sunset in the same month of
August when twelve years ago the Indiaman had been
driven on the shore.   There was a silence about the cottage
and an absence of many little trifles that showed that Polly
Grey had no children at home; indeed, there was a superstition in the village that old Mother Lee had once cursed

her, and some pretended a recollection of certain words that she had uttered when, in a fit of rage, she spat upon the ground, and said, "Yer'll get no other, Polly Grey, except what's cast up by the sea." Certain it was that Polly had never had a child since the death of her first and her adoption of the little castaway.

The small land-locked bay was quite empty—not a boat floated upon the clear blue water, but a few skiffs lay upon the beach, where nets were spread out to dry, and the smart lugger, the "Polly" of olden times, was nowhere to be seen. In the silence of the moment, Polly was startled by the rattle of pebbles on the steep zigzag path. This was almost immediately followed by the appearance of a fine, bronzed-looking man about forty years of age in the uni-form of a revenue officer, with the empty sleeve on his left pinned up to the shoulder.

"Good-evening, Mrs. Grey. Are you alone? for I have a few words to say to you in particular," said Captain Smart.

"Ah, my good friend," said Polly, "I am glad to see you, for I was just feeling melancholy; the boat should have returned yesterday, and, although the wind is fair, I see no sign of a sail even yet; what can have happened? The weather is fine, and Paul promised me that he would not be away two days—this is the third!"

Joe Smart, the old friend of the family, looked serious; and sitting upon the bench by Polly's side he explained his errand.

"My dear Mrs. Grey, don't be alarmed about his safety, but as your oldest friend I have come to give you a timely warning. A revenue cruiser has been sent to capture the 'Polly,' and Paul is either taken at this moment, or he is chased by the government cutter, as the 'Polly' is declared to be a smuggler. Now, as Paul's old friend I have often given him advice upon this point, and as his majesty's officer I have hardly done my duty; but let me implore you, should he escape this chance, prevent him from such a course, which must lead to ruin."

Polly shook her head.

"I fear that I have not the influence that I once had," said she. "Paul is always kind, but I feel sure that there are thoughts on his mind that he does not share with me. It is good of you to be our friend, but that will do but lit-

tle good should Paul be caught. Do you know where the
' Polly ' went?''

" The information we have received is this," said Captain Smart. " Although we are at war with France, there
is a league between the French smugglers and those of this
coast. They have their private places of appointment,
and they meet at sea out of sight of land, where they exchange cargoes. The French then run English goods upon
their coast, while our people smuggle spirits, lace, silks,
and other valuable articles that pay a high duty. The
' Polly ' has always been suspected, but nothing could be
proved until evidence was given a week ago that has con-
firmed their suspicions; thus an order has been received
from head-quarters to chase and board her, and to capture
her should contraband goods be found."

Although Polly Grey was anxious at this intelligence it
was not absolutely new to her. In those days there was
nothing that was considered dishonorable in a smuggler's
occupation among the fraternity, and now that Polly heard
of the intended capture of her husband's boat her sailor's
blood was up. " It will be no revenue cutter that will
catch the ' Polly,' " said Polly Grey; " there's nothing on
the south coast that can touch her, and there's no man
that dare lay a hand on Paul!"

Joe Smart smiled at her woman's pride, and rose to say
good-bye. He good-naturedly shook her hand, and said,
" I'm your true friend, Mrs. Grey; there's no friend like
an old one, and I have done my duty in giving you a hint.
Heaven forbid that I should ever be forced to act as a
revenue officer against Paul Grey! Good-bye, and may
he have no ill-luck!"

As Joe Smart disappeared Polly could not help looking
once more anxiously toward the sea, at the same time she
pondered over the warning of their old friend. The real
fact was that Paul had gradually increased in his daring
adventures, and he had now engaged in the contraband
trade to an extent that a few years ago he would have believed impossible. He had never confided these acts to his
wife, although he had frequently brought packages to the
cottage which he confessed he had purchased from French
boats without paying the duty; these were usually secreted
in a long but narrow cave, which entered the cliff from the

kitchen. This room, being built directly against the rock as a wall, was arranged, as usual in kitchens, with many cupboards. One of these against the rock had a false back, so that the door when open merely showed what appeared to be the cupboard itself arranged with shelves. By removing a bolt, the entire affair moved backward upon hinges, and opened into the gallery of the cliff. This cave was about fifty feet in length, and, although only the width of the cupboard at the entrance, it widened toward the extremity to a chamber of about twenty feet square. It was in this chamber that Polly had originally concealed the necklace and locket, together with the bag of two hundred guineas that had been found in the box with the child after the wreck. They were carefully packed together with the shawl in the same case in which they had been washed ashore.

Although Polly had no more idea of the disgrace of smuggling on a small scale than a lady might have in landing with a dozen pairs of gloves, she had always been afraid that Paul was more deeply engaged in contraband than he chose to admit, and she had now no longer any doubt, after her conversation with Joe Smart, that he was embarked in a most dangerous course. Paul had drifted so gradually into the trade that he could not see the dishonesty. He was like many others in those days who, scrupulously correct in all other matters, yet thought it no sin to cheat the government. Thus with his great experience of the coast, and his excellence in seamanship, combined with the fine sea-going qualities of the " Polly," he was one of the most successful in his trade. He had long since paid off the sum advanced upon his boat by his friend Joe Smart, and he was now sole owner, with a crew of eight picked men.

The sun was just sinking half imbedded in the sea in a broad glare of ruddy light when a sail was suddenly descried, illumined by a red glow which rapidly sunk, and shortly gave place to gray; it was now no longer visible, and the anxious wife strained her eyes along the darkening horizon, almost believing that the sail had been a fancied apparition. The breeze was blowing freshly from the sea, and the twilight having ceased, the night became perfectly dark, as there was no moon.

Polly lighted her lamp, which she hung at the window, in addition to the candles that burned upon the table.

"They will see that light far out at sea," she thought; "it's a dark night to find the entrance to the cove!"

More than one hour passed away; there was no sound except the whistling of the wind and the sullen roll of the breakers against the rocks. Somehow the sound that night reminded her of the storm twelve years ago. There was a moaning in the air that recalled the commencement of the disastrous hurricane. Another hour struck, and although for many years she had known the tone of the old wooden clock, it seemed to beat the hour with a peculiar sound that again recalled the scene of that fearful night when old Mother Lee had appeared like an evil spirit and prophesied disaster. The wind was now blowing a gale; another hour passed. Again the old clock struck; it was eleven, and the sea was now roaring against the cliffs; but there was no sound of man. She rose in a great state of nervous excitement and looked out of the window; it was pitchy dark, and the wild, peculiar moan of the gale betokened a sou'-wester. Borne down with anxiety, she sat at the table and buried her face in her hands as she offered a fervent prayer for the protection of all she loved. Suddenly, with a suppressed scream, she started from her chair as a horrible chuckle struck upon her ear, followed by the low muttered tones, "Luck comes from the sou'-west, ha, ha!" For an instant she had covered her eyes, but upon withdrawing her hands the hideous figure of Mother Lee stood before her.

"What brings you here, Mother Lee, at this late hour?" exclaimed Polly; "has anything happened? Do you come with evil news?" she asked, her anxiety for the moment overcoming her repugnance to the old woman.

"That's as you choose to take it; but you're a pretty watcher!" said Mother Lee. "Yer eyes are like a mole's that yer haven't seen them coming! You're a pretty sailor's wife, to mope in the house when the storm's brewing, and yer husband's running before the cruiser! Fy on yer! yer not the wench for Paul Grey. To go moping over yer Bible! That won't help him like a fire on the Point! Look out and see what Mother Lee has worked! The cruiser won't be long before she strikes the rock! Blow out your lights!" Polly had hardly recovered from her surprise before the old woman, having suited the action to the word, had extinguished the candles and the lamp—

they were in total darkness. "Now you'll see Mother Lee's handiwork! Come out and look at the Point. I came here to blow out your stupid lights!"

Polly instinctively followed the old woman as she left the house. She could hardly stand against the wind, but she at once saw two bright lights; one upon the extremity of either point that formed the narrow entrance to the cove, while far out at sea she observed something like a star that occasionally disappeared. In a few minutes a long streak of fire ascended from the sea at a great distance, and burst into a number of red balls.

"What a bright meteor! or was it lightning?" exclaimed Polly.

"There's meaning in the flash," muttered Mother Lee; "yer'll see another presently." In a few minutes a similar light shot up from the dark sea. "Now look to the east," said Mother Lee, "and yer'll soon understand it." Hardly had she spoken the words when on the high cliff about five miles distant, occupied by the coast-guard station, a rocket flew to the clouds and burst into a cluster of blue stars.

"Now, Paul Grey, lead 'em a dance! and steer straight between the fires!" chuckled Mother Lee, "while I go and put 'em out when all's right. She'll break her bones if she follows—yes—ha, ha! ha, ha! What a night! There's all luck from the sou'-west! Mother Lee knows a trick or two—ha, ha, ha!" and the old woman with astonishing activity disappeared down the steep declivity, and left Polly alone in the dark and stormy night. All other feelings now gave way to the wife's anxiety; she saw that the old woman had better information than herself. There could be no doubt that Paul's boat was chased by a revenue cruiser that now exchanged signals with the coast-guard on shore; thus he would run a double danger, as, although he might possibly avoid the cruiser, he would most probably be met upon arrival in the cove by a party that would be immediately dispatched from the coast-guard station to search his vessel. Polly now understood Mother Lee's reason for extinguishing her lights; there could be little doubt that the two fires to guide the entrance to the cove were the result of a preconcerted arrangement with which her third light would have interfered; but she could not help feeling hurt that her husband had not reposed the same confidence in her that he had evidently shared with others. This corroborated all that she had heard from Captain Smart, and she had no longer any doubt that Paul was far more deeply engaged in smuggling enterprises than she had imagined.

She had been watching nervously for about half an hour since Mother Lee had departed in the midst of the violent storm, when suddenly a bright cloud of sparks flew from one of the fires upon the Point, and it was almost immediately extinguished; a similar effect was nearly at the same time produced on the opposite fire, and the two bright lights disappeared; the entire scene was total darkness, while the wind and waves roared louder than before. Polly withdrew into her cottage, and striking a light she once more waited anxiously. She could not sit down, and she paced the room in intense excitement. What could have happened? Had the boat arrived? She had neither heard nor seen anything, only the sudden extinction of the fires. The noise of the storm and the darkness had obscured all else.

The old clock struck one, and hardly had the vibration of the bell ceased, when the sound of hurried footsteps was heard on the outside. Polly flew to the door as it opened suddenly, and Paul Grey quickly entered the room, carrying on his broad shoulders an immense bale. He was immediately followed by a handsome young sailor boy, who appeared to be about fourteen years of age, and who also carried with difficulty a heavy package, which he threw down upon the floor, and in the next moment he was embraced in the arms of Polly Grey.

"Now, Polly, this is no time for kissing," cried Paul; "there's much to be done, and little time to do it. Open the cupboard as quick as you can; for this is a heavy load, I can tell you, and there's more to come."

As Paul said, there was no time for kissing, for six men now entered the room, each laden with a heavy bale, which by Paul's directions they deposited upon the floor, and immediately withdrew. In the meantime Polly had gone into the kitchen and opened the secret door of the gallery, into which, after about ten minutes' labor, Paul, with the assistance of his wife and the young sailor, had carried and concealed the eight packages.

With great dispatch Polly then spread a clean cloth upon a round oak table, upon which in a few minutes appeared a large round of cold boiled beef, with a loaf of brown bread and a huge jug of ale.

"I must have a pull at the beer before I can speak," said Paul; "but here, Ned, you must be thirsty too," said he, as he poured out a large hornful for the lad before he drank. In the next instant both man and boy were silent —the only sound was the rapid gurgling as the grateful drink poured down their throats.

"Now, then," said Paul, giving a deep sigh as he replaced the half-emptied jug. "Polly, we've had a sharp run for it; haven't we, Ned? But there's nothing afloat that can catch the 'Polly,' especially when it's blowing a gale like to-night."

"I didn't like the running, mother," said the boy; "I would rather fight the cutter than see the 'Polly' run away." The bright blue eyes of the lad sparkled with excitement, at the same time a deep blush tinged his cheek when he added: "I don't like the work of to-night, for, although not ashamed to be beaten in a fair fight, I should have felt disgraced had we been taken by the cruiser. I hope we are not doing wrong, mother, but I felt as though we were not in the right."

Paul took another long pull at the ale to avoid the necessity of a reply.

"Tell me what has happened, Ned," said Polly, as she drew her chair to his side, and parted the bright waving hair from his forehead. "How hot and tired you look, my dear boy! What made you so late? Tell me the whole story, for I have had a miserable time since your father left."

Although Ned Grey was only twelve years old (as it was exactly that time since he had been first pressed to Polly Grey's bosom when she recalled the unconscious infant to existence from the memorable shipwreck), he looked at least fourteen. He was remarkably tall, and powerfully and gracefully built; his features were almost too regular, as the small mouth and curled lip and delicately arched nose would have been almost feminine had they not been contradicted by a brow of most decided character, with deep-blue eyes that, although large and soft, brightened with unmistakable fire in a moment of excitement. There was an air of noble frankness and honesty of expression that, independently of other attractions, would have stamped him as a boy of high character at first sight. This, combined with his handsome and manly appearance, had gained him friends among all who knew him.

"Well, mother," said Ned, "it was simply this: When we left the cove the other day we went to the Coast of France, and on our way back we spoke a French lugger about half-way between this and France, and father made some purchases from her captain—those very bales that we brought home to-night, and a dozen kegs of brandy; but hardly had we got them stowed on board than a strange sail hove in sight, and the French lugger was off in a minute. We followed her. The strange sail chased us; and, as the French lugger could not sail as fast as the 'Polly,' we went on another tack, and the strange sail that father thinks was an English brig-of-war chose the slower boat, and went after the Frenchman. We were now free; but the wind being northerly we had to beat up against it to get home. However, at day-break this morning we met a fishing-smack from this coast, from which we learned that the revenue cutter had been sent out on purpose to look after the 'Polly.' Sure enough a few hours later we saw a fine, smart-looking cutter bearing down upon us, with the English flag flying, and as we did not alter our course, she fired a gun. As we took no notice, she fired another. This time it was shotted, and we could see the white spray leap three times from the water as the shot bounded along the surface, quite a mile and a half too short to reach us.

"Suddenly the wind dropped, and it turned calm for hours, and neither of us could go ahead. At length the wind changed, and came in puffs from the south west; this soon turned to a gale, and the race began in earnest. The cutter sailed well, and the 'Polly' could just hold her own until the sea got up; then we had the best of it, for nothing can touch her in a heavy sea; the cutter plunged bows under, while the 'Polly' hardly wetted her decks, but scudded along like a bird. Night came on, and although we could not see the cutter we could now and then distinguish a light on board. We knew we were running on the land, and the gale had turned to a storm. It was awful work, as we knew the danger of the coast, when all of a sudden we saw a bright light to the north; then we saw another close to it, as though they were almost touching. At this time we saw a rocket sent up from the cutter, which, as nearly as we could guess, was about three miles astern. Again she fired a rocket, which was quickly answered from the shore.

" ' This is touch and go!' said father; still on we flew with the gale right abeam, and the lugger in her best trim going like a racehorse. ' Hurrah!' cried father, ' Mother Lee has got' her lamps trimmed;' and as we approached the two lights widened apart. ' That's the mouth of the cove,' said father; ' we are all right if we can see to clear the Iron Rock.'

" Father had the helm, and not a word was spoken on the deck as we went hissing through the water. The lights were now pretty wide apart, and we knew we were getting close in. ' Starboard!' shouted a man at the fore-mast, as we could just see the white foam surging in a huge breaker over the Iron Rock within a cable's length of us; in another moment we passed within thirty yards of the breakers, and presently we shot direct into the mouth of the bay between the two fires on the cliff. We could see the old woman at one fire and a man at the other; directly we had passed both fires were suddenly put out. We anchored in the bay; father left two men in the ' Polly ' with orders to sink the kegs of brandy, while we landed in the pinnace with the bales which we have just put away; and glad I was, mother dear, to see the light at home, and to find you waiting for us. But I don't like the work, mother; and I don't think it's all over yet. "

" Well, Ned, you sha'n't go again unless you like," said Paul; " but there's no harm in buying and selling fairly. All's honest and above-board; and if the ' Polly's ' too long in the legs for the king's boats she has a right to earn a penny for a new set of sails. We don't rob the government of the duty; if we didn't bring the silks through the Frenchmen would, so the country loses nothing and we gain."

The conversation was suddenly interrupted. At this moment the windows of the cottage shook violently at the loud report of a cannon that appeared almost close to the cliff. All sprung to their feet, and looking through the window, rocket after rocket whizzed high in the air. Again a vivid flash was followed by the concussion of a gun, and as Paul and Ned rushed out to the terrace a fearful sight was presented. Brightly illumined by the burning of a

blue light which rendered not only objects on the deck but
every rope distinctly visible, the fine revenue cutter lay
fixed upon the Iron Rock. A wave rolled completely over
her, and at once extinguished the light that had for a few
moments exhibited her distress; at the same instant a tremendous crash was heard as her mast fell over the side.
Again a flash and heavy report, then once more a blue light
burned, and showed the fearful havoc that had been
wrought in a few minutes; dismasted, and with her decks
confused with the fallen sail and rigging, and her immense
boom lying across the quarter-deck. The crew were attempting to save themselves on the spars. Several men
clung to the mast; but again the sea broke completely over
her, and swept away not only the light but the unfortunate
man that held it. All was complete darkness; but above
the tumult of wind and waves a cry of distress could be distinctly heard.

Without loss of time Paul and Ned had seized two coils
of rope from the cottage stores, and were making the best
of their way along the edge of the cliff to the projecting
point at the right of the entrance to the bay upon which
Mother Lee had originally lighted the fire. This point was
not far from the Iron Rock, and should any strong swimmer be able to reach it he would either be able to enter the
cove, or should he miss the mouth he would be dashed to
pieces against the perpendicular cliff. Paul thought that
the mast with the clinging crew might be driven in this direction. He had therefore taken ropes to haul them up the
rock should it be possible to save them. He had also provided himself with a crowbar to drive into the ground, to
which he could make fast a rope should it be necessary for
him to descend. Ned carried a lantern, but the way was
so dangerous along the edge of the cliff that much caution
was required in their advance.

In the meantime a person was already at the extremity
of the Point, exactly opposite to the Iron Rock upon which
the cutter lay. Mother Lee, after having extinguished her
fire, had remained upon the spot to revel in the calamity
that she had expected.

As the "Polly," guided by the two fires, had scudded
through the mouth of the bay beneath her feet, she guessed
that the cutter would approach so near in pursuit as to be
unable to weather the Iron Rock in so violent a gale on a

lee shore. Mother Lee was always in ecstasy amid scenes of suffering; but as her husband had been hanged for piracy and murder, she bore an internal hatred to all officers of the crown, but more especially to those of the coast-guard, by whom he had been captured. She now sat crouched like an old owl among the loose fragments of rock upon the extreme point of the cliff; but could her face have been distinguished an intense earnestness would have been observed as she bent her head on one side, and with one hand raised to assist her hearing she strained her ears for any sound that should be heard beneath. At length she started. There could be no doubt—it was a voice, then another still more distinct, from the raging sea, two hundred feet below!

"Hold on, my lads, never fear! stick your feet out when we near the rocks!"

"I can't hold on much longer. Oh, my poor Sarah!" exclaimed a despairing voice in reply.

At this moment the mast, with six men clinging to it, including the captain of the cutter, was washed against the cliff exactly below the Point upon which the old woman was perched. Fortunately the spar was brought at right angles across the extreme point of the entrance to the bay, so that, could the men only retain their hold in the frightful surf that beat against the perpendicular rock, both the mast and themselves would have a good chance of being washed directly into the mouth of the cove, in which case they might be saved.

"Hold fast, my lads! Never say die!" shouted the same manly voice of encouragement from below, as one end of the mast struck violently against the rock.

"Lord help us!" screamed a voice of agony; "help!"

"Hold fast!" was again heard, as the breakers forced the entire length of the mast broadside on against the rocks and jammed the unfortunate men against the cliff.

Old Mother Lee had stood up, and she leaned over the cliff, listening to the terrible struggle for life.

"Ha! ha!" she chuckled.

"Lord help us!"

"I'll help ye! Yer helped my Stephen, didn't yer? Here's help for yer! and here! And here's more help! Curses on yer! here's more help! Ha! ha! I heard that strike! D'ye like it? Here's another!"

The old woman, with incredible strength, in a frenzy of fury lifted large blocks of stone from the rocky ground, and showered them at random upon the unfortunate sailors below. A fragment of stone of many pounds' weight fell upon the head of the gallant captain with a dull crash, and his lifeless body slipped from the mast and disappeared amid the surf. Another, and then a third, succumbed to the pitiless shower of stones which the old hag rolled without intermission from the height. Two men had been crushed to death against the cliff by the mast driven by the surf. Only one remained; several rocks bounded past him, and two had struck the mast within a few inches of his hands.

Just at this moment Paul and Ned arrived, and found Mother Lee in the act of heaving another piece of rock over the edge of the cliff; in her excitement she had neither heard them approach nor had she seen the light, as her attention had been directed below.

Startled at the unexpected sight of the old woman, Paul halted for a moment just as she hurled a large stone over the precipice. At the same time a loud cry of distress from beneath rang upon his ear. The horrible truth flashed upon him as Mother Lee turned round, and he read the deed in the fearful expression of her features.

"Cursed old fiend!" shouted Paul, as he seized her by the waist, and lifting her like an infant in the air, he swung her above his head; and in another moment Mother Lee would have been flying over the rock into the boiling surf had not Ned caught Paul's arm, and checked his first impulse of retribution.

Throwing her upon the ground behind him, Paul hallooed out, "Who's below?"

"Help me! I'm nearly done, massa," replied a foreign voice.

"Hold on, my good fellow!" shouted Paul, "I'll be with you directly! Don't give in."

Just at this moment a heavy sea sweeping round the corner turned the mast end on against the Point, and another sea striking it quickly after, it was driven directly into the mouth of the cove against the face of the cliff. Once more Paul leaned over the precipice with the lamp in his hand. "Are you all right?" he shouted.

"Nearly done, massa," was the only reply.

NED SAVES TIM FROM THE WRECK.

"Hold on for a couple of minutes, and you're safe," cried Paul; at the same time with a few vigorous strokes he drove the iron bar deep into a fissure of the rock. Taking a round turn of the rope upon the bar, he slipped a noose between Ned's legs. "Now, Ned, my boy, prove yourself a man; all depends on you; take this spare rope with you while I lower you down, and secure it round the poor fellow's body. Mind yourself when you get near the mast that you don't get jammed, and halloo to me when you're all right."

Without a moment's hesitation Ned fell upon his knees and hands, and crawling to the edge of the cliff he grasped the tightened rope, and, as Paul slacked it off rapidly, in a few seconds he was swinging in the air descending quickly to the rescue.

The noise of the waves increased as he drew nearer to the water. "I'm coming! Cheer up!" he shouted to the person below, whom he could presently distinguish as a dark object clinging to the cross-trees of the mast; this was so frequently and violently driven against the cliff as to render it impossible for him to reach the man in distress. Accordingly, when only a few feet above the water, he shouted to Paul, "Hold hard!" at the same time he threw an end of the spare coil to the nearly exhausted sailor, and told him to make the loop fast by putting one leg through it and holding on. Three times he threw the rope without success, but on the fourth time it was caught, and in a few instants it was properly secured. "Haul away on the spare rope," he shouted to Paul. "I'm all right."

Almost immediately the dark object was raised from the boiling surf, and swinging in the air. It for an instant struck against Ned as it continued to ascend. "Hurrah!" shouted Ned, as he patted him on the shoulder as he passed, dragged quickly up the cliff by the tremendous strength of Paul's muscles. In the meantime Paul worked like a machine; "Take care of your hands now!" he shouted, "you're just at the top! I'll give you a hand over the cliff." In another moment Paul had caught him by the wrist, and dragged him in safety to the surface.

"T'ank God, massa! t'ank God!" said the dark object, as it fell and clasped Paul's knees.

"Halloo!" exclaimed Paul, as he held the lantern to the face of the new arrival; "a nigger boy, I declare! Poor fellow! why, he's nearly perished with cold! Here, my lad, give us a hand, and help me to haul up the boy, for you owe your life to Ned, who's down below."

"Look out, Ned!" cried Paul, "hold fast! Now haul away, boy!" and in a few minutes Ned arrived safely on the top, and warmly shook the nigger boy by the hand.

The young negro was a fine lad of about fourteen, and he immediately grasped the hand that Ned had given him, and pressed it to his thick lips, while he endeavored to express his gratitude in a few sentences rendered almost unintelligible by the excitement.

"Nigger boy almost gone—hear good massa call—then nigger pray to God, and hold fast like de debbel. Then big stones come down from rock, kill de poor cappen—break his 'ed, all smash close to nigger boy. All de people knocked off de mast by de waves—only nigger stick tight. Oh, my poor cappen! he's gone! only cappen love de nigger boy—he my fader and my moder." At this painful remembrance the boy burst into a fit of sobbing, and looking over the edge of the dark cliff he wished to descend again, in the hope of finding the body of the captain, his late master.

"It's of no use," said Ned; "there's no one left, and nothing can be done. But cheer up, lad," he continued, "if the poor captain's dead, my father and mother will be good to you."

"Yes," said Paul; "come along, boy, and get some dry clothes; we'll do the best we can for you. Be a man; it's of no use crying over the bad job; but if that isn't a cold-blooded murder I never heard of one, and old Mother Lee should swing for it. If it hadn't been for you, Ned, I think I should have chucked her over; but I'm glad I didn't, for she'll come to a worse end if there's justice in the world."

They now cautiously picked their way among the loose stones on the dangerous path, and soon arrived at the cottage, where Polly Grey was anxiously waiting for their return. The negro boy was made comfortable and fed, and was shortly snoring upon some clean straw in the kitchen, forgetting all his troubles in sound sleep.

About two hours before day-break a party of the coast-guard arrived, under the command of Captain Smart; they had heard the guns and seen the signals of distress, but they were too late to see a vestige of the cutter, which had already broken up and totally disappeared. Not a soul had been saved, with the exception of the negro boy.

It was hardly light when they shoved off from the beach in a skiff, and quickly boarded the "Polly," that was lying at anchor and rolling heavily in the bay. Her decks had already been washed, and every rope was in its place; the strictest search could discern nothing except a supply of provisions and water, together with a certain amount of pig-iron ballast.

"You don't often use the trawl-net," said Captain Smart to one of the "Polly's" men; "your decks are as clean as a man-of-war."

"D'ye like 'em dirty?" replied the sailor, "cos if you do you must come along with us when we're fishing."

"When's that? Not often, I think," answered Captain Smart.

"We'll send up to the station and let you know," said the sulky smuggler, who was by no means pleased with the visit. "You'll be safer on board along with us than on the king's cutter."

"That's very likely," said Captain Smart; "how did the cutter manage to get ashore?"

"It don't want much management to get ashore here in a sou'-wester," replied the dogged sailor; "it don't want much larning on a dark night to bump on the Iron Rock; even a king's officer knows enough for that."

"What brought her here?" asked Captain Smart, in the hope of getting some account of the chase.

"Well, I suppose it was the same wind as brought us here," continued the ill-tempered fellow; "and sarve her right that she's broke her bones, for her conduct was what I call ungenteel.

"Yer see, the 'Polly' was waiting for a chance to fish on a good bit of ground that we knows of, when up comes a cutter with a fine breeze, and without more ado she bangs a shot right into we, that came so close between the captain and me that it knocked the pipe out of my mouth, and took his cap off.

"'That's purliteness,' says I; 'p'r'aps she's been educated in France,' says I; when bang! comes another shot, which luckily missed us.

"'It's only the French that has such uncivil manners,'

says the captain; ' it's a privateer; so we'd better show 'em
the " Polly's " stern, and run for home; p'r'aps we'll meet
with a king's ship that'll be a match for her.'

" So off we went, and the ' Polly ' showed 'em the way,
I can tell you. Well, it blowed a gale to be sure, in a short
time, just what the ' Polly ' likes, and we came in like a
duck through night as dark as pitch; but the ' Polly '
knows her way. Then yer see it turns out that the cutter
wasn't a Frenchman, after all, more's the pity she began
talking French; so yer see she got in a mess, and I say
sarves her right for her unpurliteness as a king's ship in firing at we just as though the ' Polly ' had been a Frenchman!"

Having delivered himself of this veracious account, Dick
Stone proceeded to fill his short pipe, that had apparently
recovered from the shock of the cannon-ball, and, having
struck a light, he leaned against the mast, and shortly became enveloped in a cloud of tobacco-smoke; nothing
would induce him to utter another word.

Joe Smart was rejoiced in his heart that his search had
been unsuccessful. Nothing pained him so deeply as the
necessity of acting in his official capacity against his old
friend Paul; but such stringent orders had been received to
keep a watch over the proceedings of Sandy Cove that he
had no choice. Returning to the shore he left his men,
and ascended the zigzag path to visit Paul's cottage on the
high cliff. The smoke was already issuing from the
kitchen chimney as he arrived, and Paul Grey met him at
the door.

" Ha, Joe!" he said, " you're up betimes this morning!
But I don't wonder; we had but little sleep ourselves last
night."

" Is no one saved?" asked Joe Smart.

" Only a poor little nigger," replied Paul, " and it was
a wonder that we rescued him." He then narrated the
entire adventure faithfully from the commencement, differ-
ing considerably from the account of Dick Stone on board
the lugger.

While the two friends were sitting together on the bench
at the cottage door Polly was preparing breakfast. In the
meantime Joe Smart took the opportunity to explain to
Paul the severity of the instructions he had received, and

to implore him to consider the position in which not only he, but also his wife, would be placed should detection lead to their ruin.

But Paul had his own private opinion concerning smuggling; he had persuaded himself that any tax was an act of oppression, and that the principles of free trade should be supported to the fullest extent; thus no argument of Joe Smart's had the slightest influence upon his mode of reasoning, and he remained obstinate in his dogma that every man had a right to supply his wants from the cheapest market, and that any impost upon foreign goods that had become the private property of an Englishman was a direct robbery. He would not deny that he had dealt in contraband articles; but " Never mind me," he replied to his friend Joe Smart; " friends or not, if you ever catch the ' Polly,' don't hesitate to seize her if you find smuggled goods on board. I'll take my chance, Joe; you do your duty, and I'll look after mine. But now come in to breakfast, and Polly 'll give you such a cup of tea as you won't get every day, and what's more, it never paid the government a penny."

In a few minutes the party were sitting at the table. Polly had prepared a substantial breakfast of fried soles fresh from the bay; while a huge brown loaf and masses of bright yellow butter, with a sturdy joint of cold beef, were ready for the sharp morning appetites.

There was a curious contrast in the fair waving hair and the large blue eyes of young Ned Grey and the black woolly head and the dark eyes of the negro boy as they sat together at the table; but Tim, as the latter was called, was looking his best, and was no longer the miserable half-drowned object of the previous night; he had washed his black face with soap till it shone like a well-polished boot; he was dressed in a suit of Ned's clothes, and as he looked at the well-spread table a grin of happiness exposed a long row of snow-white teeth, and for the moment the affectionate but hungry Tim forgot the loss of the captain of the cutter.

Tim was an abbreviation of Timbuctoo. At the time of our story the West India Islands were the gems of our colonies, as the labor required for the plantations was supplied by negro slaves imported from the west coast of Africa. These people were collected at various stations on the African coast by native dealers, who purchased them for beads, fire-arms, cotton cloths, etc., from the native chiefs, who brought them from the interior. As the whole of Central Africa is composed of separate tribes who are constantly at war with each other, the prisoners taken are invariably retained as slaves unless they are sacrificed as offerings to the fetish or god of the victor. A special demand for slaves naturally aggravates the existing anarchy, as every prisoner becomes of additional value; thus man-hunting, although a natural institution of Africa, has been extended by the necessities of European colonists. As the greater portion of the west coast of Africa was the regular slave-market for the supply of the French, English, Portuguese, and Spanish American possessions, man-hunting became the all-engrossing profession of every petty negro chief; razzias were carried into the very heart of the African continent for the sole purpose of kidnaping slaves, who were exchanged for the necessaries of the country, and handed from tribe to tribe until they reached the agents of the coast dealer, who kept them like cattle penned in certain stations until the arrival of ships that were to carry them to their various destinations across the Atlantic. The distances from which these unfortunate people were marched were almost incredible. They generally arrived in long strings, fastened by leathern thongs from neck to neck like a living chain; and, being perfectly ignorant of geography, they had no idea of the countries through which they passed; but upon arrival few slaves could give any description of the route beyond the simple name of their native places obscured in the wilderness of Africa. The sufferings on the march were frightful. If poor women were foot-sore, or broke down under the weight of some burden they were forced to carry, they were first cruelly beaten, and if too weak to proceed they were killed by the blow of a club or the thrust of a spear: children who fell ill were thrown into the thick jungle, and left to die or to be devoured by the wild beasts. It was thus that Tim had been captured when about twelve years old; and, being a well-grown and powerful boy, he had arrived with a large gang of slaves in sufficiently good condition to fetch a high price at Sierra Leone, from which port he was shipped with many others to Jamaica. In the latter colony he was purchased by a rich sugar-planter, a kind-hearted, good man, who would neither have harmed an animal nor human being; but unfortunately it was poor little Tim's lot to be handed to the care of a cruel overseer.

For more than a year Tim had led a life of bitterness; not a day passed without some severe lashes of the whip, accompanied by the uncalled-for abuse of the nigger-driver. It was in vain that he did his utmost to please—he received nothing but threats and blows; he would sometimes steal away and hide among the thick sugar-canes, and think of his little village so far away in Africa, and cry till his heart nearly broke when he thought of his distant home that he should never see again, with his mother, and the flock of goats that he was minding in the forest on the day that he was stolen away. It was too much for Tim, and he longed to die. Once he had complained to his master, who had accordingly reprimanded the overseer; but from that time his lot was even worse than before, as the natural cruelty of the tyrant turned to actual hatred. At length Tim determined to run away; he knew not where to go, but anywhere was better than his present position. He left the plantation one night, and ran and walked alternately until at sunrise, tired out and foot-sore, he reached Port Royal. A man-of-war's boat was just pushing off from the shore, and Tim rushed into the water, and in a few broken words explained his distress and implored protection. The lieutenant who commanded, with sailor-like charity, took him on board, and Tim quickly found himself on a first-class frigate, which sailed that day for England. During the voyage Tim, who had learned to cook in the cruel overseer's service, made himself useful in the ship's galley, and soon became not only a great favorite with his master, but with the rest of the crew. A few days after quitting Jamaica the frigate fell in with a French ship, which she captured after a severe engagement, during which Tim's master (the lieutenant) distinguished himself greatly, and was badly wounded. Tim nursed him with much devotion until their arrival in England, when the lieutenant was rewarded with an appointment to the command of a revenue cutter. From that time Tim regarded his brave and kind-hearted master with intense affection, and, having learned a sailor's work, he formed one of the cutter's crew, of which he was now the only survivor, the gallant commander having been destroyed by the rock rolled down upon him by Mother Lee.

After breakfast was over he told this simple story of his career, which at once gained him Polly's heart, while the bright eyes of Ned sparkled at his description of his adventures, more especially at the account of the action with the French ship, when the brave lieutenant was wounded. From that time Tim became a member of Paul Grey's family; he made himself generally useful, sometimes assisting Polly Grey in the cooking, but more frequently he attended Paul and Ned in fishing when the " Polly " went upon a cruise, or when the boats pushed out with the seine-net to capture a shoal of mackerel.

Tim did not forget his old master. Although happy, he had fits of gloom when his thoughts wandered back to that fatal night when he clung to the drifting mast in the raging storm, and heard those last manly words of encouragement: " Never say die! hold fast, my lads!" before he lost sight of his brave captain forever.

CHAPTER IV.

NED GREY AT SCHOOL.

THE holidays were over. Ned Grey had had a happy time during the past seven weeks that had been full of adventure. In addition to the ordinary pleasures of his home, and the occupation of fishing, he had made several voyages to the coast of France in the fast clipper " Polly," and had escaped two or three French cruisers after an exciting chase; his holidays had wound up with the wreck of the cutter and the rescue of " Nigger Tim," as he was now called, in Sandy Cove.

Ned Grey excelled in all manly pursuits—there was no better swimmer in the cove, neither was there a more active sailor or better fisherman; at the same time he ranked as high at school in the more serious branches of education. No mother could have surpassed the fondness of Polly Grey for her adopted child, and she was now well repaid for her care, not only in the physical perfection of the boy, but in the filial affection that he returned. She had taught him herself until he was nine years old, by which time he could read and write fluently, although it must be confessed that his juvenile industry was less visible on his slate and copy-book than in his untiring energy and resources in setting lines for fish, making crab-nets and lobster-pots, and in catching the said crabs and lobsters, with which the rocky coast abounded. In all these pursuits he had been an apt pupil of Paul Grey's. But, as the watchful Parson Jones had often warned Polly, the time had arrived when he must be sent to school; therefore she had to part with her much-loved boy, and resigned herself to the solitude of home.

Thus Ned had first gone to school as a boarder in the house of Parson Jones when he was nine years old. Polly had prepared his mind for his entrance among his fellows by the simple but stern principles of morality: that he should be too proud to tell an untruth, or to do a mean action; that he should be rigidly honorable in all his dealings; and that he should never bully, nor allow himself to be bullied. With this advice, which he never forgot, Ned parted from his parents, as he considered Paul and Polly Grey, and went to school. Although Parson Jones and his wife were the perfection of kindness, Ned felt the difference between home and school. He had never known the want of a mother until then; and there were many hours when his thoughts returned to the little white cottage on the cliff, and he longed to feel her loving arm around his waist and her warm kisses upon his cheek. Then, as the scene of his dear home appeared, he would recall all the fond words of advice that had fallen from his mother's lips, and these he resolved should always be his guide.

Four years had passed, and Parson Jones declared that Ned was the best boy in his school. He was exceedingly gentle in his manners, clever for his age (he was just turned thirteen); at the same time he was the best cricketer and the fastest runner, although there were boys several years his senior. With such qualifications it was natural that he should be a general favorite; but there was one exception to the rule, which had for several years been a source of much annoyance to Ned Grey. The largest landed proprietor in the neighborhood was a certain Squire Stevens, whose eldest son was a boarder in Parson Jones's school. This lad was slightly older than Ned, to whom he had, without any valid reason, taken a peculiar aversion. It was in vain that Ned had at first endeavored to win his friendship: there was a jealousy in the unmanly heart of Jem Stevens that nothing could remove. The fact that Ned excelled him in the various games of football, cricket,

and others that tested the activity of boys was sufficient to
make him an enemy.   Added to this meanness of disposition, he was a notorious liar; and had not Parson Jones
hesitated to offend his father, who was the great man of
the parish, he would on more than one occasion have expelled him from the school.

The holidays being over, Ned Grey once more left home
and returned to school.   It was only five miles from the
cove; therefore, as the "Polly" was going out fishing,
Paul managed to put him and his trunk on board, as he
could land him within half a mile of Parson Jones's house.

"Good-bye, Ned," shouted many voices, as having taken
leave of his mother he descended to the beach.   The children ran out of several huts to shout "Good-bye" likewise, and to shake hands with Ned, who with Tim's assistance carried his heavy trunk along the beach and placed it
in the boat.   They soon got on board the "Polly," taking
the pinnace in tow; and with a light but fair breeze they
sailed out of the cove, and waved a parting farewell to
Polly Grey, who stood upon the terrace on the cliff watching their departure.

In less than an hour they landed, and, assisted by a
powerful sailor, who carried his trunks Ned followed the
well-known path up the cliffs, and shortly arrived at the
village.   It was a lovely spot.   Sheltered in a deep dell,
the gray spire of the old church rose above the rich green
foliage of the woods; a clear rippling stream flowed through
the bottom of the glen, where Ned had often caught a bas-
ketful of small trout upon a holiday afternoon; at times
the brook was hidden between cliffs of reddish and gray
limestone, upon which grew a rich fringe of underwood,
broken at intervals by a noble oak; in other places the
water was as smooth as glass, in deep black pools in some
sudden bend of the stream where the torrent had hollowed
out a resting-place.   Crossing a rude bridge, formed of a
tree felled across the brook, Ned passed the meadow that
bordered the high-road and arrived at the church, close to
which stood the rectory—Dr. Jones's school.   It was a
large gable-ended house, with lattice windows, and was
completely covered with ivy except in several places where
the exuberant growth had been checked for the cultivation
of the myrtle and magnolia which were carefully trained
upon the walls.   The garden was beautifully kept; a small

but rapid stream flowed through a large lawn ornamented with flower-beds tastefully arranged, while the natural undulations of the ground were in some places leveled into terraces of fine turf that descended to the rippling brook. Several ancient mulberry-trees afforded a delicious shade, beneath which rustic seats were arranged; it was on one of these that Ned had been accustomed to sit in the heat of the day and read, when Dr. Jones permitted the boys to enjoy themselves in his private grounds. The sailor had carried his trunk to the back entrance, and Ned, having opened the garden gate, advanced quickly along the approach to the front door. As the gate clanged when Ned had closed it the sound attracted the attention of a light and youthful figure that was seated in Ned's favorite spot upon the lawn, beneath the spreading branches of a venerable mulberry. She had been reading, but upon seeing Ned approach she quickly closed her book, and springing up—

"Ah! Ned," she exclaimed; "how you startled me! I was just reading about Edward the Black Prince, and I was wondering whether he was called 'Ned' when he was a boy, and then the gate slammed, and I jumped and saw you!"

"I am sorry that I startled you, Edith," said Ned. "I didn't know that you were here until this moment when I first saw you rise; pray forgive me."

"Oh, yes!" replied Edith, laughing; "it was no great sin, but I'm so glad you have come home again! Papa and mamma will be so very glad also, for you know you are their great favorite. Come in: I think papa is in his study."

There was a blush of pleasure on Edith's lovely face as she thus welcomed her old playfellow, and led him toward the house. Edith Jones was born a month after that fatal night, now thirteen years ago, when Ned was rescued from the sea. She was, therefore, nearly the same age, and as both her father and mother had taken the warmest interest in Ned, and had frequently told her of the extraordinary manner in which he, a helpless infant, was saved, she had regarded him with a tender sympathy ever since he had first entered the school, when they were both children of nine years old. Both Dr. and Mrs. Jones had treated Ned more like one of their own family than an ordinary school-boy; therefore it was natural that Edith, as an only child, should have regarded Ned almost in the light of a brother; in fact, as they now walked together hand in hand across the lawn, they matched as though sprung from the same parents. Edith was tall for her age, and beautifully formed, while her long, waving blonde hair, that fell in a dense mass below her shoulders, agreed exactly in color with the rich locks of the handsome boy by her side. She had the same large blue eyes, fine complexion, and delicate features; and, better than all, the same warm heart and generous disposition.

In a few minutes they entered the house, and upon Edith's knock at the study door being quickly answered they entered.

"Here's Ned come back, papa," said Edith; "he's looking as brown as a gypsy, and so grown, isn't he?"

"Ha, ha, Ned, my boy!" exclaimed the delighted school-master, "I'm very glad you've come to us again; we have been quite dull without you; even the canary won't sing as usual when you're away. How are your father and mother? All well, I hope?"

Ned having replied, now gave them an account of the wreck of the cutter and the rescue of the nigger boy, Tim. Edith's eyes brightened during the description.

"Where is he?" she presently exclaimed. "Oh, Ned, how I should like to see a black boy! And does he love you for having saved him?"

"Oh, yes," replied Ned. "I've heard that niggers don't feel, but I'm sure that's not true, for Tim's as fond of me as possible, although we've only had him a few weeks, and he loves father and mother like a dog."

"Like a dog!" exclaimed Edith; "but is he not like us? Is he not better than a dog in his affection?" asked the hesitating girl.

At this moment there was a rush against the half-closed door; in another instant it burst open, and a large black Newfoundland dog, bounding into the room, at once recognized Ned, and, springing toward him, it almost knocked him down as it placed its fore-paws on his shoulders and attempted to lick his face.

"Ah, Nero! down! down!" cried Edith.

"Poor fellow!" said Ned, as he returned the dog's caress, and patted his silky sides and neck; "don't drive him away. Nero, my boy, how did you know that I was here again?" said Ned, as he affectionately hugged the faithful dog. "I wish all people were as good as dogs," said Ned. "I believe Tim is; and both Tim and Nero are niggers, for they're both the same color, only Nero's not so woolly."

"Well," said Edith, half convinced, "Nero loves me dearly, too; don't you, Nero? Nobody loves me so well as you, Nero, do they, old boy?" This she said as she caught the dog by both his ears, and looked lovingly in his face.

Somehow Ned blushed deeply as he was about to make some remark, which was interrupted by the entrance of Edith's mother.

Mrs. Jones was a good-looking woman of about thirty-eight. There was a great excitement in her manner as she merely shook hands warmly with Ned, and then addressed her husband.

"My dear, you're wanted immediately; there's a terrible affair. Really that boy Stevens must be expelled; he has nearly or quite killed little Norris. They had a quarrel, and he has stabbed him with a knife!"

In an instant Dr. Jones left the room accompanied by all present, and upon arriving at the school-room they found a crowd of boys around the wounded boy, who had fainted from loss of blood, and was lying on the floor, while a tutor supported his head. The doctor, who lived close by, had already been sent for, but before he arrived young Norris had revived, as the usual remedies of cold water and smelling-salts had produced an effect. In the meantime the culprit, Jem Stevens, who had been disarmed by the other boys, stood sulkily in a corner with his arms pinioned behind him. He was an ill-looking fellow, very pale and freckled, with a quantity of tightly curling, sandy hair; his features were coarse, and the expression of his large mouth, with exceedingly thin lips, was peculiarly forbidding; he was tall, but clumsily made, and his general appearance was far from prepossessing. The doctor quickly arrived, and happily pronounced the wound to be trifling, although the hemorrhage had been alarming. The blade of the knife had entered the shoulder, and had fortunately been stopped by the bone.

"Now, then," said the doctor, as he strapped the wound tightly together with plaster, "as Horace says, ' *Jam satis terris nivis* '—' Now we've had enough of knives,' and as Virgil says," he added, looking sternly at Jem Stevens, "*Arma virumque cano!*'—'Cane him on the arms and the rump!'"

It was seldom that Dr. Jones had recourse to corporal punishment, therefore whenever such a course was absolutely necessary it had ten times the ordinary effect as an example. But on this occasion he considered it to be his duty; accordingly he now appeared with the cane, and he called upon Stevens to stand in the middle of the room.

"I didn't do it, sir," faltered the cowardly fellow. "I was cutting a stick when Norris tried to snatch it from me, and he fell against the knife."

This was quickly proved to be a complete falsehood, and the cane was about to descend with extra warmth for the lie when the wounded boy Norris interceded in his behalf, and endeavored to save him from punishment. He was quickly joined in his petition by Edith, and for the moment the school-master's arm was arrested.

"James Stevens," he said, "I regret to say you are a disgrace to your family and to this school. I have pardoned many of your faults, and I have corrected others, trusting that you would improve; but after nearly five years' trial you have ended in an act of cowardice, cruelty, and in falsehood. I have little hope of you, but I give you your own choice. Will you receive a severe chastisement, and then ask pardon of the boy you have injured, and endeavor to improve during this half year, or will you rather be expelled the school at once?"

"I hate the school," said the sullen coward, "and I'd rather leave!"

A yell of contempt burst from the crowd of boys, while the good Dr. Jones grew pale with emotion at the thought of this lamentable result after all the care he had bestowed on the wretched boy.

"Untie his arms," said he. "Go, Stevens, to your room, and at once pack up your things while I write to your father."

The culprit left the room amid the general hissing of his comrades, in which Ned Grey and little Norris were the only two who did not join. In the meantime Edith had also disappeared, while Dr. Jones sorrowfully retired to his study to write the final letter to Squire Stevens of Heron Hall.

Jem Stevens quickly packed up his clothes, and doggedly determined that, when the fly should come to the door, he would depart without taking leave of any one. Accordingly, having prepared his things, he descended to the garden, and entered the shrubbery, as he imagined, unseen; in this he was mistaken, for he had been watched by two persons, who, although unconscious of each other's presence, were actuated by the same feelings. Edith quickly followed him. She hoped to soften his hard heart, and to persuade him to ask her father's pardon and to be friends with little Norris.

Ned Grey had no idea that Edith had such an intention, and although if he had an enemy in the world Jem Stevens was the person, he was generously determined, if possible, to persuade him to act like a boy of honor, and to apologize and receive the punishment in a manly manner. As Ned followed in the direction where Stevens had disappeared, he started at seeing the figure of Edith for one moment as she vanished among the trees. She was evidently searching for Jem Stevens.

Now it would be difficult to explain why, but the fact remained that Ned did not like to hear Edith intercede with her father so warmly for Stevens when he was about to be flogged; and now that he had caught sight for an instant of her pretty figure hurrying in the direction that Stevens had taken, a bitter feeling seized upon his heart, which beat double time at that same moment.

"Why should Edith take so much interest in Stevens—that blackguard, Jem Stevens?" as he could not help muttering aloud, as he now angrily followed through the thick shrubbery. He heard voices close to him, on the other side of a clump of trees; before he could appear in view he heard Jem Stevens rudely reply to Edith:

"l wish the knife had been through Ned Grey's ribs!"

In an instant he rushed through the bushes, and appeared on the small lawn upon which Edith and Stevens were standing.

"Through Ned's ribs, you cowardly brute!" cried Ned, as in the same instant he threw off his jacket and waistcoat. "You may try those tricks on poor little Norris, but not on me, you coward. Now come on; and Edith, you stand on one side," said Ned, in a voice so stern and so different to the soft tone to which she was accustomed, that the tears started to her eyes.

" Off with your coat!" shouted Ned to Jem Stevens, who did not appear very impatient for the fray; however, in another minute the two boys stood in sparring attitude, opposed to each other. Stevens was the heavier of the two, and equally tall, but there was a superior activity in Ned that made up for his inferiority in weight; both were fair boxers, and the fight began with a considerable amount of skill. Although Ned was angrily earnest he did not lose his temper, and he walked round his antagonist, coolly waiting for his opportunity. With his left hand well forward and his right ready, and keeping steady time with each step, as Stevens with great caution kept on the defensive, Ned suddenly made a feint with his left which Stevens attempted to stop, at the same moment he received a heavy blow with Ned's right in the chest that sent him reeling backward. Without a moment's loss of opportunity Ned followed him up with a heavy left-hander straight between the eyes, that fairly knocked him down. Stevens's cold blood was now heated, and springing from the ground he rushed forward utterly regardless of science, and with his head down, protected by his bended arm, he closed with a swinging right-handed hit that unfortunately caught Ned upon the ear, and sent him reeling, and for the instant half stunned, upon one side. Stepping back with consummate coolness and dexterity, with both hands well forward on guard, Ned waited, and defended himself until he lost the buzzing sound in his ears, and recovered from the serious blow.

" Stop!" cried Edith.   " Ned! Stevens! dear Ned!" she cried, " do stop—that's enough—for my sake, Ned!"

At this appeal Ned looked on one side fondly at the peace-maker; but, taken off his guard for that instant, he received a crushing hit from his opponent straight in the face.

" Don't talk now, Edith," he replied, " till I've polished this fellow off!" and, rendered doubly steady and determined by the blow that stung him, he lashed out left and right, after stopping a wild attempt from Stevens; both blows told, and Stevens staggered several paces backward, but, profiting by his first success, he again guarded his

THE FIGHT.

bowed head with his bended arm, and rushed in with great fury, once more delivering a swinging right-hander. Ned sprung quickly on the right, and met him with an upward cut with the left exactly on the nose; at the same instant he turned, and floored him with a right-handed blow on the ear. Jem Stevens lay upon the ground thoroughly beaten.

"Get up!" cried Ned, "don't cry craven yet!" but Stevens only replied by sitting upon the grass and allowing the drops to fall from his bruised nose.

"Do you give in?" said Ned; "if not, get up and finish it like a man."

"Ned, that's enough; he's beaten!" cried Edith; but at those words from her even Jem Stevens's soul was aroused, and starting suddenly up he rushed desperately at Ned with his head down. Ned this time stepped quickly on the left, meeting him with a sharp right-handed blow, at the same time that he caught him round the neck with his left arm, and secured his head in the unpleasant position that is known by the name of "chancery," owing to the fact that the property must be seriously damaged before it can escape from the court. A sharp dig with Ned's right in the face of Stevens was quickly followed by a cry, "I give in!" Ned released him. The fight was over. At this time the sound of wheels was heard as the fly arrived that was to take Jem Stevens from the school.

Both boys were disfigured by the fight. Ned had no marks that could not be immediately removed by soap and water; but Stevens had a pair of swollen eyes that would be perfectly black in a few hours.

"I'm sorry for it, Stevens," said Ned, as he advanced and offered him his hand. "We've had a fight once before, and I had hoped that we had made it up; but don't let us part as enemies now that you must leave school."

"That's right, Ned," said Edith, who had picked up his jacket and waistcoat from the ground; "shake hands together and make up, and go and wash your faces. Now, Stevens, it is not too late; be friends, and go and ask pardon of papa; I'm sure it may be all mended even now."

For an instant Jem Stevens regarded the lovely Edith as though he hesitated in his decision, but his evil disposition overcame the first good impulse. He replied. sullenly: "No, Edith! I love you, but I hate the school; and I

hate you, Ned Grey—forever!" he added, as he looked
spitefully at the fine, generous countenance of his con-
queror.   If Ned had been beaten in the fight he would not
have felt so hurt as he now did when his friendly hand was
thus contemptuously spurned.

"Come away, Edith," he said.   "Doctor Jones will be
very angry, but I'll take the blame; if Stevens won't be
friends I am sorry for it, but it's not my fault."

Ned then put on his jacket and waistcoat that Edith gave
him, and went away.   Edith lingered for a moment in the
hope of yet being able to soften Stevens; but he only pressed
her hand, and said, "Good-bye, Edith; I hate every one but
you, and sometimes I even hate you because you love Ned
Grey better than me."   Confused by such a confession,
Edith could only reply by a cold "Good-bye, Stevens; I
hope you will live to grow more generous;" and she turned
sorrowfully homeward.   Half an hour afterward the noise
of carriage-wheels was again heard as the fly took Jem
Stevens and his trunk away from the school.

CHAPTER V.

CHOICE OF BUSINESS FOR NED.

TWELVE months had passed away since Jem Stevens was
expelled the school, and from that time nothing had disturbed the quiet happiness of Parson Jones's flock.   As
to Jem Stevens's career, his father, the old squire, had
found him incorrigible; he had therefore sent him to sea
very shortly after his disgraceful return from school.   He
was now a midshipman on board one of his majesty's frigates.   Ned Grey was upward of fourteen, and Dr. Jones
had already advised that he should be placed in a merchant's office in some great sea-port, in which capacity he
would have a good chance of improving his position.   To
this proposal Polly had agreed, as she wished that he might
be brought up to some profession that might eventually lead
to competence.   On the other hand, Paul, who had suc-
cessfully evaded the revenue authorities, claimed the active
and adventurous boy as his own son, and would not yield
him to what he called "an old woman's trade."   For Ned
the position was extremely perplexing.   He could not
please all parties.   To his mother he owed everything; to
Dr. Jones much; to his father, as he considered Paul,

hardly as much as others, although he had been always kind. And then there was another. Edith had been almost a sister. What did she wish him to do? They had often walked together in the lovely green lanes, and strolled among the romantic glens and cliffs to gather wild flowers, at which times they would sometimes sit beneath some shady rock overlooking the blue sea, while Edith arranged the flowers in tasteful nosegays. It was then that Ned would gaze at the boundless horizon, and his boyish impulse yearned to wander far beyond, when suddenly a change would come over his features as he looked at the lovely Edith, and thought how hard it would be to separate from her. On the other hand, it would have been difficult to define Edith's feelings; she was so perfectly innocent and yet loving, that she had always looked upon Ned as one that was inseparably connected with her parents and herself. The idea of his ever belonging to any one else had never been suggested to her imagination. They had grown up together for years without the slightest restriction placed upon their intimacy; and, now that they were approaching the age of fifteen, for the first time the warning had been given her that Ned would have to part.

It was a calm Sunday evening in August. The sun was low and constantly shaded by fleecy clouds that traveled slowly across the disk. There was hardly any perceptible breeze. The cattle stood or lay lazily in the meadows, and all Nature appeared to enjoy the calm rest of the Sabbath. The afternoon service had been concluded for about an hour, and the usual throng of idlers that were wont to congregate and chat at the church-door had retired to their respective homes, and the church-yard appeared forsaken. It was not entirely deserted. There were two figures sitting on the greensward, within a few feet of a stone in the form of a cross. Upon this cross was written, "A lady unknown, aged about twenty-two. Cast up by the sea at Sandy Cove."

"How sad this always seems to me!" said Ned. "Poor lady, only twenty-two! I wonder who she was? Even her name was unknown; perhaps she had a husband who may even now be alive, and be grieving for his lost wife without knowing what became of her; perhaps," added Ned, thoughtfully, "she had a child, who lost its mother, and will never know where she lies!"

"I have always heard," said Edith, "that this poor lady was a beautiful person, who was wrecked and drowned. Papa recollects having seen her, and he has told me how lovely she looked when she was brought to shore, and he saw her lying dead, as pale as marble, and almost covered with her long, fair hair. You were wrecked, too, Ned, when you were a little baby," continued Edith; "at least, I have heard so."

"I don't think it is true," said Ned. "Some people have told me so, but my mother must know best; and when I have asked her she has only pressed me in her arms, and asked me if I wish for any other mother; there can not be a dearer one than she."

Edith and Ned had been working a wreath of flowers upon a circle of ivy; the evening was darkening. "Give me that wreath, Edith," said Ned, "if you don't want it. I should like to hang it upon that cross, it seems so desolate. That cold inscription, 'Unknown, cast up by the sea,' chills me to the heart. To think that she should lie here, so utterly forsaken!"

"Let us clean that moss from the stone before we arrange the wreath," said Edith. "I wish we had some everlastings, as those flowers will so quickly fade."

In a few minutes the wreath hung upon the cross.

"Shall we always attend to this?" asked Edith.

"I shall be gone," sighed Ned, "but you will remain at home. Perhaps, Edith, you will forget it; and—you may forget me also—I may not see you for years; and," continued Ned, hesitating, "you may some day marry before I shall return; and we may never meet again."

"Marry! marry! did you say, Ned? how could I marry if you go away? who should I marry if you forsake me, Ned? I would rather die, and lie somewhere here next to this lonely grave; and then if ever you should come back again, you might perhaps come here, and think how we once sat here together, and you might make a wreath for me like that we have now hung upon this cross."

"I'll never marry any one but you, Edith, if you will have me," answered Ned; "but first I must work to earn a livelihood, for I could not see you in want; and I have nothing; but no one loves you as I do, Edith."

As Ned spoke he gazed intently in Edith's large blue

eyes, and then suddenly clasped her in his arms, and kissed her unresisting lips.

"Halloo, that's nice goings-on!" said a peculiar hoarse voice; "ha, ha! ha, ha! Nice goings-on! But I was once young myself, although you mayn't believe it. But, Ned Grey, yer'll have bitter times, and may be yer'll never see the day so long as Mother Lee's alive."

"Out, you old witch!" cried Ned; "be off with your croaking tongue, you wicked old hag, whom I could hang for what I saw when you stoned the drowning men!"

"Don't quarrel with Mother Lee," said Edith; "she's a witch, they say; she'll do some harm after this," continued Edith; "I saw her spit upon the ground as she hobbled off, and she scowled at us like a demon."

Mother Lee had in fact hobbled off, and as she retreated, muttering curses, she clinched her skinny fingers, and shook her withered fist at the innocent pair, and then vanished among the tombstones.

"What can she want here?" said Ned. "She's up to some mischief, or she would not wander so far from Sandy Cove."

"Come, Ned," said Edith, "I do not like to remain on this spot; it's getting dusk, and that horrible old woman frightens me; she may now be hiding behind some gravestone."

As Edith spoke two dark figures were seen to glide stealthily by on the other side of the church-yard; they appeared to be men, but they were quickly concealed by an intervening hedge.

"Come home, Ned," said Edith; "it may be foolish, but I have a curious feeling of uneasiness that I never felt before—a kind of dreadful foreboding of misfortune. God grant that it may be only my weakness, but that horrible old woman has chilled me through and through." She seized Ned's arm, and, trembling in every limb, she hastened toward her home.

"I must run over to the cove to-night," said Ned. "Doctor Jones gave me permission to spend a day at home, to talk over the future with my father and mother, and I promised to be there this evening; but I will see you safe at home first, Edith."

"Oh, Ned, don't go to-night," exclaimed the nervous girl. "I don't know why, but I feel that something's coming. I am certain—yes, positive—that something dreadful is hanging over us; don't go until to-morrow, Ned!"

"This is foolish, Edith," replied Ned. "Why, how is this? You who are so brave, you are frightened at old Mother Lee? Shake off this silly feeling. Never give way to nervousness; it grows upon one if indulged in. Do you think I am so weak that I could not defend you from that old woman?"

Edith felt abashed, and, clutching Ned's arm, with rapid steps she soon reached the rectory. Ned hastily said "Good-bye," and taking a small bundle slung upon his stick, he set off at a trot toward the cove. It was just early night, but the moon was nearly full, and Ned could easily run the five or six miles within the hour. As he left the rectory Nero came bounding after him, and seeing him run the dog considered that he was in pursuit of some object, and accordingly followed him, sometimes running on in advance. Presently Nero gave a short bark, and growling fiercely he returned to Ned with his hair bristled up, looking angry and yet frightened.

"What is it, old boy?" said Ned; "go at it, Nero!"

The dog did not fly forward, as was his custom at such a command, but he walked a few paces in advance, and suddenly dashed back again to Ned, giving at the same time a sharp bark, followed by a deep growl, as a curious shadow like the figure of an old woman with a long stick glided along the clean surface of the ground in the clear moonlight. Ned for the moment felt a chilly sensation creeping over him; but recovering quickly he rushed forward with the dog, but nothing was visible, and Nero, refusing to search, would only keep resolutely at his master's heel.

"The dog's bewitched," exclaimed Ned. "That shadow looked like old Mother Lee; but perhaps it was only the shadow of a cloud crossing the moon."

With this assurance Ned trotted on, followed by the dog, and without any adventure he reached his parents' cottage on the cliff at Sandy Cove. He was greeted with the accustomed warmth of welcome from Polly Grey and the nigger Tim. The latter was much grown, and was a fine strong lad. But Paul was not at home; he had sailed about an hour before Ned's arrival upon some sudden and unexpected errand. Tim, who was slightly unwell, had been left behind.

Before retiring to rest Ned had confided to his mother his boyish love for Edith, with all the youthful hopes and fears that attended his uncertain future. From many little expressions that she had frequently remarked Polly Grey had almost suspected that he was too fond of his old play-fellow, but, her experience having taught her that a boy's heart was easily cured of love's wound, she had attached but little importance to the fact; however, she now received his confession with maternal tenderness. At the same time with much judgment she cautioned him of the many difficulties that lay in his career, and yet gave him hope that Edith might some day become a prize when he should have earned her by such industry as would raise him to a position worthy of her.

Ned went to sleep that night without a fear. As he laid his head upon his pillow Edith's image was in his mind, and in his dreams life seemed to hurry through each successive stage, until he again stood hand in hand with her, who then belonged to him. All was bright—a happiness that was indescribable pervaded his heavenly vision. Could such love only last, such beauty as was painted in his sleep, what other heaven could he wish? But the magic touch of sleep is most inconstant. Presently the bright image began to fade; a mist obscured the fairy-like form with which he had been wandering through infinite space. The scene grew gloomy, then dark; he was among cliffs and precipices; there was a roar of angry waves deep beneath him, but he could not see; he could only feel the warm soft hand that he guided on the dangerous path. Ha! his foot slipped! he lost the hand! one desperate clutch, and again he held it fast, but it was cold and bony; it felt as skinny as an eagle's foot. The moon now rose blood-red, and he could see; but he led not his Edith; it was the horrible hand of old Mother Lee that was in his grasp. "Ha! ha! ha!" sung in his startled ears as he felt a sudden push; he overbalanced from the precipice, and fell—down! down! down! always falling, with the roar of water below, in the darkness and the blood-red moon; at length a crash! and he awoke. He was in bed in his mother's cottage. It was about half past four in the morning; and, feverish with the bewildering dream that he could not at once shake off, he rose and dressed himself, and calling Tim, who was quickly ready, he sought the fresh air of the sea-beach.

The tide was low, therefore upon reaching the bottom of the cliff they could walk some miles upon the rocky beach. Nero had accompanied the two boys, and, delighted with the opportunity, he dashed into the sea, and amused himself with bringing mouthfuls of long sea-weed to the shore. It was not long before the invigorating sea-breeze completely chased away the effects of Ned's miserable dream, and he had regained his usual spirits. They had strolled about two miles, when Ned suggested that it was time to return for breakfast, as they were far from home. Just at that moment they turned the corner of a projecting cliff, on the other side of which was a small sandy beach that formed one of the few landing-places along the rock-bound coast. Upon the sand, but half afloat, lay a large boat, in which were two or three men, while reclining on the beach was a party of twelve sailors; these men were dressed in blue shirts and trousers, and evidently belonged to a ship-of-war that was standing off the shore, about six miles distant. The loud barking of Nero at once attracted the attention of the party.

" Good-morning, youngsters," said a good-natured, stout-looking fellow, in a lieutenant's uniform; " what's brought you here?"

Ned explained that they had merely strolled in that direction, without any particular object, and were now about to return to Sandy Cove.

" We'll give you a lift," said the lieutenant, " we may as well go to the cove as stay here. Come along, my lads; shove the boat off!" And before Ned had time to reply, he found himself surrounded by the party, who had taken his acceptance of their offer for granted. " Jump in," said the lieutenant, as they pushed the boat off the sand. " Never mind the dog, he can find his way back." But Nero had no idea of being left behind, he therefore sprung into the boat, and took his place by Ned, dripping with water.

The lieutenant sat in the stern, but instead of steering for Sandy Cove he kept the boat's head in a direct line for the ship-of-war in the offing; while the steady stroke of eight oars rapidly increased their distance from the land.

"That's the way to France, and not to Sandy Cove!" said Ned, who began to be suspicious.

"Never mind, young fellow; you hold your tongue," said the sailor; "we know our way better than you can tell us."

"You seem to be a bit of a sailor," said the lieutenant.

"I know how to handle a lugger," replied Ned; "but I've never sailed on any other craft than my father's."

"Oh! you are a real sailor, are you? That's right, then, we'll soon make a man of you on board the frigate. You can see Sandy Cove at any time; but it isn't every day that you can see such a ship as the 'Sybille!'"

The truth now flashed upon poor Ned; he was entrapped by a press-gang, and kidnaped into the king's service. The blood rushed to his face as the thought struck him, and the next instant he turned deathly pale as he thought of his mother and of Edith, who would not even guess his fate, and whom he might never see again. He turned to the lieutenant. "For God's sake do not deceive me," said Ned, despairingly. "It will be my utter ruin—my mother expects me even now, there, in that white cottage on the cliff," continued the almost heart-broken boy, as he pointed eagerly to his little home, now plainly visible. A loud shout of laughter from the crew was the only reply to this appeal.

"Jump, Massa Ned! make a swim!" cried Tim, who had slyly slipped off his shoes, and at the same moment he dashed head first into the water; but a powerful hand seized Ned firmly by the collar, and rendered it impossible for him to follow this advice.

"Back water, all!" shouted the lieutenant: at the same time he seized a long boat-hook and caught Tim by his collar as he reappeared upon the surface. Poor Tim was hauled ignominiously into the boat like a black porpoise, amid a roar of laughter; and to prevent any further attempts at escape his wrists were secured with a piece of rope.

"You'd better make up your mind to it," said the lieutenant to Ned; "there's many a lad as good, and perhaps better, than you, who's proud to serve the king; now you have a good chance without your own seeking. You will be as happy as a prince when you're once on board."

"Shall I be able to write a letter home?" asked Ned,

whose tearful eyes were straining fixedly at the white cottage on the cliff that was rapidly diminishing to a mere speck.

"Well, perhaps you may, if anything should detain us. You see we took some letters ashore this morning, and left them with the coast-guard; but we are bound on foreign service, and only left Plymouth yesterday, so there's not much chance for writing."

Poor Ned sat with his head resting upon his hand that shaded his aching eyes. Was it a dream?—a part of that disturbed vision of the past night? He could hardly believe in the reality of the situation. What would Edith think of his mysterious disappearance? What would his mother and father think? They would naturally suppose that the tide had overtaken them, and that both he and Tim had been drowned, as there was deep water at high tide, and no footway beneath the cliffs. If Edith thought him dead, and received no intelligence for years, she might marry some one else!

As these crushing thoughts passed through his brain Ned felt as though his head was being pressed within a vise, and for some minutes he closed his eyes, overpowered with the deepest distress. This prostration did not last long. Ned was a boy of the most undaunted courage, both moral and physical; his most tender feelings had been tortured by an outrage that he could not resist, and he had yielded to the agony of the first shock; but he now brushed his eyes roughly with his jacket-sleeve, and assumed a manner of perfect coolness and determination.

"Don't think me a fool, sir," he said to the lieutenant, who had been calmly watching him; "it's all over now, and I'll do my duty, whatever it may be. She's a fine-looking ship. What guns does she mount, sir?"

"Bravo! that's our sort," said the lieutenant. "You'll do, my lad, there's no fear; you're none the worse for thinking of your mother; she'll be all right; we'll manage to let her know somehow or other, and you'll bring her home a lapful of prize-money some fine day. We'll soon have a brush with a Frenchman when we clear the coast. What's your name, my boy?"

"Edward Grey, sir; but I am always called Ned."

"And who is the young nigger?" continued the lieutenant.

Ned replied, "He is called Tim, sir. He was wrecked, and was the only one saved of the crew."

"Yes, sar," exclaimed Tim, who now broke into the conversation; "de poor nigger Tim nearly dead; then Massa Ned come down de rock like a monkey, and pull de nigger out. Dat a long time ago, when my poor captin dead. Him swim like a fish. He cry, 'Hold on, my lads!' Captin nebber 'fraid. Captin cry out, 'Nebber say die, my boys!' den a big rock tummle on my poor captin's 'ed. Break him like a pumpkin. Nebber see him more!"

"That's a long story," replied the lieutenant, "and I'm not much the wiser for it—what's it all about?"

Ned then explained the catastrophe, and for the first time Tim heard that old Mother Lee had thrown the stone that killed the unfortunate captain. The effect was extraordinary. "Let me go! let me go!" he shouted, as he strove to release his hands from the rope. "I stick a knife in Moder Lee! Oh, cuss de old moder debbel! Why Tim not know before de ole debbel kill the poor captin? Oh, my poor captin! Nebber mind! One day Tim stick a knife in old debbel beast, Moder Lee!"

The lieutenant and crew had already taken a more than usual interest in their prisoners, and Tim's excitement had already made him a favorite with the sailors, especially as they witnessed his affection for his late captain. In about half an hour from this time they neared the frigate, which presently bore down upon them, and backing her main-topsail she waited for the boat. As they approached her Ned could not help admiring her beautiful lines and her taut spars, with the numerous guns on either side peeping wickedly from her open ports. At this moment the shrill boatswain's whistle was heard as a rope was thrown from the vessel, while a man in the bows of the boat hooked on to the rope-ladder that hung over the gangway, and in less than a minute they stood upon the frigate's deck.

"Take the lads for'ard," said the lieutenant, as he went to the quarter-deck to report himself and the new arrivals to the captain. Ned now found himself upon the broad white decks of one of the crack ships in the king's service. There was no more gallant captain among the many fine fellows that thronged the English navy than Cooke, of the "Sybille." He was what the sailors called a tight hand, at

the same time he was the sailor's best friend by enforcing
a rigid discipline.   Ned was a sailor; therefore he had no
sooner cast an admiring glance at the rows of polished
guns, that shone like bronze with a varnish of boiled oil,
and the ropes all neatly disposed in Flemish coils upon the
deck, than his eyes wandered instinctively aloft to the immense yards and the taut rigging of the beautiful ship.
The sails had just bellied out with a fine breeze; the boat
that had brought them on board was already hanging on
the davits; and the foam was now rolling from her bows as
the "Sybille" held her course W. S. W., running at about
ten knots an hour.   Ned looked toward the land; for a few
minutes he could just distinguish a faint white spot apparently not very far above the sea; he knew this was his home,
in which his mother was even now awaiting him; again he
strained his eyes, it was gone!   A faint gray outline like a
bank of clouds was all that remained of the lofty cliffs of
Cornwall, and in less that half an hour there was nothing
to be seen but the boundless blue sea, through which the
noble ship was flying like a bird.

Although Ned was distressed at the sudden and unexpected change in his situation, he was nevertheless excited
by the scene that was entirely in sympathy with his tastes.
As he followed his conductor to the fore part of the vessel
in company with his two black companions, Tim and Nero,
he was full of admiration.   The sailors were beautifully
clean, and dressed exactly alike; the red-coated marines
were on guard in various parts of the ship; the hammocks
were neatly stowed along the nettings, as though they
formed a portion of the bulwarks, while the grateful smell
of cooking as they approached the forecastle betokened the
hour of breakfast.

Just as Ned was passing the fore-hatchway, a midshipman who had been mast-headed for some misconduct was
descending the shrouds, and he sprung upon the deck exactly facing him; for an instant he started backward, and
stared him in the face, as Ned in his turn gazed upon him
with astonishment.

"Jem Stevens!" exclaimed Ned.

"Why, what brought you here? and the dog? and the
nigger?" replied Stevens, recovering himself.

"Kidnaped by the boat's crew an hour ago near Sandy

Cove," said Ned, who in a few words explained all that had taken place.

"Oh, that's it, is it?" replied Stevens; "then I suppose you know your position: you're a common sailor, and I am an officer bearing the king's commission. You and the nigger will do well by giving strict obedience, and you'll be so good as to look sharp when I give you an order. D'ye hear?" continued Stevens, as Ned looked at him in amazement without making a reply.

Ned turned pale with suppressed emotion. Never had such angry feelings boiled within him as at this moment; at the same time he clearly perceived his position. It was too true: Stevens was an officer, while he was in an inferior position; therefore he must obey the bully whom he had thrashed heartily at their last parting.

"Here! look after these fellows, and tie that dog up," cried Stevens to the men, as he rudely turned his back upon Ned, at the same time that he bestowed a kick upon Nero's ribs.

But Nero was no judge of navy discipline, and he immediately replied to the kick by a short growl; at the same time flying at Stevens's throat, he threw him on his back, and pinned him to the deck before Ned had sufficient time to interfere.

"Loose him, Nero! loose him! drop it!" shouted Ned, as he caught the furious dog by the neck, and with both hands upon his throat he succeeded in choking him off. "Down, Nero! Ah, would you again? Down!" he cried, as the dog showed an evident intention of returning to the attack.

"Throw him over!" shouted several voices.

"No, don't," cried others. "It warn't the dog's fault; he kicked him first!"

"You shall throw me over with the dog," said Ned, "if you drown Nero. He is the best dog in the world, and would never bite if not ill-treated." As Ned said this he hugged the dog round the neck for protection, while Nero growled, and seemed prepared to fight all comers.

"He set the dog at me," cried Stevens; who now began to recover from the sudden attack, while the blood trickled from several wounds in his neck.

"That's a lie, if ever I heard a good 'un," said a sailor in a loud whisper to a comrade. "I saw and heard the whole of it, and it warn't the dog's fault; no, not at all; the dog's a good 'un, I know, and so's the lad."

At this time Lieutenant Manger, who had commanded the boat that had captured Ned, appeared upon the scene.

"What's all this about?" asked he, as he looked at the discomfited Stevens, who was generally disliked on board the frigate.

"May I be allowed to explain, sir?" asked Ned, as he stepped boldly but respectfully forward. "I have just recognized an old school-fellow in Stevens, who when we last parted, a twelvemonth ago, expressed a wish to run his knife through my ribs. As that was rather un-English, I made him take his coat off, and after a few rounds he gave in like a coward; he now insults me, as he says he is an officer while I am a common sailor, and to prove his importance he kicked my good dog in the ribs. If I had not saved him, the dog would have torn his throat out in a couple of minutes; he rewards me by declaring that I set the dog on. I can only say it is a willful falsehood, equaled by many for which he was celebrated when at school."

"Well, it's not the first he has told here," replied the lieutenant; "but don't let us have any rows on board. Go and get your breakfast, Ned. And," said he, turning to a sailor, "see that the dog is taken care of."

In a week from that time there were three special favorites among the officers and crew of the "Sybille:" Ned, Jim, and Nero.

CHAPTER VI.

POLLY GREY WATCHING THE MAN-OF-WAR'S BOAT.

WE must leave the "Sybille," with a fair wind, steering for the Cape of Good Hope, on her way to the India station, while we return to Ned's home at Sandy Cove.

On the morning that he had been carried off by the frigate's boat Polly Grey was sitting upon the terrace wall overlooking the sea, awaiting his return to breakfast. The breeze was off the shore, therefore the sea was calm, and from the high cliff upon which the cottage stood Polly Grey enjoyed the grand sea view, and watched the snow-white sails of a large ship in the distance, which her experienced eyes discovered to be a man-of-war. Presently, on the smooth surface of the deep-blue sea, she perceived a boat pulling from the shore about two miles distant. It was so unusual for a boat to pull directly out to sea from that particular direction that she could not help observing it with curiosity. It never altered its course, and at length it became a mere speck in the distance as it steered toward the king's ship. Little did Polly know that Ned's eyes were at that moment straining toward the white cottage on the cliff from that boat she was so curiously watching. At last she lost sight of the boat; she saw the frigate in full sail until, hull down in the far distance, the white canvas merely resembled a sea-gull's wings; it then grew faint, and disappeared below the horizon.

"How late Ned is for breakfast!" said Polly to herself; "what can have become of the boy? The tide is coming in, and should he be too slow his retreat will be cut off, as the high water rises to the cliff!"

As this thought struck her she looked anxiously at the sea below. Already the tide had reached the base of the cliff, which rose from the water perpendicularly like a wall. She felt convinced in her suspicion; and, on the impulse of a moment, she rushed into the cottage, and, seizing a coil of rope, she hurried down the zigzag path to the cove, where she collected several men to assist her in her search. Women and children joined the party, as Ned and Nigger Tim were general favorites, and the danger of the rising tide was well known to the fishermen of Sandy Cove.

They arrived, breathless, on the summit of the high cliff, and presently looked down upon the natural terrace upon which Paul's cottage was built; then continuing along the edge, they skirted the precipice with great rapidity, constantly looking below in the hope of discovering Ned and his companions.

The tide had already risen above the beach; but as the sea was calm there was no immediate danger, as the water was still shallow at the base of the cliff; but Polly hurried forward with increasing anxiety, until she at length became so excited that she wildly shouted his name as she looked over the precipice in despair.

"Ned! Where are you, Ned?"

There was no answer. Sometimes a sea-gull screamed, and for a moment gave her hope, as she imagined it to be a voice; but the time passed, and the tide rose still higher; and as one of the men rolled a large rock over the cliff it fell into the water with a hollow sound that proclaimed its depth. Still they might have climbed to some rock, and be clinging to the side of the cliff. At this thought Polly redoubled her shouts, and urged her companions forward in the hopeless search. They had already passed the spot where the frigate's boat had landed; but the waves had risen high above the sandy beach, and now broke against the sides of the cliff. Polly Grey was frantic with despair; nothing would induce her to give up the search. Hours passed away; and, thoroughly worn out with fatigue and anxiety, she sat down and sobbed bitterly as she gazed hopelessly at the sea. Many of the women and children did the same.

"Who knows?" suddenly exclaimed one of the men who had been the most active of the party, "perhaps Ned may have gone back to school. Cheer up, Mrs. Grey; don't begin to cry for him yet. Ned's not the lad to get drowned; depend upon it, he's forgotten something, and run back to the school; he thinks nothing of five or six miles, and may be we'll find him looking for us by the time we get back to the cove."

This idea, which was generally accepted by the sorrowing party, now gave them courage, and it was decided that they should at once return, while two men should be dispatched to the school; accordingly, with vigor renewed by hope, Polly Grey retraced her steps.

Upon arrival at Sandy Cove they found the little village in great commotion; those villagers who had not accompanied them were standing together in a crowd, discussing some topic with great animation; and upon seeing Polly Grey they immediately shouted:

"Run up to your cottage, Mrs. Grey! You've got some unwelcome visitors there, and we'll just chuck 'em over the cliff if you'll say the word!"

"Is Ned come back?" cried Polly, who was bewildered with her anxiety.

"No, no, there's no such luck; they're looking after him and Paul," replied a woman in the crowd.

Half crazy with this wild intelligence, Polly hastened up the steep path and arrived nearly dead with fatigue at her cottage. Several persons were sitting on the terrace wall; the cottage door was wide open, and when she entered she found old Mother Lee and half a dozen constables in possession of her home.

"What insult is this?" exclaimed Polly. "Where is Ned? Who are you that dare to enter Paul Grey's house in his absence? You, Mother Lee, leave the house immediately! How often have you been warned never to set foot upon the terrace?"

As Polly in a state of intense excitement uttered these words, old Mother Lee merely grinned at her with a ghastly smile of contempt as she quietly took her seat upon a wooden chair without replying a syllable. The head constable of the party now came forward, and, delivering a printed paper, he explained that it was a search-warrant, upon which his party must examine the premises of Paul Grey.

"I am nearly distracted," said Polly, as she gazed abstractedly upon the warrant. "I understand nothing; where is my boy Ned? Oh, tell me, I beseech you, where he is! What does all this mean?—what does all this mean? Tell me the worst at once, I can bear anything but the misery of this suspense. Say what has happened!"

Polly was a beautiful woman, although no longer in her youth; she was hardly thirty-five, and as she now appealed to the constable her face was flushed with excitement, and her large blue eyes shone with a brilliancy and tenderness that softened the hearts of all present except the wretched hag, Mother Lee.

"Sit down, Mrs. Grey, I beseech you, and be calm," replied the constable, "and I will relate all I know in as few words as possible."

Polly seated herself upon a sofa, and with an expression of calm despair she listened anxiously to the explanation.

"In the middle of last night," continued the officer, "the village was disturbed by the loud ringing of the alarm-bell at the rectory, accompanied by violent screams and shouts of 'Help!' and 'Murder!'"

"Good heavens! what next?" exclaimed Polly.

"The watchman quickly sprung his rattle and ran toward the spot, shortly followed by others, who had heard the alarm. Upon arrival at the rectory they found the door broken open, while the screams continued. At this time I myself arrived upon the scene, and upon rushing up the stairs I entered a room by a door that was wide open, where I found Miss Edith Jones endeavoring to support her father, who was lying on the ground bleeding from a wound in his left breast. Several maid-servants were screaming for help, and a strong smell of gunpowder filled the apartment. At the same time Mrs. Jones had fainted, and was lying helpless upon the floor.

"It appeared that the house had been broken into and robbed at about one o'clock in the morning, and that Parson Jones, hearing a noise in the room where his papers were kept in a chest with a large sum of money, got out of bed, and upon entering the room it is supposed he must have disturbed the robbers in the act, as a large parcel of plate packed up in a blanket was left behind in their flight. At that time one of the robbers fired a pistol, which struck the unfortunate gentleman in the left breast. A few moments after the report of the pistol Mrs. Jones and Miss Edith arrived with a light, and found the poor gentleman dying. Mrs. Jones fainted on the spot, and Miss Edith endeavored to raise her father from the ground; but he was at the last gasp, and could only press her hand, and with a struggle for utterance, he whispered faintly, but most distinctly, 'Ned Grey.'

"The robbers had escaped with all the money, which amounted to two hundred guineas, and the poor gentleman is now lying dead; while Mrs. Jones is gone almost frantic, and Miss Edith won't hear of it when her mother says it must be Ned Grey who did it, because the parson said so in his last moments."

During the relation of this dreadful narrative Polly Grey had stared fixedly at the constable as though she were in a dream. At the conclusion she uttered, incoherently, as though thinking aloud, "Ned Grey! Ned Grey! What Ned Grey? Not my Ned! But where is Ned?"

"That's exactly the question," replied the officer; "as his presence is required before the magistrate, also that of his father."

"Paul left the cove last evening in the 'Polly,' and I do not know when he will return; but Ned arrived here last night after his father's departure, and this morning at a very early hour he, with the negro lad Tim and the dog, started along the sea-beach, and they have never since been heard of. I am almost distracted with anxiety, as I can not tell what has become of them, and I fear some terrible accident from the high tide."

A hoarse chuckle was succeeded by a murmur from Mother Lee: "He's not born to be drowned, not he! more likely for the gallows! and Paul 'll swing in company if he gets his right!"

Polly looked at the horrible countenance of Mother Lee with undisguised contempt; but the old woman, who had vowed vengeance upon Paul and his family ever since the night of her narrow escape, when she heaved rocks upon the cutter's crew, now glared at Polly with a malicious triumph that made her naturally repulsive features still more hideous.

At this moment the constable, having risen from his seat, apologized for the intrusion, but declared that he could not avoid acting upon the search-warrant, therefore he must proceed to examine the premises.

"With all my heart," replied Polly, who could hardly realize her situation; "search the house and out-buildings. There is no one here—I wish there were!"

Without more delay, the officer with four of his men proceeded to search the various rooms, while a constable remained with Polly and Mother Lee. It is needless to add that nothing could be found that threw the slightest suspicion upon the house, and the officer shortly returned and requested Polly to unlock certain cupboards in the kitchen that were erected against the cliff, which having been cut perfectly straight formed a natural wall.

Polly handed him the key, and he opened the right-hand door; there was nothing but a few jars, with sundry bottles and other domestic articles. Perfectly satisfied with the result of his examination, the officer opened the left-hand cupboard. The shelves were nearly filled with trifling articles that belonged to a fisherman's occupation: sail, needles, skeins of twine, packets of sail-cloth, etc.; and having cast a hurried glance at the contents the officer carelessly closed the door.

"Ha! ha! ha! Ha! ha! ha!" yelled a harsh, shrill voice, as Mother Lee, who had been eagerly watching the examination through the open door, now hobbled into the room. "Your eyes ain't worth much if yer can't see through an inch plank," said the old woman, as she threw open the door of the cupboard that the officer had closed;

at the same time she struck the back with the end of her
stick, which resounded with a hollow tone like a large
drum. "There's music for yer to dance to! if your eyes
are no good, your ears may help yer if yer ain't deaf as
well as blind," screeched the wretched old hag, who to the
astonishment of Polly knew the secret of the cave.

The constable approached the cupboard with curiosity,
and, half incredulous, he obeyed the direction of the old
woman as she cried:

"Push the bolt back under the bottom shelf, and put
your shoulder to it—that's the secret."

In an instant the back of the cupboard together with the
shelves flew open, and exposed the dark and narrow gallery
in the rock, to which it formed an entrance.

"We must have a light!" said the officer. "Perhaps
you were not aware of this secret, Mrs. Grey," he continued, as Polly, deathly pale and trembling, struck a light,
and shortly handed him a candle without making him a
reply.

The officer, followed by several of his men, cautiously
entered the cave, as though fearing a surprise. In about
five minutes they returned heavily laden with various packages, and again entered the gallery, as much remained to
be removed.

On the completion of their task it was discovered that
contraband goods of considerable value had been concealed,
and a list was immediately made out, specifying the number of bales of silk, kegs of brandy and hollands, and packages of tobacco that had been seized, while notice of the
event was immediately dispatched to the coast-guard station.

There was one old box that was hardly worth examination, as it appeared to contain little beyond some loose cotton-wool; but, as this was brought into the kitchen from
the cave, Polly immediately rushed forward.

"You must not touch that!" she cried. "That box is
Ned's own, although he does not know it; the contents are
sacred. For Heaven's sake do not interfere with that, as
all depends upon it!—his future—his very identity—everything in the world."

As Polly, in great excitement, thus addressed the constables, their suspicions that had already been justly aroused
were rendered still more keen, and the chief officer calmly

but determinedly insisted upon an examination of the contents. In another instant a bag containing two hundred
guineas was discovered lying as though for the purpose of
concealment among the loose cotton-wool which nearly
filled the box. Hardly had the gold been produced, than
a small parcel containing a valuable diamond necklace,
several rings, and a gold locket were likewise brought forth,
to the amazement of the officer.

A large sum of gold had been stolen from the rectory;
here was a bag, evidently concealed, containing the exact
amount (two hundred guineas), also diamonds that could
not possibly belong to a person in Polly Grey's position.
Contraband goods, also concealed, proved that Paul Grey,
and probably Ned likewise, had been engaged in lawless
and desperate adventures; both were now absent. The
whole affair looked extremely suspicious. Polly might
have misled the constables respecting their absence; they
might possibly be concealed in the neighborhood; decidedly
she had not volunteered any information, and the cave had
been discovered simply through the instrumentality of
Mother Lee.

There was only one course to pursue; in spite of Polly's
entreaties, the officer declared that he must take possession
of the gold and diamonds, as he suspected them to be a
portion of the property stolen from the rectory, and he
would wait for the arrival of Captain Smart, of the coast-
guard, to whom he should hand over the articles of contraband.

About two hours passed, during which Polly Grey was in
an agony of suspense, and she at length hailed the arrival
of Captain Smart with unrepressed delight as the door
opened and he entered the room.

"Thank God you are come at last!" cried Polly. "Before you speak a word, drive that insolent old hag from the
house. Begone!" shouted Polly to old Mother Lee, who
had hitherto sat like an evil spirit watching her misery.

Joe Smart, without more ado, seized the old woman by
the arm, and in spite of her curses he bundled her out of
the door; at the same time he remarked to the chief constable upon the gross impropriety of allowing her to have
remained so long against the wishes of the owner of the
cottage.

"She is our principal witness," replied the constable;

"and without her we should never have discovered the
cave. Look at this mass of property; we owe the whole
to Mother Lee. Take your share. All the contraband belongs to you; and this comes to my department," exclaimed the constable, as he produced the bag of guineas
and the glittering necklace of brilliants.

It would be impossible to paint the surprise and conster-
nation of Joe Smart at this intelligence. He glanced first
at the numerous articles that lay upon the floor, and then
he turned inquiringly to Polly, with an expression of
mingled curiosity and despair.

"Judge for yourself," continued the officer, as he led
the way to the cave, followed instinctively by the astonished
friend of the family.

There was no possibility of doubt respecting the smuggled
goods; but upon Joe Smart's return to the room Polly immediately called him on one side, and in a few words she
confided to him the long-kept secret of the gold and diamond necklace, with the locket, and all that had been discovered in the box when the infant was washed ashore; and
that her only object in secreting them was to insure their
safety in case they might at some future time be required to
prove Ned Grey's identity.

"As to the other goods," continued Polly, "they belonged to Paul, and he will explain all concerning them
upon his return. I do not presume to interfere with his
affairs. The existence of the cave he always wished to remain a secret, and I should be a faithless wife to divulge
what he concealed."

At the first glance Captain Smart, as a revenue officer,
perceived that the affair was exceedingly grave, for,
although he had not the slightest doubt of Polly Grey's
integrity, he saw that the absence of both Paul and Ned,
together with the young negro, would be a natural cause
for suspicion, especially as Paul's antecedents would not
add to his good reputation. He thoroughly believed Polly's
explanation of the bag of guineas and the diamond necklace. The latter was worth at least a thousand pounds,
and he saw that the fact of its possession by Paul would
render such a story as that of the shipwreck most improb-
able, if not actually incredible. At all events, it would
not be believed by the hardened authorities of the law. It
was now his painful duty to seize as articles of contraband

the large amount of property that lay before him, and, even worse, it would be necessary to take the person of his old friend into custody immediately upon his arrival. How should he be able to lay hands upon Polly's husband? Joe Smart had always loved her, first as a suitor, but after her marriage with Paul he had resigned himself to his fate, and had controlled his affection to the strict degree of friendship; he now saw her in distress, and in Paul's absence she had hailed his arrival as a deliverer; but it would be his own hand that must press most heavily upon them, while his heart burned with the keenest sympathy.

"My dear Mrs. Grey," said the straightforward Joe Smart, "this is a very serious affair, and you must make up your mind to bear many severe trials before it can be concluded; at the same time depend upon me as your truest friend, although, as the king's officer, I may be forced to act in a manner that may belie such a profession of friendship. I am obliged to retain in custody the whole of the articles that have been discovered in the cave, and I only trust that my old friend Paul will land upon some other part of the Cornish coast, where I have not the command."

"But where is Ned?" asked Polly, in a voice of unnatural calmness, as though the oppression of so many misfortunes had rendered her callous to adversity. "You can not suspect Ned; neither would Tim do anything that was wrong. The dog also is with them, and they all slept here last night, and only left the house early in the morning. What can have become of them? I fear that horrible old woman is at the bottom of this," continued Polly. "She vowed vengeance against Paul for having threatened to throw her over the cliff on the night when the cutter was lost with all the crew. Me she has always hated; and Ned told me that he saw her in the church-yard by the rectory only last evening. What business had she so far from the cove? The whole affair is a fearful mystery. You know how Ned loved dear old Parson Jones and Edith. It was only last night that the boy opened his heart to me, and told me how he loved her, and how he would try by industry to win a position worthy of her. Edith loves him. Perhaps her poor father suspected it, and would have spoken of him to her with his last breath, as he died with the name of ' Ned Grey ' upon his lips. The mother is a good but foolish woman, and she is carried away by her distress. But Edith knows. She knows as well as I do how good and true is Ned. I must go to her this moment; perhaps she can throw some light upon his absence. At all events, it will be a comfort to see some one who loves my boy!"

Joe Smart could find no words of comfort. He knew that it would be impossible for such a boy as Ned to commit a crime. At the same time he saw that the circumstances of the case would naturally throw a certain amount of suspicion upon parties who had been seen at the rectory on the previous night, but who had disappeared as mysteriously a few hours later, during which interval robbery and murder had been committed, while the exact sum of money that was missing had been found concealed in the house occupied by those who were now suddenly absent.

"When do you expect Paul home?" asked Joe Smart.

"I have no idea. His return is always uncertain," replied Polly.

"Well," said Joe, "in the meantime, Mrs. Grey, it will be better to return these heavy parcels to the cave. You will give me the key of the cupboard entrance, and I will trust to your honor that they shall not be removed until I can bring the men necessary for the purpose."

Captain Smart now turned to the constables, and explained the affair of the shipwreck nearly fifteen years ago, how Ned had been saved as an infant, and the gold and precious stones now discovered had been found with the child, and secreted for an excellent purpose by Polly Grey and Paul, who had acted throughout as though they were the parents of the boy.

"That's all very well, and it may be perfectly true," replied the chief officer; "but under the circumstances it is my duty to deposit the valuables with a justice of the peace. If the tale can be proved, it will be all right; but surely Mrs. Grey must be aware that such valuable articles as diamonds and a large sum of gold should have been placed in the hands of a magistrate at the time that the infant was saved, when the discovery was first made. The neglect of this caution is now manifest, if the tale be true; but as a burglary and murder have been committed, and a sum of guineas stolen, while her son Ned was supposed to be at the rectory and he is now suddenly missing, what other conclusion can be arrived at but that he is in some way implicated in the affair? Especially as we have now found a bag of guineas carefully concealed, with other suspicious property, while the last words of the murdered gentleman appeared to point to the lad in particular. "

" It's of no use arguing the question here," said Captain Smart; " the affair will be sifted and decided by the proper authorities. I know Ned Grey, and I would stake my life upon his character. It is very distressing, Mrs. Grey," added he, turning to Polly, " but it will all come right in the end, you may depend upon it; only have patience, which I confess is sorely needed, and if I can help you in any way only point out the manner, and it will be my greatest happiness to serve you.

" Just put back those packages into the rock, my lads," continued Captain Smart, as he addressed the constables; " and give me the key."

In the meantime the chief officer made up the gold and jewels in a sealed packet, and gave a receipt in writing to Polly Grey. The party then withdrew, leaving Polly and Joe Smart alone.

" I don't like the complexion of this affair, Mrs. Grey," said Joe Smart. " I have no fear for Ned, as he is a boy who can take good care of himself; but I feel sure that there is some underhand work that must be brought to light. I can not allow you to walk alone to the rectory; the goods are all safe now that they are replaced in the cave, and you must permit me to accompany you. As you say, Miss Edith may be able to throw some light upon Ned's absence."

" You were always a good friend," said Polly, " but I never appreciated kindness so much as now;" and hastily throwing a shawl over her shoulders, she took Joe's arm and started for the rectory.

It would be useless to describe the meeting between Polly Grey and Edith. There was a natural sympathy between them which their distress only served to strengthen. Edith could give no other account of Ned than the fact of his having parted with her late in the preceding evening, when he had been followed by Nero.

" Oh!" exclaimed the sobbing girl, " if Nero had only remained here no thieves could have entered the house, and my dear father might have been still alive!"

On the other hand, her mother, who was naturally weak, and a woman of impulse, leaned to the opinion that Ned was in some way implicated in the burglary because her husband had mentioned his name; and the fact of the dog having been allured away from the premises on the fatal night only served to rivet her suspicion. Edith was furious at the idea, and in the evidence that she had given before the magistrates she laid much stress upon the appearance of old Mother Lee, that had been so quickly followed by the figures of two men who had furtively passed by the church-yard on the previous evening, when she and Ned had conversed together. This testimony was but slightly regarded, and, in spite of her protest, the general opinion leaned strongly toward the guilt of the absentees.

One fisherman declared that he had seen a vessel in the dusk of the evening which he could not exactly swear to as the "Polly," but he thought it was the lugger hovering about the coast. Thus a party might have landed, and effected their escape by sea after having committed the burglary. Rumors of all kinds more or less extravagant found credence throughout the village; but when toward evening the news spread of the discovery of a bag containing two hundred guineas, together with jewels and a quantity of contraband articles in a secret cave connected with Paul Grey's dwelling at Sandy Cove, there was a general conviction that the Grey family were concerned in the robbery. One woman said that she had dreamed a few nights ago that a black man was cutting her throat, therefore she believed that the negro Tim had shot the parson; another woman had had a cold shiver run down her back as she crossed the church-yard on the Sunday afternoon, therefore she knew that a murder was to be committed; while a third had always said from the beginning "that no good would come of Ned Grey, as he was a deal too handsome to live." However absurd! there was nothing that could be too ridiculous to be believed; even the watchman declared that, when he took his quart of ale at the White Hart just before midnight, he had a taste of blood in his mouth, and so he "thought as how there'd be a murder before morning;" but this warning had not kept him on the alert, as he had been fast asleep until awakened by the pistol-shot and screams from the rectory.

That night was one of misery for many. Although

Polly Grey was fatigued with the bodily exertions of the day, she was far too troubled to be able to close her eyes, and she begged the widow Mrs. Jones to be allowed to remain at the rectory, to sit up with her and Edith, as all were too sorrowful to sleep.

Although Mrs. Jones, in the agony of her distress, had given way to the first impulse of her suspicion owing to the simple testimony of her husband's last words, which were entirely unconnected, she was naturally a kind and warm-hearted person, and when closeted throughout the midnight hours with Edith and Polly Grey, she mingled her grief with theirs, and before the gray light of morning gleamed through the shutters she had been almost converted to a belief in Ned's innocence.

The day following only increased Polly Grey's suspense. No tidings could be heard of Ned. It was difficult to say which suffered most deeply, whether those who mourned for one dead, or those who lived in the torture of a constant anxiety. Unfortunately Edith had to bear the double trial; she had lost a father whom she had loved tenderly, and not only was Ned missing but his name was blackened with suspicion.

That same afternoon the jury at the coroner's inquest brought in a verdict of willful murder against Paul and Ned Grey, together with the negro, Tim. The principal witness had been Mother Lee, who swore that she had seen all three persons lurking about the premises shortly before midnight, and that they afterward took the road in the direction of Sandy Cove. A warrant was immediately issued for their apprehension.

The news of this danger and disgrace, added to her father's death, was too much for the excited nerves of Edith. On the day of her father's funeral she was seized with a violent fit of shivering, and a few hours later she was prostrated by a burning fever. In addition to other calamities, Polly Grey had been arrested upon suspicion of connivance at the robbery and concealment of stolen goods; and this innocent and lovely woman had been taken to the common jail, until she was bailed out by the promptitude of Captain Smart and the widow, Mrs. Jones. The latter had now insisted upon her remaining at the rectory until some news should be received of her husband and Ned.

Polly was now able to repay this kindness by the careful

nursing of her youthful patient, Edith, who lay in delirium for several days, almost beyond the hope of recovery. Although she was in a state of perpetual suspense at the unusually long absence of Paul, in addition to the mysterious disappearance of Ned, Polly Grey's spirit rose against the pressure of adversity, and she sought consolation in that trust in Providence which religion taught her was the only help in the hour of need. Bereft of all that had made life happy, she now devoted herself to the care of Edith, whom she loved with increased affection as the sharer of her anxiety for Ned.

For three weeks Edith lay in the greatest danger; but at the expiration of that time a sudden change took place, and as the restless and weary night passed away the morning dawned upon a pale, thin face, which had suddenly lost the deep scarlet flush that for so many days had overspread the features. For a moment, as Polly opened the shutters and looked upon the finely chiseled face that looked like the whitest marble, she thought the spirit had fled forever, and she hastened to the bedside and gently took the slender hand that lay upon the coverlet. There was a faintly perceptible pulse, and the sharp, hard throbbing of fever had ceased; she leaned over the lovely face, and placed her cheek close to Edith's lips; she breathed gently and regularly; the breath was no longer hot, and the patient calmly slept; it was the first natural sleep that she had had for many days.

"Thank God!" whispered Polly to herself, and she quietly left the room to carry the happy intelligence to the mother, who had been so broken down with sorrow as to be almost helpless.

From that hour Edith mended; she woke from her sleep refreshed; her mind was calm and clear, and as she saw Polly's thankful face beaming over her, she gently placed her thin white arm around her neck, and drew her lips toward her.

"You have been very kind to me, dear Mrs. Grey. But how tired you look; lie down and sleep; I am well now," said Edith, as she endeavored to sit up, but fell back exhausted in the bed. Polly was a careful nurse, and she had already prepared a stimulant to refresh the patient upon waking, and after a short time she again fell asleep. That day dated the commencement of her recovery.

In a few weeks Edith was once more in the open air, but the rectory was no longer the same. The noisy shouts of school-boys had long ceased, as the school had been broken up, and a profound stillness made the formerly happy spot almost unbearable. It was a large house, that required a considerable family to enliven it, and now that this sudden desolation had taken place, it appeared like a miserable solitude. Polly Grey had become almost one of the family since the general affliction, and Edith could not sufficiently express her gratitude for the tender care that had saved her in her dangerous illness. The good but weak Mrs. Jones now leaned upon Polly as her right hand, and she had not only forgotten her suspicions of Ned Grey, but upon hearing of the valuable diamond necklace, she had taken a vast interest in the boy's fate, as she felt no doubt that he was the child of some person of considerable position.

Dr. Jones, as has before been stated, was a man of independent fortune; the rectory, together with a farm of several hundred acres, was his own freehold; in addition to which he had left a fortune of nearly fifty thousand pounds. A life interest in twenty thousand pounds had been left to his widow, while the remainder was bequeathed absolutely to his only child, Edith.

As Edith was now sufficiently recovered to bear the open air the doctor proposed a change, and Polly suggested that they should retire to her pretty cottage on the cliff at Sandy Cove, where they could rough it in a snug and clean dwelling, with the beautiful view of the sea, and a fresh breeze that was a finer tonic than all the doctor's drugs. This proposal was at once adopted: a cart-load of sundry little luxuries was dispatched to the care of Captain Smart, of the coast-guard station, who not only received them, but with a sailor's neatness and assiduity he arranged everything in readiness for the reception of the party, so that the cottage never had looked so pretty as when they all arrived, and found the proud and good-natured face of Captain Smart to welcome them at the door.

There was a certain excitement in the move and the change of scene that had a marvelous effect in quelling the pangs of their recent affliction. There is an extraordinary power in the nerves of the eye that exerts an immediate influence upon the mind, and the scene being changed, the

4

miseries of the past were for the moment left behind in the localities with which they were associated.

On the following morning they sat together at breakfast, looking out of the open window upon the blue and now peaceful sea. Polly Grey was the saddest of the party, as she was in her old home, and her eyes were fixed upon several articles that were arranged upon the walls which belonged to Paul and Ned. There was a new red woolen comforter that she had knitted for Paul when he had started. This was to have been given to him on his return; it had now been folded carefully by Joe Smart and placed upon the mantel-piece beneath the picture of the "Polly."

At this moment Edith started as a figure passed the window. "Mrs. Grey!" she suddenly shouted, "take care!"

The next instant the figure of old Mother Lee stood peering into the cottage. "You're a pretty thing to call yerself a wife!" screamed the old woman, in her most horrible key. "Doesn't luck come from the sou'-west?"

Polly rushed to the door. "What did she mean?" cries the almost frantic wife, as the figure of the old woman vanished before she could unfasten the latch.

"I see!" cried Edith, "it is a ship!"

Polly Grey gazed intently from the window at a small white spot on the horizon.

"It is a sea-bird," said Mrs. Jones.

For some minutes not a word was spoken; all eyes were fixed upon the vessel. Presently Polly Grey turned pale as death as the vessel, altering her course, distinctly exposed the three masts and rig of a lugger.

"It is the 'Polly!' it is Paul!" shouted Polly Grey, as she fell heavily on the floor, overpowered by hopes and fears.

CHAPTER VII.

LUGGER AND CUTTER OFF SANDY COVE.

THE wind was blowing hard from the north, and the lugger presently stood off on another tack. At this moment the white sails of a revenue cutter were suddenly perceived as she rounded a point, and with a spanking breeze she bore down direct upon the lugger. Polly had quickly recovered from her emotion, and the three now watched with intense interest the movements of the two vessels, feeling convinced that Paul was within a few hours of home.

As the lugger was close hauled to the wind, endeavoring to beat up toward the shore, she had no chance of escaping the cutter, should that be her intention, unless by altering her course and running before the wind. This she presently did, and in a few minutes she disappeared below the horizon, while the cutter in full sail chased in the same direction. This was a terrible disappointment to Polly Grey, who with natural eagerness had expected her husband's quick return. More than a month had passed without the slightest tidings since Paul had left Sandy Cove. At that time the channel was full of British cruisers and privateers which preyed like falcons upon the French commerce, while on the other hand the French ships-of-war were ever on the lookout for British merchant vessels returning deeply laden from the colonies. Accordingly there was much risk attending unarmed vessels that ventured too near the coast of France. Polly Grey's chief anxiety was, that Paul might have been captured by the French; but as she had now recognized his vessel, she had no longer any fear of the common enemy; the danger lay in the revenue cutters. There was a real cause for apprehension; should he return in safety, he might be immediately arrested upon the charge of smuggling, even should the ridiculous accusation of complicity in the burglary fall to the ground. This latter charge was only supported by the false evidence of Mother Lee, who had sworn that she saw him near the rectory on the night of the murder.

The day passed away in watching the sea; the cutter had quickly disappeared in chase of the lugger in the morning. It was now past six in the evening, and for the last two or three hours the wind had changed; and although there was no appearance of actual bad weather, it was blowing hard from the south-west, and, as usual, a heavy surf was breaking upon the rocky coast.

As the wind was now fair, Polly, and other inhabitants of the cove, who were experienced in the locality, expected that the lugger would run for the bay during the night. Among others, Mother Lee was also of this opinion; and, true to her natural instincts, she had already collected some staves of old tar-barrels and a quantity of inflamma-

ble material for the purpose of making the fires necessary
as guides.

As has been already described, this wretched woman had
vowed vengeance against Paul and all that belonged to him
ever since the memorable night on which he had dashed
her to the ground when caught in the dastardly act of
stoning the drowning crew of the cutter. From that moment there was no villainy that Mother Lee would not have
perpetrated in order to effect his ruin. Thus she had endeavored to swear away his life, together with that of Ned,
in the false evidence given in the case of the burglary. She
also had betrayed the secret of the cave; and this night
she intended to complete his ruin and death by an act of
treachery still more diabolical.

Paul Grey, as is well known, was a daring and hitherto
a successful smuggler; and whenever it had been necessary
to run straight for Sandy Cove on a dark and stormy night,
when all other vessels would have avoided the coast, he
could depend upon his knowledge of the locality, and upon
the fires which were generally lighted on the heights upon
either side to guide the " Polly " into the entrance of the
bay.

Mother Lee felt certain that the " Polly," being chased
by the cruiser, would, as usual, run for the bay during the
night, as the wind was blowing hard directly upon the
shore, therefore the cutter would hesitate to approach the
rocks. She accordingly determined to arrange a snare that
must inevitably wreck the " Polly," and destroy all on
board. Having collected a large quantity of fuel, which
she tied in many bundles, she left word in the village that
she would take care of the fires as usual, if a couple of men
would give her a hand in carrying the fagots to the proper
points. This was done without loss of time.

Immediately after dark the old woman, unseen by any
one, busied herself in carrying several bundles of shavings
and a quantity of barrel-staves to the cliff against which,
upon a former occasion, the mast of the cutter had been
dashed, with the clinging crew.

She found the pile of fuel properly arranged by the
fishermen upon the edge of the precipice overhanging the
narrow entrance of the bay. On the opposite side, upon a
corresponding height, they had piled the fagots for the
parallel fire; but this it was not Mother Lee's intention to

light. Guessing as nearly as possible the width of the entrance to the bay, the old woman carried her fagots to an equal width from the fuel already piled upon the cliff. Here she carefully arranged the shavings and the staves of tar-barrels in readiness for the occasion.

There were now three piles of fuel instead of two; thus should that on the left of the bay remain dark, while the other two on the right were lighted, the unfortunate vessel, that might trust to the fires as guides, would be led at full speed directly against the cliff, instead of to the mouth of the harbor. Such was the snare that the treachery of the old hag had designed.

It was a dark night; there were neither moon nor stars, and a heavy surf roared against the rocks, while the cliffs trembled with each heavy shock as the waves dashed against their sides.

"Ha! ha! ha!" chuckled the woman, as she leaned over the pile of dry wood and smeared a quantity of fresh tar from a small keg upon the shavings. "This'll make it burn brightly, and keep the fire alight till it's all over, I know. Mother Lee knows a trick or two, cuss them all!" she muttered, as she continued to dip small pieces of wood into the keg of tar, which she arranged beneath the pile, wiping her skinny fingers occasionally upon her tarred and greasy old rags, with which she was thickly clothed. "Mother Lee knows a trick or two," she continued. "I'll have revenge to-night. It was here down below I paid 'em out; just here where the cutter's people caught it, cuss 'em all! and here, Paul Grey, you'll catch it too. It was here you laid hands on Mother Lee, and here she'll teach you that she knows a trick or two."

Thus the old woman muttered to herself as she arranged her yet unlighted beacons. She had prepared herself with about a gallon of tar, in order to keep up a strong blaze by pouring it upon the fire whenever it should be required.

In the meantime the villagers had gone to sleep, and the only persons who watched were Mother Lee upon the Point and Polly Grey from the cottage window; Edith and her mother had retired to rest.

The wind had increased in violence, and nothing could be seen in the thick darkness. Mother Lee was shivering with cold, but she had never ceased muttering curses through her chattering gums. "He's sure to come with this wind; I never knew a stiff sou'-wester without some luck." These words had hardly escaped from her thin lips when a bright light flashed like a fiery thread into the dark clouds far out at sea.

"Ha! ha! ha! There's a rocket! I said so, I knew it. Here's luck from the old quarter! p'r'aps we'll catch 'em both; p'r'aps it's the old story again, and the cutter's chasing; then we'll catch 'em in the same net, and make a night of it. Here's luck from the sou'-west with a vengeance!"

As the excited old wretch now speculated with delight upon the probability of wrecking both vessels, she drew out a tinder-box from a deep pocket in the many and intricate folds of her clothes, and, with hands trembling with devilish eagerness, she struck a light with a flint and steel. "Rot the sparks, they won't catch!" exclaimed the old woman, in a rage, as she vainly struck the flint, and cut her knuckles in the dark with the steel. At length the tinder caught, and shading the box carefully with her hands, she placed it under the shelter of the shavings beneath the pile; she then blew the spark while she applied a match, and in a few seconds the tarred shavings took fire and ignited the entire pile. Taking a lighted stick from the fire she carried it to the remaining beacon; presently it blazed brightly, and the snare was completed.

Polly could see from the cottage window the rocket at sea quickly answered by one from the coast-guard station and by the beacons on the cliff, but she could not detect any unusual change in their position, as the entrance to the bay was so exceedingly narrow that the wrong direction of one fire could not be appreciated in the darkness. She accordingly waited in earnest expectation of Paul's safe arrival, as she knew that his vessel would sail straight for the entrance of the bay. Polly's heart beat so loudly that she could hear it throb as every half hour increased her anxiety, and clasping her aching breast with her hands she prayed fervently for her husband's safe return. Once she thought of waking Mrs. Jones and Edith, but on second thought she wished to clasp Paul in her arms on his arrival without other witnesses to her joy; thus Edith and her mother slept soundly.

In the meantime the vessel neared the shore, running straight for the beacons at about ten knots an hour.

DESTRUCTION OF MOTHER LEE.

Mother Lee stood upon the cliff, and vainly strove to pierce the darkness.

"She can't be far off," said the old woman. "I'll put another dose of tar upon the fires to give 'em a blaze. That'll do it!" she muttered. "Ha! ha! ha! Mother Lee knows a trick or two, cuss 'em all!" She chuckled as she poured a quantity of tar upon the second fire at the point of the harbor's mouth, which was followed by a roar of flame. "Now for the other fire, so they'll make no mistake and come in prettily!" she again muttered, as she approached the other beacon; but on her way among the loose stones her foot stumbled, and she fell over her open keg and became covered with the contents. "Rot the stones, and rot the tar!" she exclaimed, in a rage, as she wrung her saturated clothes into the keg lest she should lose a drop of her precious fuel. At this moment the clouds parted, and the moon in all its unexpected beauty burst upon the scene and illumined the hitherto dark surface of the sea. "Here they come! ha, ha! Close in! It's all right!" almost shouted the old woman in ecstasy, as, having thrown the tar keg into the blaze, she shaded her brow with both her skinny hands so as to keep out the dazzling light which was directly behind her. The fire now roared upward with increased fury.

The brilliant moonlight plainly discovered a vessel within a quarter of a mile of the rock, driving in full sail directly upon the cliff, with the evident intention of passing between the beacons. Mother Lee crouched down lest her figure should be seen in the bright light. "Cuss your light!" she muttered, as she shook her skinny fist at the unwelcome moon; "yer'll be showing 'em the rocks;" and she stooped still lower to avoid being seen. In doing this, with her back to the fire, her thick stuff dress, already saturated with tar, became ignited behind without her knowledge, until the violent wind rapidly spread the flame. Quickly springing to her feet, she turned round, and in an instant the rush of air lashed the flames into forked sheets, which caught with wonderful velocity every portion of her inflammable dress. The awful truth flashed upon her, and with a yell that might have been heard a mile distant she rushed away from the edge of the cliff in a volume of red fire that ascended high in the air. Thick wreaths of black smoke reddened by the bright glare rolled upward in a murky volume. Shriek succeeded shriek in the wildest agony of fright and bodily torture, as the fire now thoroughly enveloped her and searched out every portion of her clothing. In a waving pillar of flame she rushed to and fro in her frantic endeavors to escape from the relentless enemy, and the hitherto bright beacons sunk into insignificance before the blazing pyramid of fire.

The apparently doomed vessel was within three hundred yards of the cliff when this third beacon startled the captain and crew. "Luff!" shouted a powerful voice on board the ship. "Let go the anchor!"

Almost in the same instant the sudden order was obeyed, and the bows of the trembling vessel were brought quickly to the wind, as a heavy sea struck her and washed her decks. At this moment, as she lay broadside on the waves, the rattle of the anchor could be heard as it fell. Once more a sea struck her and washed clean over her, but as it passed she was seen to swing to her anchor, and ride easily with her head to wind. Another anchor was let go, the cable veered out, and the vessel was saved when in the jaws of certain destruction.

In the meantime Polly Grey, having seen the frightful calamity that had befallen some one (she knew not whom), had rushed instinctively toward the spot. Some few minutes elapsed before she neared the still screaming figure. The fire burned with a steady blaze, although the clothes were nearly consumed, as the quantity of tar had converted them into a torch; but before Polly reached the spot the figure was reduced to a blackened mass, with bright patches of fire adhering to many portions of the flesh; there was no semblance to a human form, excepting the fact of two black skeleton arms and legs which were moving with frantic energy as the figure danced to and fro in attitudes of the wildest madness.

Polly was horror-stricken. She knew not who it was, as the face was burned to a cinder; but as she approached within a few yards without knowing what to do, the monkey-like figure uttered a terrific yell, and bounded over the perpendicular cliff.

As the fiery body fell with increasing velocity from the height of two hundred feet, the rush of air revived the flames, which shot out from all parts of her scorched carcass as Mother Lee rushed headlong into the boiling surf.

One splash! as the waves received her, and extinguished the bright flame that had marked her fall, in the exact spot where with the rock she had once crushed the struggling captain of the cutter.

Upon the cliff stood Polly Grey, appalled with the horrible catastrophe; but as the bright moon now clearly revealed the scene she regarded with dismay a revenue cutter lying at anchor in the heavy breakers, instead of the long-expected lugger. She took a hasty glance in the harbor; it was empty. The "Polly" had not arrived; all her hopes of seeing Paul, and of pressing him in her arms once more, were gone! Sickened by her vain desire, and by the scene she had just witnessed, she sat down by one of the fires that had destroyed the infamous designer of the snare.

The truth now flashed upon her that the false position of the beacons could only have originated from Mother Lee, and she had no longer any doubt that the attenuated and dreadful figure that she had seen dancing and writhing in the flames could have been no other than the old woman, who had met with this just but fearful retribution.

It now began to rain violently, and the wind suddenly changed to the north, blowing off the shore; the beacon fires hissed as the heavy rain-drops blackened the hot embers, and Polly, cold and shivering, was driven to the shelter of her barren home. Tired with watching, and saddened with constant anxiety, she threw off her wet clothes, and fell asleep as soon as she lay upon her bed.

The next morning found the inhabitants of the village in great excitement, as, instead of the "Polly," the revenue cutter, commanded by Captain Smart, was lying snugly within the bay. The wind off the shore had produced a calm sea, and they had towed the cutter into the cove for better security.

Joe Smart was a welcome guest at the cottage on the cliff, and Polly Grey had met him at the entrance full of eager curiosity.

"Where is Paul? where is the 'Polly'?" she exclaimed, as she opened the door. "Tell me all you know, I beseech you," she added, as she gave him a chair by the window overlooking the sea.

"I know nothing, unfortunately, my dear Mrs. Grey," replied Joe Smart. "My story is simply told. It was my duty to examine the character of a suspicious-looking lugger that we observed in the offing as she appeared to be beating up for the coast. We ran toward her with a fair wind, but she sailed like a witch, and upon seeing our approach, it was a case of ' up stick and away;' for she altered her tack, and, going free, she left us out of sight, and we have never seen her since. The wind then changed, and as evening came on, it blew hard from the sou'-west. I knew that the good people of Sandy Cove were attentive in lighting the beacons to guide the ' Polly,' or any other friend, into the bay upon a dark night, so I thought I might as well take advantage of their lamps and come in myself. The night was stormy, and so dark that we could not make out the coast, therefore I sent up a rocket, which was not only answered by the station, but by two fires that were almost immediately lighted on the cliff; these we all considered to be the guides to the harbor's mouth. Accordingly we steered directly for them, with the intention of sailing straight into the cove. As we neared the fires within a cable's length I suddenly caught sight of a horrible figure that looked like some old witch, that sprung from the earth blazing with fire, dancing in tremendous flames with frantic gestures to and fro, actually between and on a level with the beacons. Thus providentially warned of our danger, I knew that the beacons were false guides, as there was the high cliff between them instead of the harbor's mouth. We were running at nine knots, and apparently close to the danger; but luffing quickly we checked the cutter's way in time to let go a couple of anchors; after a good ducking, as several seas swept us before she came fairly round, we rode out the gale until the wind changed. If the gale had increased we must have been lost, as the cables must have chafed through upon the rocks; even now a couple of strands are cut through, although we remained but a short time at anchor. I now find," continued Captain Smart, " that I am indebted to old Mother Lee for the false beacons, as I have just heard in the village that the pile on the east side of the entrance was never fired, although the two real beacons were prepared by the fishermen. Thus the old woman had laid a trap that had nearly proved fatal to us, although there can be no doubt that it was intended for the ' Polly.' For what reason this diabolical scheme was prepared I can not say."

Polly Grey now described the sight she had witnessed, and there could be no doubt that Mother Lee had perished by a frightful death. She also explained the uncalled-for hatred that the old woman had entertained for her and Paul, and the endeavor she had made to wreck the "Polly" was only the climax to a long career of crime which had now met with its reward.

During this conversation Edith and her mother joined the party, and learned with astonishment the startling events of the past night. Some weeks had elapsed after this event, and the affection between Edith and Polly Grey had increased to a degree that rendered the idea of parting insupportable. The widow, Mrs. Jones, proposed that Polly Grey should live with them at the rectory, and that occasionally they should pass a month or two at the cottage on the cliff for change of air and scene; but that at any rate Polly should not reside alone until something should be heard of her missing husband and her boy Ned.

In the meantime, as week after week passed by without any intelligence of her husband, Captain Smart lost no opportunity of soothing Polly's anxieties, and he proved his affection for his absent friend and his devotion to his old love by buoying up her hopes with plausible suggestions as to the cause of Paul's absence and the probability of his return; at the same time he took care to supply all that she could possibly require. This was the more important, as Polly was entirely without money; several debts were pressing; as Paul had suddenly disappeared, those who were his creditors sent in their bills and demanded a settlement of accounts. Joe Smart had foreseen this difficulty, and he at length prevailed upon Polly Grey to intrust him with the management of her affairs until the happy day should arrive when Paul should appear in person. At first Polly had declined his well-meant offer, as she knew that it placed her in a difficult position. Joe Smart was a man of honor, but at the same time he had been her unsuccessful suitor; thus, in the absence of her husband, it was an affair of exceeding delicacy to define the exact degree of intimacy that should exist between them. At the same time it was necessary that the debts should be paid; but how was that possible without money? She had no claim upon Mrs. Jones, the widow, who, although rich, was totally ignorant of business affairs, and she herself required advice; therefore, although much against her inclination, Polly had no alternative but to accept the assistance of Joe Smart until her husband should return.

While pondering over her difficulties she was struck by an idea which in some measure relieved her position; it occurred to her that the Widow Jones might be equally assisted by Joe Smart, should he consent to undertake the management of her property, in which case his attentions to her individually would be shared by another, and would not appear so personal.

To her great satisfaction Mrs. Jones agreed to the proposal. The indefatigable Captain Smart was always ready to render assistance; and the arrangement was shortly concluded that he was to have the entire control of her affairs, and that a small room at the rectory was to be fitted up as an office to which he could at all times have free access.

Accordingly there was no restriction upon his visits, and he contrived that he could attend to his new duties three times during the week without interfering with his official occupation.

This was a source of much comfort to the Widow Jones, and she quickly learned to rely upon the one-armed captain with implicit confidence, and even to look forward to his periodical visits with pleasure and almost impatience; while, on the other hand, as the hopes of Paul's return grew more distant, it can not be denied that Joe Smart's sympathy for Polly Grey was fast returning to the warm affection that had caused the disappointment to his youth. He would hardly dare to acknowledge to himself that he loved her in any other light than as his old friend and the wife of his friend Paul; but as he secretly analyzed his feelings he started at the throb of his own heart when the thought passed through his mind "that Paul was, perhaps, still alive, and might again return!" It was a dangerous position for the generous and sensitive Joe Smart. He was now thrown constantly in the society of the love of his boyhood, who was still beautiful, and who always met him with a warmth of welcome that evinced her gratitude for the many kindnesses she had received from his hand. But in Polly Grey's breast there was only one feeling: this was a devotion to the true objects of her affection, Paul and Ned; not a thought of another love ever crossed her mind. Next to them her heart clung to Edith, and she regarded Joe Smart with the warm but pure feelings of an old friend.

Edith had grown sad. She loved Polly Grey as a new mother, and this love had sprung from a common sorrow. She now frequently visited the church-yard to sit by her father's grave, which was built by the side of the cross-stone where she and Ned had last parted. This she had tended with care, as had been proposed by Ned when they last sat together and read the mysterious epitaph, " A lady unknown, aged about twenty-two. Cast up by the sea at Sandy Cove."

Polly Grey had since told her the whole sad story, and her suspicions that the poor lady was Ned's own mother. Edith had planted some myrtles around the spot, and with her pretty white hands she kept the grass closely clipped; and every Sunday she twined a new wreath and hung it upon the cross, for it was on the evening of a Sabbath that she had promised Ned to attend to the lonely grave.

CHAPTER VIII.

RETURN TO PAUL ON HIS VOYAGE TO THE FRENCH COAST.

WE must now return to Paul Grey, who some months since had sailed from Sandy Cove, expecting to return after an absence of a few days, but of whom nothing had been heard.

On the evening that he sailed the wind was northerly, and the " Polly " quickly lost sight of the English shore; by day-break on the following morning they could plainly distinguish the coast of France. The " Polly " now hoisted French colors and stood in for Ushant. As the lugger neared the land a rowing boat was seen to approach from the shore; Paul stood upon the deck, and carefully examined the suspicious object with the telescope.

" It's all right," he at length exclaimed to Dick Stone, who stood at the helm; " keep your course and meet her; it's Dupuis's boat."

The " Polly " accordingly held her course, and the spray dashed from her bows as with a brisk breeze on the quarter she flew gayly over the waves toward the advancing boat, that belonged to Paul's French partner in the contraband trade. There had been some slight alteration in the lugger's equipment since we last described her. Around the main-mast by the deck was a rack for muskets and boarding-pikes; an arm-chest, well filled with pistols, muskets, and cutlasses, and rendered water-proof by a thick tarpaulin cover, was securely lashed and cleated in front of the mizzen-mast; while amidships was a long brass six-pounder, fitted upon a traversing carriage upon a pivot, which could be trained upon any point of the horizon. There could be no doubt that the vessel was arranged for a determined defense in the event of attack, as the crew consisted of fifteen men including Paul. These were carefully selected, and a finer set of sailors would rarely be seen; among them was the surly Dick Stone, who had so stubbornly resisted the inquiries of Captain Smart on his visit to the lugger. This man was an extraordinary character; he was devoted to Paul, and to the clipper lugger in which he sailed; he was brave to a fault, and his coolness in the midst of danger was remarkable; he hated the entire nation of Frenchmen, whom he termed "the Mounseers;" next to them he disliked the whole race of revenue authorities. For several years he had served on board a man-of-war; but the varied occupations of smuggling and fishing, with the dangers attendant upon such professions, formed an excitement that was the charm of his existence. He was seldom seen to laugh, neither was he ever in a passion; if anything disturbed him he invariably turned to his pipe as his counselor and comforter; a few deep puffs from the ever-present companion would either be followed by perfect silence and contentment, or by some carefully considered reply.

Dick Stone was at the helm, and, as he had been directed by Paul, he kept a course that would meet the advancing boat. "Take the tiller for a moment," said he to a sailor who stood by on the further side; and without moving from his place he took from his pocket a blackened clay pipe about three inches long, at the same time he inserted a plug of tobacco; then, striking a light with a flint and steel and a piece of burned rag, he gave two or three sharp and rapid puffs, that brought a brilliant glow to the mouth of the bowl. He then took a long and steady suck at the never-failing adviser, until his cheeks became quite hollow with the exhaustive effort; this was followed by a dense cloud of smoke, as though from the explosion of a gun. He rested for a moment, and took the pipe from his mouth as though to give his brain an opportunity of testing the effect. Once more it was applied, with a similar result as in the first instance; and as the wind carried the smoke to leeward he quietly handed the magic instrument to the sailor from whom he now took the helm, and with invigorated intelligence he directed his attention to the boat.

"She's made the signal," said Paul, who still observed her with the glass. "She has hoisted the English flag in exchange for the French."

"Can you see the Mounseer Captain Doopwee?" asked Dick.

"I can't swear to him," replied Paul, "but there's some one very like him, in a pilot coat, in the stern."

"Perhaps we'd better have the muskets ready," continued Dick, as he again took his pipe from the sailor, and asked fresh advice by a vigorous puff. "Just put a pistol and a cutlass on the deck by my side," said Dick to the sailor who had assisted him, as though the tobacco had suggested the idea. "I don't trust those Mounseers, they're too purlite by half; and I can't see Captain Doopwee."

Although Paul had no supicion of the boat that was now rapidly approaching, he saw no objection to Dick's practical advice.

"Are those muskets all loaded?" he asked, as he pointed to those in the rack around the main-mast.

"Yes," replied Dick; "if a musket ain't loaded, it's like a pipe without baccy. I loaded those muskets myself early this morning, as I don't trust the Mounseers."

"Well," said Paul to a sailor near him, "unlock the arm-chest, and let each man strap on his cutlass and put a pistol in his belt; lay a dozen muskets on the deck, in addition to those upon the rack, and keep a bright lookout as we near the French boat."

In about twenty minutes the boat was within a pistol-shot of the lugger; Captain Dupuis was not among the crew. A man in the bow of the boat now waved a small English flag, at the same time he held a letter in his outstretched left hand. The lugger now hauled close up to the wind, and lay to, as the boat was allowed to come alongside, and the person in command nimbly leaped on board, while the boat dropped astern, and was secured by a rope to the " Polly."

"*Bon voyage, Monsieur le Capitaine !*" said the sprightly individual who now accosted Paul.   " 1 have de plaisir to introduce to you von lettre of de part de notre ami Monsieur Dupuis, who makes to you ses compliments, but is engaged vith les mégrimes, or vith some seekness detestable, dat ties him to his bed."

With this introduction the dapper little Frenchman presented his letter, which Paul immediately read.

M. Dupuis described that he was unwell, and therefore could not meet him in person, but that the bearer was a trustworthy agent, who would act as pilot, and guide the " Polly " to a secure hiding-place, where she could disembark her goods and receive a fresh cargo without fear of interruption.   After having asked a few questions, which were satisfactorily answered, Paul ordered Dick Stone to obey the directions of the French pilot; and the lugger, having been allowed to fall off the wind, immediately filled her sails, and once more she scudded over the waves with the French boat and crew towing astern.

" Vest-sou'-vest, if you please, *mon ami,*" said the polite pilot to the imperturbable Dick, " till I show you von leetle port vare no one know."

As Dick slightly altered the lugger's course he took a long puff at his pipe, and emitted a cloud of smoke that for a moment obscured the Frenchman, under cover of which he muttered:

" Too purlite, too purlite by a long chalk, these Mounseers;" then, as the smoke cleared, he addressed the pilot direct.

" What's become of Captain Doopwee, mounseer?"

" Ah, *mon cher ami,* dat is my deer fren," replied the vivacious Frenchman, " our fren le Capitaine Dupuis has caught a *coup d'air,* he has taken to him a cold vith *mal à la tête,* vat ve call de ' mégrimes,' together vith a spasm in his ventre, vat you call de intestines."

" What we call the bellyache," replied Dick, thoughtfully.   " I never knew a Frenchman without the bellyache.   It's along of their sour wine.   But what's the name of the place you're taking us to?" continued Dick.

" Ve go to one *charmant petit endroit,* von leetle basin *caché deniere* dat high rocher."

" Very likely!" replied Dick, suspiciously; " but, moun-seer, what have you got to do with us? Captain Doopwee's the mounseer that I want to see."

" Ha! ha! ha!" laughed the Frenchman. " Patience, patience, *mon cher*, vait von leetle half hour, *nous verrons*, Monsieur Dupuis, *tout à l'heure*—all in de hour. You understand?"

" Too purlite, too purlite to be honest," muttered Dick Stone, as he mechanically obeyed the directions of the French pilot. In the meantime the lugger rapidly ap-proached the bluff headland, behind which lay the secure harbor described. It was in vain that Paul scanned the rocky coast with his glass; no sign of a dwelling could be seen; all appeared dangerous and desolate in the extreme. They now neared the high cliffs of a long projecting head-land.

" Give me de helm, *mon ami*, dis is one vary bad place," said the pilot, as the " Polly " just passed a sunken rock, over which the surf broke in curling foam; and taking the tiller from the unwilling Dick, he now steered along the coast direct for the rocky headland, which rose abruptly from the water to the height of about two hundred feet.

In a few minutes the lugger neared the point. The breeze was brisk, and the spray dashed high upon the face of the cliffs as the heavy waves of the Atlantic burst against the rocks; but the pilot evidently knew the coast, and steering within a hundred paces of the rocky point, he sud-denly rounded the headland, and turning sharp he ran be-fore the wind direct into a long and narrow bay. A lofty rocky island presently lay before them; the " Polly " flew along in the calm harbor, and suddenly rounding the island she passed within fifty paces of a large vessel that had been concealed by the high cliff; at the same instant the pilot brought the lugger sharp up to the wind, and she lay help-less under the guns of a French eighteen-gun corvette. All this had happened so quickly and unexpectedly that the trap was first discovered when they were fairly caught. As the " Polly " had rounded the rocky island, and the corvette first burst upon their view, a cloud of smoke had puffed from Dick's pipe; but now that the fatal truth flashed upon them as the lugger lay motionless, with her sails flapping in the wind, he quietly took his pipe from his mouth, shook the last remnants of tobacco ashes from the bowl.

and muttering, "Too purlite by a long chalk, these Mounseers," he suddenly seized the little French pilot by the collar, and catching one leg with his left hand he swung him overboard as though he had been a child. Hardly had he splashed into the deep water than the French boat, that had cast off the rope astern, pulled to his assistance, and hoisted the polite pilot on board like a drowned cat. In the meantime a boatful of armed men approached them from the corvette, that was only a few yards distant. There was no chance of escape. They were fairly caught by a well-planned trap, devised by the treacherous Captain Dupuis, who owed Paul a considerable sum of money, and who thus intended to avoid the debt, at the same time to gain the prize, by consigning Paul to a French prison.

"The Mounseers sha'n't take my pipe without a fight for it, I know," said Dick, as a number of Frenchmen suddenly boarded the lugger. As he said this he replaced his trusty ally within his pocket, and picking up the cutlass and pistol from the deck he advanced in front of the helm in an attitude of defense. "Come on, Mounseers! Komprenney, where's Captain Doopwee? I'll cure his miggrims, the purlite varmint."

Dick Stone was perfectly ready to fight either one or all, but Paul, who had at once perceived the trap into which they had fallen, and the utter impossibility of resistance, immediately gave the order that all men should lay down their arms, as several of the most desperate had followed Dick's example, and had already drawn their cutlasses.

A French officer now approached Paul, and formally announced that the "Polly" was the prize of the corvette; at the same time he assured him that both he and the crew would be well treated. Without further delay they were ordered to pack up their clothes, and to go ashore in custody of a guard of marines.

In an hour after the arrival of the "Polly" in the deceitful port Paul and his entire crew were marched through the streets of a French village, and were drawn up opposite the prison entrance.

It was a curious old building, in the Norman style of architecture, with tall conical towers of great height, in which were numerous small grated windows; a heavy iron gate closed the entrance to a gloomy court yard, and a large crowd of people thronged the approach to this uninviting spot to see English prisoners led in triumph to the jail.

Upon their arrival at the gate they were met by the governor and the principal jailer, who received them formally, and entered their names upon the prison-books; after which a receipt was given to the officer in command of the escort, and they were allotted to various cells in separate parties. Paul, as their captain, was placed in a superior apartment, together with Dick Stone, whom he had requested might be permitted to accompany him.

As the door of the prison had closed upon their admittance to the court-yard Paul had noticed a remarkably pretty girl about eighteen who had fixed her eyes upon him with extreme earnestness. As he was now led with Dick Stone to the room that they were to occupy he observed that she accompanied the jailer, and appeared to observe him with great interest. Taking from his pocket a guinea that was pierced with a hole he slipped it into her hand, at the same time laughingly he told her in a few words of broken French to suspend it as a charm around her neck to preserve her from everything English.

Instead of receiving it with pleasure, as he had expected, she simply looked at it with curiosity for an instant, and then, keeping it in her hand, she asked in her native tongue with intense feeling, *A tu vue Victor? mon cher frère Victor, prisonnier en Angleterre?*"

"Silly girl," said the jailer, her father, "England is a large place, and there are too many French prisoners to make it likely that Victor should be known:" at the same time the feelings of the father yielded to a vague hope as he looked inquiringly at Paul.

"There are many fine fellows," answered Paul, "who have had the misfortune to become prisoners of war, but they are all cared for, and receive every attention in England. When was your brother taken?" he asked, as he turned to the handsome dark-eyed girl who had just questioned him.

"A year ago next Christmas," she replied; "and we have only once heard from him; he was then at a place called Falmouth, but we do not know where that is."

"Falmouth!" said Paul; "why, I know the place well: with a fair wind the 'Polly' would make it in a few hours

from the spot where I live. Your brother then is imprisoned only half a day's sail from my house!"

"Oh! what good fortune, *mon Dieu !*" exclaimed the
excited girl, as she clasped her hands in delight, as though
the hour of her brother's deliverance was at hand. "How
can we reach him? surely you can help us?"

"Alas! I am also a prisoner," replied Paul. "At this
moment my wife is sorrowing alone in our cottage on the
cliff, and she is looking vainly upon the sea expecting my
return. How can I help you? Believe me, if it were possible, I would." At the recollection of Polly's situation
Paul hastily brushed a tear from his eye with the back of
his rough hand, which instantly awoke the sympathy of
the sensitive girl before him.

"Ha! you are married," she exclaimed. "Is she young,
and perhaps beautiful?"

"Young enough for me, and handsomer than most
women," replied Paul.

At this moment Dick Stone had lighted his pipe, and as
he gave two or three tremendous puffs he screwed his face
into a profoundly serio-comic expression and winked his
right eye mysteriously at Paul.

"I know the young man," said Dick, who now joined
in the conversation, and addressed the jailer whom he had
been scrutinizing closely; "I saw him once at the prison
in Falmouth. Rather tall?" said Dick, as he surveyed the
six-foot form of the jailer.

"Yes," said the jailer, eagerly, "as tall as I am."

"Black hair?" continued the impassive Dick, as he cast
his eyes upon the raven locks of both father and daughter.

"Yes, as dark as mine," exclaimed the now excited
jailer.

"Roman nose?" said Dick, as he looked at the decided
form of the parent's feature that was shared by the handsome girl.

"Precisely so, well arched," replied the father.

"Had not lost an arm?" said Dick.

"No, he had both his arms," said the jailer.

"And his name," said Dick, "was Victor?"

"Victor Dioré!" exclaimed the jailer's daughter.

"Victor Diarrhœa! Precisely so—that's the man," re-
p'ied the stoical Dick Stone; "that's the man. I know'd
him soon after he was captured; and I believe he's now in

Falmouth Jail. I'd almost forgot his name, for you Mounseers are so badly christened that I can't remember how you're called."

The jailer and his daughter were much affected at this sudden intelligence; there could be no doubt that their new prisoner had seen their lost relative, who appeared to be imprisoned not far from Paul's residence, and their hearts at once warmed toward both the captives.

They were led into a large but rather dark room, scantily furnished with two trestle-beds, a table, and a couple of benches.

"We must talk of this again," said Paul to the jailer's daughter; "perhaps an exchange of prisoners may be arranged at some future time that may serve us all."

"Yes," added Dick Stone, "I think we can manage it if we're all true friends; and may I ask your name, my dear? for you're the prettiest Mounseer that I've ever set eyes on."

"Léontine," replied the girl.

"Well, Leonteen," continued Dick, "if you'll come and have a chat sometimes up in this cold-looking room I dare say we'll be able to hit off some plan that'll make us all agreeable. I've got a secret to tell you yet, but I don't want to let it out before the old 'un," said Dick, mysteriously, as he winked his eye at her in masonic style; then, putting his lips very close to her pretty ear, he whispered, "I can tell you how to get your brother out of prison: but you must keep it close."

The door had hardly closed upon the jailer and his daughter, who had promised to return with breakfast, than Paul turned quickly toward Dick Stone and exclaimed, "What do you mean, Dick, by such a romance as you have just composed? Surely all is false; you never met the French prisoner at Falmouth?"

"Well," replied Dick, "may be I didn't; but perhaps I did. Who knows? You see, captain, all's fair in love or war, and it struck me that it's as well to make friends as enemies; now you see we've made friends all at once by a little romance. You see the Mounseers are very purlite people, and so it's better to be purlite when you're in France. You see the pretty little French girl says her brother's in jail in Falmouth; well, I've seen a lot of French prisoners in Falmouth with black hair, and two arms apiece, and a Roman nose; so very likely I've seen her brother. Well, you see, if we can make friends with the jailer, we may p'r'aps get the key of the jail! At all events, it ain't a bad beginning to make friends with the jailer's daughter before we've had our first breakfast in the French prison."

As Dick Stone finished speaking he looked out of the narrow grated window that in the thick stone wall appeared as though it had been intended for musketry; from this aperture he had a beautiful view of the bay and the French corvette, near to which the unfortunate "Polly" was now lying at anchor with the French colors flying at the mizzen.

"Well, that's a bad lookout, I must say," said Dick. "Look here, captain, there's the 'Polly' looking as trim and as saucy, bless her heart! as though we were all aboard: and there's the ugly French flag flying, and she don't seem to care more about it than a woman with new ribbons in her bonnet."

Paul looked at his beautiful lugger with bitter feelings. He had sailed in her for many years, and she had become like a member of his family. Although fifteen years old, she had been built of such well-seasoned timber, and had been kept in such excellent repair, that she was better than most vessels of half her age, and he sighed as he now saw her at anchor with the French flag fluttering at her masthead. For a long time he gazed intently upon her without speaking a word; at length he turned sharply round, and in a quick, determined voice, he said, "Dick, I'll never live to see the 'Polly' disgraced. If you'll stick by me, Dick, we'll retake her yet, or die!"

For some moments Dick Stone stared Paul carelessly in the face without a reply; he then tapped the bowl of his empty pipe upon the prison wall, and carefully refilling it with tobacco, he once more lighted it, and puffed for about a minute in perfect silence; he then spoke, after emitting a dense volume of smoke.

"If I'll stick to you, captain? Well, p'r'aps I never have, and p'r'aps Dick Stone's a coward? Well, you see, of course I'll stick to yer; but there's other things to be thought of. What's your plan, captain? It's of no use doing anything without thinking well first. Now if you'll tell me what you mean I'll have a little smoke, just half a pipe, and I'll tell you my opinion."

"My plans are not absolutely defined," said Paul, "but I think that by making friends with the jailer's daughter we may induce her to risk much in the endeavor to rescue her brother. We might prevail upon her to assist in our escape—she might even accompany us to England. Could we only free ourselves from these prison walls on a dark night, when the wind blows strong from the south, why should we not surprise the French crew, and carry off the 'Polly'? Once at sea, there is nothing that could touch her!" Paul's eyes glistened as he spoke, and the muscles stood out from his brawny arm as he clinched his fist, and added, "If I could only once lay hold of Dupuis's throat, and save the 'Polly,' I ask no greater fortune!"

Puff, puff, puff, came in rapid succession from Dick's pipe at these words; at last, the long exhaustive suck arrived in its turn, and the usual cloud of smoke enveloped his head, which always exhilarated his brain.

"Well, captain, d'ye see," replied Dick, "I'll stick to you in anything, and there's no doubt that there's a chance of success if the pretty little Mounseer will only help us. But, you see, from what I know of womankind, they're very fond and very purlite for their brothers, but they won't run much risk for 'em. Now if they're in love they're as good as bull-dogs; and so I think it's a pity as how you told her that you'd got a wife a-looking out for you at home! If you'd have told her that you were a single man, and p'r'aps given her a kiss when you gave her the lucky guinea, we might have got a little love to help us, and then we'd have had a better chance, as she'd have gone off with us all of a heap."

"Dick, you have no conscience," replied Paul; "you surely would not deceive the girl in such a heartless manner? No!" continued Paul, "I have told her the truth, and if she can help us I'll do my best to save her brother; but, on the other hand, why should not you, Dick, make yourself agreeable to her? You're not a bad-looking fellow, why should you not do the love-making?"

Dick made no reply, but thoughtfully puffed at his pipe; then laying down his smoking counselor upon the window-sill he thrust his right hand into a deep breeches pocket, and extracted a black horn pocket-comb, with which he began at once most carefully to arrange his hair.

Despite the loss of the "Polly" and the misery of his

situation Paul burst out laughing as he witnessed Dick's cool determination to prepare for love-making.

"I don't know how these Mounseers begin," said the methodical Dick; "they're a very purlite people, and so they mayn't like our customs. In England we take 'em round the waist with both arms, and give 'em a kiss; but p'r'aps it's better not to begin all at once. I'll just ask her to sit on my knee at first, so as not to frighten her."

"Better not, Dick," said Paul, laughing; "I'm afraid she wouldn't understand your modesty. Only make yourself agreeable, but don't touch her, and let time do the rest."

They were interrupted in their conversation by the turning of the creaking door-lock, and the jailer and his daughter entered with a loaf of black bread and two jars of water and of milk, which they placed upon the table. Léontine had already strung the guinea upon a cord, which was now suspended from her neck.

"Ha! that looks very well!" said Paul; "few French girls wear the English king's image round their necks."

"I know an Englishman who wears a French girl's picture in his heart," said Dick, who, with a sly wink at Paul as a preface, thus made his first bold advance.

"A what?" inquired Léontine.

"A poor devil," replied Dick, "who doesn't care how long he's shut up in a French prison with such a pretty little Mounseer for a jailer."

"Ha! ha! you English know how to pay compliments," answered Léontine, who knew just sufficient English to understand Dick's attempt at French.

"Yes, we're considered a very purlite people," replied Dick, "and we have a purlite custom when we goes to prison of shaking hands with the jailer and kissing the hand of his pretty daughter." As Dick said these words he first grasped the hand of the jailer, and then raised to his lips, redolent of tobacco, the hand of Léontine; at the same time he whispered, "Don't forget that I have a secret."

Far from being disconcerted at Dick's politeness, Léontine naïvely remarked: "You can't tell a secret before three persons; but we shall have plenty of opportunities, for you may pay us a longer visit than may be agreeable."

Dick in reply to this remark suddenly assumed one of

his most mysterious expressions, and winking one eye at Léontine, he placed his forefinger upon his lips as though to enjoin silence, and whispered in her ear: " Make an opportunity: the secret's about your brother."

CHAPTER IX.
THE " POLLY " AT ANCHOR.

MORE than two months had passed wearily in the French prison, during which both Paul and Dick Stone had been buoyed up in inaction by the hope of carrying into execution a plan for their escape. The only view from the prison windows was the sea, and the street and beach in the foreground. The " Polly " still lay at anchor in the same spot, as some difficulty had arisen between Captain Dupuis and the captain of the corvette that had to be settled in the law courts.

In the meantime both Paul and Dick Stone had not only become great friends of the jailer, Jean Dioré, and his daughter, but Dick had quickly found an opportunity to disclose his secret, which succeeded in winning the heart of the enterprising Léontine. Dick had made a declaration of love, and to prove his sincerity he proposed that he should conduct her direct to her brother in the English prison, whose release should be effected by an exchange; and he had persuaded her that, if she should aid in the escape of Paul and the entire crew of the " Polly," there would be no difficulty in obtaining her brother's release when the facts should become known to the English authorities. Paul had added his persuasions to those of Dick Stone; he had excited the sister's warmest feelings by painting the joy she would feel in rescuing her brother from a miserable existence, and he had gained her sympathy by a description of the misery and suspense that his own wife must be suffering in her ignorance of all that had befallen him. Léontine was won. She was brave as a lion, and, her determination once formed, she was prepared to act without flinching.

Many times Dick Stone had lighted his pipe, and puffed and considered as he took counsel with Paul on the plan that the latter had proposed. All was agreed upon.

Paul had thus arranged the attempt at escape. All was to be in readiness for the first gale that should blow from either west or south. Léontine had provided him with a couple of large files and a small crowbar about two feet long, which she had purchased in the village with money supplied by Paul; these she had introduced to his room by secreting them beneath her clothes.

At various times she had purchased large supplies of strong twine in skeins, which to avoid suspicion she had described as required for making nets; these she had also introduced daily, until sufficient had been collected for the manufacture of ropes, at which both Paul and Dick Stone worked incessantly during the night, and concealed them in the daytime within their mattresses, by cutting a hole beneath. Whenever the time should arrive it had been arranged that Léontine was to procure the keys of the cells in which the crew of the "Polly" were confined, and she was to convey the prisoners at night into the apartment occupied by Paul and Dick, whence they were to descend from the window by a rope into the fosse that surrounded the prison; fortunately, this ditch was dry, and Léontine was to fix a stake into the ground about the fosse, from which she was to suspend a knotted rope after dark, to enable the prisoners to ascend upon the opposite side.

The great difficulty would be in avoiding the sentry, who was always on guard within fifty paces of the spot where they would be forced to descend, and whence they must afterward ascend from the ditch. The affair was to be left entirely in the hands of Léontine, who assured Paul and Dick that she would manage the sentry if they would be ready at the right moment to assist her. When freed from the prison, they were to make a rush to the beach, seize the first boat, of which many were always at hand, and board and capture the "Polly;" once on board the trusty lugger, in a westerly or southerly gale, and Paul knew that nothing could overtake her.

Such was the plan agreed upon, and everything had been carefully prepared and in readiness for some days, but the favorable weather had not yet arrived. Daily and hourly Paul looked from the grated windows upon his beloved "Polly," which lay still at anchor idle in the bay, about fifty yards from the French corvette.

At length, as one early morning he as usual looked out from his prison, he saw a boat pulling from the shore, followed quickly by several others conveying cargo, and steering for the " Polly;" the bustle upon the deck, and the re-fitting of ropes and rigging, plainly discernible from the prison window, left no doubt upon Paul's mind that the " Polly " was about to leave the harbor, and perhaps be lost to him forever.

At this painful sight Dick lighted his pipe, and smoked with violence until the tobacco was half consumed, when suddenly, in a fit of excitement that was quite unusual, he hastily put his adviser in his pocket, and seizing a file from beneath his mattress he immediately commenced work upon the bottom of an iron bar that protected the narrow window.

" That's right, Dick," said Paul; " now or never! The clouds are hurrying up from the sou'-west, and I think it's coming on to blow.; as old Mother Lee says, ' Luck comes from the sou'-west;' so bear a hand, and give me the file when you get tired."

As Paul had observed, the scud was flying rapidly across the sky from the right quarter, and both men worked hard alternately, and in an hour they had divided the thick iron bar close to the base.

" Now for the top," said Dick. " We'll soon cut it through, although it's harder work, as we can't put our weight to the file."

" Never mind the file," said Paul, who now grasped the severed bar in his iron hands; " with such a purchase I could wrench the bar asunder. Something shall give way," he said, as with the force of Samson he exerted every muscle, and wrenched the bar from its loosened base. The stone in which it was fixed first crumbled at the joint, and then suddenly cracking, Paul fell sprawling on his back with the bar in his hands, while a heavy fragment of stone fell upon the floor.

" Take care, captain," said Dick; " gently with the stones. We shall alarm the jailer if we make so much noise. Why, you've settled the job in one pull!"

" Here, Dick," continued Paul, as he sprung from the floor, " take the bar while I move a stone from the side with the crow. We won't take it right out lest the jailer should notice it if he comes with the breakfast; but we'll loosen it so that we can remove it quickly when necessary, as the window is too narrow for our shoulders."

Paul then inserted the thin edge of the crowbar, and by

gently working it backward and forward he removed the stones and enlarged the aperture sufficiently to admit the passage of a man; he then replaced the stones, together with the bar, and so arranged the window that no one would have observed any disturbance unless by a close inspection. Hardly had they completed their work when footsteps were heard without, succeeded by the turning of the key in the creaking lock of their door. In an instant Dick, who had lighted his pipe, leaned upon the window-sill and looked steadfastly out of the window, at the same time he puffed such dense clouds of smoke as would have effectually screened any damage that had been done by the work of the crowbar.

The door opened, and fortunately Léontine appeared instead of her father. She brought the breakfast.

"Quick!" she exclaimed, "there is no time to lose. The wind has changed, and people say we shall have a gale from the sou'-west. The 'Polly' is to sail to-morrow. Captain Dupuis has loaded her, and he will himself depart in the morning should the wind be fair. You must all get ready for the work," continued the determined girl, as her large eyes flashed with energy.

"We have not been idle, my pretty Léontine," said Paul, as he exhibited their morning's work, "but we now depend upon you. It will be quite dark at eight o'clock. You must have the rope ready secured to this small crow-bar, driven into the earth on the other side of the fosse; the bar is sharp and heavy; it will make no noise if you can manage to strike it into the ground in exactly the same spot three or four times, and simply hang this loop upon it, pressed close down to the base." At the same time he gave her the bar, and a rope coiled, about twenty feet in length. Paul continued. "You must also be punctual in bringing the other prisoners here at half past eight, and tell them to take their shoes off and to tie them round their waists. But how about the sentry?" asked Paul.

"Don't be afraid," said Léontine; "I have already arranged everything this morning. Fortune has favored us; François is to be on guard to-night; the guard is relieved at eight o'clock, at which time he will come on duty, therefore we have nothing to fear for some hours. I will manage François; leave him to me. He is an old lover of mine, and I have appointed to meet him to-night."

At this confession, thus boldly made, Dick Stone puffed violently at his pipe, and was almost concealed by his own smoke, when Léontine continued:

"He is a sad fellow, and has given me much trouble, but I shall pay him out to-night. Look here, Dick," she continued, "if you are worth having you'll help me quickly to-night, for I shall depend upon you. I have agreed to meet François this evening at half past eight, as I have pretended to accept his love. To avoid detection (as he will be on guard), I am to be disguised as a soldier, and he will send me the clothes and arms to-day. I shall keep my appointment, and engage him in conversation so closely that he will not hear you; but at the last moment you must be ready to rush upon him and secure him, while I endeavor to prevent him from giving an alarm. At the same time," continued Léontine, "you must promise not to hurt him, for François is a good fellow, and is very fond of me."

"Only let me get hold of him," cried Dick Stone.

"Will you?" replied Léontine; "then the enterprise ceases at the very beginning. You shall not escape unless you swear that no harm shall befall François."

"Do not be afraid," said Paul; but he continued: "It may be a difficult affair if he is a powerful man—what size is he?"

"Oh," replied Léontine, laughing, "a little fellow, about as big as I am. You could soon manage poor François; he would be a mere child in the grasp of such a man as yourself."

"All right," said Paul, "then there's no fear of murder; depend upon me, Léontine, no harm shall touch him."

"Mind you seize the right man," said the gay Léontine, "when I give the signal, as I shall be in a soldier's uniform, and you may mistake me for François. The signal will be, 'A friend;' the instant that I give the word, seize and disarm him before he can fire his musket. You will then have two muskets, mine and that of François, with which you must take your chance in boarding the 'Polly.'"

"That will do," said Paul; "let me only set foot on the 'Polly's' deck, and I'll soon settle accounts with Monsieur Dupuis. But now," added Paul, "we are agreed upon all points, and we depend upon you, Léontine; do not forget to visit the beach, and see that the oars and a boat-hook, with a sharp ax to cut the cable, are placed in readiness within a large boat, to which you must guide us when we leave the prison."

"Never fear," said Léontine; "I shall not fail in my part, and I shall give the signal as the clock chimes half past eight; you must be ready on the instant. Here is a letter," continued the girl, as the tears started to her eyes, "that I have written for my father; you must leave it on the table when you escape, and it will explain all; he will then, perhaps, forgive me when he knows that I risk my life for Victor." Saying which, she left the room and locked the door behind her.

Léontine now hurried her preparations, while the day passed wearily away to those who were awaiting the hour of their deliverance.

Paul and Dick Stone counted the hours as the neighboring church clock struck heavily on the bell.

"We shall run to the cove in twelve hours," said Paul, "if this breeze lasts; it's blowing a gale out at sea, and the 'Polly' 'll fly like a witch on a broomstick."

"We've got to take her first," replied the wary Dick. "There's many a slip 'twixt the cup and the lip!"

"We are short of weapons, no doubt," said Paul; "but we must take off the sword-bayonets from the muskets, and give them to two of the men. I will be first on board, and knock down Dupuis. Let the men rush to the main-mast and secure the arms from the rack the moment that they reach the deck, while you, Dick, seize the helm. I will tell off four men to loose the sails and to cut the cable directly that we get on board. This will leave us ten men to do the fighting. If all goes well we shall find the better part of the French crew down below, and, once in possession of the deck, they will be at our mercy. This gale of wind will start the 'Polly' like a wild duck the instant that the cable is cut, and we shall be round the corner of the island before the corvette can bring her guns to bear upon us. Then, with a dark night and a heavy gale, the 'Polly' can take care of herself."

The day at length passed away, and the sun set. The wind roared through the narrow streets of the town, and whistled loudly around the pointed towers of the old prison. "There could not be a better night," said Paul; "the wind roars like a lion, and nothing will be heard by the sentry."

As he was speaking the clock struck eight. As the last tones of the bell died away the lock of the door creaked as the key turned from the outside; and presently without a sound of footsteps, thirteen strapping fellows, who had been liberated by Léontine, softly entered the room, carrying their shoes strapped to their belts, as had been directed by Paul.

No time was lost in useless greeting; but the severed bar of the window was at once made use of as a lever to remove the heavy stones, and in less than ten minutes an aperture was made sufficiently large for an exit.

Paul now fastened the rope that had been concealed in his mattress to the center of the iron bar; then, lowering the other end from the window until it reached the fosse, he fixed the bar across the base, so that it was secured on either side by the masonry.

All was now ready, and, lest they should be disturbed, Dick Stone, having received the key from Léontine, locked the door on the inside.

Paul went first. It was with some difficulty that he squeezed his broad shoulders through the narrow opening; but once without the wall he nimbly lowered himself to the bottom, a depth of about sixty feet.

In a much shorter time than might be supposed the active sailors had succeeded in reaching the bottom of the fosse, without having made the slightest noise. The wind blew louder than before; there was no moon, and merely a faint light was given at intervals by the stars that every now and then peeped from between the driving clouds.

Carefully leading the way, Paul crossed the broad fosse, and felt with his hand the opposite wall, against which he expected to find the rope that was to have been arranged by Léontine. He was followed noiselessly by the crew for about twenty yards, when he suddenly halted as he caught the dangling rope.

With extreme care Paul now climbed, hand over hand, to the top, having previously whispered to Dick Stone to hold the end of the rope, and to ascend when he should give a jerk as a signal of safety.

Arrived at the top, on the soft green turf at the edge of

5

the moat, Paul lay flat upon the ground, and listened. He
could see nothing, therefore he knew that he could not be
seen; but he fancied that he could hear a suppressed voice
in the direction of the sentry. He gave a slight jerk to the
rope, and presently Dick Stone arrived, and crept to Paul's
side, quickly followed by all the others. They all remained
flat upon the grass, which, being about a foot in height,
effectually concealed them in the darkness of the night.
Paul now crept forward upon his hands and knees, followed in the same manner by Dick Stone; the other men
had received orders to jump up and join them immediately
upon hearing the signal, "A friend."

In a few minutes Paul was within a dozen yards of the
sentry; and as he and Dick then lay flat upon the earth they
could faintly distinguish two figures standing close together, and in intervals between the gusts they could hear
voices.

We will return to Léontine.

She had not failed in any of her arrangements. The
unsuspecting François had fallen into her snare, and, delighted with the assignation, he had run great risk in the
hope of securing the love of the charming Léontine. He
had borrowed for her a comrade's uniform and arms; and
thus accoutered as a soldier she had met him at the appointed hour. They were now standing together by the
edge of the moat, and Léontine had listened to his warm
declarations of affection. François was enraptured; for
more than a year he had vainly sought to win her love.
As the belle of the village, Léontine had many admirers;
a certain lieutenant was reported to be a favored suitor;
thus what chance was there for a private such as François?
True or false, the jealous heart of François had believed
these reports, and he had yielded to despair. Judge of his
transport when, within the last few hours, he had been led
to hope; and now, when he had nearly given her up as lost,
he almost held her in his arms. Alas! for military discipline when beauty leads the attack! François thought of
nothing but his love. There was a railing by the edge of
the moat, against which Léontine had rested her musket;
the unwary sentry did the same; and the two weapons
leaned peacefully side by side, as the soldier, intoxicated by
his love, suddenly caught her round the waist with both
arms and pressed his lips to her cheek. At this moment

the dull clang of the prison clock struck the half hour. Struggling in his embrace, Léontine exclaimed:

"Oh, if I could call ' a friend!' "

At the same instant with both her hands she slipped into his mouth a wooden instrument called a gag, that was used to silence uproarious prisoners.

The signal, " A friend," had been given in a loud voice, as though in reply to the usual challenge, and before the unlucky François could relieve himself from the gag he was caught from behind in the tremendous grasp of Paul's arms, while Dick Stone by mistake rushed upon Léontine; a vigorous smack on the face from her delicate hand immediately undeceived him.

"Take that musket," whispered Léontine, quickly, "and come along."

At the same time she seized the remaining musket, while Paul pinioned the arms of their prisoner with his handkerchief, and threatened him with instant death should he resist.

No time was lost. Paul threw the sentry over his shoulder as though he had been a lamb, and the whole party hurried after Léontine, who had led the way to the beach.

This affair had been managed so dexterously and quietly that no sound had been heard except the reply, " A friend," that was the preconcerted signal of attack; but upon arrival at the beach the rattling of the shingle as the large party hurried toward the boat threatened to attract a dangerous attention.

A large number of boats were drawn up upon the beach, but Léontine, without a moment's hesitation, led Paul and his party to one that had the oars already arranged; and the powerful crew, seizing it by the bow and the stern, ran it along the steep incline and launched it through the waves.

Not a word had been spoken, but there was a sound of many feet as the crew jumped into the boat that could not be mistaken. Paul laid his struggling burden upon the beach, and Léontine, before she leaped into the boat, whispered in the captive's ear:

"François, if you give the alarm I'll never love you again." With this coquettish adieu she followed Paul and Dick Stone, who were the last of the party.

"Steer straight for the ' Polly,' and give way, my lads!

for there's no time to lose," said Paul, who had taken his position in the bow of the boat with Dick Stone, both of whom were armed with muskets, while two men with sword-bayonets were ready to follow them.

" Make a rush on board," said Paul, " and knock down everybody without asking questions; then seize the arms from the rack and chest."

The water was deep in the rocky bay, thus the " Polly " was moored to a buoy little more than two hundred yards from the shore; a light was visible on board, and the lanterns of the corvette were also burning about fifty paces distant, where she lay moored by stem and stern.

They now pulled swiftly but silently toward the lugger. Paul's heart bounded with hope, while Dick Stone, as cool as ice, but determined upon the event, waited for the command. They neared the vessel. " What boat's that?" was the sudden challenge from the lugger's deck, as their boat came within a couple of oars' length. " A friend!" shouted Léontine in French, and almost in the same instant a man in the bow of the boat caught hold of the mizzen shrouds of the lugger with his boat-hook, and held on.

Paul seized a rope, and in one bound he was upon the lugger's deck, while Dick Stone followed like his shadow. To knock down the first man with a double-handed thrust with the barrel of his musket was the work of a moment, at the same instant Dick struck and felled a Frenchman who had rushed to the arm-chest. A shot was now fired by one of the French crew, and several men made a dash at the arm-rack, but Paul was there before them, and with the butt end of his musket he struck down the leader of the party. At this moment a loud shrill cry of alarm was heard from the shore.

" *Ha, le sacre François !*" exclaimed Léontine, who had in the meantime attached the deserted boat to the lugger's stern. " *Ha, le misérable !*" she cried; " this is a return for my love!"

·Two or three shots were now fired by the French crew, but without other results than to alarm the ship-of-war; the drum beat to quarters, lights were seen at her ports; a tremendous flash was accompanied by the report of a cannon as she fired an alarm-gun; this was quickly answered by a shot from a battery above the town.

The bells of the church and the prison rang wildly as

shot after shot was fired from the battery, and the alarm spread like wild-fire throughout the port.

In the meantime, while the fight had been hot upon the "Polly's" decks, Captain Dupuis, who had been asleep when the vessel was first boarded, now rushed up from the cabin, and meeting Paul he fired a pistol within a few feet of his chest; fortunately, at thav moment Paul was in the act of raising his musket, and the ball lodged within the tough walnut stock; the next instant the weapon fell with a crash upon Dupuis's skull, who reeled backward, and stumbling against the low bulwarks he fell overboard and sunk.

Dick Stone, with his musket in one hand that he had not yet discharged, was now standing at the helm. The English crew had gained the arms from the rack, and several shots were fired as they drove the French toward the bows of the lugger, following them up with the bayonet. Many of the French jumped overboard, calling loudly to the man-of-war for assistance, and those who were down below were already helpless, as the companion-ladder was guarded by two armed men. The surprise was complete; Léontine had hauled her boat alongside, and had climbed on board; the cable was cut, and the sails were let loose; but the danger had increased. The French crew who had jumped overboard called to the corvette to fire and sink the lugger. This they had hitherto been afraid to do, as their own countrymen were on board. A blue light was now burned upon the decks of the corvette, and distinctly illumined the scene just as the sails of the "Polly" filled, as her head turned from the severed cable, and she met the full force of the gale from the shore. In an instant she leaned over, and as the water rippled from her bows and the boom was slacked off she started like a wild duck frightened from its nest.

"Hurrah! hurrah! hurrah!" rang three hearty British cheers as the clipper lugger glided rapidly through the dark water and passed the terrible broadside of the corvette within fifty or sixty yards. But hardly had the "Polly" cleared the deadly row of guns, when, a flash! and the shock seemed to sweep her deck as the dense smoke rolled across her in the midst of the roar of a twenty-four pounder fired from the last gun of the tier.

A terrible crash almost immediately followed the shock,

and the painter or rope that attaches the boat to the stern
of the lugger suddenly dangled loosely in the water, as the
shot had dashed the boat to atoms; fortunately the
"Polly" had just passed the fatal line of fire. Another
wild "hurrah!" replied to the unsuccessful gun, as the
lugger, released from the boat's weight, seemed to fly still
quicker through the water.

"Take the helm for a moment," said Dick to a sailor
by his side, and running amidships he called upon Paul,
"Give a hand, captain, and we'll get the Long Tom
round."

In an instant Paul put his powerful shoulder to the long
six-pounder that worked on a pivot, and together, with joint
exertions, they trained the gun upon the stern windows of
the corvette. Dick Stone had just beforehand lighted his
pipe when standing at the helm, and as the long gun bore
upon its object he suddenly pushed Paul upon one side,
and emptied his fiery bowl upon the touch-hole. Bang!
went the gun, as the six-pound shot crashed through the
cabin windows of the corvette, and through the various
bulkheads, raking her from stem to stern.

"Hurrah!" again shouted the crew, who like true
British sailors were ready for any fight without reckoning
the odds when the cannon once began to speak, while Paul
and several men sponged and reloaded the long gun, as the
corvette had lowered several boats to give chase.

"Hurrah for the saucy 'Polly!'" shouted Paul, as he
and Dick now trained the gun upon the leading boat; but
at that moment they turned the sharp headland of the
rocky island, and both the corvette and her boats were obscured from their view.

It was blowing hard, but the water in the bay was perfectly smooth, as the wind was directly off the shore, and
the "Polly" flew like a race-horse toward the open sea.
In a few minutes she passed the last headland, and rushed
at foaming speed over the long swell of the Atlantic. With
the gale fairly on her quarter, there was nothing that could
touch the "Polly." There was no fear of a chase,
although the heavy booming of the alarm-guns could still
be heard in the distance.

Three Frenchmen had been killed in the fight, and their
bodies, which now lay on deck, were thrown overboard;
two were prisoners down below; the remainder of the crew

had escaped by jumping overboard, with the exception of the treacherous Captain Dupuis, who had sunk when knocked down by Paul.

Dick Stone was now at the helm; his pipe was well alight; and could his features have been distinguished in the dark they would be seen to wear an unusually cheerful expression as he said to Paul, " It wouldn't have been purlite of us to leave the Mounseers without a salute, and without my pipe we couldn't have fired the gun. It's a wonderful thing is a pipe! Ain't it, captain?"

" Nor'-nor'-east is the course, Dick," replied Paul, who was at that moment thinking of his wife, and the happiness it would be to meet her on the following day; at the same time he was anxious lest any misfortune should have occurred during his long absence.

" Nor'-nor'-east it is, captain," replied Dick, with a sailor's promptitude; " but I can't help larfing when I think of Captain Doopwee, who has put a cargo on board the ' Polly ' all for nothing, and has got knocked on the head into the bargain. Well, sarve him right, sarve him right," continued Dick, musingly; " he was a very purlite varmint, too purlite to be honest, by a long chalk." After this curt biographical memoir of the late Captain Dupuis, Dick Stone applied himself to his pipe, and kept the " Polly's " course N.N.E.

While Paul and Dick Stone were upon deck Léontine was lying upon a cot within the cabin. The excitement of the day had nearly worn her out, and despite the uneasy movement of the vessel, which tried her more severely than any danger, she fell asleep in the uniform of a private in the French chasseurs, and she dreamed happily that her brother Victor was released.

CHAPTER X.

PAUL GREY IN SIGHT OF HOME.

AT day-break on the following morning the gale, that had moderated during the last hour, suddenly changed its quarter, and chopping round it blew directly from the north. The lugger had run at such speed throughout the night that the high cliffs of Cornwall were now distinctly visible; and Paul, who had not yet slept, felt the bitterness of disappointment as the head wind now checked their way, and the " Polly," instead of rushing swiftly toward home, was forced to tack. Dick Stone had steered so carefully that he had exactly made the right point, and shortly after sunrise Paul's heart beat doubly quick as he descried with the telescope a speck in the distance which he knew to be his white cottage on the cliff. The time went wearily as the lugger, close-hauled to the wind, made each successive tack, but the cottage grew larger as they gradually approached, and Paul fancied that perhaps his wife might, by this time, have descried the well-known " Polly," and that she would be waiting to receive him with joy upon his arrival.

"I'll tell you what, captain," exclaimed Dick Stone, suddenly, " we mustn't forget the cargo; if we can run it through it will be a pretty haul, but we must keep a sharp lookout for the revenue cruisers now we are getting near the coast. Wouldn't it be safer to stand off a little and wait till dark?"

Paul's heart yearned for home, and instead of adopting this cool advice he determined to press on for another hour against the head wind, until they should be within an easy distance of the coast, when they would be able to run in and land the cargo after sunset. Accordingly they stood on the same tack; and as the lugger worked well to windward, they gradually neared the shore.

Paul's eyes were riveted upon his cottage on the cliff, and he vainly endeavored with the telescope to descry some figure on the terrace that might resemble the form of Polly Grey. He could not distinguish more than the dwelling, even the terrace wall was invisible in the distance. He now swept the line of coast carefully with his glass, and presently he fixed upon some object with peculiar attention.

" What do you see, captain?" inquired Dick, who had his suspicions.

" A cutter bearing down upon us in full sail, with a spanking breeze from the shore," replied Paul, thoughtfully, as he lowered his glass.

" Then we may make up our minds for another night at sea," said Dick. " That's a revenue cruiser, I'll be bound; and if the wind is fair for her, it'll be fair for us when we 'bout ship, and the ' Polly ' shows them her legs."

" Take the glass, Dick, and try to make her out, while

I take the helm," said Paul; saying which he handed the glass to Dick Stone.

For about a minute Dick peered steadily through the glass; he then slowly lowered it, and returning the instrument to Paul, he said:

" They are steering so as to reach us on our next tack, so we'd better not come upon it, I'm thinking. There's no doubt about her; she's a revenue cutter, so the less the ' Polly ' sees of her the better. We'd better wear, captain, and we'll run out of sight in an hour; nothing can touch the lugger going free."

Paul was quite of this opinion, and he decided immediately to alter the course, and run S.W. with the wind on the quarter. He thus hoped to lose sight of the cutter, and should the wind change he would be able to return, and run into Sandy Cove during the night. In an instant the order was obeyed, and the " Polly," that had been thrashing the crest of the waves as she had been pressed close to the wind, now bounded forward like a greyhound slipped from the leash. In less than an hour the coast of Cornwall had disappeared, neither could a trace be discovered of the revenue cutter; nevertheless, Paul thought it advisable to continue on the same course, as the cutter might be still in chase. Accordingly the " Polly " was kept running toward the S.W. until about three o'clock P. M. At this time the wind slackened, and then came in puffs from various directions; the sails constantly flapped, and in expectation of a change Paul determined to lie to. The " Polly " now rode easily with her sails trimmed, so as to keep her head to the sea.

She had been lying for about half an hour in this position, awaiting a change of wind that would enable her to turn to the north, and perhaps reach Sandy Cove during the night, when a vessel was observed in the distance with a fair breeze from the south-west; she was coming along at a rapid pace, and had the advantage of the approaching south-west wind, that had not yet reached the " Polly." She was quickly made out to be a schooner of about a hundred and forty tons, and she neared the " Polly " to within a mile before the latter vessel felt the breeze.

" That's a nice-looking schooner," said Paul; " and she has the union-jack at the peak; what kind of a craft can she be?"

"Well," said Dick, "she's a pretty smart-looking thing as ever I saw; painted all black; raking masts; and the biggest main-sail for her size that ever 1 set eyes on. She ain't a revenue cruiser, anyhow; and she ain't a man-of-war; and she looks too trim for a merchantman. I'm blowed if I know what she is," said Dick, as he gave the helm to a sailor and lighted his pipe, while he kept his eyes fixed on her.

"I can't see a man on board," said Paul, who had been watching the fast approaching ship with the telescope; "but get the decks cleared, and have some cartridges ready for the Long Tom, and a match lighted; we may just as well be prepared. Call the men on deck, and let all be ready for action in case of necessity."

Dick left the helm to a sailor, and in ten minutes' time the entire crew of the "Polly" were on deck; the long gun was already loaded, and many rounds of ammunition were stowed in readiness in a large chest. The men were at their places around the gun, while the remaining portion of the crew were thoroughly armed. Paul had stuck a brace of pistols in his belt, while a well-sharpened cutlass lay near at hand. The breeze now reached the "Polly" in its full strength, but the suspicious schooner was within half a mile, and was sailing at a rate that would test the best powers of the lugger.

"I don't like the look of her," said Paul. "We have the breeze now, and we may as well let the 'Polly' take care of herself."

In an instant the lugger came round to the wind, and in a few moments she was hurrying along at full speed toward the English coast, with the British flag at the mizzen. Hardly had the "Polly" altered her course than the union-jack on board the schooner was run down, and the French tri-color was seen flying in its place. This change was effected with great rapidity, and at the same time a puff of dense smoke from her bows was followed by the roar of a shot, that flew above the masts of the "Polly" and plunged into the sea some hundred yards ahead.

"That's purliteness!" said Dick Stone; "that's the Mounseer's way of saying bong joor! I suspected this all along, but the 'Polly' knows a word or two of French as well as she does. Suppose we send the Mounseer a message!"

Paul had already taken his stand by the long gun, which he now trained carefully upon the pursuing schooner. "Now, Dick," said he, "give the Frenchman a steady shot well into the rigging, and try to break a wing."

Dick squinted along the gun, and presently, as the "Polly" steadied herself before the wind, he touched the priming with the match. The brass gun rang with a loud report. All eyes watched eagerly for the effect, as the strong breeze cleared the smoke forward; in about two seconds the topgallant-mast of the schooner was seen to fall in two pieces, which dangled loosely in the rigging.

"Well done, Dick," said Paul; "load away, my lads, and let me try my hand!"

"That's my answer to the Frenchman," said Dick, who now puffed at his pipe. "Yer see, he very purlitely said in French, 'Bong joor!' so I says, 'Very well, I thank you; komprenney, mounseer?'"

Dick Stone had hardly finished his sentence when a cloud of smoke shot from the schooner's bows as she fired a gun, and presently the ball struck the water within a few yards of the lugger, and actually dashed the spray over her deck.

"They have the range now," said Paul, as he quietly aimed the gun with extreme caution, and quickly applied the match. A loud hurrah burst from the crew of the "Polly" as the schooner's foretop-mast suddenly broke off in about half its length, and was carried overboard by the force of the gale as the shot struck fairly through its center.

"That's 'Bong swore' to the Mounseer!" exclaimed Dick; "we'll now leave 'em to mend their stick as well as their manners." At this moment another puff of smoke dashed from the schooner's bows. The gun was fired almost at the same instant that the foretop-mast came down; and as the French had obtained the exact range by the preceding shots, the ball came screaming through the air with fatal precision, and striking the mizzen-mast of the "Polly" about ten feet above the deck it cut it off like a carrot, and then passed through both the lug-sails, and ricochetted along the sea. The spanker, together with the sail and a portion of the mast, fell overboard, and at once checked the "Polly's" way.

"Cut all adrift," said Paul, who at the same moment

severed several ropes with his cutlass; " we can't let them
close. Clear away, my lads!" and his men with great
alacrity hauled upon the sail and cut it off the spanker,
allowing the wreck to float astern.

In the meantime the schooner had likewise cleared herself, and she evidently gained upon the lugger, which
severely felt the loss of her mizzen-mast. Once more Paul
fired the long gun, and the shot passed through the
schooner's foresail, doing no serious damage. Again the
smoke issued from the schooner's bows, which had now decreased her distance to about six hundred yards, and luckily
the shot flew too high, and missed its aim; but after a running fight of about a quarter of an hour, during which the
" Polly " hulled her adversary twice, there could be no
doubt that, unless some lucky shot should cripple the
schooner's speed, she would shortly succeed in bringing the
" Polly " to close action, in which case there would be little chance for the lugger against so powerful an enemy as
the French privateer of six carronades and one long six-
pounder bow-chaser. During this time the brave but helpless Léontine lay in the cabin utterly unable to stand; the
misery of seasickness had quenched a spirit that nothing
on land could have subdued.

There was an expression of stern determination on Paul's
face as he once more fired the gun, and the shot crashed
into the bows of the schooner, that was now within three
hundred yards of them. Paul threw off his coat and waistcoat, and turning up his shirt-sleeves close to the shoulders
he exposed a pair of arms with the muscles of Hercules;
he then clutched his cutlass in his right hand, and whispered to Dick Stone, who prepared himself in the same
manner for the struggle.

Paul turned to his men, and said, in a loud, clear voice:
" Now, my lads, the ' Polly ' has lost a leg, and it's no use
trying to run. Let those who would like to return to a
French prison lay down their arms at once; but those who
are men follow me, and rush on board the schooner as she
closes. Leave one man at the helm, and fourteen fine fellows like yourselves will clear the Frenchman's decks in
five minutes. Three cheers for the ' Polly ' and Old England!"

At these words a loud hurrah rose simultaneously from
the gallant crew, who at once divested themselves of their

PAUL GREY BOARDING THE FRENCH SCHOONER.

upper clothing; and with pistols in their belts and sharpened cutlasses in their hands, they prepared for the desperate attempt of boarding the French schooner.

" Let's have another shot at her before we close," said Dick Stone. " Luff a little," cried Dick to the man at the helm; " not too much; that's it; now I've got her." At that moment the gun fired, and the shot once more entered the bows of the schooner. " Too low," said Dick, discontentedly.

" Reload, and close with her," said Paul. " Fire the gun as we touch her sides, not a moment before; and spring upon her decks with me under cover of the smoke."

The schooner was now within a hundred and fifty yards of them, when the " Polly " luffed suddenly up, but as her broadside became exposed a shot from the enemy's bow-chaser struck her fairly in the forecastle, and, passing through the vessel, it killed both the unfortunate French prisoners, who were sitting together on the cabin deck. A few moments later, as the schooner came up, the " Polly " luffed sharp up and ran as though attempting to cross her bows, then, suddenly falling off, the schooner passed her within a foot; and the grappling-irons being thrown into the fore-chains, the two vessels hung together. In the same instant Dick Stone fired the long gun as the muzzle almost touched her side; and in the cloud of smoke he followed Paul, who sprung at the given signal into the lower rigging.

The maneuver of the " Polly " had been so sudden and unexpected, and the shock of the gun fired against the schooner's side was so great, that her crew were taken almost by surprise as Paul's powerful form appeared for an instant upon the bulwarks, and quickly discharging a pistol, which killed the first man opposed to him, he leaped upon the deck, sword in hand, and without reckoning the fearful odds he slashed right and left in all directions. Before the French crew had recovered from their surprise Paul had cut down three men and wounded a fourth. Dick Stone was the first to support him; and discharging a pistol with extreme coolness at the only man that he saw in uniform, he killed the captain of the privateer almost as soon as he set foot upon her deck; dashing his empty pistol into the face of a sailor, which sent him staggering backward, he then rushed into the fight with his cutlass. Three of the "Polly's" men jumped upon deck almost at the same instant; and had the entire crew been able to board, as originially intended, although the schooner's crew consisted of forty men, it would have been impossible to deny that the "Polly" might have had a chance of success. Unfortunately, as the crew were endeavoring to follow their impetuous leader, one of the French sailors fired a carronade through the very port before which they swarmed up her sides. The sudden explosion killed two men, and not only blew several others back upon the "Polly's" deck, but burst the grappling chains, and likewise carried away the lugger's main-mast close by the board.

The "Polly," utterly disabled, now drifted away before the wind, and parted from the schooner with only five able men on board; five men were fighting like bull-dogs on the schooner, while two men were killed by the shot, and three badly wounded by the explosion. In the meantime a sailor at the schooner's mast-head descried a large vessel bearing down upon them in full sail, and he immediately gave the alarm.

In the heat of the fight, surrounded by tremendous odds, Paul had, by his immense strength beaten back all who opposed him. He had fired both his pistols with fatal effect, and although wounded in several places, he fought with undiminished vigor, well seconded by Dick Stone, and the only survivor of the three gallant fellows who had followed them on board; the others had fallen. Dashing his way through the opposing crew he reached the quarter-deck, and felling with a blow of his left hand a man who stood upon the step of the raised deck, he quickly seized the stock of an immense ship's blunderbuss that was fixed by a pivot on the quarter-deck rail. "Stand clear!" he shouted, as Dick fought his way to the spot; but at the same moment Paul saw the last of his men shot through the head, and fall. He hesitated no longer; and turning the heavy blunderbuss upon its pivot, he fired it into the crowd on the main-deck, only a few feet distant. About twenty bullets crashed from this one discharge into the middle of the enemy, and they fell like birds from a flock, some killed, and several wounded. Had the "Polly's" entire crew now been on deck one gallant charge would have won the day; but Paul was alone. Dick Stone had just fallen to a shot fired from the main-top.

The cry of "A sail!" was heard, and as Paul, who was growing weak from loss of blood, for an instant looked at the sea, he saw the "Polly," with two masts gone, drifting disabled some hundred yards away before the wind. His eyes became hazy; a giddiness seized his brain as the blood flowed rapidly from his wounds; he knew no more; he fell upon the deck by the side of the stanch Dick Stone.

The loss of life had been fearful in this desperate hand-to-hand struggle; out of a crew of forty men the schooner had lost her captain and twelve men killed and fourteen wounded, leaving only fourteen sound men on deck. The shots from the "Polly's" long gun had hulled and raked the French vessel repeatedly, and upon every occasion there had been a loss of life; the discharge of the blunderbuss alone had killed three men and wounded six, and the schooner's decks were strewed with dead, and slippery with blood. The remaining portion of the crew were demoralized at the loss of their captain, and upon seeing the large vessel that had been reported as a strange sail now rapidly approaching, they determined to leave the "Polly" to herself, and to run from what they correctly suspected to be a British man-of-war. The schooner at once altered her course, and with the loss of her fore-topmast, she attempted her escape, leaving the "Polly," whose crew were busily engaged in repairing damages.

Hardly had the French vessel sailed a quarter of a mile when a cloud of smoke for an instant obscured the "Polly," as a shot from her long gun passed through the schooner's rigging. The English crew had seen the approaching succor, and they continued to fire shot after shot in the hope of disabling a spar or yard to enable the cruiser to overtake the enemy.

In less than three quarters of an hour a brig-of-war, with the English colors flying, hailed the "Polly," and heaving to she lowered a boat, and upon hearing an account of the late fight she took the lugger in tow. The French schooner was out of sight, and as the captain of the brig was under orders to proceed to Falmouth he declined to begin a chase that would lead him in an opposite direction, especially as the schooner might have altered her course, which would render her discovery most uncertain.

Within an hour of the action the brig was under full

sail toward Falmouth, with the disabled lugger in tow, while the wounded men had been transferred to the king's ship, and placed under surgical treatment.

We must now return to the schooner, which steered direct for Dunkerque. As she lost sight of the English cruiser the crew regained their spirits, and heaving the dead bodies overboard they washed the soiled decks and carried the wounded down below. As one by one the dead were examined and stripped prior to being committed to the waves, the sailors who were thus employed came upon the bodies of Paul and Dick Stone. They had just commenced their examination, and had turned Paul upon one side, when blood was observed to flow from one of his wounds, and upon a closer inspection it was discovered that he was not yet dead. As buckets of water were thrown upon the deck in all directions, the heave of the vessel occasionally rolled the water in a considerable depth into the scuppers, where the bodies of Paul and Dick Stone were lying. Having left Paul, they now attempted to lift up the apparently lifeless body of Dick for the purpose of throwing it overboard; with this intention two men laid hold of it by the shoulders and the heels, and dragged it toward the open gangway on the main-deck. Before heaving it over they laid the body down, and one man exclaimed, " *Mon Dieu!* what heavy people are these English! We could throw two Frenchmen overboard with less trouble than one rosbif Englishman!"

As he said these words, to the horror of the Frenchmen the body of Dick Stone suddenly sat up, and looking around with an expression of extreme coolness, he appeared to understand the unpleasantness of his situation, as he exclaimed, in a calm but faint voice:

" You Mounseers are a very purlite people, but I'll not trouble you to heave me overboard, as I can do that for myself whenever it's agreeable."

Having said this, he instinctively put his hand into his trousers pocket, and drew forth his faithful pipe, which he deliberately filled; he then searched in his other pocket, and produced his flint and steel; striking a light with difficulty, he faintly puffed his pipe, and then asked:

" Where's my captain?"

The Frenchmen pointed to Paul's body. Dick stared mournfully at his commander's lifeless figure.

"Where's the 'Polly'—the lugger?" continued Dick, still more faintly.

The Frenchmen pointed to the far horizon: "Gone!" they exclaimed.

Dick's eyes glazed and became fixed; the pipe dropped from his mouth; he fell backward on the deck, and his features became rigid; a dense puff of smoke issued from his mouth; the gallant spirit of Dick Stone had parted forever!

"What droll people are these English!" said the Frenchman, who now examined the body with much curiosity; "at last he is dead! Give me a hand, and lift his feet while I take his shoulders; now! one! two! three!"

A dull splash was heard as the schooner steadily continued upon her course.

CHAPTER XI.

NED GREY, NIGGER TIM, AND NERO AT SEA.

WHEN we last parted from Ned Grey the "Sybille," one of the finest frigates of the British navy, was plowing along with a fair wind at the mouth of the Channel on her voyage to the Indian station. Although strangers on board, it was not long before an incident occurred that raised the new-comers in the estimation of both officers and crew, with whom they had already become favorites. It would have been hard to say which was the greater pet of the sailors—the nigger boy Tim, or the dog Nero. The former had become cook's mate, and was domiciled in the galley, while the latter was allowed to range anywhere except upon the quarter-deck, which sacred spot Nero learned to respect after he had been only a few days on board, and nothing would induce him to trespass beyond the forbidden limit unless called by the captain, who had specially adopted him.

Captain Cooke was one of the brightest ornaments of the service. Beloved by his men, they were ready to follow him through any danger; and although he was well-known to be heedless of a superior force, his attack was invariably attended with success; he was accordingly considered to be a lucky captain, and when others found a difficulty in manning their ships, the "Sybille" was always certain of a superior crew.

The frigate had passed the boisterous Bay of Biscay, and had made a rapid run to the Cape Verde Islands. It was about an hour before sunset that the high peak of St. Antonio was first observed by a man at the mast-head bearing S. S. E., and as the evening closed this lofty landmark faded from view, and mingled with the gray bank of clouds that concealed the horizon.

The night was fine and starlight, and the noble vessel flew through the water, as with studding-sails set she sailed like a huge white swan over the phosphorescent waves that sparkled with ten thousand lights, as though in mockery of the bright stars above. The foam rushed from her bows in sheets of mimic fire, while a brilliant stream of light washed her dark sides and glistened in her wake like a river of molten metal as the " Sybille " woke from their sleep the billions of animalculæ—those glow-worms of the deep that light the sailor's path in the dark and fathomless sea. Now a huge polypus gleamed in the depths as though some mermaid wandered with a lamp below; then smaller lights twinkled in the creaming waves, and huge and fiery serpents seemed to chase each other in wild speed as the swift porpoises left their long and brilliant trail illumined in the dark-blue sea.

It was a lovely sight; it was one of those glorious ocean scenes that are unknown by those whose lives are passed on shore. Each drop of water teemed with life: there was the so-called barren sea, the watery desert peopled with its countless myriads; the bright universe above; the heavens with their hosts of brilliant worlds so distant, so incomprehensible, equaled only in their infinity by the ocean waves, each of which contained a thousand worlds—life within life —world without end. " The Spirit of God moved upon the face of the waters."

Ned Grey stood upon the quarter-deck and gazed below at the sparkling current as the ship flew rapidly on her way; he thought of home, of his mother, and of Edith; every instant the distance increased between them as the wind hurried the noble vessel further and further away. When, if ever, should he see their loved faces again? These thoughts engrossed his attention, and although he still looked fixedly at the phosphorescent water beneath, he almost ceased to observe the brilliant scene, but merely gazed abstractedly, until a dark object struggling in the silvery stream roused him from his reverie; almost at the same instant a loud cry was raised in the fore part of the ship: "A man overboard!" Instinctively and without a moment's hesitation Ned threw off his jacket, and repeating the alarming cry he sprung boldly into the sea.

Rising quickly to the surface after his deep plunge, Ned struck out in the direction of the object that had first attracted his attention—this had vanished.

"Where are you?" shouted Ned. A voice was heard far astern, at the same time Ned felt himself seized from behind by the shirt near the collar; in another instant he felt a mass of silky hair as he reached back, and found himself grasped by the strong teeth of his faithful dog. Nero was by his master's side, apparently sleeping on the deck, when Ned had sprung over the ship's gangway; but upon seeing him disappear the dog immediately leaped overboard, and had succeeded in catching him quickly after his reappearance on the surface.

"Good old boy!" cried Ned, as he endeavored to free himself from the dog; "loose it, old fellow! Let go, old man!" he continued, as Nero resolutely maintained his hold. After some difficulty he released himself from the dog, who then accompanied him toward the object of their search, which could now be clearly made out by the extreme brightness of one particular spot in the water, caused by the struggles of the person in the phosphorescence.

"Keep up till I come!" shouted Ned, to encourage the individual in question, who was about sixty yards distant, and without a thought for his own safety he struck out with increased vigor, with Nero swimming by his side.

"Help! I'm sinking!" cried a despairing voice as Ned arrived within twenty strokes of the struggling sailor.

"Don't give in!" cried Ned, "I'll save you!" and he redoubled his exertions to reach the drowning man; he was within a few feet of him when he suddenly threw his arms above his head, and he disappeared just as Ned was about to seize him by the hair. At that moment Ned dived, and following the bright light caused by the struggles of the sinking man, he caught him by the shoulder and dragged him once more to the surface. Without an instant's delay Ned grasped him by the collar. "Hold him, good dog!" cried Ned, who found it difficult to support the weight; but to his astonishment Nero relaxed his grip, and quitting the man he caught Ned by the shirt at the shoulder-sleeve. At this moment the head of the half-drowned man turned, and the bright starlight shone upon the pale features of Jem Stevens. The dog had recognized him quicker than Ned, and nothing would induce him to assist. It was in vain that Ned urged him on. Occasionally he relaxed his hold of his master and swam by his side barking loudly, but he avoided Stevens with a stubborn determination. Several minutes elapsed in a severe struggle for life. Jem Stevens was an enemy, but this fact only served to awaken the chivalrous nature of Ned Grey, who clung to him with a gallant tenacity that endangered his own life. Stevens was utterly helpless, he was half dead, and Ned would have been unable to support his head above the surface had not the dog added to his buoyancy by holding him by the shoulder: even with his assistance he was nearly exhausted. Several times he had swallowed large quantities of water, as for a few seconds the dog relaxed his hold, when the shirt gave way, and Ned sunk until Nero once more grasped a fresh portion of his clothes; he was almost done, and he feared that for self-preservation he would be forced to relinquish his prize; he felt heavy in the water, and his limbs became almost leaden. Whenever the dog lost his hold he barked loudly, as though calling for assistance; but the " Sybille " was far away; she had come sharp up to the wind at the cry of " a man overboard," and had laid her foretop-sail aback; but she was nearly half a mile away from the spot before she could come round and lower a boat.

Once more Ned's shirt gave way, and again he sunk, and for an instant he loosed his hold of Jem Stevens; the dog barked loudly, and again he seized and supported his young master, who once more clutched the almost lifeless form of Jem Stevens, although himself in the last stage of distress. At that moment, when it became positively necessary to sacrifice Stevens to save his own life, he heard a voice at no great distance.

" Hold on, Massa Ned! Lord hab mussy 'pon us! Hold on, my dear Massa Ned! Tim got de life-buoy! Tim coming quick catch Massa Ned!"

There was no mistaking the voice; it was hardly a hundred yards distant, and the hope of succor instilled fresh vigor into the sinking frame of the exhausted Ned. Nero had also heard the well-known voice of Nigger Tim, and for an instant relaxing his hold, he barked loudly in reply, and then again supported his master.

"Come quick, Tim, I'm very nearly done!" cried Ned.

"All right, Massa Ned; t'ank God for Tim and de life-buoy! I's a-coming!"

In another minute, when Ned could no longer have supported his burden, the dark and welcome figure of Tim was seen within a few yards. He was swimming in the center of the life-buoy with all his strength, and, gaining Ned, he slipped from his position, and assisted him to the secure place that he had vacated; at the same time with their joint endeavors they supported Stevens above the surface. Tim held on stoutly, while the dog, released from his labor, swam easily by the side of the party.

In the meantime a boat was hurrying to their assistance from the frigate. The barking of the dog was the first guide, but upon a nearer approach the extreme luminous appearance of the water caused by the friction of the struggling swimmers directed the rowers to the spot. Although comparatively safe when clinging to the life-buoy, much exertion was required to support the almost inanimate body of Stevens, and it was with a joyful sense of relief that Ned Grey hailed the arrival of the boat.

"Back water!" shouted a voice as the boat neared them; at the same time a sailor in the bow reached Ned with a boat-hook, grasping which, the floating party were gently towed to the side and taken on board.

Stevens showed no signs of life, and upon arrival at the frigate his body was hoisted on deck by a sling, and at once consigned to the care of the doctor, while Ned and Nigger Tim quickly changed their clothes, and refreshed by a glass of grog they soon forgot their recent danger and escape. Nero had given himself a good shake, after which he was rubbed dry by several admiring sailors with a new swab.

Ned Grey had only just reappeared on deck in a dry suit of clothes when he was summoned to the captain's cabin; the door was opened by the steward, and Ned found himself in the presence of Captain Cooke, who was engaged in the examination of a chart of the Indian seas. As Ned appeared he rolled up the chart quickly, and looking steadfastly for some moments at the lad without speaking, he at length asked his name.

"Edward Grey, sir," replied Ned.

"You joined the ship against your inclination?" said the captain.

"I was sorry to leave my home without a chance to say good-bye, sir; but I'm proud to serve the king under you, sir," replied Ned.

"Well, Ned," continued the captain, "the king may be proud of such a lad as yourself. You have done a gallant act to-night, and I'm glad to have the command of one so young who has shown such courage and devotion. There are many men who shine in the heat of action, but few who will risk their lives as you have done to save another. Tell me," continued the captain, "is it true that the lad you have saved is an old school-fellow and a personal enemy?"

"He was a school-fellow, sir," replied Ned, "and I am sorry he is an enemy. I trust he may now forget the past, for I never gave him cause for dislike."

"Where do you live, and what is your occupation in England?" asked the captain.

Ned in a few words explained, and gave a short outline of his career, including the history of the nigger Tim's escape.

"Well," replied the captain, "I congratulate you. There are few lads of your age who have already saved two lives, and I trust that you will yet earn other laurels on board the 'Sybille.' I need not tell you to do your duty, but I trust the opportunity may soon arrive when you will prove yourself as brave under fire as you have been under trials by water. Go, Ned, do your duty, and I wish I had many like you."

Ned's heart beat with an honest pride as he left his captain's presence. He felt at that moment as though he could dare the whole world to win his approbation, and he yearned for the moment when in the smoke of battle he should be able to gain a smile from his gallant commander. At the same time that these feelings occupied his thoughts he longed to stretch out his hand to his old enemy, Jem Stevens, and to bury all enmity in the deep from which they had emerged.

He had no sooner gained the dark than he requested to

be allowed to visit Stevens, who was slowly recovering under the doctor's care. He found him lying in the berth only half conscious, and apparently with a desire to sleep.

The doctor had other patients to visit, and as all immediate danger was past he gave Ned a bottle that contained a stimulant combined with a gentle narcotic, of which he ordered him to give a table-spoonful should he remain awake for more than half an hour. Ned sat by his berth, and watched the pale features of Jem Stevens by the dim light of a lamp.

The half hour passed, and as he was still awake Ned wished to give the draught that had been prescribed. He therefore gently took the hand of Stevens that rested on the bed-clothes, and pressing it effectionately, he whispered:

"Stevens, take this from me. I promised the doctor to attend to you. Are you feeling better?"

There was no return on the part of Stevens to this friendly greeting; but after gazing fixedly at Ned for a few minutes, he coldly withdrew his hand, and turning upon his side with his back to Ned, he muttered sullenly that he required no medicine, but would go to sleep if left alone.

Ned felt a pang as he quietly left the cabin and ascended to the fresh air of the deck. There was an unmistakable feeling in the withdrawal of the hand, and he knew that the stubborn nature of Jem Stevens was proof against all generosity.

From that day Ned Grey held a high position in the opinion of both officers and crew of the "Sybille;" his ready obedience and alacrity in the performance of his duty, together with his more than ordinary strength and activity, insured him the good-will of his superiors, while his general good-nature and cheerful disposition, added to his well-proved courage, gained for him the admiration of the men. He had become an especial favorite with the captain, who had been much struck with his gentlemanly appearance and demeanor. Upon several occasions he had drawn from Ned certain descriptions of his former life that increased the interest he had taken, and he comforted Ned with the assurance that upon their arrival at the Indian station he would be able to write home to his parents, and thus relieve their anxiety. At the same time he advised him to stick to the profession, and that he would apply for

his promotion to enable him to enter as midshipman on the
next voyage.

There was only one individual among the entire crew of
the " Sybille " who did not share the general feeling toward Ned Grey. This was Jem Stevens, who, although he
had in some degree abated the insolence of his former demeanor, now sullenly passed him upon every occasion without condescending to notice his presence.

Generosity of character is one of a sailor's virtues, and
the ingratitude of Jem Stevens, thus publicly exhibited,
increased the dislike with which he was generally regarded.
In the midshipmen's berth he was positively hated; by the
superior officers he was despised; and the sailors had on
more than one occasion declared that the dog Nero had
shown more discretion than Ned in refusing to assist so
worthless a fellow.

This was the state of feeling among the officers and crew
of the " Sybille " when, after a prosperous voyage, during
which she had captured several prizes, she arrived off the
coast of Ceylon, which was the first land she had sighted
since leaving the Cape Verde Islands.

The frigate had coasted the southern portion of Ceylon
at a distance that obscured all but the beautiful deep-blue
mountains of the interior, which rose to an altitude that
concealed their summits in the clouds. Upon rounding the
eastern point the " Sybille " steered directly north, and as
the south-west monsoon was blowing strong she coasted
within ten miles of the shore to make the harbor of Trincomalee. Nothing could be more beautiful than the appearance of this paradise of the East. At times the lofty
mountains, although upward of sixty miles distant, appeared to be within a day's march of the vessel. The sea
was the deepest blue, and as the frigate stood close in shore
when passing a projecting headland the white surf was seen
to break upon the coral reefs almost at the feet of the waving cocoa-nut palms which forced dense groves even to the
water's edge. At times the native villages could be perceived nestled among the shady palms. At length the
latitude of the wished-for harbor was reached, and the
" Sybille " steered direct for the shore toward the heights
that rose near the entrance to Trincomalee. As the frigate
approached the scene increased in beauty; the palms appeared to spring from the surface of the waves, and the

hills, clothed with verdure to their summits, were reflected in the calm waters of the magnificent harbor which, completely land-locked, lay like an inland lake surrounded by the most lovely vegetation of the tropics.

With her sails close-hauled, the "Sybille" steered through the narrow entrance, and shot after shot rang from her decks and re-echoed from the surrounding hills as she saluted the fort upon the Point; she then came sharp up to the wind, and cast anchor within a hundred yards of the shore, while the men swarmed up the rigging at the sound of the boatswain's whistle, and in a few minutes every sail was furled, and the "Sybille" looked as snug as though she had been lying for a month in port.

At that time the beautiful island of Ceylon had not been long in our possession since England had wrested it from the Dutch. The latter people had contented themselves with the seaboard and adjoining lowlands, as they considered that the great importance of Ceylon consisted in the peculiar harbor of Trincomalee, which not only would contain a powerful fleet to command the Indian seas, but was sufficiently large to float half the navies of the world; in addition to its vast capacity, the water was of a sufficient depth within a few feet of the land to enable a first-class ship of the line to lie with her bowsprit overhanging the shore. Trincomalee may be called the key of India; in the hands of a powerful enemy a fleet would lie in perfect security that could defy attack, as the vicinity of the harbor is specially arranged by nature for defense. At the time of which we write there was no other protection than the Dutch fort at the Point, which exists at the present day, and it is a curious instance of neglect that this magnificent harbor remains otherwise unprotected.

With a fleet of fast cruisers concentrated at Trincomalee by an enemy the trade of India would be almost annihilated, as such vessels would scour the seas like falcons, and when chased by a superior force they would run for the impregnable nest. On the same principle the possession of Trincomalee affords incalculable advantages as a great depot and arsenal for naval and military stores. There is no other safe harbor in the island, neither is there any secure port nearer than Bombay; thus, in the event of a naval action in the Indian seas, there are no ports to which the crippled ships could retreat for repairs, except those of

Port Louis in the Mauritius, Trincomalee, and Bombay; it was accordingly of vital importance to our Indian possessions that these three harbors should belong to England.

Unfortunately for our Indian commerce, at that time Mauritius belonged to the French, with whom we were at war, and the extreme importance of our position was painfully exhibited to the English by the havoc committed on our trade. In the strongly fortified harbor of Port Louis a French fleet of powerful frigates was established, with which our vessels of inferior force upon the station were unable to cope. In consequence of our inferiority several actions had been fought in the Indian seas which added more to French renown than to the glory of England: nevertheless our Admiralty authorities continued to send to the Indian station a number of second-class frigates and corvettes that were totally unadapted for a collision with the large ships and heavy metal of the enemy.

Although this inferiority was admitted, it did not interfere with the ardor of our captains, who with a reckless intrepidity hovered around the coasts of Mauritius, and challenged every combat without considering the overpowering odds. Thus many severe losses had befallen us.

Among those French vessels that had gained a high reputation was a powerful frigate, the "Forte." This vessel had been newly built in France expressly to harass our commerce in the Indian seas; and as our naval supremacy was generally admitted, the French had constructed this ship upon a scale and armament so superior to anything that the English possessed that without some gross mismanagement success would appear almost certain.

As the English losses had become of serious importance it was resolved that the fleet upon the Indian station should be re-enforced. Thus, among other vessels, the "Sybille" had been dispatched from England, and it was the determination of her caption to seek out and fight the renowned "Forte" upon the earliest opportunity.

CHAPTER XII.

NEWS OF THE FRENCH FRIGATE "FORTE."

A WEEK after the "Sybille" had arrived in the harbor of Trincomalee she looked as though she had only just been rigged and fitted for sea; her lower rigging had been tightened and retarred, her top-masts fresh varnished, and the vessel had been newly painted from stem to stern. There was not a ship in the British navy that looked more like a perfect specimen of a man-of-war; her guns were not only in beautiful neatness and finish of polish, but her crew were constantly trained in their use, as Captain Cooke was of opinion that a shot thrown away was worse than wasted: thus he instructed his men never to fire at a useless range, but to wait patiently for close quarters: " Close quarters and good seamanship will win the battle " was a well-known saying of the " Sybille's " captain, in which his men had learned to thoroughly believe.

During the frigate's stay at Trincomalee she on several occasions put to sea to exercise her guns, until at length the day arrived when she was to sail in search of the renowned depredator, the " Forte."

At that time the French Indian squadron, under Admiral Sercey, was cruising with great success in the neighborhood of Manilla and throughout the China seas, in which direction our losses of homeward bound Indiamen had been most severe; it was reported that the " Forte " was also in those seas, and the " Sybille " left the quiet harbor of Trincomalee with her officers and crew in high spirits at the expected rencontre.

After a rapid voyage to Manilla, to the great disappointment of Captain Cooke he heard that the " Forte " had left, and that she was cruising in the Bay of Bengal. Without losing a day the " Sybille " ran for Madras, where she expected to gain some intelligence of the proceedings of her enemy.

Upon arrival at the Madras roadstead Captain Cooke heard to his intense satisfaction that the " Forte " was cruising along the coast, and that she had already intercepted several vessels. Having gained this welcome intelligence he sailed without delay for the mouth of the Bengal River.

When near the Sandheads the " Sybille " met a vessel containing French prisoners, some of whom had been on board the " Forte;" these upon seeing the armament of the " Sybille " ridiculed the idea of an encounter with their heavy frigate. Upon the same vessel was an English captain of a merchant vessel that had been captured by the " Forte;" he also expressed an opinion that the risk of an engagement would be most dangerous to the " Sybille," at the same time he gallantly volunteered his services. The " Forte " was reported to be near at hand off the Sand-heads.

It was on a dark night that the " Sybille " was standing under easy sail, with the wind light but steady from the sou'-sou'-west, when flashes were remarked in the far distance which resembled sheet lightning. At first this appearance attracted no more than ordinary attention, but upon their quick and repeated occurrence Captain Cooke concluded that they originated from the explosion of cannon; it was therefore natural to suppose that, as the " Forte " was within a short distance, the flashes must proceed from her in some engagement with an English vessel.

Having carefully extinguished all lights on board, the " Sybille " tacked to the west at 9 P.M., and at 9:30 P.M. she distinguished three vessels in a cluster in the south-east; these were the " Forte " and her two valuable prizes, the Indiamen " Endeavor " and the " Lord Mornington " from China. In her action with these ships the flashes from the " Forte's " guns had attracted the attention of the British frigate.

The " Sybille's " drum beat to quarters, and as the crew stood at their guns a finer lot of seamen could never have been selected. Not a light was to be seen on the English ship; but standing on the quarter-deck, in a silence in which a pin might have been heard to fall, the gallant Captain Cooke addressed a few spirit-stirring words to his brave followers:

" My lads," he said, " you've long been looking for the ' Forte;' there she lies before you; go in and take her! Double shot your guns, and don't fire until you rub against her sides."

" Rightly conjecturing that one of these ships would prove to be the object of his search, Captain Cooke continued to stand to the westward in order to get the weather-gage; and soon afterward the ' Sybille ' passed about two miles to leeward of them. At 10 P.M., having brought the three ships sufficiently on her quarter to enable her to weather them by going on the other tack, the ' Sybille ' put about, and taking in her top-gallant sails and courses, kept the center ship, which from her superior size and the lights in her stern marked her out as the ' Forte,' on her lee or larboard bow.

"The water was at this time quite smooth, with a light and steady breeze still blowing from the sou'-sou'-west, and the ' Sybille ' under her topsails, jib, and spanker, was going about two knots an hour. At 11:30 P.M. the ' Sybille ' saw that the three ships were lying to on the starboard tack, or that on which she was standing.

" At midnight, when the ' Sybille ' had approached within a mile of the ' Forte,' the latter's two rows of ports, lighted up as they were, gave the ship a very formidable appearance. The ' Forte ' then filled, hove in stays under the ' Sybille's ' lee bow, and as her larboard guns began to bear, fired six or seven of them, the instant and principal effect of which was to bring down her opponent's jib. The ' Forte ' as she passed on fired also her after guns, and one of the prizes opened her fire; but still the ' Sybille,' as a proof of the judgment of her commander and the steadiness of her crew, reserved her fire for a shorter and more effective distance.

"The patience of the latter, however, was put to no longer a trial than until the ' Forte ' passed abaft the beam of their ship; when, at three quarters past midnight, the ' Sybille ' put her helm up, and fired the whole of her broadside into the ' Forte's ' stern, at less than pistol-shot distance; so close indeed that the French ship's spanker-boom was scarcely cleared. Luffing quickly up, the ' Sybille ' was presently close alongside her antagonist to leeward, and poured in a second broadside, as well directed as the previous raking one. The bearing-up of the ' Sybille ' had been so sudden and unexpected that several of the ' Forte's ' larboard or weather guns went off after the former had passed to leeward.

"Thus this furious night action commenced. For nearly the first hour, during which the two ships lay broadside to broadside, at a distance that never exceeded point-blank musket range, and was sometimes much nearer, the ' Forte ' returned a spirited but far too elevated, and consequently an almost harmless fire. At 1:30 A.M., on March 1, Captain Cooke was mortally wounded by a grape-shot, and the command devolved upon Lieutenant Lucius Hardyman. About ten minutes after Captain Cooke had been carried below, Captain Davies, of the army, an aid-de-camp of Lord Mornington's, and a volunteer upon this occasion, while encouraging the men at the quarter-deck guns, of some of which he had charge, was killed by a cannon-shot that nearly severed his body."

Ned Gray was splashed with his blood, as, stripped to the waist, he fought his gun with the brave fellows around him, with that cool intrepidity that has won all of England's battles. He had seen his beloved captain struck down by a shot, and for the moment he would have rushed to his assistance; but a stern sense of duty overcame this first impulse, and as others supported his captain's sinking frame Ned cast a sorrowful look behind him, and then lent double strength to his work as they ran the gun out, and the shot crashed into the sides of the French frigate. For upward of two hours there had been an uninterrupted roar of artillery, but at this time the fire from the "Forte" began to slacken, and at 2:30 A.M. it entirely ceased.

"On this the 'Sybille' discontinued her fire, and hailed to know if her antagonist had struck. Receiving no reply, although the ships were still so close that the voices of the 'Forte's' people were distinctly heard, the 'Sybille' recommenced firing with renewed vigor. Finding no return, the British frigate a second time ceased, and a second time hailed, but again without effect. At this moment, perceiving the 'Forte's' rigging filled with men, and her topgallant sail loose, as if with the intention of endeavoring to escape, the 'Syblle' recommenced her fire for the third time, and set her own foresail and top-gallant sails.

"In five minutes after this the 'Forte's' mizzen-mast came down, and in another minute or two her fore and main-masts and bowsprit. The 'Sybille' ceased firing, her crew gave three cheers; and thus at 2:28 A.M., being about two hours and a half from its commencement, the action ended.

"The 'Sybille' immediately dropped her anchor in seventeen fathoms, and all hands began repairing the rigging and bending new sails. At about 3 A.M. one of the English prisoners on board the 'Forte,' finding that the ship was drifting upon the 'Sybille,' hailed the latter to request that a boat might be sent on board, as all theirs had been shot to pieces. Although no doubt existed on board the 'Sybille' as to the name of the ship of which

she had made such a wreck, the question was put, and
the French frigate " Forte " was the answer returned.
While taking possession of the prize, we will give some
account of the damage and loss of the ship that had so gallantly captured her.

" The ' Sybille ' had most of her standing and all her
running rigging and sails shot to pieces, all her masts
and yards, particularly the main and mizzen-masts, and the
yards on them badly wounded, but with all this the
' Sybille ' had only received in the hull and upper works
six shot; one of which, however, had dismounted a gun,
and another, a twenty-four pounder, having entered one of
the officer's cabins, had shivered to atoms a large trunk and
a smaller one near it, carried away two legs of a sofa, and
passed out through the ship's side. The ' Sybille ' had lost
Captain Davies, one seaman, one marine, and two soldiers
killed; Captain Cooke (mortally), fifteen seamen, and one
soldier wounded; total, five killed and seventeen wounded.

" When Lieutenant Nicholas Manger, third of the
' Sybille,' with his boat's crew, went on board the ' Forte,'
the scene of wreck and carnage that presented itself to their
view was such, by all accounts, as no other persons than
the actual spectators could form an adequate idea of. The
bowsprit had gone close to the figure-head, the fore-mast
one foot above the forecastle, the main-mast eighteen feet
above the quarter-deck, and the mizzen-mast ten feet above
the poop. As the masts had fallen with all the sails set, it
was remarked that the three topsails were very slightly injured; the ' Sybille's ' shot had taken a lower and more
fatal direction. All the boats, booms, the wheel, capstan,
binnacle, and other articles on deck were cut to pieces.

" The ' Forte's ' upper works were lined with cork to
prevent splinters; and for the same purpose nettings were
fixed fore and aft as well on the main-deck as on the quarter-deck, forecastle, and gangways. Another stout net-
ting was spread like an awning over the quarter-deck.
This is common on board French ships; and being put
up to prevent blocks and other heavy articles from falling
from aloft, is appropriately named ' la sauve-tête.' The
starboard quarter-deck and forecastle barricades were completely destroyed; and the same side of the ' Forte ' from
the bends upward was nearly beat in. Upward of three
hundred round shot were counted in her hull; several of

6

her guns were dismounted; and the very cables in her tiers
were rendered unserviceable.

"The loss on board the 'Forte' may well have been
severe. Her original crew, including a portion of Malays
taken on board at Batavia, amounted to five hundred and
thirteen men and boys. Of this number she had sent away
in various prizes, according to the account given by her
officers, one hundred and forty-three; leaving three hundred and seventy as the number present in the action. Of
these she lost, as appears, sixty-five killed, including her
captain, first lieutenant, and some other officers, and eighty
wounded, including also several of her officers."*

At the close of the action the two prizes, now manned
with French crews (the "Lord Mornington" and "Endeavor"), made sail and effected their escape after an in-
effectual chase by the "Sybille," the shattered condition of
her rigging preventing the possibility of carrying sufficient
sail to overhaul them.

The joy of the "Sybille's" crew was terribly damped
by the grievous wound received by their captain; a grape-
shot had entered the fleshy portion of his right arm, and
tearing its way through the ribs it had passed out at the
back near the spine; the doctor had no hope of his recovery.

A few days were passed in rigging the "Forte" under
jury-masts, after which she was taken in tow by the "Sybille" to Calcutta, where she could be repaired sufficiently
to enable her to proceed to England. Upon arrival at Calcutta there was universal gratification at the sight of the
dreaded "Forte" thus brought in as a capture by the gallant "Sybille." But the unfortunate Captain Cooke could
enjoy no share of the honors that were heaped upon them.
The glory of this world was passed; and he gradually sunk,
and died a few days after his arrival. Before his death he
had requested to see Ned Grey, in whom he had taken the
warmest interest, and he confided him to the care of Lieutenant Hardyman, requesting that, as he had been forcibly
taken from his home, he might return to England on board
the "Forte," together with Nigger Tim and the dog Nero.
The latter had so attached himself to the captain that he
had seldom stirred from his cabin since the day he had received his mortal wound.

* The description of this celebrated action between the "Sybille"
and the "Forte" is extracted from James's "Naval History."

The body of Captain Cooke was buried at Calcutta with military honors, followed to the grave not only by the "Sybille's" officers and crew but by an enormous assemblage of people, among whom there was no more sincere mourner than Ned Grey, who had lost his best and most powerful friend.

True to the instructions that he had received from Captain Cooke, Lieutenant Hardyman, who had succeeded to the command, placed a prize crew upon the "Forte," including Ned Grey and his party, that had originally been kidnaped, together with Jem Stevens, who had shown so much nervousness in the late fight that the officers requested to be rid of him, and the vessel, having been partially repaired, set sail for England.

The "Forte" was commanded by the same officer who had taken Ned Grey from the beach on the morning that he and Tim had left Sandy Cove with the intention of returning home to breakfast, and the good-natured lieutenant now looked forward to returning to his friends the same lad covered with honor that he had originally misled; as he had left England on board the "Sybille," so he would return on board the "Sybille's" prize, which he had bravely helped to win.

On the 25th of March the "Forte" sailed, and had fair weather until she arrived in about seventeen degrees south latitude. Ned Grey was acting as midshipman, having received this temporary promotion for the voyage. Nigger Tim was, as before, in the galley as cook's mate; and Jem Stevens was as sullen as usual, but ever since the action with the "Forte" he had very little to say, as during the fight he had been found lying upon his back, at first supposed to be killed, but upon examination there was no wound, and he could only explain the situation by declaring that he had been knocked down by the wind of a shot at the commencement of the action, and that he had not recovered his senses until it was over. Various remarks had been made by the officers and crew, who were sufficiently uncharitable to attribute his prostration to fear; the word "coward" had been used by more than one in connection with this affair, and even Nigger Tim had ventured a remark that had become a by-word with the sailors—"Massa Stevens smell de powder, Massa Stevens get de bellyache." Ned Grey had long since discontinued his attempts at reconciliation; and to avoid unpleasantness he said as little to his old school-fellow as possible.

It was on the 22d of April that the "Forte" suddenly lost the wind, and lay becalmed. The barometer had fallen in an alarming manner since the morning, and it continued to sink with great rapidity, although the sky was perfectly clear. At about an hour after noon snow-white and dense clouds, like mountains of frozen snow, rose upon all quarters of the horizon, and were it not for the oppressive heat the scene might have been imagined in the Arctic regions. Quickly ascending from the sea, and darkening as they rose, the clouds massed together, and uniting from all directions, in about an hour they formed the densest canopy, that totally concealed the heavens. The sky was solidly black, as though covered by thick folds of velvet, only in certain points the color varied to a dark purplish gray, as one edge of an overlapping stratum was exposed. It was the hurricane season in that particular latitude and longitudinal position, and there could be no doubt that a cyclone of the most fearful description was about to burst upon them. The "Forte" was badly manned, as few could be spared from the "Sybille," and the greater portion of the crew were Lascars; in addition to this disadvantage she had only been patched and otherwise hastily repaired since her recent engagement, in which she had been terribly shattered, and her rigging was made up of old stuff that had been procured at Calcutta simply to enable her to complete the voyage to England preparatory to a general refit. Altogether, the "Forte" was in no condition to contend with a tropical cyclone.

There was a painful stillness in the air, and the vessel rolled heavily in the long, irregular swell of the sea, as there was no wind to steady her. Suddenly there was a scream as though ten thousand furies yelled and flapped their wings high up in the dense mass of inky vapor; but still the sails hung listlessly without a breath of air; these were a storm stay-sail, double-reefed foresail, and spanker.

It was nearly dark, although hardly 3 P.M.; the sea was black. Presently, in the far distance a bright white streak appeared low upon the horizon, which increased with amazing rapidity until it resembled an endless line of rolling snow. There was no doubt in the minds of all on board —the hurricane was upon them! There was no breath of air to trim the sails and bring the vessel's head to the advancing squall. She lay helplessly rolling in the disturbed and heavy swell.

In the meantime the roar of the approaching storm could plainly be heard as the ghastly line of foam swept over the darkened sea with incredible velocity. Every man was on deck and at his post, but as yet nothing could be done. The roar increased, and as the white line advanced the surface of the sea behind was like a sheet of snow after a heavy fall; the water appeared compressed and flattened by the enormous pressure of the gale. On it came! nearer and nearer, in all the madness of the hurricane, until, with a shriek of wind and tumultuous rush of foaming water, the white line reached them, and pressed the noble frigate on her beam ends.

The fore-mast snapped short off by the deck; every sail had been blown to shreds; the bowsprit was gone; and thus relieved the ship slowly recovered her position, and drifted at a fearful speed before the storm. It would be impossible to describe the tempest which now hurried the frigate from her course; the sea, that had at first been vanquished by the wind, now rose in all the ocean's majesty; mountain and valley could be reckoned as the overwhelming masses of water swept in wild waves before the hurricane, their curling crests blowing off into misty spray as their tops became exposed to the force of the wind. Nothing more could be done than to loosen a few reefs of the main-topsail, and run before the storm.

Night came on. The darkness was hardly felt, as every half minute a bright flash of lightning illumined the scene, succeeded by roars of thunder, before which the artillery of the ship would have appeared like a faint echo. Running before the gale, the frigate rolled to such an extent in the heavy sea that no one could stand upon the decks without holding on. Upon several occasions she had shipped great seas that rushed bodily across her decks from port to port; everything was battened down securely, and thus the "Forte" rushed headlong before the resistless storm.

When day broke the hurricane, if possible, increased, and a little before noon a sudden whirlwind carried away the main-topmast. Cutting the wreck adrift, the "Forte" rolled worse than before, and it was considered necessary to heave some of her guns overboard to reduce the deck load. This was effected with great difficulty, and one by one her heavy guns plunged into the deep. All those from the upper deck had disappeared, and the effect was quickly observed. Although she still rolled heavily, she no longer shipped a sea at every lurch.

Three days and nights thus passed away in the gloom and misery of the hurricane. The world appeared to be made up of thunder, lightning, wind, waves, and darkness!

On the fourth morning the storm began to abate, and the wind, although still blowing a violent gale, was no longer the hurricane which had driven them from their course. As yet the sky had been completely overcast, thus no observation could be taken, and the position of the ship could only be vaguely guessed by dead reckoning. The vessel had been running at about an average of eleven knots an hour throughout the storm, and as the direction, although varying, tended principally to north-west, it was considered that she must have either run past the northern extremity of Madagascar, or be still on the east of that island. In either case it was a most dangerous position, as the storm still blew with great violence, and was driving them toward a lee shore. The sea was exceedingly heavy, as the hurricane had forced it toward the west; thus the full power of the India Ocean was surging in that direction.

The day passed away as usual in deep gloom, but as night came on there was a decided improvement in the weather, which, although bad, was as nothing compared to the storm to which they had been for so long exposed. The men began to breathe again; the ship had leaked badly, owing to the numerous shot-holes, some of which were insecurely stopped; thus the pumps had been kept going throughout the storm, and the men were nearly worn out. As the night closed in all hoped for fine weather on the morrow, and Ned Grey, who had had little sleep, swung in his hammock, cheered with happy dreams, in which he saw the cottage on the cliff, and Edith and his mother. Suddenly he was almost thrown from his hammock by a sharp jerk, and waking quickly he heard a confused noise and trampling of feet, together with the sound of a heavy rush of water. He sprung from his hammock, but hardly had he reached the deck than a tremendous shock sent him staggering against the bulkhead; at the same instant he heard a loud crash upon the upper deck.

DESERTION OF NED AND TIM BY STEVENS.

Recovering from the shock, he rushed up the companion-way. At the moment that he arrived he fortunately grasped a rope in the pitchy darkness, as a heavy wave swept across the vessel and carried several men overboard, which would also have been Ned's fate had he not held on firmly. Nothing could be seen. The wind was blowing hard, but it had much abated, and the storm was evidently dying out; nevertheless, the sea was running very high, and presently the vessel rose upon a tremendous wave, and once more Ned felt a shock that for the moment threw him off his legs. Again a heavy sea swept the decks, and rolled completely over the hapless frigate, which, having weathered the storm, had now been driven on a reef in the darkness of the night. The main-mast had fallen overboard at the second shock of striking; the vessel now rested immovable, the fore part firmly wedged upon the coral reef, while every sea swept over her with fearful violence.

Some of the crew were in the mizzen rigging; this was the only remaining mast, and there was no fear of its loss, as the vessel was now stationary; a crowd of men had therefore occupied the mizzen-top.

As the night wore on the clouds began to break, and the stars peeped out from the thick veil that had so long concealed them; the wind had also sensibly decreased, but the sea struck heavily upon the frigate, and as the stern hung in deep water, while the fore part was fixed upon the reef, she had already broken her back and had filled with water; her sides had opened amidships, and there was great danger of her going to pieces.

When morning broke, after a long and weary night, the first person that Ned saw was Nigger Tim, shivering with wet and cold and clinging to the windlass, to which he had secured Nero with a rope. The sea still broke over the ship at intervals; but as daylight had dawned Ned left his secure position and went aft to receive orders.

Amidships the deck was torn up, and the stern was hanging lower than the fore part of the ship. The lieutenant in command was missing, with many of the crew, who had been washed overboard during the night, and the scene of confusion was beyond description. There was no one to command except Jem Stevens and another midshipman, and the men had lost all discipline, and merely thought of

saving themselves by the boats, of which few were left, as
they had been dashed to pieces by the surf. It was in vain
that Ned attempted to restore order. The Lascars had attempted to push off from the ship unobserved, upon the
discovery of which a fight ensued, and the English, being the
stronger, threw many of them overboard. The men would
listen to no commands, and simply united in their endeavors to launch the cutter, as they momentarily expected the
vessel would part asunder and sink in deep water.

Others of the crew succeeded in launching two smaller
boats, and leaping wildly into them they pushed off from
the ship; but being overcrowded they almost immediately
filled and upset, disappearing with all hands in the raging
surf. At length, after many fruitless efforts, the cutter
was safely lowered, and kept away about three boats'
lengths from the ship; Jem Stevens was already in her, and
many men now sprung into the water, and endeavored to
reach the boat by swimming. About twenty were taken
on board, and, seeing the necessity of self-preservation, Ned
called to Tim to follow him, and both lads, accompanied
by the dog, sprung into the sea and swam toward the boat.
In a few strokes they arrived at her side just as the crew,
having manned the twelve oars, were preparing to pull away
from the ship. Ned clung to the stern, his example being
followed by Tim.

"Give a hand!" cried Ned to Jem Stevens, who was
seated in the stern.

"Hands off!" cried Stevens; "the boat's full! you're
too late!" at the same time he threatened to cut Ned's
fingers with his knife (which he quickly opened) unless he
let go his hold. "Give way, my lads!" he cried at the
same time to the crew, who had not observed Ned Grey,
who was concealed by the stern of the boat; at the same
instant the ten oars dipped in the water, and the large boat
started forward at a powerful stroke. Ned had clung to
the boat; but seeing that Stevens actually cut at his fingers, he relaxed his hold just in time to avoid the knife,
and the boat left him swimming in the water.

Tim was still clinging to the gunwale, but upon observing Ned deserted, he relinquished his hold and swam back
to his young master, at the same time he shouted, "Catch
de ship, Massa Ned! nebber mind de boat. Debbel take
care of Massa Stevens!"

Ned followed Tim's advice, and struck out for the frigate, and fortunately both lads caught hold of a floating mast just as the vessel parted amidships and the after portion disappeared entirely in deep water.   Had they not clung to the mast they must have been sucked under by the vortex of the sinking hull.   Nothing now remained but the fore part of the frigate, which was firmly fixed upon the reef.   To this portion of the wreck the two lads swam, and climbed on board by means of the broken shrouds hanging from the fore-chains; they then secured the dog by a rope, and hauled him upon deck.   Another boat in addition to the cutter had succeeded in leaving the wreck.   Many people had perished with the sunken stern; others had been drowned in their attempts to reach the boats; some had been washed overboard during the night; and as Ned and Tim now stood upon the forecastle with the faithful Nero they were the only living beings that remained upon the wreck of the once-powerful frigate "Forte."   The boats had pulled out to sea in a direction north-west.

By degrees the wind died away as the sun sunk in the evening; the clouds had broken, and as the moon rose they gradually dispersed; the stars shone brightly; the stormy sea had spent its rage, and subsided into a long and sullen swell, and peace once more reigned among the exhausted elements.   Hungry and tired, the three living creatures on the wreck lay down and slept upon the deck of the forecastle.   The sea no longer broke over the fragment of the hull, but simply dashed harmlessly against the sides, and splashed into the interior of the hold where the vessel had parted amidships.

CHAPTER XIII.

NED, TIM, AND NERO ABANDONED.

ANOTHER morning broke; it was clear and beautiful. Not a cloud dimmed the sky in the gray dawn, and the sun rose upon a calm sea; no vestige of the tempest remained but the broken wreck— the "Sybille's" prize, that was to have conveyed Ned to England and his home.

Ned and Tim had both slept soundly, in spite of the chill of wet clothes; the weather was warm, and as the sun rose, the heat soon dried them.   Ned Grey was not deficient in romance, but he felt that, however exciting the adventure, much remained to be done to save their lives. Tim was entirely practical, and as he felt extremely hungry he desired something to eat. Judging from Nero's demeanor, he was of the same opinion, as he constantly pawed his young master Ned, and looked wistfully in his face, as though he thought he had forgotten to order breakfast.

All the fowls had been washed overboard together with the hen-coops and half a dozen sheep that had been taken on board for the officers; there was literally nothing to eat, unless they could discover some casks of provisions among the mass of miscellaneous cargo that occupied the fore-hold. Descending into the interior of the wreck among a chaos of barrels, Ned broke in the head of a cask with a heavy iron marline-spike, and to his great joy he found that it contained biscuits, which were perfectly dry and uninjured; accordingly, lest the sea should again rise, both he and Tim employed themselves in carrying up a large quantity, which they piled on deck, nor did they relinquish their work until, by means of a piece of canvas cut from a sail, they had conveyed away the whole contents of the barrel. Upon a further search they discovered a cask branded " Indian Mess Beef," whereupon the head was removed, and a sufficient supply was transported to the upper deck. Fortunately several casks of fresh water were discovered, therefore their immediate wants were supplied. They had no means of lighting a fire until a further search should yield the materials, therefore they breakfasted off biscuits and uncooked salt beef, and never had they eaten with better appetites. Nero feasted upon biscuits soaked in water, with a few pieces of meat chopped small.

Having satisfied their hunger, Ned carefully surveyed their position. The vessel was lying upon a sunken reef, many portions of which were within two or three feet of the surface. About two miles from this spot there was a long but narrow reef that formed a coral island, to which Ned at once determined to transport all that they would require lest another storm should destroy the wreck. From this reef he trusted they might be able to reach the main-land.

Without any delay both he and Tim set to work. Several empty water-casks were floating about in the fore-hold, and having selected ten, Ned, with Tim's assistance, succeeded in lashing them together with spars, so as to form a most buoyant raft, twenty-two feet long by ten in width. The sea had sunk to a complete calm by the afternoon; and as the fore part of the vessel was thrown high upon the reef, it was rather above its natural level, therefore the water only covered the bottom cargo. Fortunately the lower deck was dry, as the ship, having parted in the middle, the water that she had shipped during the storm had run out when the sea subsided. When Ned descended he at once found the carpenter's tool-chest, with a large quantity of all kinds of stores, and forcing away the bulk-heads he made use of the planks to cover the raft so as to form a deck. From sunrise to sunset the two lads worked without ceasing, by which time they had decked their vessel; but much remained to be done.

On the following morning they again set to work, and having discovered a spare boat's mast among the carpenter's stores they fitted it securely on the raft, and arranged a sail. At the same time Ned constructed a rude rudder with an oar, and improvised a false keel by running a plank perpendicularly through the deck, both fore and aft, so that it should project about three feet below the bottom of the raft, and thus prevent it from drifting to leeward.

By the evening of the second day the raft was thoroughly complete. Ned had arranged two empty water-casks amidships, to which the mast was lashed. Both he and Tim then busied themselves in carrying fresh water in buckets from the full casks on board the wreck, until they had completely filled the casks on the raft.

Everything was in perfect order by the evening of the second day, and Ned looked forward to the morrow with eagerness, as he would then try the sea-going properties of their vessel.

Before sunrise both Ned and Tim were engaged in collecting all that they considered useful. They had discovered a couple of double-barreled guns among the gunner's stores; and having selected half a dozen good muskets and pistols, they took a barrel of gunpowder, a hundred flints, and a large quantity of bullets and shot, together with a couple of cutlasses and a quantity of fishing-tackle, including a shark-hook and harpoon. They then emptied the carpenter's chest, together with several of the sailor's boxes, and carried them to the raft, where they stowed them around the mast, after which they replaced the tools in the carpenter's chest, and filled the others with biscuits and salt beef.

Tim, having been cook's mate, did not forget his pots and pans, but visited the galley, and selected a good kettle and a couple of saucepans, with a gridiron. By noon they were ready to sail, and having carried down a large parcel of the best clothes they could select from the sailors' kits, together with a supply of needles, thread, buttons, etc., they placed several large sails upon their cargo, that would afterward serve as an awning on shore, with a quantity of small spars and ropes, and pushed off from the wreck.

The wind was light and the sea smooth; thus the raft, although very heavily laden, sailed easily, without wetting her cargo; and as the breeze set directly toward the coral island, there was no difficulty in the navigation. The two boys were in high spirits at the success of their raft, which both sailed and steered well; and although alone on the wild east coast of Africa, with no other companion than the dog Nero, such is the elasticity of youth, and the excitement of vanquishing a difficulty, that they were for the moment thoroughly happy and free from every care.

The water was as clear as glass, and as they passed over the coral reefs at various depths they could be seen below like gardens of brilliant flowers glistening with every color, while the fish of many kinds, also varying in bright colors of gold, red, and blue, swam in large shoals among the coral groves, and sometimes sprung high from the water in their delight at the warm sun and the calm surface of the sea.

Sailing quietly along the beautiful gardens of the deep the raft approached the coral island, which appeared to form the center of the surrounding shallow reefs. It was a long and perfectly flat island, that might be upward of a mile in extent, although not many hundred yards in width; it was protected by an outer reef, which girded the island like an artificial outwork upon which the waves broke as upon a breakwater, and left a perfectly smooth harbor within, but extremely shallow. Such are the wonderful works of the minute coral insects, those apparently insignificant but mighty engineers, whose works are never washed away, and who alone can safely struggle with the power of the ocean.

Although the sea was calm, the swell broke with considerable force upon the outer reef, and it required some caution in coasting along the line, until an entrance could be discovered through the natural breakwater. The raft now felt the advantage of Ned's false keel, without which it must have drifted directly upon the reef.

After having coasted about a quarter of a mile a gap was discovered in the reef, through which the raft safely steered, and in the next minute they found themselves in a perfectly calm basin of crystal water of that beautiful pale green that is exhibited in the precious stone called aqua-marina. The basin was shallow, and once or twice the planks that formed the false keel touched the rocky bottom as the raft slowly glided over the lovely corals and disturbed the numerous fish. Beautiful shells were seen among the coral branches, while in many places large rocks were entirely covered with dense masses of oysters, that looked as though they had swarmed like a hive of bees. Many delicate but widely spreading branches of coral were a brilliant scarlet; others were a deep blue, some were variegated with several colors. But Tim, who could not resist the temptation of dragging some on board, quickly discovered the deception, as the bright tint rapidly faded upon being exposed to the air; these flowers of the ocean, like the flowers of the earth, soon lost their beauty when broken from the stem.

Gliding over this fairy-like sea they neared the island, and as the water was very shallow Ned took in the sail, and both boys, jumping overboard, gently towed the raft to the land, and moored it to a large mass of coral. There was no necessity for precaution, as the natural but well-protected harbor could never be disturbed, and the island, that was flat and sandy, was perfectly uninhabited. A large quantity of drift timber, portions of the wreck, had drifted through the gap, some of which was stranded on the island, while much was still floating in the calm basin; among other things Ned observed a box that had evidently belonged to the late frigate. As the raft was secured, and both boys were already wet, they waded toward the case and dragged it from the water. It was a strong and well-finished oak chest, and being locked they were obliged to break it open. It contained several suits of officers' clothes; with shirts, socks, shoes, a looking-glass, brushes and combs, a brace of beautiful pistols with ten-inch barrels carrying an ounce ball, a bag of bullets, powder-flask, a telescope, sextant, and compass, a silver pint drinking-cup, and a Prayer-book and Bible, in the latter of which was written the name, "James Stevens."

"Jem Stevens's chest!" exclaimed Ned, in astonishment. "What luck to find the sextant and the compass!" he continued, as he examined both the instruments, of which he had fortunately learned the use when on board the "Sybille" and the "Forte."

Tim had in the meantime taken the looking-glass, in which he was scrutinizing his own countenance with evident satisfaction; but upon hearing that it was Stevens's property that had thus fortuitously come into their possession, he burst into a fit of laughing, exclaiming: "Ha, ha! Tim knows. Debbel take care of Massa Stevens, God take care of Massa Ned, send him Massa Stevens's chest! Ha, ha, ha!" continued the delighted Tim, "what Massa Stevens do? Get no chest! no clothes! no looking-glass! can't see his ugly face! Ha, ha, ha! don't want Massa Stevens, got his chest. Debbel catch Massa Stevens, Tim catch his box! Ha, ha! dat's what Tim call de right t'ing 'xactly!"

No one would have supposed from Tim's merriment that they were two wretched castaways on a desolate coral reef upon the savage coast of Africa. Although Ned did not share the full extent of Tim's hilarity, he was delighted at the inestimable treasure that had fallen into his hands in the shape of a sextant and compass, which was further increased by the discovery of a small bottle of mercury and trough for an artificial horizon, which had been packed up by the optician in case astronomical observations on shore should be requisite. Not only were the instruments of vital importance, but the box likewise contained the "Nautical Almanac" and the charts of the Indian Ocean, including the east coast of Africa, together with drawing and writing materials. Next in value to the astronomical instruments was the brace of excellent pistols.

People in civilized life have but a faint idea of the happiness that such an unexpected treasure can afford. Riches depend upon their actual value, and at that moment all the gold of the earth would have been utterly useless to Ned; but under their present circumstances no gift could have equaled that which had providentially fallen into their hands. Rejoiced at their good fortune, the boys commenced work, and having fixed four poles into the ground, which they had brought from the ship for that purpose, they steadied them by cross-pieces firmly lashed across, over which they stretched a couple of sails, which, being doubled, effectually protected them from the burning sun; the roof of their tent being completed, they strained the canvas upon either side at an angle, and pegged it to the ground. In some places the rock preventing them from driving in the pegs, accordingly they rolled large masses of coral into convenient positions, to which they attached the cords that stretched the sides of their tent. They now arranged a few chests which they carried with some difficulty from the raft; and having heaped up two masses of sand in an oblong shape like raised asparagus beds, they threw a sail over each, and forming a pillow by an extra hillock at the end, they completed a couple of couches more roomy and comfortable than the hammocks in which they had been accustomed to swing on board the frigate.

By the time their work was complete they were hungry and thirsty. Taking a draught of water they determined to boil a piece of beef, and choosing a nice fat joint from their stock, Tim collected a quantity of fire-wood from the drift-timber on the shore while Ned prepared a fire. He had no tinder, neither were there any small twigs nor anything that is requisite to light a fire; however, they had plenty of wood, and as some fragments of deal cases had been cast ashore, and thoroughly dried in the sun, he selected a piece with a straight grain, and with his large and sharp knife that hung from his side he split it into fine slips; he then took a plane from the tool-chest, and with another portion of the wood he supplied a few handfuls of fine shavings. Cutting off a portion of dry canvas from the ragged end of a sail, he bruised about a tea-spoonful of gunpowder, with which he rubbed the sail-cloth until it was perfectly blackened; he then spread a small pinch of powder on the surface as he placed it in the pan of an unloaded musket, and pulled the trigger. In an instant it ignited and burned fiercely. Ned now rolled up the burning cloth, and placed it in the center of the shavings like a bouquet, which he swung rapidly round with the full force of his arm until the draught of air fanned it into a blaze;

upon this he placed the small wood that he had already prepared, and as it readily took fire he piled cautiously larger pieces in proportion to the strength of the flame, until a large oaken log at length rested on the top of the pile.

The fire now blazed brightly about ten yards distant from the tent. It was near sunset, and the great heat of the day was past. There were no sharks in the shallow water within the outer reef, therefore Ned took off his clothes to bathe while Tim was cooking the dinner. He plunged into the clear water, and reveled in the luxury of a bath, especially as he would be able to change his clothes and enjoy a clean shirt from Jem Stevens's stock. He dare not put his feet to the bottom on account of the sharp coral and shells; but having incautiously done so as he was coming out, he discovered that the object that had cut his foot was a huge mass of fine oysters cemented together so as to form a rock of about two hundredweight. Calling to Tim for assistance, after much labor by their joint exertions they rolled it to the shore, and surveyed their prize in some perplexity, as the oysters were curiously contorted and most difficult to open. Ned had already broken the point of his good knife, when an idea happily struck him. "Give a hand, Tim," he cried, "and let's roll the rock close to leeward of the fire; the wind will blow the heat upon it, and the oysters will open by themselves!"

"Massa Ned know de trick!" replied Tim, exultingly, as he put his shoulder to the work, and they presently rolled the rock to the desired position. The heat was intense; the surface of the mass first became dry, then several oysters gaped widely, and in a few minutes the example was generally followed, and as Ned turned the other side toward the fire the entire rock bristled with gaping shells.

Tim was delighted, and enjoyed the feast; but being a cook he contrived a good dish, and stewed some of the oysters with broken captain's biscuits and small portions of salt beef. Salt they had none, but they had a fire, a kettle, and the sea-water; thus they kept the kettle boiling briskly, which they refilled as it evaporated, until the brine became strong, when it was boiled nearly dry, and a considerable supply of salt was procured of excellent quality. After an excellent dinner, which they finished as the full moon rose, Ned determined to discover the latitude by the meridian altitude of a star. Accordingly he walked some distance from the blazing fire, and looking attentively at the heavens, he singled out Capella as the brightest star near the meridian. After a careful observation with the sextant he completed his calculations, and found that the reef upon which they stood was situated in south latitude 10° 30′.

He could only guess vaguely at the longitude; but upon considering the run of the frigate during the hurricane, upon reference to the chart of the east coast of Africa, he came to the conclusion that their position was not more than fifty miles from the main-land, and that the current must have carried the ship into the northern mouth of the Mozambique Channel, to the west of the extreme point of Madagascar. The latitude of Zanzibar was 7° 20′. This being a Portuguese settlement, Ned hoped to reach it either by sea should the wind be fair, or should they gain the main-land he trusted to arrive there on foot. In either case the voyage upon the raft would be most hazardous; but as the weather would most probably be settled after the recent storm, Ned resolved to start without loss of time, lest the present fair wind should change. He accordingly communicated his intention to Tim, and he arranged to start on the following morning. The night was cool and delightful, and as bright as the full moon of the tropics could shine, without a cloud. Ned wished to stroll round the narrow island before he left on the morrow, therefore, calling Tim and Nero to accompany him, he walked along the edge of the coral reef.

They had proceeded about half a mile when they arrived at a spot where the rock was no longer abrupt, but a beautiful snow-white sand; the *débris* of wasted and wave-worn coral formed a wide shelving beach for some hundred yards in length. Upon this plain white surface were a number of low dark objects that looked like casks, which, washed ashore, had become half imbedded in the sand. The nearest was about a hundred yards from them, and as they approached, to their astonishment, it began to move toward the sea.

"Turtle!" shouted Ned, as he dashed forward to cut off the creature's retreat. "Go at him, Nero!" he cried, as the dog shot ahead of his master in the race. In a few

seconds Nero was vainly attempting to hold by the hard
and slippery shell; but as the turtle had withdrawn its head
under cover, it stopped until Ned arrived, when he dexterously turned it upon its back. In the meantime Tim
had run on and cut off the retreat of several others, which
he had turned upon their backs, in which position they
would be helpless until righted. In about a quarter of an
hour eight large turtles had been thus captured, and Ned
quickly discovered that this bank of fine sand was a favorite spot for depositing their eggs. There were numerous
holes that had been freshly scraped in the sand to a depth
of about eighteen inches; in some of these were several
hundreds of eggs, that had been laid from time to time
during the nocturnal visits of the turtles. These curious
creatures are in the habit of visiting the shore after sunset,
but seldom or never during the heat of the day, during
which they remain either floating lazily on the surface of
the water or in the cooler depths below. At night the
female seeks some sandy beach, in which with her horny
head and fins she excavates a hole some distance above
high-water mark; in this she lays the number of eggs that
may be ready for the deposit, after which she carefully
covers them with sand, and conceals the recent excava-
tion. Every night she returns to the same spot and reopens
the hole, in which she deposits a fresh batch of eggs, as a
hen daily visits her nest, until from three to six hundred
have been laid. When the number is complete the female
leaves the nest to the action of the sand heated by the sun's
rays, and by this simple process of incubation the young
turtles, when no larger than a crown piece, free themselves
from the eggs and work their way through the sand. Upon
arrival at the surface they follow their natural instincts,
and scramble to the sea in crowds, where a great portion
are devoured, not only by the larger fish but by other
turtles. The eggs are good eating, and are extremely
rich; as the exterior is never hard like the egg of a bird,
but is tough and flexible like fine white kid, they are easily
packed without danger of breakage.

Ned rejoiced in this unlooked-for supply of fresh food
for their voyage. Several turtles could easily be stowed
upon the raft, and be kept alive by simply pouring a few
buckets of sea-water over them during the day. Food they
would not require, as the stomach of the turtle has a won-

derful power of contraction; and one of the peculiarities of this creature is that it can continue for many days without eating, and still retain its original weight, if only wetted with salt water.

Ned determined to leave his immovable captives on their backs during the night, and to call for them with the raft early on the following morning, as he perceived a much wider and more practicable outlet from the reef than that by which the raft had entered. It was through this wide entrance that the waves had washed the sand that allured the turtles as a resting-place.

Delighted with their evening's work, Ned and Tim returned to their tent, and in the cool and bright night they replaced the chests upon the raft, struck the tent, and got everthing on board in readiness for their departure at sunrise. At the same time they did not forget to lay a piece of canvas upon the deck, on which they piled about two hundredweight of sand. The canvas beneath was to prevent the sand from running through the crevices between the planks, and disappearing like water through a leak; the pile of sand was to be the foundation for the cooking fire. After this, all was completed by the stowage of a quantity of fire-wood around the foot of the mast.

Ned rose after a sound sleep in the fresh open air. The stars were still faintly twinkling in the gray sky, and the moon was bright, although as pale as frosted silver. It was an hour before sunrise, and he woke Tim, who was snoring like a young pig.

As all preparations for departure had been wisely made on the previous day, there was nothing to be done but to shove the raft off the shore, and with a delightful breeze the sail filled, and they glided pleasantly along the smooth water. In about ten minutes they arrived at the sandy beach, where they found their turtles as they had left them. Some were so heavy that they could hardly carry them; but as the great object was to keep a supply of fresh provisions, they rejected the largest, and selected three that weighed about seventy pounds each. These they carried down to the raft, and then turned the rejected and heavier turtles upon their flappers, which they at once made use of by waddling down to the water, in which they disappeared.

Both Ned and Tim hurried in their work, and they were

not long in collecting several hundred eggs, which they stowed in one of their chests. They then set sail.

The exit from the basin was broad, and as the wind was fair, the raft steered into the open sea without any difficulty. The extra weight of the turtles, and the sand, firewood, etc., had made the raft so heavy that Ned determined to steer for the nearest shore. He therefore directed the course due west, in the hope of reaching the African coast within about fifty or sixty miles. The wind being light was extremely favorable, as the sea was smooth, and the steady pressure upon the sail propelled the raft at about three miles an hour. Although this appeared tedious, Ned computed that twenty hours of even progress would bring them to the land, and he only trusted in the continuance of the breeze.

The raft was well supplied; they had about eighty gallons of water, which would last twenty days at a fair consumption for three, including that required for cooking. They had a large quantity (about one hundred and fifty pounds) of salt beef, three turtles, and some hundred eggs. Thus there was no fear of starvation, and the only danger rested in foul weather. Ned arranged that one should sleep while the other steered in alternate watches of four hours, thus neither would be fatigued.

It was about seven A. M. when the raft fairly cleared the coral island, and as she insensibly glided along the water they soon lost sight of the wreck of the frigate, and then of the hospitable but dangerous reef; around them was the sea horizon, with the burning sun above. While Ned had the helm Tim placed some thickly folded sails across the chests and barrels, and creeping into the shade beneath, he soon fell asleep. At the expiration of the watch he relieved Ned, who in his turn crept into the snug shade and slept till three P. M., when he once more took the helm.

The evening came, and with it the same cloudless sky and the bright stars. At length the moon rose, and continued with them throughout the night, and the wind blew steadily, but a little fresher than before; the water rippled as the raft increased its speed. Nothing could be more beautiful than the night; they floated quietly on as though in a dream, and the placid sea glistened tranquilly in the moonlight, and looked as though it must forever rest in peace.

As Ned stood at the helm alone, and his faithful companion and his dog sleeping side by side, he looked steadfastly at the heavens and their countless revolving worlds, and with a heart overflowing with gratitude he fervently thanked the Almighty Creator for the preservation of his life, and prayed for His help and guidance in the unknown path before him. The breeze blew steadily and fresh, and the night passed away; the raft had never altered her course from the west; once more it was Ned's turn at the helm before the sun rose.

A haze from the sea covered the horizon; the morning was gray, and the first red streaks shone low upon the eastern sky; the wind was faint, and the raft moved slowly forward. The morn grew lighter, and soon the crimson flashes in the east turned to a golden blaze as the sun rose glorious from its ocean bed, awakened for the day. The haze dissolved as the warmth increased, and clear and blue the long wished-for scene burst upon Ned's view. "Land!" he shouted. Tim sprung from his hard couch at the startling sound, and Nero too rose, and, although ignorant of the cause, the dog shared the enthusiasm of his master.

Apparently not far distant were lofty mountains, the outlines of which were sharply defined upon the sky as the sun shone vividly upon them. Within six miles of the raft the shore was distinctly visible; unfortunately, at this moment it fell calm, and the sail hung listlessly upon the mast at the very time when they longed for a brisk breeze to conclude their voyage. Ned determined to lighten the raft and to paddle her forward with oars. Accordingly they threw overboard the sand and fire-wood, together with a quantity of the salt beef, also one of the heavy chests; this made a great difference in the buoyancy of the vessel. The water was the heaviest portion of the cargo, but this they dare not waste, as there might be no supply on shore. "Throw over some more beef," cried Ned; "we have three turtles, and biscuits enough to last a couple of months."

Tim looked wistfully at the good beef, as one by one he threw the large pieces overboard.

"Dat's enuff, Massa Ned," said he; "don't t'row all de good meat away; 'pose we get hungry one day, eh?"

"Suppose the wind should change and blow off the shore before we land," replied Ned, "what will become of us?

We must lighten the raft as much as possible; throw all the beef overboard except half a dozen pieces; then heave the heavy chest away likewise."

Tim obeyed the order in exceedingly low spirits, and being of a careful disposition, and deeply interested in the commissariat arrangements, he pushed the large chest overboard first, after he had emptied the contents, and then he reluctantly threw another piece of beef into the clear water. Hardly had the joint splashed into the sea, when a dull, cloud-like appearance was seen in the deep water close to the raft; this became more dense, until a distinct and huge brown object rose rapidly to the surface, and turning upon its side, a long white belly was exposed as it opened its huge jaws and swallowed the piece of beef that Tim had just thrown overboard. It was an enormous shark, and as the water was as clear as crystal it could be distinguished as minutely as though it were in a glass case as a specimen. The long, cimeter-shaped back fin frequently protruded above the surface as it swam fearlessly and apparently lazily around the raft, with its large white eyes gleaming as it hunted for fresh prey.

"Oh, my eye, Massa Ned!" cried Tim, "dere's a big shark been and swallered de beef! T'ank God Tim's not de beef!"

"Shoot him with one of the muskets," cried Ned, who was at the helm, and on the instant Tim snatched a loaded musket from the chest in which they were stowed, but upon second thoughts he laid it down, and diving among the miscellaneous articles in the carpenter's tool-box, he quickly produced a large shark-hook about sixteen inches long; a chain of about two feet in length was already attached with a swivel, and Tim with great quickness fastened it to a rope.

Having prepared his tackle within a couple of minutes, he now stuck a fat and tempting piece of beef upon the hook; but the shark had disappeared.

"Why didn't you shoot him as I told you?" asked Ned; "now we've lost him!"

Tim replied by throwing his large bait far into the water, and the fat beef could be distinctly seen deep below as it hung about four fathoms beneath the surface.

"He'll come again, Massa Ned," said Tim, "don't be 'fraid—if he see Tim take a swim, de shark come catch him quick, I knows; now Tim catch de shark. I seed him when he swim round de raft, winked his big eyes, he thought, ' Dere's Tim, like to swaller 'im!' Now, Massa Ned, wait a little, see Tim swaller de shark."

As Tim gave this little programme of the entertainment he slowly drew in one line, and as the piece of white beef came near the surface several small fish striped like perch, of about two pounds weight, followed the bait, which, having smelled, they darted away as though afraid. " Ha, ha!" exclaimed Tim, " his little frens gone to tell him Tim cooked de beef ready; now de shark won't be long."

Tim was well up in shark-fishing, as he had seen many caught; and as he saw the arrival of the pilot-fish that almost invariably accompany the shark he was not wrong in expecting its return. In a short time the monster issued from directly beneath the raft where he had most probably been concealed, and swimming slowly toward the bait he first smelled it, then with a quick and sudden turn he bolted it, together with the hook and chain, and dashed off into the deep water.

" Ha, ha!" roared Tim, " now's got it tight! now Tim swaller de shark!" at the same time he allowed the rope to run from the coil on deck until about eighty yards had been expended; then, as the fish had halted and turned, he drew in some slack line, with which he took a turn round the base of the mast; after this he drew in line hand over hand until he felt a tug that would have pulled Tim overboard had he been unprepared, and away dashed the shark once more. This time Tim was determined to make him work for his line, and having grasped the rope between a portion of a sail to prevent it from chafing his hands, he held on with all his might, and merely allowed it to slip through his grasp as he felt himself compelled.

The fish was not many feet shorter than the raft, and as he ran out the entire length of line that Tim had fastened to the mast he now dragged the raft slowly along in whatever direction he chose to take. As it was perfectly calm Ned left the helm and came to Tim's assistance, and the two strong lads of sixteen gave the shark some trouble, as they hauled together on the line with all their might. At times they were obliged to let the fish run, until once more it had regained the full extent of the rope; but as the raft acted as a buoy against which the shark had to pull, it be-

came exhausted, and the united strength of Ned and Tim
at length prevailed.

For about half an hour the struggle had continued, when,
having hauled in the greater portion of the line, the shark
was seen within ten yards of the raft; it still persisted in
keeping in the depths; but as the two lads were equally determined that it should come to the surface, they hauled
away with such vigor that by degrees the immense creature was secured by a short rope, and it lashed about in the
rage of its capture within a few feet of the raft.   Ned now
prepared a bowline which he threw over the shark, and
slipping it cleverly over the tail, he drew the noose tight,
and fastened the line to the stern of the raft.

"Now, Tim, give me a musket," cried Ned, as he tied
the knot, " and I'll finish him off."

In an instant Tim handed the musket, and Ned went to
the center of the raft to obtain as close a shot as possible at
the nape of the neck, if we may so describe that portion of
a shark where the first vertebra of the spine is connected
with the head.   Taking a steady aim at a moment when
the fish was quiet, Ned fired, and the shark gave a convulsive shudder, and then stiffened like a log of timber, as
every muscle strained in the pang of death; the ball had
divided the spine at its junction with the brain.

Ned and Tim now surveyed their prize in triumph as it
lay by the side of the raft; it was about seventeen feet in
length, and so heavy as to be perfectly unmanageable.
Tim proposed that they should cut off as much as they required for food, and then set the carcass adrift.   Ned did
not see the force of the argument; as they had just thrown
the beef overboard to lighten the raft, why should they exchange weight for weight?   They were thus arguing the
question, when an event occurred which relieved them from
the difficulty.   As Ned looked toward the shore, which appeared much nearer, as a current had taken them closer to
the land, he was surprised to see hurrying toward them six
canoes, which he had not before observed, as he had been
so busily engaged in the capture of the shark.   They were
about a mile distant, and there could be no question that
the raft was the object of their attention.

Although both Ned and Tim expected assistance upon
arrival on the shore, they were somewhat disturbed at the
appearance of so many canoes, and they immediately held

a council of war. Tim was as brave as a lion, and was ready for a fight should Ned only give the word; but the latter wisely considered that fighting should only be resorted to in the last extremity. They were utterly helpless, unless they could make friends; therefore it was of the first importance that they should establish amicable relations with the natives. Having well considered their position, Ned determined to load all the muskets, and be prepared for a resolute defense should it be necessary; at the same time he cautioned Tim that he should avoid all chances of dispute. The muskets and double-barreled guns were quickly in order; spare ammunition was arranged so that it would be immediately at hand, and Ned loaded Jem Stevens's handsome pistols, which he at once stuck in his belt.

The canoes approached with great quickness, and with the telescope Ned discovered them to be full of blacks.

"If dey real niggers, Massa Ned, we make 'em frens," exclaimed Tim. "Tim knows de niggers; fill de nigger's belly, make de nigger frens; dat's de trick 'xactly! Tim knows! fill de nigger's belly wid de shark! dat's de trick 'xactly; niggers dance and sing when dey see de big shark."

There was much truth in Tim's philosophy.

CHAPTER XIV.
NERO'S RECEPTION OF THE STRANGERS.

THE canoes, quickly paddled by a number of men, neared the raft, which still lay helplessly becalmed. As the leading boat approached within a hundred yards both Ned and Tom made signs of friendship, and as the latter was as black as themselves, the negroes no longer hesitated to come alongside. Tim now called to them in his own language, which they did not appear to understand, but a small amount of pantomime quickly explained the capture of the sharp, and as they caught sight of the huge fish floating in the water, they paddled rapidly to the raft.

Without a moment's hesitation many leaped on board, and, hardly noticing Ned or Tim, they seized upon the shark, and with their sharp lances, which they used as knives, they at once began to separate the flesh from the bones. There was a third party, however, who had no

idea of submission to this sudden invasion of the raft; this
was Nero, who, having bristled up his back at the rude intrusion, presently fastened his teeth in the naked thigh of
a savage who had roughly run against him. In an instant
the negroes sprung back to their canoes in fear, as, never
having seen a powerful Newfoundland dog, they had no
idea that Nero belonged to the race, and they regarded
him as a ferocious animal.

At this sudden retreat Tim burst into a roar of laughter,
while Nero barked his loudest at the discomfited blacks
until he was quieted by Ned. Tim's merriment quickly
restored confidence, but not a negro would again venture
upon the raft, and they set to work in earnest upon the
shark from their canoes.

In a much shorter time than could be imagined they had
divided the flesh into large pieces, which were distributed
among the canoes; these were heavily laden: then cutting
off the head for the sake of the teeth, which they prized as
ornaments, they allowed the bones to sink, and taking the
raft in tow, they paddled to the shore in high spirits, singing and chattering in delight at the prey they had unexpectedly gained.

A heavy surf drove upon some reefs that protected the
land, but the canoes avoided the danger by passing through
an opening which presently led them into still water; this
narrow bay ran inland for a considerable distance, and was
surrounded upon all sides by dense groves of cocoa-nut
palms.

The water was beautifully clear, and as Ned looked over
the side he could distinctly see the bottom at a depth of
about twenty feet; this was a mass of coral, and the low
shore around appeared to be of the same peculiar formation; it had become covered with a poor sandy soil, upon
which the cocoa-nut palm invariably thrives.

The canoes towed the raft for about half a mile along
this lovely inlet, until, bending to the left, a small village
of circular huts was observed close to the water's edge, beneath the shade of the cocoa palms; to this spot the canoes
slowly paddled, as the raft was heavy, and they were themselves deeply laden.

A long, shrill, tremulous cry was now raised by a crowd
of women who stood upon the bank to welcome them, and
as the canoes touched the shore many sprung into the

water and assisted to unload them, which they completed with wonderful quickness, and laid the masses of fish upon a row of neat palm mats, which had been immediately prepared. As the women were naked, with the exception of a small ornament, composed of fringe and cowrie-shells that formed a short apron from the hips, they could move with great activity, and they took to the water and washed themselves like amphibious animals after they had arranged the oily fish upon the mats. They would now have unloaded the raft had not Nero barked angrily as they approached, which sent them hurrying back amid the laughter of the crowd of men, who had been similarly repelled when they first boarded from their canoes.

Ned and Nero, the white boy and the black dog, were now the objects of the women's curiosity. As Nero could protect the raft, that was now moored to a palm-tree close to the shore, Ned jumped on land and took his seat beneath a shady tree, at the same time he made signs to the crowd that they should sit down. At this moment a girl brought him a new mat, neatly woven with the split leaves of palms, upon which he was requested to sit instead of on the bare ground. He now attempted to explain by signs and gestures the shipwreck and their escape. The chief now appeared; he was a gray-headed old man, of a tall and commanding figure. Upon his arrival Ned rose from his seat and offered him his hand, but instead of receiving it according to European custom, he took both his hands and raised them three times above his head as the native form of welcome; he then made a sign that Ned should resume his seat, upon which he also sat down upon a leopard-skin that one of his followers carried for that purpose. Once more Ned was obliged to go through the pantomime that he had already performed, to explain the accident that had befallen them; in this he was assisted by a number of volunteers, who conceived that they had understood the story: accordingly they broke in upon the conversation as interpreters, and concluded by a general chaos of noise and confusion.

The palaver ended by the old chief's expressing a wish to examine the raft: accordingly Nero was whistled for by Ned, and as he came bounding toward him the whole crowd took to their heels in a general panic. The old chief had followed the example; but being at length reas

sured as Ned fastened the dog to a tree, he ventured on
board the raft with a few of his people, the rest of the
crowd obeying his orders by keeping at a respectful distance. Ned exhibited the various articles that he had
saved from the wreck, but nothing pleased the old chief so
much as the sailcloth, of which he immediately begged a
portion. A large sail was at once presented to him, which
he ordered to be carried to his hut. It was now proposed
by the chief that the raft should be unloaded, and the
stores arranged within a hut set apart for that purpose,
while another dwelling should be prepared for Ned and
Tim. There could be no objection to this; as the two lads
were entirely in the power of the natives; the best policy
was to secure the chief's good-will, therefore Ned at once
conceded to the proposal. A number of men were called,
and the process of discharging cargo was quickly accomplished.

Two huts were set apart for Ned and Tim with their
effects, in one of which the heavy luggage was stowed,
while the tool-chest, ammunition, and Jem Stevens's box
were placed in Ned's own hut, together with the guns.

Ned's hut was exceedingly pretty. Like all the others,
it was circular, and about fifteen feet in diameter; the
walls were formed of large bamboos neatly fitted together
like the pipes of an organ; the inside was smeared with a
mixture of clay and cowdung, with which the floor was
thickly cemented, and the roof was built of a frame-work of
bamboos neatly thatched with plaited palm leaves. Around
the two huts was an inclosed garden, in which were gourds
and water-melons of different descriptions: these climbed
as creepers over the high bamboo fence by which the little
garden was inclosed on three sides, while the fourth was
protected by the water, as the hut stood within a few yards
of the margin. Although there was no view behind the
hut, owing to the height of the inclosure, the greater portion of the inlet could be seen from the front, from a beautiful position beneath a thick clump of palms which produced a delightful shade.

Ned was well satisfied with their reception, and both he
and Tim busied themselves in arranging their only room.
A sail was spread upon the floor, upon which were laid two
sleeping-mats; beneath these the women placed a quantity
of palm leaves stripped from the stalks, which formed

clean and comfortable beds. The large chests served for both chairs and table, and as bamboos were plentiful, Ned soon contrived a neat gun-rack, against which he placed a row of loaded muskets and the two double-barreled guns. Pegs were then driven into the wall in many places, upon which were hung pistols and cutlasses, with the shark-hook, harpoon, and a variety of objects.

After a couple of hours' work, the hut was converted into a comfortable home. Tim, true to his occupation, arranged his cooking utensils in the other hut, where he constructed two simple fire-places by cutting a trench in the floor about six inches deep to create the draught, on either side of which he placed some blocks of coral to support his pots.

Two of the turtles were secured by a rope to one fin, and were then allowed to enjoy themselves in the water, while the third was killed for the day's consumption; a portion of this was sent as a present to the old chief.

Tim's original proverb of "fill de nigger's belly, make de nigger frens," was proved to be correct. There was great feasting in the village; pots were boiling in all directions filled with sharks' flesh and pumpkin, and the natives were in the best of humors, and had taken a great fancy to the new-comers. The women and girls were much struck with Ned's handsome appearance: his rich fair hair and blue eyes had been discussed by a crowd of admiring ladies, who had already declared that he must become a member of their tribe. Tim was also a favorite; his good-humor and fearless, straightforward manner had at once gained their confidence; and the fact that the two lads unassisted had been able to capture so large a shark was in itself the best introduction to a people who held all hunting exploits in the highest estimation.

It was their first night on shore, and Tim's turtle-soup and boiled beef were nearly ready for dinner. He had cut the under-shell of the turtle into small pieces, which is the most delicate portion when well boiled; this had been simmering for some hours, together with the green fat and a few of the turtles' eggs. A quantity of red chilis grew in the garden: he had accordingly added sufficient of these hot peppers, with salt, and a species of wild thyme, with the peel and juice of small ripe lemons, that grew in profusion around the village. There were few better dishes than Tim's turtle-soup, when it appeared on table in a large gourd shell, steaming hot. They had no spoons; but Ned had strolled along the shore before dinner, and had collected some long mussel-shells, which were admirable substitutes, and far more beautiful than silver. Ned had also scooped out some cocoa-nuts, and had converted them into drinking-cups. That night they mixed a little rum which they had saved from the wreck with cool water and fresh lime-juice, together with some honey which the chief had presented to them, and in this impromptu punch Ned silently drank the healths of all those left at home.

When the moon rose the natives were sitting round their fires reveling in the feast, and the night was subsequently employed in singing and dancing, with a beating of drums, blowing of horns, and the usual wild sounds that accompany savage festivities.

Several weeks passed away, during which Ned employed himself, with Tim's assistance, in perfecting his dwelling and arranging the gardens, while his leisure hours were devoted to fishing in one of the native canoes, and in shooting the wild fowl that swarmed upon a small lake within a mile of the coast. In all these excursions he was generally successful, and the return of his boat was eagerly looked forward to by the negroes, who had learned to regard him with much respect, especially as he supplied their wants and added to their commissariat. As time flew on Ned gained so high a position in the estimation of the old chief that he determined to give him one of his daughters in marriage; and as matrimonial arrangements in those countries are reduced to the most practical simplicity, Ned was one evening astonished, while sitting in his garden by the sea, upon observing a crowd of women, who advanced toward him raising the loud and thrilling cry that is used upon all joyful occasions. They led a pretty young negress of about fourteen. As they approached two of the women brought her in advance of the crowd, who had now sat down, and upon arrival before Ned they took both his hands and placed them within those of the young girl, after which they again raised their disagreeable cry, and the girl took her seat upon a mat by Ned's side, who, not having received any warning of the intended ceremony, was at a loss to understand its meaning. A loud burst of laughter from Tim attracted his attention, and Tim's mirth having in some degree subsided, he explained to Ned that this was the marriage ceremony of his own country, and common among many tribes: thus the young negress, who was the chief's daughter, was now his wife.

It would be impossible to express Ned's astonishment and confusion when the girl suddenly rose, and throwing her arms round his neck, she half smothered him with her embrace. This was too much for Tim, who once more burst into a fit of merriment, at the same time he exclaimed, "Now Massa Ned got de nigger wife, wot Massa Ned's moder say when take her home? Ha, ha!" continued Tim, "why de chief not send Tim one wife? all for Massa Ned, not'ing for poor Tim; 'cos he's black he get not'ing—nigger don't like de nigger!"

This was great fun for Tim, but very unpleasant for Ned, and he quickly found out the truth of the saying that "it is much easier to get married than to get *un*married." Determined, however, that he would not be led like a lamb to the slaughter, he now rose from his seat, and taking the girl by the hand he led her through the village toward her father's hut, accompanied not only by the women who had brought her, but by a great crowd, who followed them with the usual yelling to the old chief's dwelling.

Upon arrival at his hut the old man was found busily engaged in deciding a controversy between two of his people, but upon seeing the approaching crowd, headed by Ned and Tim, he immediately directed his attention to the deputation. Tim endeavored to act as interpreter, but to no purpose; then Ned attempted an explanation, which was so imperfectly understood that the chief imagined Ned was not satisfied with his daughter's personal attractions.

"Ah!" he at length exclaimed, as an idea struck him as to the real cause, "you do not like Fernina; you shall have the ox-eyed Bokha instead. Here, Bokha!" he cried; and almost immediately a large-eyed, handsome girl approached from a neighboring hut.

"Go to the white man and take his hand," said the chief; "and you, Fernina, go to your hut, he don't like you." But the latter had no idea of yielding her claims so easily, and she clung to Ned with a determination not to forsake her prize. At the same time the ox-eyed Bokha seized his hand, and Ned was fairly captured by the swarthy

7

beauties, who at once commenced to quarrel for his possession. The women of the crowd now interfered; some took
the part of Fernina, others sided with Bokha, until the
argument grew so hot that they proceeded to blows, and
the authority of the old chief was obliged to be exercised
without delay to quell the riot. "Silence!" he cried, in
a loud and commanding voice, and at once the tumult
ceased, and the chief, who was a Solomon in his way, addressed them.

"Women," he said, "the white man declines Fernina,
but on the other hand she desires the white man: he would
prefer the ox-eyed Bokha, she also desires the white man of
the yellow hair; do not quarrel among yourselves, for I
have decided that he shall have them both, thus all parties
will be satisfied."

Upon this judgment, delivered by their chief, a pro-
longed yell of satisfaction was raised by the crowd of
women, in which the men also joined, and the two young
girls, now rendered happy, held the unwilling Ned by each
hand. Never did a marriage tie appear more binding than
when he thus stood in the firm grasp of his would-be wives.
It was in vain that he endeavored to offer an explanation:
not one word was understood, until Tim once more came
forward and apparently cleared the mystery, as the old
chief drew a long breath, and having obtained silence, he
exclaimed, "Ha, now I understand; at length I understand! The black lad also demands a wife! he shall have
one. Call Goolah of the thick lips!"

Almost immediately a fat, unwieldy girl, whose name of
the "thick lips" was thoroughly deserved, was led forward by two women to be presented. This was more than
the patience of Ned could bear; a third offering had now
been added, although he had waited upon the king to de-
cline the first; he therefore led his two lady candidates to
an empty hut, and made signs that they should enter,
which they immediately did. "Goolah of the thick lips"
was then requested to follow, and when all the three were
within Ned closed the door, against which he placed with
Tim's assistance an immense block of coral. The wives
were prisoners, and Ned, with unmistakable pantomime,
explained to the old chief that they should remain in that
hut, but that he would not accept them. Annoyed with
the savage hospitality, Ned then hastily withdrew, and ac-

companied by Tim he returned to his own hut amid the silence and astonishment of the crowd.

Some weeks had passed since this memorable occasion, and Ned had observed that the chief and also his people had much changed in their demeanor toward him; they no longer came to sit and stare at him in crowds, neither did the chief visit him as he had done before, but he was evidently regarded with suspicion; in fact, it could not be otherwise, as he had declined the offer of friendship that had been made by the old chief in presenting him with his daughters as wives. The women had taken a great dislike to him, as their vanity had been injured by his refusal to belong to the tribe through marriage.

Under these circumstances Ned thought that it would be advisable, if possible, to escape from the negro hospitality and march to Zanzibar, where the Portuguese had a settlement, whence he might perhaps obtain a passage to Europe in some trading-vessel. He calculated that Zanzibar was about two hundred miles distant; thus, could he only follow the right direction by compass, he should be able to reach it in about twenty days. Should he decide upon this plan it would be impossible to carry anything beyond ammunition; all else would have to be forsaken. Tim was as faithful as the dog Nero; thus all was quickly agreed upon, and it was decided that if possible they should escape on the following day, by pretending to go upon a shooting excursion, from which they would not return. On more than one occasion Ned had requested the chief to supply him with a guide to Zanzibar, but he had always been met by some frivolous excuse, after he had been asked, " why he wished to desert the tribe?" and Ned felt that although externally civil, it had been inwardly determined that he should not forsake the country: thus he was merely a prisoner unless he chose to enter the tribe by accepting a wife from the chief.

Having determined to act, no time was lost in making preparations for escape. The great difficulty lay in the lack of means of transport; but Ned was not to be beaten by any obstacle; thus he quickly decided upon the necessary arrangements. His first work was to prepare two roomy knapsacks, which, with Tim's assistance, he constructed from a piece of strong tarpaulin lined with canvas. He then formed small saddle-bags of the same mate-

rial, together with a soft pad, which he proposed to arrange
on the back of Nero, who would be able to carry twelve
pounds with great ease; thus if he and Tim could carry
forty pounds each, they could travel with ninety-two
pounds' weight of supplies.

Great management would be necessary in the arrangement of the luggage; accordingly he made six small tarpaulin bags, into each of which he packed two pounds of
gunpowder, making a stock of twelve pounds, in addition
to one pound each that he and Tim were to carry in two
horns which he had fitted for that purpose when the last
ox had been killed by the negroes. When the bags were
filled he sewed them neatly up, and rendered the seams
water-tight by smearing them with the thick milk of the
India-rubber-trees, which grew in great abundance. This
was a tree of the fig tribe, the milk of which exuded in
large quantities from the bark when incised; this rapidly
evaporated, and became solid India-rubber when smeared
upon any substance and exposed to the air, thus it formed
an excellent water-proof packing when rubbed repeatedly
upon canvas.

Having thus carefully protected the gunpowder, Ned selected his supplies: two cutlasses; two double-barreled
guns, with two dozen spare flints; two brace of pistols; two
knives; one cooking-pot; twenty pounds of bullets, and
twelve pounds of gunpowder; ten pounds of shot, two steels
for striking fire; one ax and two files, and a number of fish-
hooks and lines; two pairs of shoes; one change of clothes
for himself, in addition to others for Tim; a case containing
sextant, telescope, compass, artificial horizon and "Nautical
Almanac," with paper, pencil, etc.; a few medicines, with
two gourd bottles of rum, and about twelve pounds of
biscuits.

These stores were divided equally between himself and
Tim, while Nero carried a portion of the bullets, and a
supply of biscuits for his own use.

It was on a bright moonlight night that Ned had determined to start. At about one A. M., when the people of
the village were asleep, Ned strapped the small saddle-
packs upon Nero, and with knapsacks upon their backs
and double-barreled guns in their hands, he and Tim for-
sook the comfortable hut, and struck into the depths of
the forest. They marched till daylight upon a narrow

footway that resembled the run of sheep. This was already well known to them for a distance of about six miles, as they had often traveled upon the route during their shooting excursions, but beyond that limit all was unexplored. When day broke Ned found himself in a dense forest, where giant trees rose to the height of upward of a hundred feet, springing from a thick and tangled underwood, through which it would have been impossible to penetrate except by the narrow path already mentioned. They had marched five hours when the sun rose at six o'clock; thus Ned calculated that they had made fifteen miles: he accordingly determined to push on until eight at the same rate of three miles per hour.

The night had been cool, and they had marched almost without fatigue until sunrise, but the last two hours had been extremely hot, and Ned was thankful when he suddenly arrived on the banks of a clear stream that rippled over a bed of pebbles between two overhanging cliffs. It was a lovely spot, shaded by the dark foliage of the tamarind-trees that grew in the deep clefts among the rocks, and Ned had no sooner arrived than he unstrapped Nero's load, and quickly throwing off his own clothes he plunged into a pool of cool water that formed a natural basin in the river's bed. The dog followed his master, together with Tim, and all reveled in the luxury of the morning bath.

After bathing Ned arranged the packs upon some bare rocks beneath the shade of a large tamarind-tree, and all being extremely hungry he looked despairingly at the bag of biscuits which formed their scanty fare. Tim had already lighted a fire, although there was nothing to cook, when Ned suddenly listened to a distant sound, and, jumping up, he took his gun, which he loaded with shot instead of ball, and started along the bed of the stream in quest of guinea-fowl that he had heard cackling in the distance. He was followed by Nero, and after a rough scramble among the rocks in the bed of the winding stream he arrived close to the sound. As he carefully turned a corner in the river he observed a large number of guinea-fowl sitting close together upon the branches of a tree, from which they kept up an incessant cackling at a falcon which, having captured one of their party, was now eagerly devouring its prey upon a high rock above the stream. Creeping through the bushes while the attention of the guinea-fowl was attracted by the falcon, Ned arrived unseen within thirty yards of the tree, and aiming at the center of the flock he fired.   To his delight five birds fell to the ground, one of which being only winged would have escaped in the thick bushes had not Nero at once secured it; they were in exceedingly good condition, and as Ned felt their fat breasts with satisfaction, he tied their legs together with a strip of tough bark, which he tore from the stem of a mimosa, and then joyfully returned to breakfast.   They had now sufficient for the evening, as the birds were so large that even their appetites could hardly manage two for breakfast; therefore the pot was placed upon the fire, and two were boiled, while three were stuck upon spits for roasting. Tim was a good hand at jungle cookery; thus he placed a straight bamboo across two forked sticks which rested in the ground close to the fire; against this he laid his spits, with one end fixed in the earth; these he occasionally turned when they required it, and in about forty minutes the fowls were beautifully roasted.   Breakfast was ready. They wisely determined to eat the boiled fowls and to carry the roast upon the afternoon march, as they would better support the heat of the journey.   A few biscuits stewed up with the soup of the boiled fowls, together with the bones left from breakfast, afforded Nero a hearty meal, and both Ned and Tim lay down beneath a shady tree, against the stem of which they placed their guns.   In a short time the whole party, including the dog, were sound asleep.

They had slept for about four hours when Ned was suddenly awoke by a low growl from Nero, and sitting up he saw the dog rush into the jungle and bark furiously at some object unseen; but almost at the same instant Ned felt himself seized from behind, and before he had time to offer the slightest resistance, or even to discover the cause of attack, his arms were firmly bound, and he was entirely helpless.   Tim had been secured in the same manner.   A loud yell was now raised, and Ned was surrounded by a party of naked savages armed with spears and bows.   Nero upon hearing the noise came bounding back from the man whom he had attacked in the jungle, and seeing Ned he immediately took his stand by his side.

All this happened so suddenly and unexpectedly that Ned could hardly believe his eyes; but putting a bold face upon the matter he smiled as the leader of the party confronted him, at the same time he made signs that the twisted palm-leaves that confined his arms caused him much pain. This man was an immensely powerful negro, with a ferocious expression of countenance, but upon seeing Ned smile he examined him closely with surprise; he then looked at the dog and at Tim, as though completely puzzled at the nature of his prisoners. In the meantime Nero was growling fiercely, although restrained from attack by Ned's voice.

Having satisfied himself that the party consisted of only two persons and the dog, the negro chief gave an order to his men, who at once prepared two long forked sticks, about the thickness of a man's arm. In a few minutes Ned found his neck firmly secured in the fork by means of a cross-piece of wood that was lashed across the points. Tim was fettered in a similar manner; a rope was then attached to the extremity of the handle, and thus led by two powerful negroes, both Ned and Tim found themselves in the possession of a gang of slave-hunters. Without further delay several men took possession of the guns, knapsacks, and various effects that lay upon the ground, and they marched rapidly forward for about an hour, until they arrived at a narrow path which turned to the west, upon which they hurried without once halting until nearly sunset.

Ned was suffering severely from thirst and fatigue; the heat was excessive, and upon arrival at a considerable stream he made signs to the man who led him that he wished to drink. At that moment the party halted, and the negro descended to the river, and having slaked his own thirst, he returned with a large gourd-shell full of clear water. Never had Ned enjoyed a draught of water with such delight, and he drained every drop from the gourd. He now made signs that they should release him from the yoke, and that he would not attempt to escape. Upon this a consultation was held, which ended by the approach of the leader of the party, who, with violent threats and gesticulations, explained that, should Ned attempt to desert, he would be immediately put to death. He then drew a knife from a sheath slung upon his arm above the left elbow, with which he cut the rope that secured Ned's neck in the fork; at the same time he released his arms.

Ned was so stiff that he could scarcely raise his hands to his forehead in gratitude for his freedom; but having performed this simple act of courtesy to the negro chief, he explained by signs that Tim also should be released. Without further delay Tim's bonds were cut; at the same time he was given a gourd full of water. Having taken a long draught Tim stretched his stiffened arms, and then rubbed his elbows as he sat down by the side of Ned, who, tired out, had thrown himself at full length upon the ground.

"Dis is a pretty kettle ob fish, Massa Ned!" exclaimed Tim. "Pity Massa Ned didn't marry all de ole chief's gals! Now we run away we got into bad bus'ness. Tim knows dis work; not de fust time Tim had his neck in de fork. Dese black fellers big blackguards, Massa Ned; catched we for slaves. Tim knows dis work; catched Tim before now."

Tim's former experience had been severely practical, and he rightly surmised that both he and Ned were captured for the purpose of being sold to some neighboring tribe; thus they might be handed about from one to the other as slaves for the remainder of their existence. At the same time, when he had reflected upon Ned's want of diplomacy in refusing the old chief's daughters, he in no way faltered in his allegiance, as he was thoroughly prepared to suffer any misery so long as he could share the lot of his young master; but it was Ned's misfortune that he regretted.

"Do you think they mean to sell us, Tim?" asked Ned.

"Yes, Massa Ned, p'r'aps sell Tim to one man; sell Massa Ned to anoder."

"Brutes!" exclaimed Ned; "this slave-trade is, indeed, an accursed traffic!"

"Yes, Massa Ned," rejoined Tim, "very bad bus'ness —almost bad like King George's bus'ness."

"What do you mean, Tim?" asked Ned.

"I say," replied the practical Tim, "de black nigger fellers almost bad as de press-gang fellers, only not quite. King George's fellers steal de boys to let de Frenchmen shoot 'em; de black niggers steal 'em, make 'em do de work; press-gang more bad, take de white slaves, let de Frenchmen kill 'em."

Ned would not question Tim's logic. There was no doubt of their situation; the tribes were at perpetual warfare with each other for the purpose of capturing slaves, some of which were exchanged for ivory with distant coun-

NED AND THE LION.

tries, while others were transported to Zanzibar, which was the great Portuguese depot for the trade. One fact was clear, that it was necessary to find favor in the eyes of their captors, and to trust in Providence for their future guidance. Determined upon this policy, although stiff and tired, Ned rose from the ground, and assisted the party in collecting wood for the night fires that were necessary to protect them from wild animals. There was a large quantity of fallen timber in the forest, and in a short time the united efforts of the people had collected numerous trunks and branches of dead trees, which were arranged in several piles. All being completed, a negro commenced the tedious operation of producing fire by the friction of two pieces of wood. He first procured a stick, in which he cut a notch; he then selected a piece of straight and dry wood about as thick as the little finger; this he sharpened to a point, which he inserted in the notch, and holding this firmly upon the ground with his toes, he rapidly twirled the upper stick between the palms of his hands, so that the point revolved within the notch as though it were a drill. In about three minutes it began to smoke, but as the success in producing fire by this method depends upon the quality of the wood, much labor was vainly expended, and the friction brought no spark, as the wood was of the wrong kind. Ned immediately produced a flint and steel from his pocket with a piece of tinder formed of canvas; with this he at once struck a light, to the astonishment of the natives, who crowded round him to witness the extraordinary operation. For at least ten minutes he was obliged to continue the performance of producing a shower of sparks by the blow of the flint and steel, to the intense delight of the natives, who vainly attempted it, but only succeeded in knocking the skin off their knuckles.

It was nearly dark, and the forest appeared in deep gloom as the pile of dry wood blazed brightly and illumined the trees upon the bank of the river where the party had bivouacked. The chief, accompanied by one of his men, had been some time absent in a search for wild yams, which abounded in the forest, and climbed like gigantic convolvuli around the stems of the trees. Tim had already placed his pot upon the fire, and the water was boiling, in expectation of the supply of vegetables, when suddenly a loud shriek was heard in the dense wood at no great distance.

This was almost immediately succeeded by a terrific roar; another loud cry of alarm was heard, and all the men rushed to their arms, crying, "The lion! the lion!"

In an instant Ned seized the gun loaded with ball, and without the slightest hesitation he rushed toward the spot through the thick bushes, followed by Nero and the entire party. In the excitement of the moment his stiffness and fatigue had vanished, and he dashed forward with a speed that was hardly equaled even by the naked negroes who accompanied him. In less than a minute they heard a rush in the jungle before them. Ned immediately cocked his gun, but in that instant the figure of the powerful negro chief appeared, flying toward them as he shouted the dreaded name, "The lion!"

A loud roaring and growling was now distinctly heard within a hundred paces of them, and the negroes hesitated to advance. Ned resolutely pushed forward, followed by Tim and Nero; and presently the dog, who had heard the terrible sound, dashed from his master's side, and rushing toward the spot was heard barking loudly at the lion. In a few moments Ned arrived at a small open glade in the middle of the forest, in which to his horror he saw the lion upon the body of a man whom he had seized by the throat, while Nero stood within a few yards baying him furiously. Upon Ned's arrival in the open spot the lion angrily shook the neck of the man as a dog would shake a rat, and then slowly dragged the body toward the thick bush. Ned rushed forward, and stood within ten paces of the immense brute, who, seeing himself thus challenged, turned, and releasing his hold on the neck of his victim, he placed one of his paws upon the chest, and crouched upon the ground, facing and glaring upon his unexpected adversary. At this moment Nero sprung toward him and barked loudly; this diverted his attention, and the lion turned his shaggy head toward the dog. Profiting by the opportunity, Ned took a steady aim at the temple, a little in front of the ear, and fired.

At the report of the gun the lion rolled over upon his back, and convulsively stretched out his prodigious paws, which trembled in the palsy of death, as the ball had passed through his brain. Hardly had the smoke cleared when Nero rushed in and seized the lion by his hairy throat, which he shook and tore in desperate fury, at the same time he received a deep scratch from one of the claws that contracted in the death struggle.

At the report of the gun the natives had rushed back in terror, but now that they witnessed its effect they crowded around Ned, and taking his hand they kissed the palm and embraced him after their fashion, by raising both his hands three times above his head. The ferocious-looking negro, who was their chief, also drew near in the ecstasy of the moment, and throwing up his arms, he shouted an address of admiration, which was succeeded by a loud yell of praise from all present. The dead body of the negro who had been killed was then drawn upon one side, and left for the beasts of prey that would devour it during the night, while with exciting shouts of victory the negroes dragged the lion through the forest, and laid it by the night fire that was brightly blazing at the place of bivouac.

It appeared that the chief and the deceased negro were returning from their search after yams, when the lion suddenly sprung upon them from the thick jungle, and seizing the man by the throat, he quickly strangled him. The chief had thrown his spear without effect, as it had glanced from the stem of a tree; he had then shouted for help, which had been so quickly and courageously given by Ned.

For several hours after the moon rose the conversation continued upon the recent event, and there was a general feeling of astonishment and admiration at Ned's courage and the power of the gun. Nero also shared in the praise, as the negroes were delighted that the dog had flown so directly at the lion's throat when the fatal shot was fired. While the exciting topic was discussed by the blazing fires the heroes of the night, Ned, Tim, and Nero, were stretched upon some dry grass fast asleep, tired out with the long day's march; they had gone supperless to rest, as sleep was more desired than food; in the meantime the natives, having carefully skinned their late enemy, made use of Tim's cooking-pot, and feasted on the lion.

CHAPTER XV.

MARCHING TO THE WEST.

FOR several weeks following the recent event Ned's captors led him by long and constant marches toward the west, but since his gallant behavior in the encounter with the lion, he had been kindly treated; both he and Tim were allowed to march free, and, moreover, they were permitted to carry their arms, which were useless to the natives. Hardly a day had passed without a supply of meat, as the country abounded with game, and Ned had killed many large antelopes and buffaloes that had fed the entire party. Thus upon Tim's proverb, " Fill de nigger's belly make de nigger frens," an alliance was established between the captors and their prisoners that was exceedingly favorable to the latter.

After a march of three weeks, during which Ned calculated that they had traveled three hundred and twenty miles due west, they arrived in an elevated country, where the temperature was much cooler than any to which they had been accustomed. For several days they continued to ascend immense slopes of waving grass lands, interspersed with clumps of mimosas, whose dark-green tops were an attraction for large herds of beautiful giraffes; it was the first time that Ned had seen these stately animals, and as he sat upon a high rock during a halt upon the march he looked down with admiration on the beautiful country before him. As far as the eye could reach were undulating plains ornamented with trees, while lofty mountains formed a dark-blue chain in the distance, and abrupt rocky hills rising here and there broke the monotony of the vast prairie. Animals of great variety and numbers gave life to the scene; herds of beautiful zebras galloped over the plain when disturbed; ostriches stalked proudly upon a carpet of bright green turf, which afforded pasturage for thousands of antelopes and buffaloes that were scattered in large troops over the landscape.

The first rains had commenced, thus all was verdant; but the march was drawing to a close, as the rainy season was unfavorable for traveling.

Another week was passed in steady progress of about fifteen miles per day. Every night Ned took his latitude by the meridian altitude of a star, and as the natives watched him communicating (as they thought) with these heavenly bodies, they regarded him with feelings of profound respect, as they considered that he had brought down the recent showers that had so refreshed the land. Thus he was looked upon as a rain-maker—a most important personage throughout the interior of Africa. Ned found that they had traveled due west, as they had seldom diverged more than a mile north or south of the same parallel of latitude upon which they had first started; therefore, allowing fifteen miles per day in a direct line as the distance marched, he knew by this dead reckoning his approximate position.

It was on the twenty-eighth day of marching that a scene burst upon Ned's view that almost repaid him for the fatigues of the long journey. During the morning they had passed through a more than usually populated country, and by ten o'clock they were near the summit of a hill, to which the negroes pointed as the end of their pilgrimage. Upon several occasions the guides had endeavored to explain something important connected with this day, and they now quickened their pace as they approached the brow of the steep slope, the negroes still pointing before them as though something extraordinary would be seen. The path now wound through a narrow rocky gorge that cleft the summit of the hill; passing through this cleft, overhung with beautiful trees and climbing plants, a magnificent scene burst suddenly upon them. Ned stood for a few moments riveted to the spot. He looked down from a height of about a thousand feet upon a vast inland sea, which sparkled in the sunshine like a valley of diamonds as every ripple on the surface reflected the bright rays. On the western side of the lake a clear blue outline cut the sky, as a range of lofty mountains walled in the mass of waters; while from the spot on which Ned stood the ground sloped in rapid undulations of green turf, ornamented with numerous forest trees. Upon the rich pastures were innumerable cattle, that belonged to the many villages that were scattered at irregular intervals upon the slopes. Some of these dwellings appeared to be within a few yards of the water's edge, and upon the beach could be plainly distinguished two rows of canoes, many of which were engaged in fishing, but upon none could Ned perceive a sail.

The country was extremely populous, and as the party now rapidly descended the hill Ned observed that every village was strongly protected by stockades, while large cattle kraals were erected in the vicinity, equally fortified, with the addition of a live hedge of the impenetrable thorny cactus. There could be no doubt that he had arrived at a place of great importance, as he had seen nothing approaching to the wealth of this country throughout the long march from the sea-coast, and Ned felt that if he were to become a slave this spot would most probably be the scene of his captivity. As this thought passed through his mind he observed that the more level portions of the ground at the bottom of the valley were cultivated with various crops, which as he descended he could plainly distinguish to be the tall millet and sweet potatoes, while thick groves of bananas surrounded every village, and afforded both fruit and shade. There could not be a more lovely country; and Ned congratulated himself that his lot appeared to have fallen in pleasant places, when, having completed the descent, the party passed through a large field of millet nearly twice the height of a man, and presently entered a plantation of bananas upon a path which conducted them to the gateway of the principal town.

They arrived at a curious archway in the thick stockade. This was formed of innumerable sharp-pointed boughs of extremely hard wood, so closely fixed together, and apparently interlaced with their points outward, that it was necessary to walk exactly in the middle of the narrow entrance, which would only permit the passage of men in single file. This peculiar arrangement was to prevent a sudden surprise by a rush of men in a large body; and to render the approach still more difficult, there was a turn at right angles in the middle of the sharp-pointed passage, which continued for a distance of about twenty feet. The stockade fence was composed of a double row of large trees, firmly fixed in the ground, and laced together with bamboos interwoven with the branches of the hooked thorn mimosa, which would be perfectly impenetrable to any naked men, and the defense might be considered impregnable unless destroyed by fire.

It was through this fortified work that the party now entered the town, when they were almost immediately met in a large open space by a number of the natives, who were lounging beneath the shade of an immense tamarind-tree; they immediately rose and surrounded them with expressions of much curiosity upon seeing Ned. These natives were entirely different in appearance to those who had captured Ned and Tim; their language was perfectly unknown to the guides, and they were unable to converse except by signs until an interpreter could be found who had lived for some time among the other tribe. Suddenly Tim came forward, and listening for a few moments with intense eagerness to the buzz of voices in the crowd, he exclaimed to Ned, " Dis my people! dis my talk, Massa Ned! Tim knows de talk!" and without more ado he spoke fluently to the native who was nearest to him.

The effect of this was extraordinary. Tim was at once the center of attraction, and the people crowded round him to hear the account of their journey and capture by the band who had led them thither. The crowd increased, and as a man of some importance appeared they were at once conducted to a large open place in the center of the town, where they were brought into the presence of the chief or king. He was a fine man of about forty, and was seated upon a carpet of leopard skins beneath the shade of a large banyan-tree, surrounded by many of his people. The large crowd that followed Ned and Tim now halted, and sat down respectfully at some distance, while the two strangers, together with the band of slave-hunters, were introduced to the king. He now made a sign to a negro by his side, who at once struck a large drum three times, with slow but heavy beats. The effect was instantaneous: every voice in the crowd of more than a thousand persons was hushed.

Complete silence having been restored, the king addressed Ned in a few words, desiring the entire party to be seated, and to explain whence and for what purpose they had arrived.

Tim now became the spokesman, and in a long but clear discourse he gave an account of the shipwreck and their subsequent journey; he also described his first arrival in England, to which country Ned belonged.

The king and his people were intensely interested. They had never heard of any white nation; and he at once requested to know whether all men were white in England, or whether Ned was an exceptional curiosity?

Tim gave him a description of the people, and the immense power of the country; at the same time he endeavored to explain the nature of our weapons, and he at once exhibited his gun.

The king took it in his hands, and nodding complacently as though he thoroughly understood it, he placed the muzzle in his mouth, and pronounced it to be an exceedingly inconvenient form of tobacco-pipe. As the gun was loaded, Tim explained the danger of the weapon, and as several

fowls were running about in the open square he asked permission to exhibit the effect. At about thirty yards' distance he fired his gun, which being loaded with large shot
killed three fowls; he then quickly fired the remaining
barrel, which killed two more. At the instant of the discharge a panic seized upon the crowd, who, having never
heard a gun, were terrified at the report, and rushed off in
all directions, falling over each other in the scramble to
get away; as the first shot was repeated by a second, they
expected a continuation of the terrible noise, and having
witnessed the death of the fowls they dreaded a similar fate.

Although the king had shared in the panic, he had recovered his self-possession sufficiently to enable him to
strike the drum, at the sound of which the frightened
crowd resumed their seats, while Tim explained the nature of the weapon and the tremendous power of gunpowder.

Order having been restored, Tim continued his discourse,
and explained how the largest animals could be killed by
the gun as instantaneously as the fowls that had been just
shot. He then described the attack of the lion that Ned
had destroyed by a single bullet, at the mention of which
a loud murmur of applause was uttered by the throng of
listeners.

When Tim had finished his narrative he wisely concluded
by a petition to the king for assistance; he described how
he had been stolen as a slave when a child, and he gave the
name of the tribe to which he had belonged. Upon hearing this name the king exclaimed in surprise, as the chief
of that country was his great ally, and his principal town
was situated at the extreme end of the lake, which he described as ten days' journey for a canoe, or about two hundred and fifty miles to the west. Thus Tim was not far
distant from his own home.

After some minutes' reflection the king spoke to his
counselors, who sat at his feet, and at once gave a command that the gang of slave-dealers who had captured Ned
and Tim should be brought before him. Through the
medium of an interpreter he questioned the powerful negro
who was the chief of the party, and as he explained that he
had arrived for the purpose of buying slaves in exchange
for beads and brass coil bracelets, the king offered to supply them on condition that he should receive Ned and Tim
as presents, together with all their effects. The parcels

that had been carried by the slave-hunters were now brought forward and examined. Mats were spread upon the ground, upon which large piles of glittering beads of all colors were laid; these were sorted into numerous small heaps, each of which was supposed to represent the price of a slave. The brass bracelets were next produced; these were formed of about four feet of wire, of the thickness of a drawing-pencil, twisted into a coil to fit the arm from the wrist upward. One of these highly prized ornaments was the value of a female slave. After much bargaining, during which a small number of beads was added to each pile, and a couple of bracelets thrown into the general offer, it was decided that on the following day one hundred and fifty slaves should be delivered to the leader of the gang.

The meeting was broken up, and Ned was shown a hut that was to be appropriated by him and Tim; the crowd made way for them, as Nero growled angrily and bristled up his back when intruded upon too closely, and in a few minutes Ned found himself in possession of a clean circular dwelling within the king's private court, in which were numerous huts inclosed within a ring fence of palisades; these were occupied by the king's wives, and by other members of his family, who now issued from their doors to examine the new arrivals. There was nothing remarkable in Tim's appearance with the exception of his clothes, as the only difference between himself and the natives consisted in their nudity; the men had not a vestige of clothing beyond a scarf of tanned antelope's hide that was fastened across the shoulders and hung loosely before the body; the women wore a neat apron of finely plaited twine that was spun from the fiber of the wild aloe.

The usual thrilling cry of welcome was raised as Ned and Tim were led to their hut. It was exceedingly clean, and was surrounded by a court neatly cemented with a hard coating of clay and cow dung, which is general throughout Africa. The view was extremely beautiful, as the front of the hut commanded the lake, which was about a quarter of a mile distant; in this spot it appeared to be about twenty miles in width, and the opposite side was bordered by lofty hills which looked a rich purple in the distance. Toward evening several slave-women brought a large circular wooden bowl with a steaming mixture of kid stewed with sweet potatoes and bananas; this was exceedingly hot with red pepper, and Ned thought it almost surpassed Tim's art in cookery.

"Not too good, Massa Ned," said Tim, who was jealous of the strangers' success; "too plenty pepper got in de stoo. E-e-ché!" continued Tim, sneezing violently, but shamming, "bad cook dis people; not cook like me. Tim knows de trick 'xactly."

In spite of this criticism Tim eat heartily, and by the time that dinner was concluded the bowl was nearly empty. The boys were both tired, and throwing themselves down upon clean mats, they slept soundly.

On the following morning before sunrise Ned was awakened by the loud beating of drums and blowing of horns, and upon rising hastily he was surprised to see a vast crowd of people assembled in the king's court, headed by himself in person, who came to summon him to a council. The fact was, that during the night much feasting had been going on, and the chief of the gang that had formerly captured Ned had communicated the intelligence to the king that he was a renowned rain-maker; thus Ned's presence among the tribe would be of inestimable benefit to the country, that was subject to severe droughts. He had described how Ned conversed with the stars and moon, and how he stared at the sun with an extraordinary instrument, although the eyes of common men could not for a moment support its light. He also repeated the account of the conflict with the lion, and he declared that he had no doubt that Ned possessed the power of magic. As the king was surrounded by many of his people when this description was given an immense excitement was created, and after a long consultation it was determined that on the following morning the king and his people should visit the fair-haired sorcerer, and request him to perform some feat of sorcery. Ned had left his hut to meet the king, and Tim, who acted as interpreter, shortly informed him of the object of the deputation.

It was in vain that Ned declared he had no supernatural power; the more that he protested, the firmer was their belief; and the king requested to examine all the curious articles that he possessed, and that their use might be explained. Tim at once unpacked the knapsacks and produced the sextant, which the king declined to touch, as he was not sure that it might not explode like the gun on the

preceding day. Ned then exhibited the compass; this perfectly delighted him, as the needle followed the blade of a
knife which Ned passed around it; the king wished to touch
the needle, but was astonished that his finger could not
reach it on account of the glass which covered the surface of
the instrument. This was a matter of extreme curiosity;
glass was unknown, therefore the nature of the obstruction
was not understood. The needle could be seen but not
touched, as an invisible substance protected it from contact
with the hand; this was handed from one to the other of
the king's great men, and at once declared to be magic.
Among others in the crowd were the king's sorcerers; these
were old men whose heads were ornamented with chaplets
of dried lizards and toads, with pieces of roots of certain
trees that were supposed to be charms. Around their
necks were long necklaces composed of entire tortoise-
shells about three inches long, together with crocodiles'
teeth, lions' claws, and the black seeds of the wild plantain. When the compass was handed to them they at once
declared it to be a spell, and advised the king to return it
immediately to the owner.

Ned having already gained the reputation of a magician,
was now obliged to continue a performance which tended
to increase the belief in his power. He produced the
quicksilver that belonged to the artificial horizon; some of
this he poured into a cocoa-nut shell, which he handed to
the king, and requested him to touch it. Both the king
and his sorcerers dipped their fingers in the supposed water
without being able to wet them; this was still more wonderful than the compass; the shell was passed from one to
the other, while each attempted to moisten the tips of his
fingers, which he carefully examined after every experiment. At last a small quantity was spilled upon the ground,
which forming into numerous globules, afforded general
amusement, as they vainly attempted to secure them with
their fingers and thumbs. The mercury was at once declared to be magic water that had the power of producing
rain.

The telescope was now exhibited and its use explained.
Ned then raised it to his eye, and directed the sight to a
herd of cows that were being milked at some distance.
Upon seeing this the king suddenly snatched it from him,
and begged him never to look at either cows or goats with

such an instrument, or they would assuredly lose their milk. Yielding at once to the superstition, Ned requested the king to observe some object through the telescope. This he vainly attempted, and his example having been followed by his sorcerers with the same want of success, it was returned to Ned as a magic instrument that could only be used by himself. Accordingly Ned unscrewed the large magnifying-glass, and as the sun was bright he requested the king to stretch forth his hand; then directing the focus of the burning-glass upon his black skin, the king suddenly sprung backward with the pain. Recovering from his first surprise, the king now insisted that a similar experiment should be tried upon all his sorcerers, as their charms and spells, if potent, should protect them from the white man's magic. Each offered his arm. The first bore the pain heroically for a few seconds as the skin burned and smoked in the fire of the sun's focus; he could then support it no longer, and he suddenly cried out and quickly withdrew his arm, which was severely scorched. One by one each sorcerer was subjected to the ordeal, and all having suffered alike the king declared that their magic was inferior to that of the white man, and that they were useless in comparison with him. Ned then set fire with the glass to a piece of canvas rubbed with gunpowder; this was handed from one to the other with admiration, amid general exclamations of delight and astonishment.

"What are they saying, Tim?" asked Ned.

"Dis black niggers stoopid people, Massa Ned," replied Tim; "dey say de white man got de fire in one eye and de water in de odder eye, so he make 'em fire when he like, and rain when he please. Dat's all right!" continued Tim. "Tim knows de niggers; give 'em little 'stonishment, dat's de right trick 'xactly. Now de black king make Massa Ned a big man."

Perfectly satisfied with the treasure he had gained in Ned, the king lost no time in collecting the one hundred and fifty slaves that he had agreed to supply to the negro dealer; he at once gave an order that a certain refractory village in the neighborhood should be pillaged, and the inhabitants sold as slaves. Accordingly, at about three A. M. on the following morning, a party of a thousand men started by moonlight for the purpose of surprising the village before the people should awake. This brutal order was given because the headman of the village had refused to pay the customary tribute. A little before daybreak Ned perceived the flames of the burning huts, as the fire destroyed the inflammable constructions of thatch and wood, at a distance of about four miles from the principal town. The king was standing in his own court-yard enjoying the scene of destruction, and in a few hours his army returned, having killed many of the men, and captured several hundred women and children of both sexes. These unfortunate people were secured in a living chain, tied neck to neck by thongs of hide; others were fastened by the necks in forked sticks, similar to those in which Ned and Tim had been confined when first taken by the slave-gang. Some of the young girls were crying bitterly; there were mothers .with infants in their arms, others who had lost their children in the massacre, and many children who had seen their parents ruthlessly speared before their eyes. The prisoners were now ranged in several rows in the large inclosure that formed the court, after which they were inspected by the negro slave-dealer, who selected one hundred and fifty according to the bargain he had made with the king; these were taken without the slightest regard to the relationship of the individuals. An infant was torn from the arms of a pretty young mother, while she was led away with the lot selected for transportation, without the smallest attention to her cries of agony at the separation from her child. Children of twelve and fourteen were taken sobbing bitterly from their parents, and the whip of hippopotamus hide descended cruelly upon their naked shoulders when they struggled to remain with their mothers, from whom they were torn. At length the requisite number was complete, and the band of slave-dealers that had brought Ned to the country now commenced their return march, with one hundred and fifty slaves to supply other black dealers, who would conduct them to the Portuguese possessions on the coast near Zanzibar.

As they disappeared from the town the remaining slaves were distributed by the king among a number of his people, who were allowed to have the use of them provided that they agreed to restore them or others in their stead whenever they might be required. There were many heart-rending scenes as they saw their relatives disappear while they were themselves divided and apportioned to strangers. Ned looked on in horror at the infamous traffic, while it recalled to Tim's recollection the scene of his first day of slavery.

"So de nigger eat de nigger!" exclaimed Tim, philosophically. "Bad fellers dese black chaps," he continued; "where 'spect to go to, eh? God shut His eye, let de debbel catch de nigger. Pray God take care of Tim."

This theological sentiment closed the melancholy scene.

CHAPTER XVI.

LIFE AMONG THE NEGROES.

SEVERAL months passed away, and with them the rainy season closed, and the harvest was gathered in. The sun now resumed its sway, the clouds had given place to a spotless sky, and the vivid green gradually faded, and the country parched into a bright yellow; the smaller streams all dried up, and even the great lake sunk a few feet below the former level.

It was now the season for hunting, and parties were organized for killing elephants and hippopotami, the flesh of which was the principal food of the people; this was dried in strips, and then hung up in the smoke of their cabins in sufficient quantities to last for many months.

The harvest of meat was considered almost as important as that of corn; therefore while a portion of the men and the whole of the women were engaged in the cultivation of their fields, those who were most active and courageous formed bands of hunters and provided a supply of flesh. To be distinguished for exploits in the hunting-grounds was considered to be even more meritorious than acts of valor on the field of battle, and as Ned had gained a great reputation by the death of the lion he was expected to perform prodigies in the chase of wild animals. Next to the king he was already the greatest man in the country, as his supposed power in magic had given him an extraordinary influence. Among his medicines he had a large supply of calomel and emetic tartar; the effect of these drugs upon the sick had gained him much repute, and his success as a physician was also attributed to sorcery. Although Ned was no charlatan, he found it impossible to stem the tide of public opinion, and he was forced to allow the natives to indulge in their superstitions. There was, however, much danger inseparable from his exalted position. The king was an ignorant savage, and although he believed thoroughly in magic, his confidence in the individual sorcerer depended upon success, and the law of the country determined that three successive failures should be punished by the death of the rain-maker or magician. To Ned's horror and disgust two of the king's sorcerers had already been put to death in his presence for having repeatedly failed in their prophecies of success to the hunting-parties. The fault was considered to exist in a lying spirit in the inside of the sorcerer; the unfortunate wretch was therefore put to death before all the people, by being ripped open with a sharp knife, when his vital organs were carefully examined by other sorcerers, who pretended to discover the traces of the evil spirit.

It was not long before Ned was requested by the king to foretell the result of a hunting expedition that was about to start upon a large scale. With the horrible fate of the unlucky prophets before him, Ned declared, with much tact, that great success would attend the hunting-party should he and Tim accompany the hunters. It was accordingly arranged that he should take the entire command.

At daybreak on the following morning Ned, accompanied by Tim and Nero with fifty picked men, started upon their expedition in five large canoes, formed from the straight stems of gigantic trees.

The sun had just risen when the little fleet paddled rapidly along the shore; the men were in the highest spirits, as Ned's presence among them inspired a confidence of success. For ten hours they paddled without ceasing, merely halting to relieve each other at the oars, and Ned reckoned that they had traveled about thirty-five miles, when, at four o'clock, the leading canoe steered into a narrow bay, with a clean sandy beach, upon which the crews disembarked and dragged their vessels high and dry. A ridge of precipitous rocky hills of several hundred feet high bordered the lake about a quarter of a mile from the water, which appeared to extend to their base during the floods of the rainy season; the flat, sandy ground between them and the lake was scantily covered with a fine silky grass, and the soft earth was deeply imprinted with numerous tracks of elephants, hippopotami, giraffes, and other large animals.

This part of the country was uninhabited, and therefore it abounded with game.

While the hunters removed their weapons and light baggage from the canoes Ned strolled with his gun to the base of the rocky hills, and perceiving that they were too precipitous to ascend he concluded that the wild animals must descend to the lake by some pass from the high ground above. Continuing along the base of the hills it was not long before he arrived at the dry bed of a torrent that descended between two walls of rock that formed a ravine from the high lands to the lake; this was completely trodden down by the feet of the ponderous animals that nightly arrived by that path to drink. It immediately struck Ned that, if he were to watch the pass by moonlight, with Tim and their two double-barreled guns, he would be able to cut off any animals that should descend, as he would have the advantage of a secure position about twenty feet above them. Determined to carry out his plan, he hurried back to the party, who had already settled themselves for the night behind some high rocks which effectually concealed their fire. Ned now explained his plan to Tim and the people, and having dined off a large fish which one of the hunters had harpooned during the voyage, he tied Nero to a tree, telling him to watch his knapsack of clothes and ammunition, and with a caution to the hunters to observe the greatest quiet, he started with Tim to watch the pass.

Upon arrival at the mouth of the gorge, which formed an alley or narrow street through the hill-side, Ned climbed up the steep ascent, and took his position beneath a small tree that grew among the clefts of the rocks exactly on the edge of the ravine; thus he commanded the pass, as he could drop a pebble upon any animal that passed below. This curious pathway was of great length, as it was by no means precipitous, but descended at a gradual inclination with many windings from the table-land on the summit of the hills.

The wind blew toward the lake; thus it was favorable for the watchers.

The moon was nearly full, and not a cloud dimmed the face of the heavens; thus it would be almost as easy to shoot correctly as in daylight, especially as Ned had taken the precaution to fasten a piece of white paper cut into a sharp point as a sight at the muzzle of the guns. At length, as daylight entirely faded, the moon seemed doubly bright, and the night set in with that brilliancy that can only be seen within the tropics. There was not a sound to be heard except the occasional splashing and loud sonorous snort of the hippopotami among the reeds by the margin of the lake, and the hum of mosquitoes that tormented Ned without ceasing.

About an hour passed in fruitless watching: the moon was now high enough to throw her light directly into the ravine, and suddenly, although no sound had been heard, Ned perceived a dull gray mass that looked like a large portion of the rock moving slowly forward from an angle in the gorge. The mass suddenly halted, when, in the distance, a sound rang through the still night air like the shrill note of a trumpet. A low and deep growl, like the rumbling of distant thunder, seemed to shake the rock upon which Ned lay concealed. Suddenly a tremendous trumpet sounded from the gorge where the dull gray mass had halted, and, growling deeply, the bull elephant advanced unconscious of impending danger along the bottom of the ravine. Another and another elephant followed until the leader passed directly beneath the spot where Ned and Tim were concealed; the entire alley was crowded with the herd of enormous animals as they followed their leader in single file toward the lake.

Ned's heart beat loudly with excitement as one by one the elephants passed below him; but he reserved his fire until eight or ten had made their exit from the gorge, as he rightly conjectured that at the alarm of the first shot those who had already passed out would endeavor to return whence they came; this would create great confusion in the narrow pass, during which he would have an opportunity of selecting the finest animals.

As the elephants slowly filed below Ned whispered to Tim to hand him the spare gun as quickly as possible when he should require it, and aiming behind the ear of a large bull that was not more than five paces distant he fired. The huge animal fell dead to the shot. For some minutes the herd of elephants remained stationary, as though suddenly turned to stone; the flash of the gun and the unknown report had completely astonished them, and they waited in uncertainty of the position and nature of the danger. During this time Ned reloaded his gun, and aiming at the temple of a large elephant that stood exactly before him he again fired. To his delight this animal fell likewise; but now an indescribable scene of confusion arose. At the last flash of the gun those elephants that had already passed from the gorge turned quickly round, and charged desperately in their retreat up the narrow pass, which was blocked not only by the bodies of the two dead elephants but by the dense mass of animals which, seized by the panic, now wedged closely together in their frantic endeavors to escape.

There was no necessity for concealment, and Ned quietly stood upon the edge of the rocks, just out of reach of the elephants' trunks, and steadily selected his shots, aiming generally behind the ear as the most fatal spot. Six elephants fell to his guns before they could extricate themselves from their helpless position; then, having regained their formation in single file, they disappeared at an extraordinary pace in the gloom of the ravine.

This was a good beginning. Tim had handed the gun quickly, and had reloaded as fast as Ned had fired, and their six prizes now blocked the passage of the narrow gorge. But more remained to be done, as the night was young and the moon bright; therefore Ned proposed that they should follow the edge of the ravine for a considerable distance where it had been undisturbed; there they might pass another hour in watching before they returned to their party.

They picked their way among loose rocks until they arrived at the summit of the high ground; they then discovered what they had supposed to be a hill from the level of the lake was merely a cliff, or precipitous slope descending from a beautiful expanse of table-land, that was a combination of forests and plains. From this elevated land the torrents descended to the lake by deep gorges that had been worn through the hill-side, and Ned once more took up his position behind a large tamarind-tree that overhung the ravine which the elephants had recently quitted. The white sand at the bottom of the gorge was trodden deeply by the feet of the numerous herd that had now retreated to the jungles, in which they could be distinctly heard trumpeting and roaring in the distance.

More than an hour passed away without the appearance of any animal, and Ned was thinking of his return wher-

he suddenly heard the clatter of stones as some hard-footed beast was descending the ravine. In a few moments he observed several specter-like forms advancing along the bottom, their heads being sometimes on a level with the rocks that overhung the edge. They were giraffes who were thus descending to drink at the lake.

As they passed within a few feet of Ned he fired at the head of one that nearly touched him; this fell to the shot, and as the herd dashed round and rushed off with amazing speed, Ned fired his remaining barrel at the shoulder of another animal, but apparently without success, as it retreated with the rest. This was great luck; Ned had killed six elephants and a giraffe, and he resolved to return to the spot where his party had bivouacked, as he had done sufficient work for the night. The easiest path was by the ravine through which the elephants had arrived; Ned therefore clambered down the rock, followed by Tim, until he gained the sandy bottom of the gorge, by which gradual descent they arrived at the dead elephants. In passing these Tim cut off their tails, as he had also done with the giraffe, and with these trophies they continued on their way. After passing through a dark strip of forest they observed the light of the fires around which the natives were sitting in anxious expectation of their return, as they had distinctly heard the shots and the loud trumpeting of the elephants. Tim, in great triumph, exhibited the tails, and recounted the story of the night, to the astonishment of the natives, who had now obtained as large a supply of meat in one night as they were accustomed to collect in a fortnight's hunting. They determined to visit the spot before daybreak, to prepare the flesh and secure it from putrefaction.

At about four A.M. they sallied forth with knives, axes, and sacks to cut up the game. This they performed with great dexterity by dividing the flesh in long but thin slips, which were at once hung upon the trees in festoons to dry, while fires were lighted beneath to preserve it from the flies. While they were thus engaged Ned, with the dog, strolled up the ravine to the body of the giraffe, which had already been attacked by hyenas, whose tracks were visible in the sand. Knowing that he had wounded a second giraffe, he now continued along the ravine, and presently he discovered tracks of blood upon the stones upon the

right-hand side of the gully, which proved that the animal
was wounded. He now carefully followed upon the marks
until he emerged from the ravine among some roughly
broken ground near the summit of the table-land; this was
in some places covered with thick bush, but Ned remarked
that in one spot the white sand was reddened with blood,
and trampled in all directions by the tracks of lions mingled
with the wide-spreading hoofs of giraffes. It was evident
that some great struggle had taken place, as the sand was
marked in one direction by a weight that appeared to have
been dragged across it, as though the giraffe had been carried off by the lions. As he followed upon the track along
which the heavy body had been dragged Nero bristled up
his back, and cautiously approached a dense covert of
thorns within a small hollow among the rocks. The dog
halted, and appeared to wind something within the thick
jungle, as he advanced a few steps nearer and then barked
in great excitement. Ned felt sure that either one or more
lions had dragged the body of the giraffe within the den of
thorns; accordingly, when within twenty paces of the spot,
he threw several large stones into the middle of the bush.
With a loud roar a magnificent lion rushed out from his
lair and crouched before the bush, eying Ned fiercely, and
growling deeply as though prepared to spring. The lion
moved his tail rapidly from side to side, striking the ground
with the tuft of black hair at the extremity with a force
that made the sand fly like puffs of smoke. This was a
sign of extreme fury, and Ned momentarily expected an
attack that would have been difficult to avoid. For several
minutes they faced each other determinedly, Ned all the
while keeping his eyes fixed unflinchingly upon those of
the lion. At length, as the dog continued to spring around
him, barking without ceasing, the lion rose from the
ground and stalked proudly backward and forward before
the covert, as though to guard the entrance. This was a
grand opportunity for a side shot at the shoulder, and never
did Ned aim with greater coolness and accuracy, as he knew
that his life depended upon the shot; trusting to break the
shoulder-bone, and thus disable him, he fired. With a
terrific roar the lion charged with one bound into the smoke
of the gun; at the same time that he descended he struck
a random blow with his right paw that would have felled
a buffalo. Fortunately for Ned, at the moment of firing

he had sprung upon one side, and thus avoided the crushing blow. The lion now rolled over almost at his feet, and, recovering himself immediately, he rushed upon Ned, receiving at the same instant the contents of the second barrel in his mouth. With great activity Ned had again avoided him in the thick smoke at the moment of firing, and Nero rushing in had seized the lion between the hind legs, where he hung on with a furious tenacity that no efforts of the animal could relax. Ned had Jem Stevens's pistols in his belt, one of which he had quickly drawn; but the struggles of the lion with the dog were so great and extremely rapid that he had no chance of taking a correct aim. The blood was pouring from the lion's mouth, as well as from a wound through the shoulder, and presently, amid his tremendous efforts to turn and attack the dog, he reared, to his full height upon his hind legs, and with a savage roar he fell upon his back with the stanch dog beneath him. As quick as lightning, to save Nero, Ned rushed in, and fired his pistol within a few inches of the lion's head, scattering his brains upon the faithful dog. The lion never moved a muscle. Ned, pale with the excitement of the fight, now caressed the dog, who fiercely shook the dead lion's throat; after which he wiped the perspiration from his forehead, and looking up to the clear heavens he devoutly thanked God for protection in the strife. He was surveying the carcass of the lion with a hunter's pride when Tim suddenly appeared, accompanied by several of the natives who had heard the shots and hurried to discover the cause. They could hardly believe their eyes when they saw the lion lying dead; and upon entering the jungle they found the remains of the giraffe, which had been partially devoured. They now took possession of the prize; and having skinned the lion and cut his flesh from the bones, they severed his head from the body, together with the skin, and returned to their party, who were busily engaged in taking the meat of the elephants.

The whole day was occupied by the natives in cutting up the elephants and transporting them to the place of bivouac. In the meantime Ned, who had no taste for that branch of the expedition, took possession of one of the canoes with the assistance of Tim, and determined, if possible, to procure some fresh fish for dinner. Many drift bamboos were lying upon the beach, from which he selected one about sixteen feet long and tapered; he then lashed a thong of elephant's hide to the point, so as to form a stiff loop in the place of a ring, through which he passed a strong line made of the aloe fiber; to this he attached a large hook and a piece of light wood as a float. With a coil of about a hundred yards of line wound upon two pegs a foot asunder, that he drove into the butt of his rod in the place of a reel, Ned was ready for a day's fishing, with the exception of the bait. Tim quickly secured the latter necessary article by forming a line with half a dozen single hairs of the giraffe's tail, to which he attached a small hook baited with a minute piece of elephant's fat. The small fish of about half a pound weight bit greedily, and having caught five or six Tim kept them alive in a large gourd-shell of water, and Ned pushed the canoe from the shore. The small fish were bright and silvery, but they had a tough skin like that of an eel instead of scales; through this, just beneath the back fin, Ned inserted the large hook, and throwing his lively and alluring bait into deep water within a few yards of a bank of tall reeds he patiently waited the result.

About half an hour had passed in perfect silence when Ned was startled by a tremendous snort, accompanied by a splash in the water close to the canoe; in another instant he felt a severe shock as the head of a hippopotamus struck the bottom, and lifted the canoe several inches above the surface. As though proud of his performance, the angry old bull now raised his head above the water, and again snorted loudly. Tim snatched up his gun, and, taking a good aim, he fired into the middle of its head in a line from between the eyes. With a splash the animal disappeared. Several other hippopotami now showed their heads, but at a more respectful distance, as they were alarmed at the report of the gun.

" Dat's what I call a ugly feller," remarked Tim; " he got a pair of lips same like de nigger; got a flat nose like de nigger; he's de reg'lar water nigger—dat's a fact 'xactly."

Having expressed this opinion upon the natural history of the hippopotamus, Tim reloaded his gun, and Ned was about to make some remark when his float darted off, and the rod was nearly jerked out of his hand; fortunately he held a loose coil that was not wound round the pegs, and allowing this to fall upon the ground he grasped the line with one hand, and struck hard to fasten the fish. It was impossible to check the rush, and for the moment Ned feared that a crocodile had seized his bait, and that he should lose the tackle; but he was presently undeceived, as an immense fish sprung high out of the water, at about eighty yards distant, firmly hooked.

For about twenty minutes the struggle continued between Ned and the fish, which constantly leaped from the water, and, shaking its head violently, endeavored to free itself from the hook. At length, as Ned had kept a severe strain upon the line, the fish showed signs of exhaustion, and Tim paddled the canoe toward a sand-bank for the purpose of landing their prize in shallow water. Jumping out of the canoe Ned ran backward upon the bank, and keeping a tight line he presently succeeded in leading the fish into the shallows, where it struggled helplessly upon its side; Tim got behind it, and falling bodily upon it, he grasped the gills with both hands, and dragged it to the shore. The scales were as bright as silver, except upon the back, where they were a dark slaty blue; it was a species of perch that weighed about eighty pounds, and both Ned and Tim rejoiced in their beautiful prize. To preserve it fresh Ned fastened a piece of strong line around the tail, and then placed it in deep water secured to a peg upon the bank; thus it quickly recovered from its fatigue.

In about an hour Ned had another run, and captured a fish of the same species that weighed nearly forty pounds, which he landed upon the sand-bank in a similar manner to the first. They had again pushed off in the canoe when Tim perceived something like the back of a large turtle above the surface of the water, and upon quietly paddling toward it he discovered that it was the flank of the hippopotamus at which he had fired, which now floated. This animal always sinks to the bottom when first killed, but in about an hour and a half, when the gas has distended the body, it rises to the surface. Here was an additional supply of food; and returning to the shore Ned procured a rope, which they made fast to one of the hind legs, and towed the carcass to the bank, where it awaited the arrival of the natives.

In the evening the hunters returned, having completed
8

their task, and upon hearing of the fresh supply they immediately set to work upon the hippopotamus.

In the meantime Tim, ever mindful of the cooking department, dug a hole in the ground, about four feet deep and three in diameter, like a well with perpendicular sides, and having collected a large quantity of fuel he lighted a fire within the hole, which he fed with logs of dry wood, so that it burned fiercely for four hours: by the expiration of this time the sides of the pit were red hot, and the bottom was a mass of glowing embers. Into this natural oven he placed the two forefeet of an elephant with a portion of the trunk and the four feet of the hippopotamus. He then covered the hole with bars of green wood, upon which he piled a few armfuls of green and well-wetted flags that he procured from the lake. He then plastered the whole surface thickly with mud, upon which he piled earth and sods firmly beaten down until it resembled a grave; this was to retain the heat within the oven. This supply of meat would be thoroughly roasted in about thirty-six hours.

Having dined sumptuously off hippopotamus liver cut into steaks and grilled, with slices of the fish fried in hippopotamus fat, Ned and Tim threw themselves upon their mats close to a blazing fire, and slept during the night.

On waking upon the following morning Ned found the camp already astir. The natives had made numerous fires, upon which large earthenware pots were arranged, and the whole party was occupied in boiling down the fat of both elephants and hippopotamus. The residue of the meat, after boiling, was carefully stored in goat-skin sacks, and was considered a great delicacy. No fat can equal that of the hippopotamus in mildness of flavor; this was poured while warm into gourd-shells, and allowed to harden. The bladders of the elephants were also filled with fat, and not even the smallest portion of the numerous large animals was wasted. Another day was passed in drying and packing their harvest of meat. On the next day Ned opened the subterranean oven. Upon removing the earth the coating of mud was found to be perfectly hard like a thick crust; beneath this the flags had retained sufficient moisture to prevent them from being burned, although the oven was still hot and steaming. With some difficulty the men now lifted out the immense feet of the elephant, together with the other baked meats, all of which were laid upon a mat strewn with green reeds. The elephant's feet were extremely curious, as the soles became detached from the foot upon a gentle pressure, and exposed a white and inviting surface beneath; this was a firm, but fatty substance that was extremely rich and gelatinous. Having taken off the elephant's shoes the feet were divided among the party, and Ned thought that he had never eaten anything more delicious.

As the labor of preparing the store of meat was completed the natives wished to return home, as the canoes would be nearly filled. They accordingly launched their vessels, and loaded them with dried flesh, fat, and elephants' tusks, together with pieces of giraffe hide cut into oblong shapes that were to be manufactured into shields. Everything was ready for a start on the morrow, and Ned strolled about half a mile from the camp before sunset, and climbed a high rock to enjoy a more extensive view of the landscape. From this position he looked down upon the camp, at the same time he commanded a view of the pass in which he had killed so many elephants. As his eyes instinctively wandered to the scene of his first night's sport he was astonished to see issuing stealthily from the gorge into the low ground a long string of blacks in single file, all armed with bows and spears. For about ten minutes he watched them attentively. Some were painted a bright red; these Ned supposed to be chiefs, as they were at regular intervals in the file of men, which still continued to pour from the ravine. Marching directly for a small thicket that was near the edge of the lake the entire party of about five hundred men was suddenly concealed. This had taken place so suddenly and quietly that Ned could hardly believe his eyes. There could be no doubt that the large armed force was lying in ambush for some hostile purpose, and as Ned would be forced to pass within a few hundred yards of the thicket to regain the camp he felt that his position was extremely hazardous. It was necessary to give an immediate alarm to his party, but the great difficulty lay in effecting a junction. There was a small dry water-course that led from the hill to the lake, and Ned immediately determined to crawl along the bottom until he should gain the rushes that bordered the water, after which he would have no difficulty in reaching the canoes, where the men were still engaged. There was no time to

lose. Sliding upon his back down the steep hill-side, Ned
reached the water-course. This was tolerably deep in
parts, so that he could cover his advance by simply stooping; but in the more rocky portions of the trench it was
shallow, and he was forced to crawl upon his hands and
knees. He had gained one of these exposed positions
when he turned his head toward the thicket, and he distinctly observed two natives peering out from the place of
ambush. Ned lay flat upon the ground, and did not move
for several minutes. Again he slowly raised his head; he
could see no one, and once more he crawled along the
ground until he arrived in a deeper portion of the water-
course. He then hurried along in a stooping position, and
at length gained the reeds at the water's edge. Under
cover of the reeds, he splashed through mud and water until
he at length reached the canoes. Tim was the first person
whom he met, as he had been fishing in the lake and had
just returned with several natives. Upon hearing Ned's
account rapidly delivered Tim immediately informed his
native companions. In an instant they rushed to the camp
for their arms, followed by Ned and Tim. Upon arrival
the entire party would have been seized with a panic had
not Ned at once assumed the command.

Upon order being restored, the natives explained that
the people whom Ned had seen must be men of a hostile
tribe, who had upon a former occasion massacred a hunting-party similar to the present expedition; they had no
doubt been informed by spies of their presence, and they
would attack from their ambush during the night. It
would be impossible to resist them, as they were warriors
renowned for the impetuosity of their onset. Thus a force
of five hundred men would annihilate a small party at the
first rush.

As the canoes were loaded, Ned proposed that they should
embark at once and push off from the shore. It was growing dusk, and they would avoid the confusion of a night attack, should they be assailed when the enemy perceived
their retreat to the boats. Not a moment was lost. Ned
ordered the natives to march in a compact body to the
canoes, while he and Tim would bring up the rear. Drawing the bullets from their guns, the two lads recharged
them with buck-shot, which, in the event of a fight, would
take a greater effect upon a mass of men. Ned had the

brace of pistols in his belt that he had found in Stevens's chest, and he felt no doubt that the report and effect of fire-arms would paralyze the attack sufficiently to allow them to push off in their canoes. He gave the word "forward," and his little body of fifty men, with their arrows ready fixed upon their bows, advanced steadily but quickly forward, while he and Tim followed a few paces in the rear.

Hardly had they quitted the screen of jungle which protected their camp than their retreat was observed by the party in ambush in the thicket some hundred yards on their right. In the instant a wild yell was raised by an invisible enemy, who almost at the same moment burst from the wood, and with savage screams and shouts came rushing across the open ground to intercept the route, and to cut off the canoes.

"Steady!" cried Ned; "keep together, my men;" which Tim interpreted immediately, and the party continued their course at a quick walk.

They were much nearer to the canoes than the enemy, and Ned, with cool judgment, calculated that they would reach them at a walk before the hostile party could gain them at full speed. They would accordingly have time to push off from the shore, provided that the embarkation were conducted without confusion. They were within a hundred yards of the boats that were afloat in the little bay among rushes, while the enemy was about three times that distance from them, advancing at full speed, in a confused mass of yelling naked savages. Ned quickly gave the order that every man should run to his own boat in which he had arrived. In an instant his fifty blacks rushed forward, and dividing into tens, the individual crews of the five canoes leaped on board and took their places with the paddles in their hands by the time that Ned and Tim had reached the bank. A flight of arrows now fell around them as the enemy, already within eighty yards of their expected prey, shot wildly at full speed and happily missed all but the canoes, in the sides of which several arrows remained fixed. Ned and Tim now jumped on board two canoes, and as the paddles struck the water with the powerful stroke of ten men, both opened fire from the stern upon the crowd of savages at about fifty paces distant. Thirty buck-shot rattled among them like hail, and five or six men fell, while others were wounded. This unexpected volley for the in-

stant checked their advance, and before they could recover
from their confusion the left-hand barrels opened and scattered destruction among their ranks.   Ned now loaded with
ball as the canoes increased the distance between them, and
two or three shots fired into the baffled crowd sent them
scampering off in all directions, leaving several dead and
wounded upon the ground.   A loud cheer was now raised
by the crews of the canoes, who ceased paddling, and waved
their paddles in the air in defiance of their beaten enemy.
So excited had they become, and so thoroughly confident in
their leader, that they besought Ned to allow them to return to shore for the purpose of attacking their crest-fallen
antagonists.

Ned was unwilling to shed blood except in self-defense,
therefore he restrained their exuberant valor, and desired
them to pull steadily along the coast toward their own
home, where they would be received with a hearty welcome
as they were heavily laden with hunting spoils.   For some
hours they paddled in silence, as the night was dark and
they were obliged to keep a good lookout ahead; but when
at length the moon rose and shone brilliantly over the calm
surface of the lake they burst out into songs that lasted until sunrise.   The substance of their minstrelsy was a description of all that had taken place during their expedition.   This was generally improvised by one man who sung
in a kind of recitative, and at the end of each verse a wild
chorus was joined in by the whole crew.   Thus were Ned's
praises sung, neither was Tim nor even Nero omitted from
the ode, but all the principal performers were introduced,
and the various scenes described, even to the yells and
shouts of the attacking enemy, and the reports of the fire-
arms in the defense.

In spite of the savagery of the music, there was an indescribable enthusiasm and an energy in the chorus that was
contagious, and in the pale moonlight, with the regular
splash of the paddles that kept an even accompaniment,
Ned found himself joining with the wild voices around him;
while Tim, not content with forming one of the chorus, improvised several verses in his native tongue in honor of
" Massa Ned " that produced roars of applause.

The rowers had worked well during the night, and at
about ten o'clock the canoes were within sight of the village to which they belonged,   Their approach was quickly

observed, and crowds of people assembled on the shore to welcome them on landing. Hardly had the canoes touched the sandy beach than they were dragged in triumph to the land, while the women yelled in honor of their arrival. The cargo was discharged with great rapidity by a numerous band, and was transported to the village, where Ned was quickly brought into the presence of the king. Drums were beaten, horns blown, and great rejoicing accompanied their return. The king was seated upon his leopard skins, and he received Ned with great courtesy, while the principal man of the hunting-party recounted the incidents of the expedition. Loud shouts of applause were raised at various portions of the narrative when Ned's hunting exploits were described; but when the attack and defeat of their old enemies were told with extreme energy the crowd could no longer restrain their enthusiasm, but broke out into wild yells of approbation, and crowded around Ned to kiss his hands after their peculiar fashion, by touching the palms with the tip of their tongues.

From that day Ned was almost as great a man as the king, to whom he acted as counselor and guide in all the affairs of his territory. He was thus enabled to materially improve the condition of the people. They, in common with all negroes, were exceedingly improvident, and neglected the cultivation of their fields, rather depending upon the precarious success of their hunting expeditions than upon a system of steady industry. Thus they were liable to periodical famines. Ned advised the king to insist upon the cultivation of a certain area of ground in proportion to the number of the population, which should insure a supply of corn that would render them independent of a bad harvest on the following season. Although this law was at first extremely unpopular it was rigidly obeyed, and in the course of a few months a large tract of land was cleared and brought into cultivation. Various improvements were gradually effected, and Ned, having almost supreme power, considered it to be his duty to ingraft, if possible, in the native mind a belief in a Supreme Being. At present they were utterly devoid of a religious sentiment; they had neither an idea of a God nor of a future existence.

The task of conversion that Ned contemplated with the sanguine hopes of youth was far more difficult than he had conceived. There was a complete void in the native mind of all spiritual belief; they had neither idols nor temples, but their ideas were concentrated upon things temporal, and they could understand nothing concerning a future state, unless the God of that future should grant them the desires of the present. Thus Ned labored in vain; his descriptions of spiritual blessings were listened to with apathy, or encountered with practical remarks that entirely paralyzed Ned's attempts at theological explanations. "If your God is good," replied his hearers, "why does he kill us? why do mothers die and leave their children helpless? If you say that He will hear your prayers, call upon Him that our cows shall give more milk, and that the locust shall disappear from our crops."

Ned could make no impression upon their obtuse intellects; they were too selfishly practical to understand the theory of religion; their only idea of a God was temporal benefit that could be derived from the object of worship; to pray was to solicit a favor; to ask for a reward; to beg for some special thing. Should this demand not be granted, where was the use of prayer? They did not require a God unless He would grant them all that they desired. When Ned endeavored to convince them of a future existence they flatly denied the fact, and, moreover, they did not wish to live again when they once should die. "To live twice is to die twice; nothing can last forever. We die, and all is ended like a fire that is burned out," declared one of the king's sorcerers with whom Ned attempted to argue. It was simply impossible to make the slightest impression upon their feelings; their belief did not extend beyond the power of sorcery, which had no connection with spiritual agencies; this faculty was supposed to be possessed by particular individuals who could produce rain, foretell events, and create spells and charms that would preserve the wearer from evil.

Ned was always curiously watched whenever he referred to the " Nautical Almanac." As he turned over each leaf the king's sorcerers would gaze intently at the mysterious characters on the page, and wonder at the hidden meaning. One day as Ned was examining the book for the declination of a star he happened to observe that an eclipse of the sun would take place upon a certain day, and that it would be visible from the position of the earth which he then occupied. He at once seized upon an idea by which he hoped to explain to his obtuse hearers the existence of a God. The sun was bright and the sky without a cloud when the king and his chief people, together with his sorcerers, were sitting beneath the shade of a huge sycamore, while Ned with his sextant took a meridian altitude; as usual his proceedings were watched with great curiosity. Ned had by this time learned sufficient of the native language to converse with tolerable ease, but upon difficult occasions he obtained Tim's assistance, who was now present as interpreter. Ned had just noted down his observation when the king asked why he regarded the sun and the stars so frequently?

"Because," replied Ned, " they are the most wonderful works of God; each star is a world; many are far larger than this globe; some revolve around certain suns, as our earth revolves round our glorious sun, which is the mainspring of all life."

Tim put this into his native tongue, and the king made a short remark.

"What does he say?" asked Ned.

"He says, ' Dat's a lie!' " replied Tim.

At this flat denial of the planetary system Ned felt the impossibility of an explanation. He accordingly requested Tim to ask the king for his opinion regarding the sun. The question having been put, the king consulted the sorcerers around him, and after an animated discussion Tim interpreted his reply.

"De king say, Massa Ned, dere no such ting as one sun; got plenty suns; ebery morning one new sun come up out of de 'arth same like a pumpkin; den he climb up de sky all day, and die when de night come, and bury 'sself in de ground."

"And what does he think of the moon?" asked Ned.

After considerable discussion between the sorcerers and the king, Tim replied:

"De king say, de young moon come very thin and hungry up in de sky; den she swaller a lot of stars ebery night and grow a little fat; den at last she swaller too many stars and swell 'sself out and bust herself right off 'xactly.

"Tim," said Ned, solemnly, " these people are stupid creatures, but tell them that there shall be a sign in six days from this time that shall teach them the truth. Tell them that the Great Spirit who made all things shall darken the sun, and the moon shall pass across its face."

"Massa Ned," replied Tim, thoughtfully, "p'r'aps better not tell 'em dat story; now de nigger b'lieve all Massa Ned's talk, but tell 'em one lie den upset de boat 'xactly!"

Ned was highly amused at Tim's honest but ignorant advice, and he had some trouble in explaining to him the nature of an eclipse; but when at length he showed him the exact hour in the "Nautical Almanac" at which the event would take place Tim at once appreciated the importance of the phenomenon, although half incredulous of the fact. He now interpreted Ned's prophecy that at the expiration of six days a sign should be seen that would prove the existence of the Great Creator, as the sun should be darkened at midday.

At this announcement the entire crowd raised a shout of incredulity, and the king having applied to his sorcerers, who shook their heads in derision, turned angrily toward Ned and spoke for some minutes in great excitement.

"Massa Ned," said Tim, "better not tell dat kind of talk. De king very angry; look what he say! He say: 'How de white man dare trow de dust in de king's eye? Tell him one big lie like dat make him look like one big fool 'fore his people!' Den de sorcerers say, 'Try him! if he make de sun black, all right; if he not make de sun black, kill him; dat's de trick!'"

At this moment loud murmurs arose among the crowd, and the king rose and retired with his sorcerers without taking the slightest notice of Ned. The sorcerers had always been jealous of Ned's supremacy, and they now seized the opportunity of prejudicing the king's mind against him; several gave advice that he should at once be put to death for having attempted to deceive by so gross a falsehood; but the king, having duly considered the matter, came to the conclusion that some great evil might befall the country should he take Ned's life unjustly, therefore it would be wiser to await the time when the phenomenon was to take place. Should Ned's prophecy be correct, there could be no doubt that he was a wonderful sorcerer; but should it fail, he would be an impostor who should be justly punished. In the meantime Ned was regarded with great suspicion.

On the morning of the promised day one of the king's cows had twin calves at sunrise; and upon the intelligence being received, he immediately arose in astonishment, and beat his huge drum to summon the attendance of his sorcerers and counselors. They had hardly arrived and heard the news from the king's own mouth, as he sat upon his leopard skins beneath the great sycamore, when a messenger rushed in haste to his presence and informed him that one of his wives had just presented him with twin boys. Loud murmurs of astonishment were raised by the assembled crowd, and the sorcerers immediately advised the king to beat the drum and summon the whole population to hear the wonderful news that the favorite cow and the favorite wife had produced twins almost in the same hour. Upon this the king beat the drum, and every headman of a town quarter replied upon his drum, which general summons was almost immediately followed by a crowd of people who collected from all quarters and sat upon the ground, completely thronging the open space around the sycamore.

The king now addressed the multitude, and explained that he considered this unexpected blessing must be the result of magic; that the white man had promised a wonderful sign upon this day, when the moon should darken the face of the sun, which they all knew must be impossible. If indeed this should take place there could be no doubt that he was the greatest sorcerer that had ever lived; but if, on the other hand, the sun should remain bright, there could be little doubt that the birth of two sets of twins was a sign that must be followed by the death of the white man. A loud cry of assent from some thousand voices followed the king's address, and a messenger was immediately sent to summon the attendance of Ned and Tim. Upon their arrival the decision of the king was at once made known to them.

"Dis a very bad job, Massa Ned," said Tim; "a foolish bus'ness 'xactly; if de sun not turn black, dese black niggers kill Massa Ned. What can do to change dis bus'ness, Massa Ned?"

"Don't be afraid, Tim," replied Ned; "the eclipse must take place between noon and one o'clock; we shall triumph if you translate what I tell you without flinching. Tell the king," continued Ned, as he rose and fixed a lance perpendicularly in the ground, "that before the shadow shall reach this line" (which he marked in the dust with his foot) "the sun will be darkened; and if my words are untrue he may drive that lance through my body."

With much reluctance Tim interpreted the ominous sentence, which was received by the king and the crowd in deep silence.

With much tact Ned then demanded of the king that twenty oxen should immediately be slaughtered and distributed to the multitude to celebrate the occasion.   A loud cheer burst from the crowd at this demand, and the king having assented, the oxen were shortly brought to the spot and slaughtered; at the same time a huge fire was lighted, and long strips of flesh were thrown into the blaze and divided when half cooked among the thousands present.

This savage feasting consumed the interval, and twelve o'clock arrived by the time that the remnants were cleared away and the feast was over.

Ned now rose from the ground and drove the people from the spot in which he had placed the lance, while he deepened the line with a burned stick that was to mark the limit of the shadow.   The king and his sorcerers now anxiously watched his proceedings; but none more eagerly than Tim, who dreaded the result of failure.

At first the lance threw no shadow, as the sun was vertical; but slowly the dark line began to lengthen toward the east.   Many of the crowd now stood up in their excitement to watch the gradually increasing shadow, while some attempted to gaze at the glaring sun that shone in a spotless sky with a power that appeared unquenchable.

The time passed on, and the shadow of the lance grew longer, and stretched nearer and nearer to the fatal limit. Tim's heart beat quick, and he fixed his eyes upon Ned in despair, as at length the dark line extended within a few inches of the mark.   The crowd began to murmur, and the sorcerers whispered to the king and shook their heads in derision of Ned's presumption.   The king's features assumed an expression of angry discontent as he leaned forward to see whether the shadow had reached the defined limit, at the same time he beckoned to a huge black whom Ned knew to be his principal executioner.   This brutal-looking fellow advanced with a rope wound round his waist, with which he was accustomed to tie the arms of his victims, and he smiled grimly at Ned, as though he considered him already in his power.

Ned himself began to fear that he had made some error in the calculation of the hour, as the shadow of the lance almost reached the line; when a sudden gloom, as though a passing cloud, caused the shadow to disappear. Ned sprung from the ground, and raising his extended arms toward the heavens he invoked the protection of the Almighty in a loud clear voice that produced a startling effect upon the king. The gloom increased, and shortly a black shadow veiled a portion of the sun, and a dark sphere crept slowly but surely over its disk. It was like the dim twilight of evening gradually increasing toward darkness, and the round black object could now be seen creeping across the sun, until merely a thin crescent of its light remained.

With a loud cry the king and all his people threw themselves upon the ground, and hid their faces in their hands; Ned and Tim alone remained standing amid the crowd of prostrate savages.

"Cry out, Tim, in your loudest voice," said Ned: "This is the work of the Great Spirit that the white man serves! this is the hand of his God!"

Tim repeated these words with great energy in the native tongue; the whole crowd groaned with terror.

"Cry out again, Tim," said Ned: "Rise up and the sun will regain its light!"

At these words the king arose trembling, together with some of his people; but the greater number still remained prostrate upon the earth. Ned then approached the king, and directed his attention to the sun, which slowly resumed its brilliant proportions as the eclipse passed away.

Turning to his chief executioner the king gave some directions, and before Ned could interfere the sorcerers who had advised his death were seized and strangled upon the spot, and their bodies were dragged outside the town to be devoured by the hyenas that prowled around the entrance during the night.

The king and all his people were now thoroughly convinced that the birth of the double twins was the work of Ned's magic, and he was looked upon as the most wonderful sorcerer that had ever been known; thus from that day he had the highest position in the state, and he was hourly tormented by applicants of both sexes for charms and talismans against every imaginable evil.

With all this influence he had been unable to inculcate the true ideas of religion in their savage minds. Some few indeed professed to believe in the Great Spirit that had darkened the sun; but the death of a goat or a cow was in all cases sufficient to dispel their belief in a God who allowed their cattle to die.

Prisoners in this land of heathens, and apparently cut off from the rest of the world forever, and from his loved home and Edith, we must leave Ned and Tim and return to other scenes.

CHAPTER XVII.

LEONTINE AT FALMOUTH.

FIVE years had passed away since the memorable day when the body of the brave Dick Stone had been committed to the waves, and the dismasted "Polly" had been towed into Falmouth by the British cruiser. The gallant defense of the lugger against a superior force, and the dexterous escape of the crew from a French prison through the intervention of Léontine, had made a great sensation at a time when hardly a week passed in England without some deed of daring that claimed the admiration of the world. Léontine, upon her arrival in Falmouth, had found herself in the position of a heroine rather than a prisoner, and upon her devotion and brave conduct being made known to the authorities she was rewarded by the freedom of her brother Victor, who was in the Falmouth jail. It was a happy day for Léontine when the order for his release arrived, and she was permitted to visit the prison and throw herself in her brother's arms as his unexpected deliverer. She had been kindly received by the mayoress of the town, who had supplied her with clothes, and after a few weeks' delay both she and her brother, with other French prisoners, were forwarded to France in exchange for British sailors who had been captured in merchant vessels.

In the meantime, while Léontine had been rendered happy, a cloud of misery had shrouded the cottage on the cliff at Sandy Cove. The few men who had remained among the "Polly's" crew after the fatal engagement returned to the cove from Falmouth, and the wailing of women in the little village for husbands and sons lost in the action was the first sound that had struck upon Polly Grey's ears a few minutes before Joe Smart arrived and gently broke the dreadful intelligence. Paul Grey had been seen to fall in the heat of the fight, and there could be no doubt of his death.

Polly was stunned by the shock of this overwhelming affliction; her heart was withered by the blow, as all the fond hopes with which she had comforted herself in her husband's absence were thus crushed forever. It was long before she could weep, and for days she sat upon the terrace wall and gazed at the barren sea, as though she still hoped that the well-known sail would reappear, and that she might once more clasp her arms around Paul's neck. She would then retire to her cottage and open the drawers and look at the clothes in which she had often seen him; everything that he had worn had become dear to her, and all that had been his was now sacred: there was the red woolen comforter that she had knitted for him, and this she took in her hands, and letting it fall upon the ground she fell upon her knees, and burying her face upon the bed, she sobbed bitterly:

"Oh, God! I am a widow, and my boy Ned is also gone!" she cried, as she appealed in the agony of her grief to Him for comfort.

In this hour of deep affliction she was not alone; she had a devoted friend and comforter in Edith, who loved her fondly, and who strove with affectionate care to soothe her distress. Mrs. Jones, who had passed through a similar bitter trial, showed her the greatest kindness, and it was resolved that the cottage at Sandy Cove should be sold, as the scene of the old home only served to awaken painful recollections.

When a few weeks had passed, and the first burst of grief was over, Polly mournfully turned her thoughts to her late husband's affairs. She was in debt to Captain Smart, as he had advanced considerable sums to liquidate various claims. She therefore proposed that all the effects, together with the cottage, should be sold, and that the "Polly" should be put up to auction at Falmouth, as it would be useless to enter upon the expense of the necessary repairs.

It went to Polly's heart to part with Paul's old lugger; but as Joe Smart was her counselor, and he declared it to be positively necessary, she at length decided, and it was sold at Falmouth for one hundred and sixty pounds.

The cottage remained; and this, together with the furniture and nets, etc., was shortly advertised for auction, and upon the appointed day the people of the neighborhood assembled at the sale. Joe Smart was not only the active manager of the affair, but he had determined to become the purchaser of the cottage, which would thus relieve him from the unpleasantness of receiving money from the widow of his friend Paul for sums that he had advanced. He therefore outbid the highest offer, and became the proprietor, not only of the cottage, but of the principal articles of furniture.

When all the little property was realized through the care and industry of Joe Smart, Polly found herself possessed of about three hundred pounds. Although the interest of this small sum was only fifteen pounds a year, it was sufficient for her simple wants, as she resided with Mrs. Jones and Edith at the rectory as one of their family, while Captain Smart called twice a week to arrange the accounts of the estate.

As some months passed by Joe Smart appeared to find an increase of business that claimed a greater share of his attention; at all events his visits became more frequent at the rectory, and Mrs. Jones felt at some moments qualms of uneasiness as she imagined that she was the object of more than his ordinary attention.

Years had passed, and the widow, Mrs. Jones, had long since thrown off her weeds, and had quite resolved that Captain Smart's constant visits to the rectory were directed specially to herself. In the meantime Polly Grey had never forsaken her mourning; although saddened in manner, she still retained the sweetness of her youth with much of her original beauty; she devoted herself chiefly to visiting the poor of the neighborhood, and attending to the village school, trusting that the charitable duties of life would afford pleasures to compensate in some measure for a past happiness that could never be renewed. The world might have supposed that Polly had no care except the recollection of old times, but she had one cause of deep anxiety— Joe Smart loved her. She was the love of his boyhood, and he had proved his affection through life with unvarying devotion; he had been her adviser and guide in Paul's absence; and since his death she was under countless obligations to him, as he had stood more in the position of a brother than a friend. It was natural that Polly should regard Joe Smart with warm affection; on the other hand, although he loved her with devotion, he almost dreaded to declare his feelings, lest she should consider that she was forced to accept him after the numerous obligations she owed to him. At length the warmth of his passion overcame this generous delicacy of feeling, and Joe Smart declared his love, and offered her as honorable and manly a heart as ever beat in a sailor's breast.

It was with real sorrow that Polly witnessed the effect of her refusal. The active and sprightly Joe Smart became an altered man; his early hopes had been destroyed by her marriage with Paul, and with unchanging love he had almost worshiped her; in the distress of her widowhood he had been her comforter, and he had looked forward not only to complete his own happiness but to render her once more joyous by making her his wife. Polly had received his declaration with tender regret, and she had gently but firmly assured him of her love and respect, together with her deep gratitude for all the acts of kindness and affection that he had bestowed upon her through so many years; but she implored him as her truest friend never again to speak of marriage, as she was determined to die a widow. It was in vain that Joe Smart endeavored to change her determination. Polly loved him as a brother, but she would not hear of marriage. She had frequently declared to him that she was happy in her present position, and that she considered it to be her duty to remain a widow. She cherished Paul's memory with deep affection, and she loved to talk with Joe Smart over all the daring acts that he had performed in his adventurous life; the last scene of his bravery, when he met his death, she dwelt upon with untiring energy and pride, and she expressed impatience upon only one point—for death, that she might join him once more in heaven and tell him how true and devoted she had been. This example of her affectionate constancy only served to heighten Joe Smart's admiration and love, and although firmly refused he still hoped that at some future time she would relent and sympathize with his feelings. In the meantime, Mrs. Jones had a great regard for the handsome one-armed sailor, who was always welcome at the rectory, and was received almost as a member of the family.

In this manner five years had passed away. Polly was

now a handsome woman of forty, and was but little
changed, but there was one in whom a few years had made
a wonderful alteration. It was on a fine summer Sabbath
that Polly was on her way to church accompanied by a
lovely girl about twenty years of age, who leaned upon her
arm and shaded her with her parasol from the glare of the
morning sun; her beautiful complexion and large blue eyes
would alone have made her striking, but her regular features and the peculiar amiability of her expression rendered
Edith a perfection of charms that is rarely seen.

She was seated between her mother and Polly Grey. It
was during the second lesson, when the church was perfectly quiet, a somewhat heavy footstep sounded in the aisle
as a person entered the door and walked straight toward
Squire Stevens's pew, in which he took his seat. The old
squire had been dead for some years, and nothing had been
heard of his son. The action between the " Sybille " and
the " Forte " had been a theme of glory for the day; but
having been duly chronicled among other brilliant achieve-
ments of the navy it had ceased to be of public interest—
the dead had been mourned for, and the crape had long
since been laid aside; and as the " Forte " had never been
heard of, she was considered to have been lost with all
hands.

Nothing had been heard of Ned. In those days there
was no regular mail from India, but the letters for England were dispatched by the first vessel that chanced to sail;
thus as the " Forte " had been rapidly repaired she was
the first upon the list, and Ned had expected to bring home
glad tidings of his arrival in person.

Edith had never forgotten the love of her girlhood, and
although time and altered circumstances had so far modified her sorrow at Ned's mysterious disappearance that she
had ceased to be absolutely unhappy, she rigidly executed
her promise, and every Sunday evening she strolled with
either her mother or Polly Grey through the church-yard,
and removed the weekly weeds from the neatly kept grave
beneath the cross marked " A lady unknown." Here she
would frequently sit and recall the time when Ned sat with
her as a lovely boy and talked of the future with the enthusiasm of his age; and then a blush would tinge her
cheek, and a tear for an instant dim her eyes, when she
thought of the warm kiss he had given her at parting, and

the vows that the determined boy had made to work his way to win her.

In the night these old scenes were frequently renewed in dreams, and all the characters that were associated with Edith's early youth reappeared in their accustomed places; her father, who had been so mysteriously murdered, she had sometimes seen as though in life; Ned had again sat by her side beneath the old mulberry-tree that was still her favorite haunt; she had heard Nero's bark as he came bounding toward her; and then, in wild fitfulness, the characters had become confused and faded into nothingness and mist, through which sometimes flitted the horrible figure of an old hag that resembled Mother Lee. The events of her youth had thus left a somewhat melancholy impression upon Edith's character. Although so beautiful, she was utterly unconscious of her attractions, and her chief happiness depended upon the duties of her daily life. Deeply religious, without appearing to be so except in her general conduct and unostentatious charity, she found an intense pleasure in ministering to the wants of the poor in her neighborhood, by whom she was almost adored. Her lighter pleasures consisted in sketching and attending to her flowers, and in charming the ears of all who heard her with her beautiful voice; for of all accomplishments Edith shone most prominently in music—in fact, many of the poor people of the village declared that the Church service would be nothing without Miss Edith's singing.

At the time that the stranger took his seat in the squire's pew all eyes were for the instant turned upon him, as it had long been vacant, and it was seldom that an unknown person of the upper class appeared in the secluded village. He was a tall and powerful man, exceedingly weather-beaten, with a face bronzed by exposure to a hot sun, and much freckled; his large sandy whiskers gave him an appearance of advance manhood; but upon closer observation his age might have been guessed at twenty-two or three. As Edith for a moment observed him she could not help thinking that she had seen his face before; but chasing all other thoughts from her mind, she directed her attention to the service until it was completed.

When the throng of the congregation passed down the aisle at the conclusion of the sermon Edith remarked that the stranger's eyes were fixed intently upon her; and hard-

ly had she quitted the church-yard in company with her
mother and Polly Grey than he turned round and approached her, and stretching out his rough hand in a
familiar manner, he exclaimed, " Edith Jones, have you
forgotten me?"

Edith paused, and without accepting his hand she examined his features for a few moments, and replied, " I
hope you will forgive my want of memory. I think I may
have seen you before, but I can not recall the occasion."

At that instant a peculiar, unpleasant expression passed
over the stranger's face, and Edith immediately recognized
Jem Stevens.

She could no longer withhold her hand, which he pressed
warmly as he exclaimed to her mother, " I am your old
school-boy, Jem Stevens, Mrs. Jones!"

The latter lady looked at him for some moments with
astonishment, and then grasped his hand warmly.

" How wonderful!" exclaimed Mrs. Jones. " Why, it's
only the other day, not seven years ago, that you left us a
mere boy! and you look five-and-twenty! and your poor
father's dead! and the Hall's empty! and all sorts of
changes have taken place! My poor husband, too! but of
course you know. But no, let me see, I don't suppose
you do. How should you? You have been away from
England all this time, haven't you? When did you come
back? Come along with us and lunch at the rectory, and
tell us all about yourself!" continued the voluble and impatient Mrs. Jones, who overwhelmed him with a string of
questions without giving him time to reply.

Now, if Mrs. Jones's thoughts could have been analyzed
as they rapidly passed through her mind, they would have
discovered a natural instinct that she would have at once
denied had the fact been asserted. It really did occur to
the mother in one moment that Heron Hall would be no
bad home for Edith! In another moment she reflected
that Stevens had been a bad character when at school; and
subsequently, with the rapidity of lightning, she concluded
that he must have changed for the better, and she therefore asked him to lunch. Stevens accepted the invitation
without the slightest hesitation, and offering his arm to
Mrs. Jones while listening to her long list of questions and
her rambling conversation, he accompanied them to the
rectory.

During luncheon Stevens made himself unusually agree-able to Mrs. Jones, and gave her a long description of his voyages, and of the engagement between the "Sybille" and the "Forte," in which he described his own prowess as having in no small measure contributed to the victory. Mrs. Jones was charmed; and when he narrated the subsequent shipwreck of the prize, and the destruction of all the crew with the exception of those saved in the cutter, which he declared he was the last man to enter, the amiable but weak lady was moved to tears. Stevens then described the voyage of the cutter to Madagascar, where the crew and himself were made captives by the natives, until, after years of suffering, he was at length released by a Portuguese trading-vessel that took him to Zanzibar, whence he had only arrived on the preceding evening.

There was much in the story of his adventures that interested Edith, but she little knew how much that would have been dear to her he had as yet concealed. He said not one word of Ned.

"What a wonderful change!" exclaimed Mrs. Jones, as Stevens took his departure late in the afternoon. "I never could have believed that so bad a boy would have turned out so nice a man; he is really a charming young man! and so clever! and evidently so very truthful! There was something in his way of telling his stories that seemed to assure one of their truth. Well," continued the enraptured Mrs. Jones, "as your poor father, Edith, used to say, 'When the wicked man turneth away from his wickedness' (and of course that meant the boy, as men are only bigger boys), 'he shall save his soul alive.' He was quite right. This is a wonderful instance of the works of Providence, my dear child, that you should observe attentively. How changed! He is a very nice young man! so very gentle-manly! and so good-natured for a man who has fought the French, and seen so much of the world. Not at all proud or stuck up; and remembered you, Edith, directly, and me, too; but of course a few years make no difference at my age; as Captain Smart remarked the other day, 'An English woman never begins to look her best till she is turned forty.' A very clever man is Captain Smart; very sound judgment; if he only had another arm there would be no one like him. Then, you see, Heron Hall and a very good fortune belong to him, now his father's dead. I don't mean to Captain Smart, as he died, or rather his father died, long ago, but I mean Stevens, as we used to call him, Jem Stevens. James is a very pretty name; one of the apostles was called James; I wonder whether they ever called him Jem? I hate abbreviations, but Jem is not so very ugly; not so bad as Ned, for instance," said the discursive Mrs. Jones, thoughtfully.

"Ned an ugly name! I would not wish for a prettier!" exclaimed Edith. "Edward is quite beautiful, and Ned is a lovable name, I think."

At this juncture Polly Grey joined in the conversation and warmly supported Edith, until the argument grew hot, and only terminated by each retaining her own opinion.

From that day Stevens's visits to the rectory became frequent. By a little judicious flattery he had succeeded in captivating Mrs. Jones; and as Edith, when a girl, had been the love of his boyhood, he shortly found himself hopelessly smitten with her now ripened charms.

Edith was fond of riding; and as she daily cantered her pony along the springy green turf above the cliff by the sea-side, she was invariably met by Stevens, who joined her in her ride. After some months the object of Jem Stevens's visits to the rectory had become unmistakable. He had offered Edith a beautiful horse, which she would have declined, but her mother had insisted upon her acceptance of the present.

Polly Grey had watched the growing intimacy with anxiety. She had no fear that Edith would lose her heart, but she was much afraid that the folly of Mrs. Jones would compromise her by giving Stevens an undue encouragement. She accordingly took an opportunity of speaking to Edith on the subject, and the innocent girl was startled at the idea that she would be expected to return Jem Stevens's love.

On the other hand, Mrs. Jones was determined that, if possible, the match should come off. She had really learned to like Stevens; and as he was the great landed proprietor of the neighborhood, and Heron Hall was a fine old place, she considered that it would be a very desirable marriage for her daughter; accordingly she one day placed the matter clearly before Edith's view.

It was late in the autumn, and as Edith and her mother were returning from their evening walk they were met by a gamekeeper, who had been sent by the young squire with a leash of pheasants for Mrs. Jones.

"Really, my dear Edith," said Mrs. Jones, as, after having thanked the keeper, she passed on, "I do not think that I ever saw a more lovable young man than James Stevens has become."

Edith said nothing.

After a pause her mother continued, "I think he is a deeply religious young man, and you know, my child, that your sainted father was partial to religious young men."

Edith still remained silent.

"I think, my dear Edith," continued Mrs. Jones, impressively, "I think—that is to say, I do not think, for I feel perfectly convinced—that the good and amiable, the warm-hearted and deeply religious, James Stevens, who is now the proprietor of the Heron Hall estate, comprising, I believe, about five thousand acres, is an unhappy man."

"Unhappy!" replied Edith, "what should make him so? Surely he has enough of the world's riches to be happy. He is young, and has no cares. What can you mean, mother?"

"I mean," said Mrs. Jones, "that he is in love. I can see it in his manner; he is nervous, Edith. You should be kind to him. Your poor father was nervous, and I believe he never would have proposed at all had I not given him some slight assistance. Not that I was too forward, quite the contrary; but some men require that particular kind of courage, although brave in other respects. James Stevens requires assistance, my dear child; you alone can afford it; you would make him a happy man. Think what a blessing it would be to confer happiness upon a fellow-creature . . . especially with a large landed estate in our immediate neighborhood," added Mrs. Jones, who had wound herself up to a pitch of enthusiasm.

Although Edith loved her mother, she was not blind to her peculiarities, and she had long suspected that she favored the suit of Jem Stevens. Edith was more sensible than most girls of her age, and she well remembered the character that he had borne at school. She had often heard her father remark that "the boy was the father of the man," and she thoroughly believed in the theory that the man was merely an older boy with the same natural character, perhaps in some instances modified by circumstances; thus, although Stevens was much improved, and made himself as agreeable as most men, she could not persuade herself to trust him. Even had she liked him, there was a something which Edith could hardly have defined in the fond recollection of younger days, when her girlish heart had loved Ned Grey. The mystery of his disappearance had given a romantic interest to his name, which, although half forgotten by many, was warmly remembered by her, and if she did not consider herself absolutely bound by the vows of a childish affection, she could at present feel no other. She did not positively dislike Stevens, at the same time she had no confidence in her mother's judgment. Accordingly she replied cautiously to her enthusiastic remarks.

"My dear mother," said Edith, "I can not think that you are serious. James Stevens has never said anything that would allow me to presume that I had gained his affection, neither should I wish for his love. Although he is certainly much changed and improved, I can never forget his conduct when a boy, and his unmanly hatred of poor Ned Grey. I do not believe that boys really change in character when they become men. They may be too clever and cunning to exhibit their true feelings, but the heart remains the same."

"Edith, my dear," replied her mother, "you can not possibly know anything about men's hearts, therefore your remarks are sheer nonsense. You must be guided by me in these matters. Do you not believe in conversion? Was not St. Paul converted? and did he not become one of the most faithful apostles? St. Paul must have been an exceedingly bad boy, if he ever was a boy, for we have nothing about his having been a boy in the New Testament, and I believe nothing except what is written in the Holy Book; but, anyhow, he was converted; therefore, why should not James Stevens also have changed in disposition —especially now that he has succeeded his father to the estate?"

"I do not doubt that you are right, mother dear," replied Edith, who knew that contradiction would be useless; "but I have not the heart to love any man. In fact, I never did feel an affection of that nature, except—" Edith hesitated.

"Except what? when? who?" asked Mrs. Jones in the same breath.

"Except long ago. I was very fond of poor Ned. He was only a boy of fifteen, and I a girl; but those were very happy days. Oh, mother! what can have become of Ned; I so often think of him, and wonder whether he was drowned, poor boy, with my dear old Nero and the negro Tim, on that day when they walked on the beach beneath the cliffs and the tide came in!"

"It is a dreadful mystery indeed," said Mrs. Jones; "but life is full of mysteries, my dear. For my part, I have always believed that he was drowned, since I changed my mind about his complicity in your father's death."

"That idea was too absurd, mother. My dear father, I know, wished to give me some advice about Ned Grey at his last moment, but he had no strength to complete the sentence. I have often thought of that sad night since I have been more able to form an opinion, and I feel sure that my father knew that I loved Ned, and he would have spoken to me about him."

"Well, my dear, he would, I am sure, have said it was a very foolish thing for two mere children to talk of such nonsense as love; and as to Ned Grey, a poor little found-ling, what in the world could he expect? He was a good boy certainly, but there are plenty of good boys. Now, a good position in life is of great importance to a woman, and a good boy has seldom a good position."

"Poor Ned!" sighed Edith; "the last time that I saw him his fine honest face brightened up, and his large blue eyes sparkled like fire, as he vowed that he would win a po-sition worthy of me. I can see him now; that manly and generous heart that could think no evil, and would even have forgiven Jem Stevens, and have made him his friend, if it had been possible to soften such a— Oh, mother!" continued Edith, "do not talk to me of Stevens! When I look back to the past and compare him to dear Ned Grey, and think what he would say were he alive and knew that you counseled me to love his enemy, I feel unworthy of him, and almost despise myself that I could listen to such advice."

The color had rushed to Edith's cheek, and the tears to her eyes, as she thus compared the past with the present, and clung with fervor to the warm feelings of her youthful days. "No, mother," she continued, "I should be grieved to displease you, but my heart is my own, and I can not give it to Ned's enemy."

Although Mrs. Jones was a weak woman, she was not devoid of a certain amount of tact; and upon seeing that Edith was not in the humor to be driven, she wisely determined to postpone her attack until a more favorable opportunity; at the same time, with a pertinacity peculiar to her sex, she was resolved not to give up her point, as she had persuaded herself that the match with James Stevens, of Heron Hall, would be exceedingly satisfactory. There were several families in the neighborhood who were anxious that their daughters should be intimate with Stevens; thus, although Mrs. Jones would not have confessed it to herself, she had a feeling of pride that would have delighted in their disappointment, should Edith triumph in the love-match. She accordingly closed the conversation with the following remarks, which were really sincere:

"My only child Edith, do not worry yourself when there is no cause; my only wish is to see you happy, and I advise you in order to insure your happiness as far as I can foresee. I do not press you to love James Stevens; but as I feel sure that he loves you, I give you timely warning with the advice that you should at all events not throw cold water upon his attentions. You may like him more when you know him better; and as to his having been Ned Grey's enemy, why, I feel sure, had he lived, James Stevens would now have been his friend."

On their arrival at the rectory Edith had a long conversation with Polly, whom she regarded as a second mother, but upon whose opinion she placed a much higher value than upon that of Mrs. Jones. It was natural that Polly Grey should regard Stevens with suspicion, as she had heard much of his character in former days from Ned, but on the other hand, as she felt convinced that Ned had been drowned by the rising tide, she had no feeling of jealousy should Edith form a suitable engagement with another person. Had Ned been alive, a marriage between him and Edith, whom she dearly loved, would have been the joy of her heart. She knew that Stevens's position in life would be considered, in a worldly sense, as an excellent match for Edith, but she was unable to give her other advice than to wait patiently until she should feel assured, not only of Stevens's sincere affection, but of his altered character.

Not long after this conversation Mrs. Jones took an opportunity of sounding Stevens upon his intentions. He at once declared his love for Edith, which he asserted had never varied since the time when he was a boy at school. He expressed his regret at the bad conduct of his younger days, and showed such contrition for the past that he entirely won the heart of the weak Mrs. Jones, who thereupon explained to him the state of Edith's feelings respecting Ned Grey, and the resentment that she felt toward him as his former enemy; could that dislike be overcome, she did not doubt that in a short time Edith's heart would soften toward him.

At this intelligence Jem Stevens turned deadly pale, which Mrs. Jones attributed to the violence of his affection; and hastily filling a glass of cordial from the sideboard, she insisted upon his swallowing it, which, as it was an excellent mixture of French brandy and bitters, he did without a moment's hesitation.

A few days after this explanation, Stevens, who daily rode over to the rectory, found himself alone with Edith in the drawing-room. She had been singing at the piano with such exquisite sweetness of voice and taste in execution that even Stevens appeared to be touched with the softening spirit of her music. Mrs. Jones had prudently left the room, and as Stevens was standing by Edith's side, as though enraptured by her song, he gently took her hand and raised it to his lips; at the same time he said:

"Forgive me, dearest Edith, but the fault is yours if I am wrong; your song has driven me from my senses! I can conceal it no longer! I love you to distraction! Say that I may love you, and do not make me miserable by a refusal!"

At this sudden declaration Edith hastily withdrew her hand from Stevens's grasp, and, rising from the piano, she regarded him fixedly and blushed deeply while, with a trembling but decided voice, she said:

"I can not say who you may or may not love, Stevens; I have known you many years, and I used to think that you loved no one but yourself."

"Dearest Edith!" exclaimed Stevens, "pardon me for the faults of my boyhood. I acknowledge that I was often

wrong and bad. Say what you will, and I will bear anything from your lips except a word of coldness! Those
days are long since past. Try me in every way, and see if
I am not changed; only in one thought and feeling I am
the same—I always loved you when a boy, and I love you
now dearer than ever, Edith!"

Edith was for some moments silent; then, fixing her
large blue eyes upon Stevens as though to read his inmost
heart, she said in a calm, low voice, as though she had
screwed her courage determinedly to the task:

" James Stevens, there shall be no misunderstanding between us; we have known each other too long for unnecessary concealment. You say that you loved me when a boy;
I did not love you, Stevens, but I did love Ned Grey—the
good, generous, dear Ned Grey—whom you hated. If Ned
Grey were alive, I would love no other; if he were poor, I
am rich, and I should esteem his love as of more value than
wealth or titles. I should consider it an honor to be loved
by one so good and true, so brave, and so incapable of a
mean action as was poor Ned Grey, your enemy!"

As Edith said this with almost fierce energy, her voice
choked with emotion toward the latter part of the sentence;
then, almost overpowered with her excited feelings, she
continued bitterly, " Oh, why did you hate him? Why did
you hate all that was good and true? one whom all loved?
one who tried to be your friend? one whom I loved, and
now you ask me to love you? Oh, Stevens, Stevens, we
had better say no more; you have mistaken your own feelings!" Edith hid her face in her hands to conceal her
emotion.

Stevens turned a ghastly white, and trembling from head
to foot, he suddenly seized both her hands, and drawing
them from her face while he held them firmly in his grasp,
he said in a hoarse voice, with intense earnestness, " Look
at me, Edith; look at me, and forgive me. If you loved
Ned Grey, I have a secret that will distress you, although
it will be a comfort."

The blush that had overspread her features suddenly
vanished, and a deadly pallor that turned her beautifully
chiseled face to marble seized upon her. Releasing her
hands from his grasp, she caught him by the arm.
" Speak!" she cried, in a deep, unnatural voice; " what

secret can Ned's enemy know that he has concealed till now?"

"I am not his enemy," said Stevens, who looked like a man guilty of murder. "I was his friend. It is now nearly six years ago that I was on board the 'Sybille.' We had left Plymouth the day before, and were bound for India. We lay to off this coast to send a boat ashore with our last letters; it landed near Sandy Cove. When it returned, two lads had been found upon the beach, and the boat's crew had kidnaped and pressed them into the service. A black dog was with them. The lads were Ned Grey and the negro Tim; the dog was Nero."

Edith stared wildly at Stevens, and sighed deeply. "Go on," she said, calmly, but despairingly.

"Ned was in distress, as he had no means of communication with home. The ship sailed to India. We fought a French frigate, the 'Forte,' which I have before described to you; Ned distinguished himself in the action, and he was sent to England in the prize with myself. As you know, she was wrecked. I have never dared to tell you his fate, as I thought it better to let it remain a mystery. When the ship was wrecked, I saw him and the negro swimming in the surf. I stretched out an oar from the boat to save him; at that moment a tremendous wave rolled over him, and neither he nor the negro appeared on the surface again. We rowed for some time backward and forward in hopes of finding him at the risk of swamping the boat, but we saw no more; both he and the negro were drowned."

Edith sunk upon her knees, and clutching vainly at something for support, she fell prone upon the floor.

For the moment Stevens thought she was dead, and, terrified at the result of his story, he rang the bell violently, and then endeavored to place her upon the sofa. In a few moments the house was in a state of excitement. Edith's mother, Polly Grey, and several servants, were endeavoring to restore animation. Some time elapsed before Edith recovered sufficiently to be supported to her room, when, as her mother was questioning Stevens below stairs, she threw her arms around Polly's neck and gave way to a burst of grief. When sufficiently calm to speak she described the dreadful story in a voice broken by deep sobs, and Polly Grey became overwhelmed with sorrow.

CHAPTER XVIII.

MRS. JONES COMPARES JEM WITH NED.

A few weeks after the supposed fate of Ned Grey had been described by Stevens, Mrs. Jones, who had felt deeply for her daughter, endeavored to renew the topic that was nearest to her heart.

"A very gallant act, my dear, of James Stevens! Indeed it was an act of generous devotion; he risked his own life, and nearly swamped the boat to save poor Ned. He was Ned Grey's friend, no doubt; or, if he were his enemy, the act was doubly generous. Sailors are always gallant fellows! I am glad that Stevens was a sailor. Should I ever marry again, I should like to have a husband of that profession." Here Mrs. Jones thought of Captain Smart. At the same time she continued:

"You should make up your mind, Edith, my child; if you loved Ned, you are under an obligation to Stevens for his brave attempt to rescue him. I am sure that the reason of his long silence upon Ned's fate was his excessive modesty; he was oversensitive, and feared to extol himself. Your poor father used to say in Latin, 'Modesty is a good sign in a young man.' I believe this is in the Latin grammar. I wonder they said nothing about modesty in young women; perhaps the grammar was only written for boys' schools. However, I am sure that James Stevens is a very modest young man, and I confess that I should like him as a son-in-law. Think it over, my dear child; forget the past as much as possible. We should always endeavor to escape from painful recollections; we should look forward, and not back. Ned Grey was a charming boy; a gentleman born, there can be no doubt. I always thought so from the moment that I saw his lovely mother's corpse; but then he would have had an up-hill life, full of cares and troubles. Death has released him. Think of him only as a dream of childhood, and make use of the present time. There are many worse than James Stevens, and in my opinion few are so good. Heron Hall is a beautiful place! I don't think I ever saw such magnificent oaks or so fine a park! Then I can come and see you, my darling child, and you will be perfectly happy!

Don't say no, my dear Edith! Trust to me, for I know better than you do what would tend to your future happiness; all this cloud about poor Ned will pass away, and the future will be as bright as sunshine.''

Edith listened abstractedly to her mother's glowing picture of her future life. Since the day when Stevens had described the shipwreck and Ned's death, she had certainly leaned more toward him than before, and, as his visits to the rectory had been constant, she had often led the conversation to the sad event, and dwelt with a painful interest upon all the details of the voyage from the time that Ned had first joined the '' Sybille.'' With consummate hypocrisy, Stevens pretended an extreme friendship for Ned Grey, and appeared to sympathize with Edith in her regard for his memory; he described, with well-feigned admiration, his courage in the action with the '' Forte,'' and also Ned's daring act in plunging into the sea to save his life when he fell overboard in the voyage from England.

These, and many other anecdotes in which Ned was concerned, served to awaken a common interest between Edith and Stevens which her mother lost no opportunity of supporting; nevertheless Edith's heart was as yet free from all warmer feelings than those of a friendly intimacy.

While Mrs. Jones was endeavoring to fan Edith's first spark of friendship into a brighter flame, Joe Smart was burning with love for Polly Grey. He had used every argument that the warmest passion could suggest to persuade her to overcome her scruples and to become his wife. Polly had always regarded Smart with great affection; but although their intimacy was upon a footing that rendered the slightest hesitation dangerous, she still resisted his proposals. '' Not until some eye-witness swears that he saw Paul's body buried, will I listen even to you, Joe Smart, who were Paul's best friend!'' such was Polly's final determination.

Joe Smart was in a difficulty; how would it be possible to procure the desired witness? It at length struck him that the only chance of obtaining information would be through Léontine, assisted by one of the lugger's crew, who might have obtained the name of the French privateer upon which Paul and Dick Stone had been killed. For this purpose Joe Smart set off for Falmouth, in order to discover from the authorities of that town all the particulars of the exchange of prisoners that had been effected when Léontine returned to France with her brother Victor; this information might be a guide to Léontine's address, and she might probably discover some members of the privateer's crew who could swear to the fact of Paul's death.

It was the eve of Christmas-day when Joe Smart started upon this important mission; the snow was falling heavily, and was drifting in the wind that howled across the hill-tops, and scattered the few withered leaves that at this late season still clung tenaciously to the oaks. It was bitterly cold, and Joe Smart's fingers were so numbed that he could scarcely feel the bridle through his thick woolen gloves; buttoned tight to the chin, he had raised the high collar of his great-coat, around which he tied a large red woolen comforter that Polly had given him at the last moment of starting. This was the same comforter that she had knitted years ago as a present for Paul when he should return. Thus secured from the weather, with a sou'-wester oil-skin cap drawn tightly over his head and ears, and tied beneath his chin, Joe Smart trotted along upon a powerful cob and took the road for Falmouth. The wind was directly in his face; and as the snow froze as it fell, the mane of his horse was covered, and the eyes of the animal, like those of the rider, were so pained by the drift that it bent its head upon one side to avoid the cutting wind. The earth was white with snow, and as Joe Smart rode along, he closed his eyes to avoid the needle-like sharpness of the sleet, trusting to the sure-footedness of his careful horse. It was about three P. M. when he passed along the road above Sandy Cove, and as he glanced below, he recalled to mind the old times when Paul's clipper lugger lay anchored in the bay, and Polly had always welcomed him at the pretty cottage on the cliff, which now was his.

"Poor Paul!" exclaimed Joe Smart to himself, " he was as gallant and fine a sailor as ever lived! God rest his soul, and bring happiness to his dear wife!"

Occupied with these thoughts, he trotted steadily along, meeting no object upon the road except a man well wrapped up like himself, who bent his head before the blast as his horse cantered quickly by like a phantom, leaving no sound of hoofs in the snow that was already many inches deep.

As Joe Smart is trotting onward on the road to Falmouth, we will follow the stranger whose horse was hurrying in the opposite direction.

There was no road visible, and the recent tracks of Smart's horse were rapidly disappearing beneath the fast falling snow, but without an instant's hesitation the stranger spurred his powerful black horse over the white surface, regardless of hidden holes or drifts; he was so muffled up that hardly his eyes were visible; and thus he galloped on until he arrived at the steep footpath that led down the cliff to Sandy Cove. Springing from his horse, he drew the reins over its head and led it carefully down the zigzag path. Upon reaching the bottom, he knocked at the door of a hut formed of a well-tarred inverted boat, in which windows had been fitted.

" Who's there?" cried a shrill woman's voice from within.

" Open the door, my good woman, for I'm very cold," said the stranger, " and I won't delay you two minutes."

The door immediately opened, and securing the reins to a hook upon which crab-nets were suspended, he left the horse outside and entered the hut, closing the door behind him to keep out the cold wind. The occupant of the hut was a woman of about forty-five, with several children, the youngest of whom was a boy about six years old.

" Does a man named Paul Grey live here?" asked the stranger.

" Paul Grey live here?" replied the woman. " No, I wish he did; he's dead long ago, poor fellow, on the day that my good man fell fighting by his side, and they're both now in heaven. This child," continued the woman, as she took the youngest by the hand, " was then at my breast when the news came home that his brave father was shot through. The ' Polly ' brought some wounded men to Falmouth, but my poor man lies in the sea; God only knows the spot."

" Poor fellow! he was a brave sailor," said the stranger; " but what of Paul Grey's wife; is she too dead?" he asked, in a hollow and uncertain voice.

" No, she's alive and well, poor soul, but always sorrowing," replied the woman. " She often comes over here and sees us all, and talks of Paul as though he were still alive; and she goes up to the cottage on the cliff, and looks upon

s

the sea as though she thought the ' Polly ' would return
again as in old times."

"Is the old boat gone, too?" asked the stranger.

"Lord bless you! the boat, the ' Polly,' do you mean?
Why, she never came back to the cove after the fight; she
was almost knocked to pieces, and was sold at Falmouth to
pay Paul's debts; there's nothing left except the cottage on
the cliff, and that was bought by the one-armed captain
when all the things were sold."

"Where is Paul's wife?" inquired the stranger.

"She lives at the rectory with Mrs. Jones and Miss
Edith, who are very good to her; they come here sometimes now, and never forget the poor, God bless them! I
don't know what my poor children would have done this
cold Christmas had it not been for all their goodness. And
the one-armed captain, too, is a good man, and helps us
often; he'll make Mrs. Grey a good husband if she'll have
him, but they say she won't listen to him till she sees where
Paul's buried. Poor soul, she's a good wife, and true as
steel."

"And is it supposed that she will then marry the one-
armed captain?" asked the stranger.

"Well, it's most likely to come off, I think," replied
the woman. "You see, Captain Smart was a good friend
of Paul's, and he did everything for Mrs. Grey when she
was mourning for him; he paid all the debts, and never let
her want; and she-must have a harder heart than flint if
she doesn't love the man."

"And the lad, Ned Grey?" said the stranger; "where
is he?"

"Ned Grey?" replied the woman. "Why, there's a
long story about Ned Grey; he was missing ever since the
night of Parson Jones's murder, together with the nigger
Tim, and was never heard of since. Some say as how he
did the murder, but that I know is a lie; but for all that
they issued a warrant to apprehend all three—Paul, and
Ned Grey, and Tim—because the old woman, Mother Lee,
witnessed against them."

"Parson Jones murdered!" exclaimed the stranger.
"Ned Grey and Tim missing, and never heard of! Mother
Lee witnessed against them! Good heavens, what shall I
hear next? Where is Mother Lee?" he asked.

"Why, you know something and yet know nothing of

these parts," replied the woman. "Mother Lee hated Paul, and she tried to wreck the ' Polly ' by lighting false beacons on the cliff in a sou'-west gale; her clothes were covered with tar, and she caught fire and blazed for half an hour till she was burned to a cinder; it was the devil's work for his own that night."

"Have the murderers of Parson Jones been discovered?" asked the stranger.

"Nothing has ever been heard of them," replied the woman; "but as two hundred guineas were stolen, and the same amount was found in a bag concealed in a cave in Paul's house, together with a lot of jewels and smuggled goods, suspicion fell upon his family, and a verdict of willful murder was brought against Paul, Ned Grey, and Tim, for whom a warrant was given."

The stranger made no reply, but, giving the woman a shilling, he left the hut, and once more encountered the fierce blast. Leading his shivering horse to the summit of the cliff, he remounted and galloped hard in the direction of the village.

After the first two miles were accomplished the dusky twilight gave way to darkness, and he was obliged to slacken his speed to a walk; it was about five o'clock when he first saw the lights twinkling in the windows of the village. Riding through the quiet and desolate street of snow, he halted at the door of the White Hart Inn and put up his tired horse. Leaving a small valise that was strapped upon the saddle in charge of the boy that took his horse, he left word that he should require a room, and without changing his clothes or in any way altering his muffled appearance, he at once disappeared in the darkness of the street.

In a few minutes he entered the garden gate of the rectory, and stealthily approached the house by the lawn; he observed a bright light at a window on the ground floor, and he was soon sufficiently near to distinguish the persons within. A large fire flamed up the chimney of the drawing-room, in which were several ladies. Having drawn near to the window, the suspicious-looking stranger peered through the glass. Mrs. Jones and Edith were unconsciously sipping their tea, while Polly Grey was seated by the fire in an arm-chair reading. Presently Edith rose from her seat, and, drawing her chair near, she placed her arm round Polly's neck and kissed her cheek.

The stranger left the window, and retiring as quietly as he had arrived, he passed round the house to the back door and rang the bell.

A woman-servant answered the summons, and for the first moment she screamed and slammed the door at seeing the tall, muffled figure that looked black and huge upon the white snow.

"Open the door, my good girl," cried the stranger, "and don't be afraid. I have a message of much importance to deliver to Mrs. Grey."

Once more the timid girl opened the door, and the stranger entered the house.

"Say to Mrs. Grey immediately," said the stranger, "that a sailor who fought with Paul Grey when he fell wishes to speak with her; but show me into a room, where I can see her alone."

The girl led him into the library, and leaving the candle she left him in the gloomy chamber while she delivered the message.

A chill of surprise thrilled through Polly Grey. "How strange," she said, "that Captain Smart should only have started to-day, and that already some person brings intelligence of the event! They must have met upon the road! What kind of person is this who has brought the message?" asked Polly.

"He's a horrid-looking man, mum, if you please," said the timid maid; "you can't see anything of him except a tremendous great-coat and a slouched cap, and a big comforter, and a shawl tied round his throat that hides his face altogether, and he looks as cold as shivers," continued the girl, "for the snow's sticking all about him."

"Is there a fire in the library?" asked Polly.

"Yes, mum, there's a blazing fire."

"Then tell him that I will see him immediately."

The girl left the room, and having said a few words to Edith and Mrs. Jones (who felt rather nervous at the idea of a strange person having been thus admitted into the house after dark), Polly shortly followed her.

As Polly Grey entered the library, lighted only by one candle that the maid had left, she at first hardly distinguished the dark and muffled form of the stranger, who was standing by a book-shelf. Startled for the moment as he came forward, she said, "I believe you are the person who wishes to speak with Mrs. Grey? I am the widow of Paul Grey."

The tall figure of the stranger for an instant appeared to reel forward, but almost immediatly recovering himself, he said, in a deep and trembling voice, "Widow of Paul Grey, I was with him in the fight when he fell."

Polly pressed her hand for some moments against her forehead in silence. "I know he fell," she said, "and that bravely; but I have always hoped against all hope that he was not killed, but perhaps severely wounded, and that I might again see him in this world. Did you see him die? Oh, tell me, I beseech you, all! Hide nothing from me; for now that I know he is really dead, I can bear to hear all concerning him."

"I came here to tell you all I know," replied the stranger. "I am a sailor who fought and bled in that hard fight when Paul and Dick Stone were both struck down. Poor Dick lies in the sea, and Paul—but I will not harrow your feelings, Mrs. Grey. I had heard that you were about to marry again, and that Captain Smart was to fill Paul's vacant place. I am an old friend of Joe Smart's, and I could wish him no better fortune than to win Paul's wife."

"Alas!" said Polly, "that such reports have stirred abroad. Captain Smart was Paul's best friend, and he has well befriended me, but never was woman truer to her husband's memory than I have been; it has been a life of sorrow to me for many a long year, and I have prayed to God for death as my greatest comfort, that I might see dear Paul again in heaven. I never can marry. I could not take another vow; my heart would break; but still, there could not be a better or more honest man than Captain Smart."

As Polly spoke these words, the tall, muffled figure drew nearer to her and said, in a hoarse whisper, "Mrs. Grey, did you ever dream of Paul? Did you ever pray for him when away?"

"Dream of him?" said Polly; "I have passed such nights of happiness with Paul in my arms, only to wake and find myself alone, and the world a wilderness without him; and I have prayed till my heart has nearly broken that God should restore him to me. I have lived in hope till now; and you, evil messenger, have broken the last reed on which I leaned, now I know that Paul is gone forever. Oh, God! why did I pray? Let me die rather than live this life of anguish!" said Polly, bitterly, in her despair.

For some minutes Polly leaned upon the mantel-piece and buried her face in her hands; the tall stranger also appeared to be affected. "And if," said he, "Paul Grey were to return to life, what would become of Captain Smart? Does he not love you, Mrs. Grey?"

"Question me no more. You have delivered your fatal message; I thank you for the sad news. You must be tired and hungry; I will order supper."

"The moment is too serious for thoughts of hunger. I have yet more news to tell, but I must have your thorough confidence," replied the stranger; "tell me plainly and upon your oath, does not Smart love you, and do you not return his love?"

"He does," said Polly; "and for him I have the affection of a sister. Since Paul's death he has been more than a brother to me, and he now asks for his reward—that I should consent to become his wife."

"What is your reply?" asked the stranger. "I must know all before I proceed with my story, for the end has not been told."

Polly hesitated. "Why should I be ashamed to declare my feelings? I can not love again as I loved Paul, and yet I owe Captain Smart so much that, although I have always refused his offer, I feel that if Paul's spirit could know all he has done for me and for his interests, he would himself counsel me to accept his hand. I have told him," continued Polly, "that I can hear no more until he can discover an eye-witness who saw my dear Paul's body buried. He has left this house to-day for Falmouth, and if you came from that direction you must have met him on the road. I fear you are the witness that would have rendered his journey unnecessary; would that I were dead!"

"Mrs. Grey," said the stranger, solemnly, and in a voice broken by his excited feelings, "prepare yourself for the remainder of my tale. Can you bear more?"

"I can bear anything," said Polly; "my distress has been so great that nothing can impress me now that Paul is dead; my feelings have grown callous."

"Then hear the end, and fortify yourself for what will

be as severe a shock as you ever had to bear. Are you prepared? Is your courage screwed to its highest pitch? Can you support the trial?"

"I can bear anything," she repeated; "only tell me quickly! What can be worse than all I know?"

The stranger sat down upon a chair, and apparently overcome by emotion for some moments, he leaned his elbows upon the table and buried his face in his hands. As though feeling oppressed, he unbuttoned his great-coat and loosened the numerous wraps around his throat; then standing up, he approached Polly, who calmly awaited his mysterious announcement.

In a deep, hollow voice, he said, "This is the end of my mission. . . . Paul Grey is still alive!"

"Alive! alive! alive! Oh, for God's sake don't deceive me! My Paul not dead? Where, where is he?" exclaimed the almost frantic wife.

"Here, in your arms, my own sweet wife! God has heard your prayers! I am Paul Grey!"

In an instant he had thrown off his overcoat and shawl which concealed his features, and once more Paul pressed his devoted Polly to his heart, while she clung around his neck in a paroxysm of joy that almost approached to madness.

CHAPTER XIX.

PAUL'S ACCOUNT OF HIMSELF.

WHEN the first violent shock of delight was past Paul explained in a few words the history of his captivity and escape. After the fight with the French privateer he had lain apparently dead upon the deck; but as the water which washed the scuppers in which he lay flowed over him when the vessel rolled, he recovered sufficiently to show some signs of life, which saved him from being thrown overboard. Upon arrival at Dunkerque he was sent to the hospital, and, when sufficiently recovered, he was committed to a French prison. There he lay for years, until one day he was informed that he had permission to see a friend who had called at the prison door. He reached the barred gate, and looking through the small iron grating, he saw to his astonishment and delight his old and true friend Léontine. Upon her arrival with her brother Victor in her native town, she had been arrested and confined in jail for a certain period for having aided in the escape of the prisoners; but upon the whole affair becoming known, it caused a great sensation, and she shortly received a pardon.

The unfortunate François, her old lover, who had been on guard when the prisoners escaped, and who had borrowed a comrade's uniform and arms to aid in her disguise for the nocturnal meeting, had been severely punished; and Léontine, having recovered from the loss of Dick Stone, had rewarded the hardly treated François with her hand. They were married, and François soon forgot his hardships in the delight of his gallant prize.

Some years afterward François, who had risen to the rank of lieutenant, happened to meet at a *café* a French sailor who was describing to a comrade an action in which he had been engaged with an English vessel. Listening attentively to his story, he heard him relate the daring manner in which the English had boarded the French privateer, together with the escape of the disabled lugger, owing to the arrival of a British cruiser. François naturally concluded that this was a description of the action with the " Polly," and joining in the conversation, he gave an account of the manner in which Paul had escaped from prison and recaptured the lugger, when Léontine had played him the trick long since forgiven. He then heard that Paul had recovered from his wounds and was confined in prison. From that moment Léontine was determined to obtain Paul's release, but she could not discover the place in which he was imprisoned. At length she found that he was in Dunkerque Jail. Thither the faithful Léontine at once set off and found him as described. She at once went to the governor of the jail and related the circumstance of her brother's release and the kindness she had received in Falmouth, and she besought him to forward her petition for Paul's release to the proper authorities. Struck with Léontine's romantic tale, and with her extraordinary beauty and energy of character, the governor exerted himself in Paul's behalf, to whom he had taken a special liking from the moment that he had entered the prison, as he had heard of his daring behavior in boarding the privateer. After much delay Paul was included in a list for an exchange of prisoners, and was sent to England. Landing at Falmouth, he had hastened toward his old home.

In a few days the news of Paul's return was spread throughout the neighborhood. Edith shared in Polly Grey's happiness. Often had Polly mourned on Christmas-day, when others seemed so happy, and she was miserable, but now she had spent that day together with her long-lost husband. They had knelt together in the church, and poured out their hearts to God in humble thanksgiving for a joy that few in this world can know. But joy was not for all. Slowly and mournfully a powerful brown cob, tired with its journey in the deep snow, carried its rider along the road from Falmouth to the rectory. Although the wind was cold and piercing, his great-coat was unbuttoned, his throat was unprotected, and the empty sleeve of the left arm dangled neglected at his side. Joe Smart had heard the news, and was on his return; he was on the way to welcome his old friend Paul, and to take a farewell forever of Paul's wife. He could not trust himself again to be her friend; he knew that his happiness in this world was gone.

Thus broken down in spirit, Joe Smart traveled slowly on. He did not feel the cold, for the hard frost was nothing to the chill that was in his heart. He loved Paul, and he had thoroughly believed him dead; thus he had never curbed his passion for Polly Grey, and his whole soul had become devoted to that one object of his affection. Paul's return was an avalanche of misery to him that had crushed every hope. At the same time his love for Polly was so thoroughly devoted and sincere that, even in his misery, he rejoiced at the intensity of happiness that she must feel at her husband's resurrection from the dead. He dared not think of the future; to him the world must be a blank. Thus he rode slowly on.

It was late in the evening when Joe Smart reached the rectory and warmly pressed his old friend's hand. He would not trust himself to see Paul's wife, but he wrote her a letter of farewell, full of touching expressions of affection, concealing as much as possible his own distress, and dwelling more upon her future happiness. He explained that he had not the courage to meet her to say "Good-bye," and he concluded by begging her to accept from him, as a souvenir of many happy days, a present of

the cottage on the cliff at Sandy Cove that he had purchased at the sale of Paul's effects; in which he trusted
once more to see her and Paul together at some future day
when time should have lessened the agony of his disappointment.

It grieved Paul's heart to see his friend's distress.
" Cheer up, Joe, my dear friend, and more than brother," he said, as he almost crushed his hand in his affectionate but iron grasp.   " It might have been better had I
died, but I trust to live to repay you, if ever possible, for
all the kind acts and generosity you have shown to Polly.
You have been sorely punished, my dear Joe, by my return; but believe me how I grieve to see you feel so keen-
ly.   You must come and see us often in the old place, and
Polly will welcome you with all her heart, as I will; and
we will forget that 1 was lost, and we shall live as we did
before; the door always open to you as our truest friend."

Joe Smart choked in his attempt to reply to Paul's feeling words; but biting his lips until the blood flowed to sup-
press the emotion which this kind sympathy had awakened,
he could only return the pressure of Paul's hand, and hurriedly left the house.   As he rushed from the front door
in the dark he came in sudden contact with some person
who fell with the shock, and almost immediately afterward, although he had apologized, he felt a smart blow
with a heavy whip across the face.   Stung with the pain
and with the unmerited insult, Smart instinctively struck
his adversary a severe blow on the eye with his only fist,
but quickly found himself closed with in return.   This
had happened in a few seconds, and as Paul had followed
Smart with the intention of insisting upon his return, he
opened the door and found him engaged in a struggle with
Jem Stevens.

" Halloo, what's the row?" exclaimed Paul, as he col-
lared Stevens in his powerful grasp and separated the com-
batants.   " What? fight with a one-armed man, you coward?" saying which, he gave Stevens a push which sent
him staggering some paces distant.

Stevens was half blind with passion when he found that
his adversary was Joe Smart, of whose position at the rectory he had been for a long time jealous, as he imagined
that he counseled Edith against his proposals.   Turning
quickly upon his heel, he exclaimed, " You shall hear more

of this!" and retreating to the stable, he remounted his horse, muttering, "Coward he called me; that ruffian, Paul Grey!"

On the following morning, as Paul was sitting at the breakfast-table with Polly, Mrs. Jones, and Edith, a ring was heard at the front-door bell. In about five minutes the door opened, and several constables entered the room, one of whom exhibited a paper, and, laying his hand upon Paul's shoulder, he said, "I apprehend you, Paul Grey, upon a charge of willful murder." This was the original warrant for his apprehension that had been issued many years ago when Parson Jones was murdered.

It was useless to resist; however false the charge, there could be no doubt that the warrant was strictly legal; and Paul, rising from his seat, took leave of Polly, saying, "I shall not be long in settling this farce." He accompanied the constables, who led him before a magistrate. That worthy functionary was James Stevens, Esq., of Heron Hall.

* * * * * * *

We must now change the scene and return to Africa at a period of about twelve months before Paul's return.

It was the rainy season in the country where we left Ned and Tim, but no rain had fallen. Not a drop of dew moistened the ground; but, parched and withered, the whole land was a bright yellow glare of sunburned grass. In a large circular hut sat a tall, handsome young man of about twenty years; by his side was a clean-skinned, powerful young negro of about the same age; these were Ned and Tim. They were dressed in clothes of beautifully prepared skins divested of the hair, resembling chamois leather. These they had themselves manufactured by tanning with the fruit of a mimosa, as their stock of European clothes had long since disappeared. The king had been dead for some time, as he had been murdered by his subjects, and Ned had been, much against his will, elected chief. This was a dangerous position, as few of their governors had died a natural death; but they had generally been sacrificed to some popular superstition. Ned was at the present time in a state of great perplexity, as the people were vainly crying for rain.

Daily the sky clouded over, but when all hopes were high, the clouds would gradually disappear without yield ing a drop, and the sorcerers had declared to the people that Ned withheld the rain by magic. Added to this un- lucky drought, a murrain had broken out among the cattle, which had probably originated from the absence of green fodder; the cows died in great numbers, milk was hardly to be obtained, and the people dreaded a famine, as they would be unable to sow their crops in the burning soil. They flocked to their sorcerers, who, having always been jealous of Ned's supremacy, now boldly declared that it was he who inflicted this curse upon the land.

Thousands of natives congregated from all parts of the country, and they determined to wait upon Ned in a vast assemblage to petition him for rain.

It was early morning when a hum of distant voices, to- gether with the beating of drums and blowing of horns, approached the town. Quickly the drums of many head- men responded to the call, and an immense body of people assembled beneath a grove of large fig-trees or sycamores upon a clear spot outside the palisades, as there was no open space within the town sufficiently large to contain them. In a short time the sorcerers waited upon Ned, and requested him to appear before the people.

It was not without some misgiving that Ned, accom- panied by Tim and old Nero, responded to the call. The dog was no longer the bounding and playful animal of former days; his muzzle had grown gray, and his expres- sion had become solemn; while his eyes, deeply sunk within his head, showed the effects of age. A loud shout from the multitude welcomed Ned's appearance, and he took his seat beneath a sycamore, with Tim by his side. There was no shade, as the long-continued dry weather had withered the leaves, few of which remained upon the trees.

As Ned sat down, the air rang with the shouts of many thousand voices:

"Rain! rain! great chief. Give us rain, or we all per- ish!"

These cries continued with increasing vehemence, until the excitement became so great that many brandished their lances in menacing attitudes, as though to imply that they would have recourse to violence should their demands not be complied with. Ned had now mastered the language so as to speak it fluently; and as the tumult increased, he was about to address them, when Tim interrupted him with advice.

" Massa Ned, dese niggers not like us. Dey all same like a mad bull; just give 'em an idea, dey knock dere heads against it. Now dey got de idea ' no rain come cos of Massa Ned;' now dey run dere heads slick at Massa Ned, and kill us sartain!"

" You are right, Tim," said Ned, " they are merely brutes in impulse, and I fear we shall be the victims of their ignorant passions. I see no hope except in delay. We must endeavor to keep them patient for a few days, and take the chance of rain."

" De rain not come, Massa Ned. I know de custom of de sky in dis bad country; four or five years p'r'aps de rain come, den one year come dry as tinder; not a drop of water. Den de niggers kill de king and all de rain-makers. Dis year no rain come, and we be killed if not run away. Tim don't care for self; but bad job for Massa Ned."

" Escape is impossible," said Ned. " How often would we have escaped from this hateful land if it had been prac-ticable? Our only chance would be Zanzibar; that is at least five hundred miles from here. How could we accom-plish such a journey without means of any kind to pass through the various tribes, all of which are hostile to each other?"

" I know all dat, Massa Ned," replied Tim. " P'r'aps we get killed on de road, but dat's only p'r'aps; if we stop here dere's no p'r'aps, only killed for sartain. If we not look sharp," continued Tim, " we be killed to-day! Look at de niggers now, see how dey cuss, and hark what dey say—' Kill de white man and de black dog!' Now dey t'ink de poor Nero stop de rain, stoopid niggers!"

At this time the excitement had reached so high a pitch that, as Tim had described, the crowd were shouting for the death of Ned and the dog, as strange creatures that must have brought the calamity upon the country.

" I know de trick, Massa Ned!" exclaimed Tim sudden-ly, when the tumult was at its height, and one man had in his excitement thrown a lance at Ned, which he narrowly escaped. " Massa Ned holler out, ' Stop de row! de rain's a-coming!' Holler quick! or we be killed sartain!" con-tinued Tim, as another lance whizzed past his ear.

On the impulse of the moment Ned rose from the ground, and, throwing his arms high above his head, he shouted in a loud voice that the people should be silent. The tumult quickly subsided, as Ned's tall and commanding figure produced a sudden effect, and they expected that he would speak.

"Now, Massa Ned," said Tim, quickly, "tell 'em you call de rain in six days, but you want to go to fetch it. Tell 'em you know de place where de rain's shut up. De niggers, stoopid fools, believe all dis. Den we get six days' start, and cut and run. Dat's de trick 'xactly."

Ned qualified Tim's sagacious idea, and having obtained perfect silence, he addressed the multitude in a forcible speech, blaming them for certain crimes that they had committed, and declaring that the drought was thoroughly merited for the murder of their late king. He continued by threatening them with the vengeance of the Great Spirit should they persist in their determination to sacrifice him and the dog, and reminded them that, although the drought and the murrain had visited them, the locusts and the small-pox had not yet arrived—two plagues infinitely worse than the former—that would punish their offenses. Ned concluded by demanding six days of seclusion, during which he was to be left entirely alone with Tim and his dog, in a grove of palm-trees about three miles from the town on the borders of the lake, as he wished to observe the sun. Should no rain fall before the sixth day, he offered to become a sacrifice for the good of the people.

Wild shouts and immense confusion followed this speech. Some of the people would have agreed to the proposal, while others declared that he should be put to death at once. The tumult rose to such a pitch that the riot became general, and the parties were proceeding to blows, which would certainly have ended in the slaughter of Ned had not Tim promptly struck several loud blows upon the great drum, which important signal restored tranquillity. Tim did not lose the opportunity, but at once addressed the people, and, being thoroughly conversant with their ways, he made a proposal that met with general approbation and satisfied all parties. As he explained this suggestion to Ned: "I tell dese black stoopid niggers, Massa Ned, dis much. Says I, 'You all right on de one side, my good fellers, and you all right on de oder side, too.

Now, if everybody all right, nobody all wrong; dat's a fact 'xactly! Now one side say, 'Kill him to-day'—quite right; but de oder side say, 'Wait six days'—quite right. Now I say, 'Make it half of de one and half of de oder—dat's de proper way, den everybody's right. Wait t'ree days 'stead of six; dat's de trick! den nobody's wrong and everybody's right!' Dat's de way to talk to de niggers, Massa Ned. Now dey understand; now dey quite pleased. If get de rain in t'ree days, very good fun; if not, dey kill us all, dat very good fun too, for de niggers; but we'll cut and run, and get de start for t'ree days; dat's de trick 'xactly."

Tim's speech had completely satisfied the savages. The shouts lately so angry quickly turned to those of merriment, as they all looked forward to rain within three days. Ned lost no time in preparation, and determined to start at once.

To avoid suspicion, it was arranged that the natives should carry a certain amount of provisions to the grove of palm-trees by the lake; shelter was not required, as there was neither dew nor rain. It would be impossible to carry much, as Ned determined to make forced marches; therefore the two old knapsacks were quickly arranged with longer straps that would fit the broad shoulders of the two powerful young men, and these were packed with strips of dried meat, with a quantity of native bread that, dried in the sun, would serve in the place of biscuit during a long journey. The sextant, compass, etc., and ammunition, completed the outfit; but of the original stock of the latter no more than sixty rounds of ball cartridge remained, and the shot had been expended years ago. The cartridges were divided between them; and with their two double-barreled guns with new flints, and a sharp cutlass each, they accompanied the natives to the palm-trees, where they were to be left in perfect seclusion for the stipulated three days.

The natives quickly left them, and as the moon would be nearly full, Ned determined to start shortly after sunset.

At that hour, when the natives were engaged in penning their cattle, which they had driven within the kraals, Ned and Tim departed, followed by old Nero. They knew the country for the first twenty miles; thus they accomplished that distance in about five hours; and then continued to march throughout the night over vast plains of withered grass interspersed with large trees.

By sunrise on the following morning they had marched about forty miles, and had gained a fair start of the natives in case they should be pursued. During the entire distance they had found no water, but happily shortly after day-break they arrived at a ravine, which, although a formidable torrent during the rainy season, was now reduced to a dry rocky bed, with small pools of clear water at intervals. Having bathed in a pool, they slept beneath an overhanging rock which gave a delightful shade, which was the more grateful as the trees were all devoid of leaves, owing to the intense drought. They woke at about two P.M., and immediately buckled on their knapsacks and refilled their goat-skins with clear water for the march.

Ned's greatest anxiety lay in the want of water. The country was entirely unknown to him, and he knew that ferocious tribes of negroes existed between them and Zanzibar, but these he did not fear so much as a frightful death by thirst. The entire country was burned up, the underwood in the jungles was dead, the trees leafless, and the plains were a bright yellow; the ground was cracked in all directions into broad and deep fissures, and the ravines that generally held water were completely dry. Trusting in Providence, but finally sensible of the extreme danger of the journey, which was simply a last resource to escape certain death, Ned led the way.

They had hardly started, when he perceived a large herd of buffaloes coming across the plain toward the ravine, and raising a cloud of dust from the parched ground as they galloped toward the drinking-place. As fresh meat for themselves and the dog was sorely needed, Ned determined to obtain a shot if possible; accordingly both he and Tim concealed themselves, and watched the herd of thirsty animals, who now rushed headlong to the water. Presently they arrived at the margin of the ravine, down which they hurried in a dense mass, and Ned distinctly heard the clattering of the loose rocks which fell as the numerous hoofs dislodged them. Creeping quietly toward the spot where the herd had disappeared in the ravine, Ned reached the precipitous bank, accompanied by Tim and Nero. Looking cautiously over the edge, he observed a herd of about a hundred buffaloes wallowing in the pool below. As he required meat of a good description, he selected a cow instead of a bull, and aiming steadily at the shoulder of one that stood about fifty yards distant, he fired.   For the moment she fell to the shot, and Nero, with his usual courage, dashed forward to the attack and seized her by the ear. Recovering on the instant, the buffalo sprung upon her feet, and tossing her head with immense force, she swung the dog high in the air. Unfortunately poor old Nero had lost many of his teeth, and the ear slipped from his hold. Falling from the height of several feet, the buffalo with great adroitness caught the dog upon her sharp-pointed horns and bored him upon the ground.   The herd had in the meantime remained standing in astonishment, as they had never before heard the report of a gun, neither could they distinguish the cause; but as they saw the wounded cow attacking the dog, they were seized with a sudden fury, and one and all, headed by an enormous bull, charged desperately forward upon the unlucky Nero.   There was a savage and tremendous tumult of hoofs and horns.   The wounded cow that was streaming with blood from the shoulder became the object of attack as well as the dog; she was bored to the ground by a phalanx of maddened animals, who now fought with each other in their rage, while others tossed in the air and alternately trampled under their feet a black woolly mass that had entirely lost the shape of a dog.   All this had happened so quickly that Ned had neither time nor power to render assistance.   The rage of the buffaloes was such that he fully expected they would turn their attack upon him should he be discovered; accordingly he dared not fire until both he and Tim had climbed to the top of a large fragment of rock about seven feet above the level of the ground on the margin of the ravine.   From this secure position he fired at the shoulder of a large bull in the midst of the mélée, now within twenty paces of him. For an instant the struggle ceased, and the entire herd, leaving the cow dead upon the ground, charged recklessly toward the spot where the smoke of the gun hung heavily among the bushes. It was well that Ned and Tim had taken the precaution to secure a strong position; the herd came thundering up the steep bank of the ravine, and as a wave is broken by a reef, so the dense body divided on either side the rock upon which Ned stood, against which they were pressed by the weight of those behind. Although ammunition was scarce, Ned could not resist a downward shot in revenge at the neck of a huge bull, whose tough sides rubbed against the rock close to his feet as he rushed blindly past; the ball passed through the spine, and he fell dead, the rest of the herd galloping over his body. Following their mad impulse, the herd dashed wildly on, they knew not whither, and shortly nothing could be distinguished but a dense cloud of dust upon the plain as they disappeared in the distance.

Ned and Tim jumped from their stronghold and ran quickly down to the spot where the poor dog lay, crushed to a mummy by the infuriated herd.

It was Edith's dog, and Ned recalled the day when he left the rectory and saw her for the last time, and Nero came bounding after him. From that moment the dog had been the faithful companion of all his wanderings, and the partaker of every danger and hardship; he had slept by his side at night, and watched over his safety; and, next to Tim, Nero was his greatest friend. His soft curly coat was now a mass of matted gore, and nothing remained that bore the faintest resemblance to the fine old dog that a few minutes before was full of courage and vigor.

Tim fairly blubbered like a child as he and Ned dug a hole in the sand with two stakes that they had sharpened with their cutlasses, and they buried their faithful companion. As they covered the grave with large stones and thorn-bushes to prevent the body from being exhumed by hyenas, Ned lingered for a few minutes on the spot, and then sorrowfully buckled on his knapsack and slung his water-skin upon his shoulders. Taking up their guns, they silently commenced their dreary march; neither could speak.

It was intensely hot, and not a cloud shaded the sky. They had cut a few steaks off the buffalo, and the air was already swarming with vultures that had observed the carcasses from the immense altitudes where, themselves invisible from the earth, they soared throughout the day upon their untiring wings, and watched for prey beneath with telescopic sight.

They had marched for about four hours over arid plains almost devoid of trees, when they arrived at a broad belt of forest; passing through this, they entered upon a vast tract of high tangled grass that was nearly double the height of a man; this was perfectly impenetrable, and, after having vainly endeavored to discover a path, Ned came to the conclusion that they must alter their course, or trust to a broad track that had been made by the trampling of elephants. Tim suggested that the latter might possibly lead them to water. It was nearly dark; and after wandering fruitlessly upon the tracks which turned in various directions, there was no other course than to halt for the night. They now felt the loss of their good friend Nero, who had always been their faithful sentry; and fearful of sleeping without a watch being kept, it was resolved that, although tired, they should take it in turns to keep guard throughout the night. They cleared a small space in the high grass, made a fire, upon which they threw for a few minutes their strips of buffalo meat which served for their dinner, and Ned first went to sleep. The moon was bright, and had the country been clear, the night would have been the most favorable time for marching. Tim, being on guard, had taken his station on the top of a large white ant-hill about twelve feet high, at the foot of which Ned was asleep; from this elevated position he had an extensive view of the bright yellow plain that glistened in the moonlight like burnished gold. Lions were roaring in the distance, but Tim was so accustomed to this sound that it made little impression upon him, and for about an hour he kept a vigilant watch. As Tim was a Christian, he never omitted to say his prayers, and it suddenly occurred· to him that he had forgotten his evening devotions; accordingly, as he sat on guard on the conical summit of the ant-hill, he repeated his accustomed prayer, and, being thoroughly fatigued, he fell asleep before he had actually concluded it. How long he slept he could not tell, but he suddenly woke, as what he imagined to be the bright sunlight was streaming in his eyes. A vivid glare shone upon the sky, and an intense line of light streamed along the surface of the earth. Recovering from his sleep, Tim shouted "Fire!" and at once scrambling down from his high post, he drew his sharp cutlass and set to work like a madman to mow down the high grass by which they were surrounded.

Ned woke in an instant, and, quickly made aware of the danger, he joined Tim in his work with a desperation incited by the extremity of the moment. The wind was blowing strong from the direction they wished to pursue on the following morning, and the prairie being on fire, an immense volume of flames that extended in a long line that appeared to have no limit was driving toward them at a prodigious rate. As Tim had been asleep for some hours, he had not observed the fire until it was within a mile of their position, and the bright light had awakened him.

Keeping the ant-hill for a center, they now worked desperately, and cut down the grass in a circle until the mound stood in a clear space about seventy feet in diameter; they now dragged the cut grass to the leeward side of the circle, and piled it against the wall of dried and inflammable material that was to be ignited to clear a space before them. Taking a brand from their fire that was still burning, Ned lighted the pile to leeward, and they both immediately retreated to the windward side of their cleared circle. The grass was so intensely dry that it burned like flax, and the flames at once leaped upward to a height of about thirty feet with a loud rushing sound, accompanied by cracking reports resembling pistol-shots, as the reedy stems burst in the blazing fire. The heat was almost insupportable, and Ned was forced to retreat into the high grass to windward, while Tim sheltered himself behind the ant-hill, as the flames spread with wonderful velocity, and, swept by the strong breeze, they licked up the grass before them and rushed forward, leaving a dark and level surface behind them like a pall of black velvet, in which flared the withered stumps of numerous trees.

In less than ten minutes several acres of ground were cleared by the fire to leeward; and although the grass had ignited around the circle, so that Ned was forced to join Tim at the ant-hill, it burned slowly to windward, and did not produce the distressing heat to which he had at first been subjected.

The warning had been short, and had Tim slept a little longer, nothing could have saved them from destruction. The ground left by the receding fire was scarcely cool enough to be endurable by the feet, when dense volumes of smoke rolled over them from the advancing fire, accompanied by a terrific roar, as the flames, fanned by the wind, leaped forward as though rejoicing in their power to annihilate all before them. Ned and Tim were obliged to rush far forward upon the burned ground to avoid suffocation.

The sight was grand in the extreme, as the whole earth appeared to be in a blaze of fire further than the eye could reach. Presently it reached the cleared circle, and in an instant the flames ceased in that portion of the line, which, now broken, swept by on either side, and vanished as it met the limits already burned. They were safe! And as Ned looked forward now in the rear of the advanced line of fire, the earth was cleared of every particle of vegetation, and was covered with a light black ash, as though with a light fold of crape.

There was no longer any danger to fear from either man or beast, and the two tired and blackened figures, Ned and Tim, lay down and slept till morning.

They rose before sunrise, and, as the ground was even and perfectly cleared from all obstacles, they marched rapidly by compass, steering direct for the position of Zanzibar. Ned had his chart with him that he had preserved throughout his first journey from the coast, which he knew to be correct; therefore there would be no difficulty in discovering the right position, provided that the nature of the country should permit a direct line of march. Aware of the great importance of speed, they pushed on at a rapid pace throughout the day, and only halted when they arrived at water in a beautifully wooded hollow at about four in the afternoon. Ned calculated that they had traveled thirty-five miles since the morning.

They had now reached the origin of the prairie fire, which had evidently commenced on the high bank of the stream which they discovered in the wooded hollow beneath. In the wet season this was a considerable river, but the dry weather had reduced it to a trickling brook of beautifully clear water that rippled over the pebbly bed in a depth of only a few inches, except in certain bends where the torrent had hollowed out deep pools; these were some acres in extent, and hardly had Ned descended to the river's bed than his ears were delighted by the loud snort of hippopotami, and he noticed several of these animals with their heads above the water. He lost no time in endeavoring to procure a dinner. A large tamarind-tree grew in the steep bank above the deep pool; hiding behind this, Ned sent Tim to the opposite side of the pool to shout and to throw stones at the hippopotami, so as to drive them over to the spot where he was lying in ambush. This had the desired

effect, and presently, after a succession of loud snorts
and repeated diving, the hippopotami retreated from Tim's
side of the pool, and a large head suddenly appeared on the
surface exactly beneath Ned and within five or six yards of
the muzzle of his gun. He fired at the back of the head,
between the ears, as the animal was looking away from
him, its attention being engaged by Tim. It sunk immediately, but Ned felt certain that it was killed; he therefore
determined to waste no more ammunition, but to wait
until it should float, which would be in about an hour and
a half.

They now strolled up the bed of the stream to seek for a
convenient spot for the night's bivouac.

They were passing across a broad sandy surface, when
they suddenly arrived at a footpath well trodden by human
feet; this led to a well that had been dug in the sand to a
depth of several feet, and there could be no doubt that it
was the regular watering-place of some village in the immediate neighborhood.

As the opposite bank was thickly covered with fine forest
trees and dense jungle, Ned proposed that they should
conceal themselves and watch for the women, who in those
countries always fetch water in their jars at a little before
sunset; it was now about five o'clock.

They had hardly concealed themselves when a long string
of women appeared from the forest. They were almost
naked, and each carried a large earthenware jar upon her
head; some were accompanied by their little children, all of
whom carried jars of various dimensions proportioned to
their size.

As they filled their jars at the well Tim stepped forward
and accosted them in his own language, while Ned remained
concealed lest his strange appearance should frighten them.
At first they were startled at Tim's sudden arrival among
them, but as they spoke a dialect that somewhat resembled
his language they quickly understood him, and after some
explanation Tim called to Ned that he should join him.
Some of the women were young and exceedingly pretty,
with remarkably well-shaped noses and fine eyes, although
their hair was woolly. They showed some signs of surprise
at seeing Ned, who had appeared to Tim's summons, but
without the slightest fear they examined his white skin and
light-brown hair, which Tim had pointed out for their ad-

miration. Ned then spoke to them and explained that they were lost, and had strayed there from a distant tribe that had threatened to kill them. He ended by asking to be received as a friend, and explained that he had just killed a hippopotamus in a pool a few hundred yards distant that would supply them with meat. At this announcement several of the women started with their jars for the village, which they declared was at no great distance, and they requested the strangers to remain until they should return with some of their people.

In about half an hour a large number of men, armed with lances, were seen to issue from the forest, accompanied by the female messengers. Upon arriving within fifty yards of Ned, they stuck their lances in the sand and advanced unarmed toward him as a sign of friendship, and upon a near approach they went through the customary salute of raising both his hands above his head. When Tim had been subjected to a similar operation they all sat down, and Ned described their history from the time of the shipwreck and their escape from the tribe, which he now discovered to be their deadly enemy.

By the time that he and Tim had concluded their stories Ned expected that the hippopotamus must have floated; accordingly he led the men to the spot, and happily discovered that it had risen to the surface. The natives, having heard that it had been killed, were already provided with ropes and axes. Rushing into the water in a body with loud shouts to scare the crocodiles, they attached ropes to the legs and hauled it to the shore. It was a fine large male, and Tim's proverb of " Fill de nigger's belly make de nigger frens " was quickly exemplified as they cut up the massive animal, and, heavily laden with fat and flesh, they conducted Ned and his companion to their village with great rejoicing.

It was a small but pretty village, situated about a hundred feet above the level of the river, in the rocky hollow of a mountain that rose to the height of several thousand feet. This had been a landmark by which Ned had steered for the last two days. The ascent to the village was exceedingly precipitous, and it was entered by a narrow cleft in the rock like a small alley, the cliffs of which rose like walls on either side to the height of several hundred feet. Having ascended the rough blocks of granite that formed natural steps up to the cleft, a strong gate-way of hooked thorns that protected the narrow entrance was passed through, and the party entered the peculiar hollow in which the village was situated. This was of considerable extent, comprising about three acres, in which were beautiful groves of bananas, shady sycamores, and neat gardens, surrounding about a hundred circular dwellings constructed of bamboos thatched with reeds. The village appeared like a huge bird's-nest in the heart of the mountain, which rose abruptly on all sides, and completely encircled it with perpendicular cliffs; these could only be scaled by a narrow and dangerous pathway that had been cut out of the rock, to enable the inhabitants to escape to the top of the mountain in the event of an attack. Altogether it was an exceedingly strong position, as there was no way of ascending this side of the mountain except by the narrow cleft already mentioned.

Ned and Tim slept soundly in a clean hut that had been allotted to them. On the following morning the women brought them a quantity of fresh milk, contained in large gourd shells, and a wooden bowl or broad dish of excellent porridge, mixed with pounded hippopotamus flesh and pumpkin, and flavored with red pepper and salt. After breakfast they washed themselves in a shallow pool among the rocks in the river's bed, and returned to the village to attend a general meeting of the inhabitants.

The people were already assembled beneath a large sycamore in the center of the village, and Ned observed with surprise that a beautiful young girl of about nineteen sat upon a raised seat as their chief or queen. She rose as Ned advanced, and smiling graciously, she raised his hands three times above his head, and requested him to be seated upon a lion's skin by her side.

The whole story of the shipwreck and Ned's wanderings up to the present time had to be repeated, during which the queen's large black eyes were riveted upon Ned's handsome countenance and fine manly figure. The story was completed, and loud murmurs arose upon all sides, until an old man with snow-white hair arose and addressed the queen and her people.

"Great queen," he said, "it is the custom of our tribe to receive the stranger with hospitality, as we ourselves may require assistance when in a strange country. According to our rule, we have welcomed the man with the yellow hair; we have lodged and fed him and his companion, and we will keep them for three days, as we are bound to do by our custom, but at the expiration of that time they must depart. We are weak, and the Mazita, from whom they have escaped, are strong. There is no rain to wash away the foot-prints; they will follow on their tracks, and we shall suffer at their hands for harboring those who have escaped from their lances. Is this not true, my brothers?" said the old man, as he turned to the assembly.

"True!" shouted every voice except that of the young queen.

"We have no wish to remain," said Ned. "We thank you, great queen, for your welcome," he continued, as he turned toward her and raised her hands above her head, "and we should be sorry to bring misfortune upon you in return for your kindness. I only beg you to keep us until to-morrow shall have passed, as our feet are sore with the hard march, and that you will give us a guide across the desert on the following day."

A shout of approval followed this speech; but the queen commanded silence. She rose and spoke, and Ned thought he had never seen a more graceful figure. She was tall and rather slender, although her limbs were beautifully developed. Her head was prettily ornamented with a chaplet of various colored beads interspersed with bright feathers; the rest of her scanty attire consisted of a short fringe of about a foot in length, formed of innumerable single rows of small beads threaded upon the twisted fiber of the plantain, and fastened to a leather belt around her waist, from which they descended like a short kilt to a few inches above her knees. The beads were tastefully arranged in various colors, and their weight retained them in the necessary position to conceal the figure. She had bracelets of polished brass rings upon her wrists and above the elbows, and anklets of the same metal, ornamented with minute bells that tinkled as she moved. Her complexion was a deep copper color, and when she spoke she exposed a beautiful row of teeth as white as pearls. Looking proudly at the assembly around her, she said: "Are my people like the apes that fear the approach of the leopard, or are they like the lion that guards his own den? Did I not slay this lion upon which I sit? and am I not a lioness that will protect my cubs? The strangers that seek my protection are my children, and I will guard them as the lioness fights for her young."

As the beautiful young queen said these words with determined emphasis, she cast her eyes upon Ned, who was not slow to perceive an expression of tenderness that he at once feared might lead to a difficulty. The people whom she addressed, naturally feared their powerful neighbors; and not being smitten to the heart by Ned's personal attractions, they did not enter into their queen's feelings. But the old man who had already spoken had too much experience to contradict the passionate young Amazon who ruled them; accordingly he replied, like an old courtier, that " the queen's will was her people's pleasure, even should she command them to die."

After a long conference the assembly broke up, every one looking discontented but the young queen, who, shortly after she had retired, sent one of her maids as a messenger to request Ned's attendance in the royal hut.

After a rest of three days in this delightful village Ned requested a guide to lead them through the desert, which was described as a hard journey of three days without water. Tim had at once perceived that the young queen had fallen desperately in love with Ned, and he dreaded the consequences, as she would endeavor to detain them in her country; he therefore advised Ned to leave the village, and to push on as rapidly as possible, as the fickleness of a passionate young savage might eventually lead to a danger equal to that from which they had just escaped. Ned was equally aware of the dilemma, and he agreed with Tim that it was absolutely necessary to be off without further delay, as he had determined to push for Zanzibar at all hazards, where they would receive protection from the Portuguese, and be forwarded to England. Already Ned had discovered that the beads worn by the queen and others of the tribe were brought by Arab traders from the coast in exchange for ivory and slaves, and he trusted that when they should have accomplished the terrible desert journey, the great difficulties of the march would have been overcome, and they would meet trading-parties of either Arabs or Portuguese, from whom they could obtain assistance.

Tim had already engaged a guide who professed to know

the desert route, and it was agreed that they were to start
after sunset by stealth and march throughout the night as
rapidly as possible, so as to travel in a cool temperature
and to consume as little water as possible. The goat-skins
were in good order, and Ned proposed that the guide should
procure an ox, which should be loaded with two extra
water-skins: they could then drive the ox throughout the
night, and kill it when it should become distressed from
thirst; they could then replenish their own water-skins, and
eat what they might require of the animal.

It was about noon when these preparations were completed, and Ned anxiously awaited the hour of sunset. He
was sitting in his hut, and had just packed his few articles
of baggage, when he was sent for by the queen. When he
entered her hut she was reclining upon an immense lion's
skin; the shaggy black mane was supported by a bundle
of sweet-scented grass so as to form a pillow, upon which
she leaned her beautifully rounded arm, and without rising from her position she told Ned to sit upon a leopard-
skin by her side.

"Son of the yellow hair," she said as she looked fondly
at him, "we are alone, and I wish to speak to you on a
matter of great importance. I had a dream last night
that has disturbed me. I was sitting before my people
beneath the sycamore, when the air suddenly became dark,
and I heard a noise like thunder in the sky. I fell, and
knew nothing; but, when I recovered, I felt as though I
were falling from a dizzy height; at length, when I expected to be crushed against the ground, I was caught and
saved by a pair of strong white arms, and I found that I
was in the grasp of the son with the yellow hair. I woke,
and I was alone; he was not there! Again I slept, and
dreamed I was sitting before my people, and the son of the
yellow hair sat by my side; the crown of beads that I wear
was upon his head, and three birds with bright feathers
flew around me and cried, in a loud voice, ' Take to thyself
the son of the yellow hair, and let him sit upon the lion's
skin!' We can not disobey the birds," continued the
queen. " Now come and sit with me upon the lion's skin
and be my chief, and all my people shall obey you as their
king."

This was a climax to Ned's worst fears; the lovely queen
had determined that he should share the throne with her,

and he knew not how to reply without giving dire offense. As Ned had directed his steps toward Zanzibar and broken through his long imprisonment, his thoughts were engrossed with the fond recollections of home and the Edith of his boyish days, and he longed to see her grown into womanhood, and to prove whether her childish love had been as sincere and lasting as his own; he now found himself proposed for by a beautiful young savage from whom there appeared but a faint hope of escape.

At this difficult moment he was suddenly relieved by the loud beating of an immense drum in the court of the queen's dwelling; it was almost immediately followed by loud shouts and blowing of horns, while the old man, who had spoken at the assembly rushed into the queen's presence and shouted: "My words are true; the Mazita are upon us! Up, son of the yellow hair, and fight! We suffer for you! we shall all be slain!"

Ned started to his feet, as did the young queen also. A few moments before her eyes had beamed with love: but at the sound of war another expression took possession of them, and they brightened with a fire of determined courage. Before making a reply, she coolly took from a peg a long bow made of an elastic wood: this was already strung according to the custom of that country; she then took a piece of beeswax and carefully rubbed the string. There was a large quiver on the wall containing about forty arrows frightfully barbed and poisoned; this she slung across her shoulders, and addressing Ned, she exclaimed: "Son of the yellow hair, fight by my side! If we fall, we die together: the lioness will protect her cubs."

Following the undaunted and beautiful young savage, Ned left her hut, and, upon entering the court, he was met by Tim, who assured him that about two thousand of the Mazita were in sight, advancing upon the village; they had first been observed by the herd-boys who were minding the goats on the other side of the river, and they had immediately rushed to the village and given the alarm.

The Mazita had discovered Ned's escape on the morning after his start; and as the sorcerers declared that no rain would fall until he and the dog should be killed, they had at once collected a large force, and followed so rapidly upon the tracks that they had before the evening arrived at the skeletons of the buffaloes, to which they had been directed by the clouds of vultures hovering in circles in the air.

They guessed the direction of Ned's flight until they had at length arrived at the foot-prints of Tim and himself upon the ashes of the newly burned grass, which conducted them straight to the village in which they had been received by the Queen of the Mapondas.

There was no time to be lost; and Ned immediately armed himself, and determined to ascend the rocks that commanded the narrow approach to the village, which he felt confident he and Tim could defend so long as their ammunition lasted. He communicated his intention to the warlike queen, who was eager for the fray.

Already about two hundred natives of the village had armed themselves with bows and arrows, and waited for her commands. Ned advised that they should be stationed among the rocks, well concealed, and that they should guard the difficult approach by a constant flight of arrows, while he and Tim, with the undaunted queen, should protect the narrow defile.

In a few minutes the natives had disappeared, and had taken their respective positions among the rocks without the slightest noise, while Ned and Tim followed the active queen up the precipitous cliffs, and at length took their stations upon a broad ledge of rock about a hundred feet above the gate-way, which, although an exposed spot, completely commanded the approach.

They had hardly reached their station before the dense mass of the enemy were perceived advancing to the attack from the grove of bananas below the village: with wild shouts, intermingled with the harsh braying of their horns, they rushed up the steep ascent and delivered a shower of arrows direct at Ned and Tim, who, with the heroic queen, were the first objects that met their view.

The arrows all fell short, and struck harmlessly against the face of the cliff. It was now the turn of the defenders. The queen stood erect upon the high shelf of rock, and drawing her bow steadily, with her left arm as rigid as an iron bar, she let an arrow fly at a chief who was leading the attack; he carried a shield before him, in the center of which the swift arrow struck with a sharp sound that could be distinctly heard. Passing through the tough giraffe's hide, it nailed the shield to his breast, and he fell

backward to die after a few brief struggles. A loud cheer
from the defenders followed the successful shot. With admirable coolness, the queen exposed herself to a flight of
arrows, some of which she escaped by nimbly springing on
one side; but, quick in return, she shot her poisoned arrows
in rapid succession, nearly the whole of which buried their
points in the enemy or stuck in their tough shields. She
was a beautiful type of the Amazon, as she stood fearlessly
upon the rock, and with a face beaming with courage and
determination she sent death into their ranks at almost
every twang of her bow-string.

"Well done, son of the yellow hair!" shouted the excited Leona as Ned opened fire, and two of the enemy fell to
one bullet that had passed through them both. For an
instant this checked the attack; but as Ned's fire-arms
were nothing new to the Mazita, they again pressed bravely
forward, and that with such determination and courage
that they gained the narrow alley which led to the gate-
way. This was directly below the spot upon which the
queen stood, supported by the guns from Ned and Tim,
every shot of which told upon the dense throng which
pressed through the difficult approach. Ned requested
Leona to kneel behind a large, loose mass of rock that
would protect her as she shot: but although the arrows
were flying thick, the dauntless young queen scorned concealment, and with extraordinary strength she put her
shoulder to the heavy fragment and moved it toward the
edge of the perpendicular cliff. Ned laid his gun upon the
ground, and assisted her to roll the rock upon the heads of
those a hundred feet below. It crashed with a dull echo
into the dense throng of fighting men. This was the signal for a storm of rocks and stones that were now showered upon the attacking party from all sides, as many of
the defenders had manned the cliffs, upon which a large
store of such missiles had been prepared to resist an assault
upon the gate-way. Leona had shot away her last arrow,
and she now threw stones with great rapidity from a large
pile upon the ledge. The alley was choked with the dead,
as the rocks hurled down upon the enemy were more de-
structive than bullets from a gun. Ned and Tim directed
their fire at the leaders, and brought them down one by
one with fatal certainty as they reached the gate and attempted to force an entrance. At length an enormous rock

DEATH OF THE AMAZON QUEEN.

of several tons' weight that had been an original portion of the cliff, upon the edge of which it almost balanced, was set in motion by the united efforts of about twenty men, who had worked the supporting stones from beneath it with long bamboos. For a moment the huge mass tottered, and the next instant it fell forward, carrying with it one of those who had assisted to dislodge it from its bed. This avalanche of stone rushed through the air, accompanied by a shower of smaller rocks that had been loosened by its fall.

With a tremendous crash it descended upon the heads of those below, crushing to instant death about twenty of the enemy, and completely blocking up the alley, so that those between it and the gate-way were shut up in a prison of rock. With a loud shout of triumph Leona leaned over the edge of the cliff to watch the effect of this tremendous fall, but at almost the same moment her beautiful arms were thrown convulsively in the air as an arrow pierced her bosom and penetrated completely through her back. Ned saw the barbed point as it protruded some inches through her soft dark skin, and catching her in his arms just in time to prevent her from falling over the cliff, he supported the dying Amazon. The arrow had passed through her heart; she had instinctively clasped one arm around Ned's neck, and she fixed her large eyes fondly upon him for a few moments as she vainly strove to speak. With a smile of love and triumph upon her beautiful features, Leona's brave spirit fled. Ned laid her body gently down, and straightening her lovely limbs, he placed her bow and empty quiver by her side, and then renewed the fight.

There was little left to complete the victory. The fall of the huge rock had created a panic; those who had been hemmed within the narrow passage had been massacred to a man, and Ned and Tim now opened fire with fatal effect upon the retreating throng, who fell pell-mell down the steep approach in their frantic efforts to escape from the cloud of arrows and the bullets that whizzed among them.

The fight was over. The defenders had not lost many men, as they had been more or less protected by the rocks, but several were wounded by poisoned arrows, whose death was certain, as the slightest puncture would be fatal.

The body of the courageous queen was laid out upon the lion's skin upon which she used to sit beneath the sycamore, and all the women wept and raised their loud shrill cry of distress, in which the men joined as they mourned for the beautiful Leona. Her bow and quiver lay by her side; and although her lovely features were placid, the stern smile of triumph still lingered upon her face as Ned, for the last time, looked upon her with deep regret that he should have been the unwilling cause of her untimely end.

"Massa Ned," said Tim, "dis a bad job 'tirely; de poor queen's dead; but if she alive, dat's a worse job, she never let Massa Ned go away. Neber see in all my life such eyes! De queen love Massa Ned like mad; bad t'ing dat. I know de nigger queen. All fire one day, all water de next; love you in de night, kill you in de morning; dat's de trick 'xactly. Bad job de poor queen's dead, worse job if she alive; dat's a fact 'xactly. Now, Massa Ned, let's cut and run before anoder job begins."

The philosophic Tim having given his opinion, with which Ned could hardly disagree, however much he might have admired the beauty and courage of the unfortunate young queen, he determined to start without delay, as fortune had hitherto smiled upon their journey beyond his most sanguine hopes. Once across the terrible desert, he would have little to fear.

Ned addressed himself to the old man of the village, and declared that he would not remain any longer among them, lest he might bring fresh calamities upon their tribe; and, deploring the queen's death, he begged that he might depart at once. His determination was applauded by all present, and as the guide was a native of a tribe to which he wished to return on the other side of the desert, there was no difficulty. All was prepared for the journey; an ox was loaded with two large water-skins, and after a hearty meal, Ned and Tim took leave of their hosts and started. The guide was a fine powerful man who knew the route thoroughly; he had distinguished himself in the late fight, but he had received a slight scratch upon the arm from an arrow as it had grazed his skin during its flight; he had simply bound a piece of plaintain leaf around the scratch to prevent the flies from troubling him. After an hour's quick walking they left the forest that bordered the river, and entered upon a boundless plain of sand and pebbles, devoid of all vegetation except a few stunted mimosas, and scattered tufts of a withered, wiry-looking grass.

Although this portion of the country was a frightful desert during the dry season, it abounded with grass and water during the rains; but when the drought arrived, there was a general disappearance of all herbage, as it became so completely dry that the fine grass broke into minute pieces, and was carried away by the wind, leaving bare the hot and barren soil that did not appear capable of producing vegetation. For a distance of about a hundred and twenty miles there was neither well nor stream: thus, as no drop of water could be procured during this dry season, it was necessary to force a march of about forty miles per day to accomplish the journey in three days. Ned did not fear any distance provided the supply of water was assured, but any accident to the water-skins would terminate in the destruction of the entire party.

They now pushed forward over the barren surface of the desert; their ammunition had been reduced by the late fight to ten rounds of cartridge each, therefore they had not much to carry besides their guns, as they had fastened their knapsacks upon the ox, which, having drunk water before starting, would be able to travel for two days, or about eighty miles.

CHAPTER XX.

IN THE DESERT.

THE moon rose, and the night air was cool and delicious. It was past midnight, and the party traveled rapidly along the even surface, unimpeded by the tangled vegetation that had retarded them in some portions of their journey. There was no wind, and not a cloud upon the sky, in which the stars shone with extraordinary brightness, although those near the moon were nearly eclipsed by her extreme light. There was a silvery glow upon the wild desert that gave an indescribable beauty to the scene: the rocks that rose abruptly from the sandy plain appeared to assume the forms of monsters, as in the indistinct haze of distance Ned sometimes fancied that they moved; but in reality there was no life within the parched and dreary desert—all was solitude, sand-rocks, and rounded pebbles. The ox, laden sparingly with the knapsacks and water-skins, marched well; the tinkle of an iron bell suspended from its neck was the only sound that disturbed the silence of the spot, while the tall, powerful figures of Ned and Tim, following the guide, seemed to glide like specters along the sandy waste upon which their footsteps left no sound.

The night passed away, and the moon grew pale as the first streaks of dawn appeared in the east. Quickly the stars disappeared, and the planet Venus, lately so brilliant, faintly glimmered as the last of the bright host, and then vanished from view as the gorgeous orb of gold rose suddenly from the horizon of desert, and glowed all mighty upon the sterile scene. It was the horror of sunrise. The pitiless destroyer rose vigorous in the sky, rejoicing in his power. The air, lately so cool, now quivered with insupportable heat; the sand of the desert scorched the feet; the poisonous breath of the simoom, that destroying wind that seems to own a furnace as its birthplace, blew upon them; still on they journeyed rapidly, as there was no shade in which to halt.

For fourteen hours they had marched without a rest, as it was necessary to push on with the greatest rapidity at the early part of the journey, that the ox might carry the water and knapsacks as far as possible before it should become exhausted from thirst, when it would be necessary to kill it. All were fatigued with intense heat, and the guide suffered from the slight scratch upon his arm, which had swollen, and was extremely painful.

For some time they had seen a lofty rocky mountain in the distance among a chain of lower hills; they determined to push on for the higher ground, in which they might discover some rock that would shelter them from the burning sun. For nearly four hours they marched, until they at length reached an overhanging rock in a rugged pass through which the dry bed of a broad torrent formed a stony road. Here, tired and thirsty, the party rested. Tim cut some brittle straw that was all that remained of some wiry herbage in the bed of the exhausted stream, and this he gave to the famished ox, that was too thirsty to eat; after vainly endeavoring to swallow a few mouthfuls, it refused the food. Tim now opened a water-skin, and moistened the straw by sprinkling it with a few handfuls of the precious fluid; the ox then eat it greedily.

The whole party lay down and slept. They woke at

about three P.M., and immediately prepared to start; but all were foot-sore, as they had marched about forty-eight miles. The guide's arm was dreadfully swollen and painful, and the ox was suffering from extreme thirst. Ned commenced loading the tired animal. With Tim's assistance he strapped on the knapsacks, and then he went to the spot where they had laid the water-skins in the shade. Horror of horrors! they were empty!

It would be impossible to describe the shock that this terrible sight produced upon the whole party. The skins were literally torn to pieces by the horns of the ox! The thirsty animal had seen Tim sprinkle water from the skins upon the dry straw; during their sleep it had risen, and, discovering the water, it had attempted to drink by tearing open the leather sacks with its horns. Every drop had immediately disappeared in the sand. Not even the ox had procured a mouthful; it could only lick the damp sand and the empty water-skins.

Both Ned and Tim had a small supply in the skins which they carried on their backs; the guide had none, as he had depended upon those carried by the ox. They had at least seventy miles of desert before them.

Ned and Tim looked at each other, but neither dared to utter a word; the future appeared certain, and too horrible to think of. They agreed to put the small quantity of water that remained into Ned's water-skin, as that of Tim leaked slightly, and the evaporation from one skin would be less than from two.

The guide was in dreadful pain, but, as no time could be lost, they started, and it was agreed that they must push on for their very existence, and march the seventy miles without a halt; this Ned hoped to accomplish in about twenty-four hours, but, in his own mind, he did not feel certain of the distance, as the native accounts could never be depended upon.

The guide appeared stupefied with pain, but he pointed with his lance in the direction that they were to take, and he declared that they would arrive at a river upon which was a village and trading depot of Arabs from Zanzibar; but that it was two days' fair marching distant. Ned took the bearing with his compass, and with heavy hearts they pushed on. For about five miles they followed the steep and winding water-course until they arrived at the summit of the mountain-range, from which they had a distant view, and Ned hoped to have discovered some point that would have been the limit of their journey. The guide pointed to a far-distant cone which could faintly be distinguished on the horizon; that was the mountain beneath which the village was situated. Ned felt certain that it was at least sixty-five miles distant. He was already thirsty, but he dared not drink. For some minutes they had sat upon a rock to observe the country; they now would have started, but the guide could not rise from the ground; his arm was swollen to the size of a man's thigh, and he complained of giddiness and total paralysis of the lower limbs.

"The arrow was poisoned," he faintly uttered; "I must die. I thirst; give me water!"

"Don't give de water, Massa Ned," said Tim; "de pison kill him quick. What for give de water? Water or no water, de pison kill him. Save de water, for God's sake, Massa Ned, or we all die!"

It was a painful trial, but Ned felt that Tim's advice was just; the unfortunate guide was doomed, as the poison of the arrow had become thoroughly absorbed into the system. He was already delirious, and, raging with a burning thirst, he raved for water. His sufferings were pitiable, and Ned felt half inclined to share the last portion with him, when the guide suddenly seized his lance that lay by his side and drove it deep into the throat of the ox that was standing by him. As the animal fell from the blow, pierced to the heart, the dying guide fell upon it, and gluing his parched lips to the wound, from which the blood spouted, he drank madly his last draught.

Although each moment was precious, as delay added to their thirst, Ned could not leave the guide alone to die upon the desert. For about three hours he remained to witness the agonies of the miserable man, who, as the poison wreaked its fatal work, swelled in all his limbs, and in his body until he appeared to be inflated. At last the throat swelled also to such an extent that, after a few convulsive struggles for breath, he stretched himself out and lay upon the burning sand a corpse.

Both Ned and Tim were horror-struck; they were themselves in the agony of thirst, but no more than about a quart of water remained; it had evaporated from the near-

DEATH OF TIM.

ly empty water-skin. They pushed on down the mountain-side and reached the level ground.

The sun had sunk. Once more the air was cool; and although thirsty and fatigued, they freshened for their work and determined to accomplish the night's long march at as great speed as possible. They pushed on and marched until sunrise at the rate of four miles an hour, without drinking. The moon had been their friend, but once more she became pale, and the dreadful enemy again appeared—the sun!

As the sun rose upon the two unfortunate young men, it shone upon tired and haggard-looking creatures that had scarcely signs of youth. Their cheeks were livid and sunken, their eyes bloodshot, and their lips swollen, while they still marched forward with an expression of fearful distress and desperation.

They had walked about forty-eight miles from the spot where they had left the guide. The blue conical mountain appeared to be within fifteen miles of them; once at the foot, they would find water, as the river flowed at its base. The sun rose hot as fire, and again the dreadful simoom blew, and they felt faint at the terrible heat. They both reeled with fatigue and thirst. Ned could support the latter no longer. During the cool night the water had not evaporated, but he knew that the simoom would dry up their scanty store within an hour.

"Drink, Tim!" said Ned; "we will each share the last drop, and, please God, we may then hold out till the end, but we must not halt, or we are lost. Drink, my dear Tim, a full half, and leave the rest for me!"

Tim was fearfully distressed from thirst, and he clutched the water-skin from Ned's hands. For an instant he hesitated, as he gazed intently at his loved master, who was in a lamentable state of exhaustion; he then eagerly pressed the mouth of the water-skin to his lips and appeared to drink.

"Drink more, you have not had your share, and I will then finish it," said Ned.

Again Tim appeared to drink, after which he handed the water-skin to Ned, who ravenously finished it, devoutly exclaiming, "Thank God!" as the last drop gurgled down his throat.

"T'ank God, Massa Ned," repeated Tim, as he watched

Ned's refreshed countenance with a mingled expression of intense affection and agony.

Throwing the empty water-skin upon his shoulder, Ned now led the way, followed by Tim. They could no longer walk fast; their feet were terribly swollen, and although they had thrown away their knapsacks, and Ned had reserved nothing but his compass and chart, they could barely march at the rate of three miles an hour. The sun rose higher, and the heat increased. They walked slower and slower, until they almost crawled.

Tim lagged many yards behind; several times Ned halted and waited for him. As he came up he reeled from side to side, and his tongue was hanging from his mouth parched and furred like a hare-skin. Once more he lagged more than a hundred yards behind. Again Ned waited; he was himself also exhausted from a frightful thirst and prostration; he could scarcely feel the ground with his feet.

At length Tim staggered slowly up, and stopping suddenly, he clasped his head with both his hands, and reeling backward, he fell heavily upon the ground. Ned endeavored to raise him.

"Tim! my dear Tim, for God's sake don't give in!" cried Ned; "I am nearly done myself; but if we can only march a few hours more we may yet be saved from this horrible death."

Tim fainted, and lay for some minutes insensible. Ned thought he was dead. At length he recovered consciousness, but he could hardly articulate, as his tongue was as dry as leather. "Go on, Massa Ned!" he said; "leave Tim to die. I can't move again. I going to die, Massa Ned."

Tim's features were drawn and contracted, and he breathed with difficulty. Ned felt a giddiness overcoming him, and he feared that he should faint as the blood rushed to his head as he leaned over the prostrate Tim and endeavored to support his head.

"Pray God forgive Tim, Massa Ned; go on, go on! Leave Tim to die."

"I'll never leave you, Tim; my true, my faithful friend," said Ned, in an agony of despair, as he saw the unmistakable signs of death stealing across Tim's face. "We'll die together, if die we must. Oh, for one draught of water!" cried Ned; "one draught to save my poor Tim's life!"

A faint smile crossed Tim's haggard face as he heard these words, and, looking at Ned, he said, painfully, "Pray God forgive me, Massa Ned; I told one lie; 1 told one lie!"

"What lie, Tim?" said Ned; "you have never told me a lie."

"Yes, Massa Ned; p'r'aps God forgive me if you ask Him. I told one lie about de water, and now I die. I told Massa Ned I drink my half—dat one lie. I not touch one drop; 1 leave it for my dear Massa Ned. Dat save him p'r'aps, if go on quick and leave Tim to die. God bless you, my dear Massa Ned! Tim got no frens, only one poor nigger; nobody cry for Tim. Let him die! Go on, my dear Massa Ned! Go home; see fader and moder; de Miss Edit! see all—all—all!"

Tim could speak no more. Ned wrung his hands in an agony of despair. Now, for the first time, he knew of that heroic act of devotion in his brave and all-suffering follower. Although dying of thirst, he would not drink his share of the scanty pittance; but he had practiced the too generous deception to save his master's life.

"Oh, Tim, dear friend! too good, too generous! how shall I forgive myself for this?" cried Ned, "that you should die that I might live! Rather let us both die as we have lived, together, and trust to God to bless us both hereafter!"

At these words Tim convulsively raised himself upon his elbows, and looking up to the burning sun with fixed eyeballs that never contracted before the blazing light, he laughed wildly in delirium. For some minutes he uttered this frightful mirth, and then a change came over his face. Still looking fixedly at the sky, his features became placid and assumed an expression of intense happiness and peace. Smiling as though tasting the joy that the next world alone could give, he said, "My God! my God! I see de watersprings! t'ank God Almighty!" Tim fell gently back upon the ground; his soul was at the water-springs; and Ned wept over the body of his beloved friend.

A giddiness seized Ned's brain; his tongue hung from his mouth, and he fell insensible by Tim's side. Had he not drunk that one long draught that Tim's devotion offered, he would have been the first victim to a death by thirst.

There was a rumbling sound far distant in the air when Tim's last words spoke of the water-springs. Again it sounded louder and nearer than before, and from the southern horizon rose a cloud, like that of Elijah, no bigger than a man's hand. Again the deep muttering sound vibrated through the desert as distant thunder spoke to ears that could not hear. And now from every point of the horizon clouds arose, at first snow-white, but rapidly increasing in size and darkening in color, until they became an inky black, and the fierce sun himself was veiled. Within an hour from the time of poor Tim's last gasp, as though his spirit had petitioned the Great Mover of the Water-springs, not one speck of blue sky could be discerned, but pitch-black clouds formed a thick canopy above the earth.

The lightning played incessantly; the thunder roared and cracked enough to waken up the dead; and the rain—that Heaven-sent torrent—poured like a water-spout upon the famished earth, and almost flooded the lately withered desert. Oh! had that rain descended one hour sooner!— but no! it would have condemned to longer life on earth one who was now in heaven.

For more than two hours the rain poured in an uninterrupted deluge. Cascades of clear water fell rushing from the lately torrid rocks; and deep water-courses, filled with a muddy fluid, tore their wild course along the sandy desert; the whole of the level ground was ankle-deep in water. In this lay the bodies of Ned and Tim, side by side. Suddenly, as though awakened from a deep sleep, Ned sat up and stared wildly round him. The rain still poured, and the thunder burst heavily at intervals.

Rubbing his eyes, he exclaimed, "It is a dream! where am I? I dreamed that Tim had died of thirst in the desert. Ha! here he is. Wake up, Tim, or we shall be drowned!" saying which, Ned, half delirious from overexhaustion and thirst, placed his lips to the flood that covered the ground and drank deeply. Taking a deep breath as he slaked his thirst, he now turned toward his silent companion, and, taking one arm, he endeavored to arouse him. He dropped the arm as the fatal truth flashed upon him—the body was cold and stiff.

Ned could find no tears to relieve his feelings; but he knelt by the side of all that remained of his faithful friend and follower and gazed upon his swollen features in intense affliction. The dreamy delirium passed away, and he remembered all. He was in the desert alone, and he had lost all that had cheered his many years of captivity, together with every joy and sorrow. Tim was dead!

He heard a sudden noise—a rushing sound in the air—and, looking up, he perceived a huge vulture descending from on high, with closed wings, with the noise of a rocket, in its eagerness to be a sexton for the dead. Many of these birds were circling in the air above the spot, while several were already perched upon the neighboring rocks waiting for their opportunity. A thrill of horror ran through Ned's veins. There was a deep crevice in a plateau of solid rock a few yards distant. Thither, as a labor of love, he carried, with much difficulty, the rigid body, and gently lowered it within the narrow vault. He then fetched rocks as large as he could lift; these he placed across the crevice until he had effectually protected it with a pile of heavy fragments that would defy the attacks of vultures or wild animals.

Ned drank once more, and half filled his water-skin from a clear stream that spouted from a rock, and, slinging it upon his shoulder, he took Tim's gun and ammunition in addition to his own. Thus loaded, he took a last farewell of the fatal spot, and in a few words, as he stood by the grave, he offered up a heartfelt prayer for the dead, and for guidance on his lonely way.

Strengthened by the cool rain, and rendered callous to fatigue by sorrow, he wandered on direct for the high blue cone that had been pointed out as a landmark by the guide. This appeared to be nearer than before, as the rain had rendered the atmosphere doubly clear, but it was in reality about fourteen miles distant. Ned plodded on.

It was nearly sunset when he reached a grove of tall palm-trees that grew in a long line at the base of the mountain, and extended as far as the eye could reach. Passing through these for about two hundred yards, he perceived a considerable village upon a high rocky ridge, which looked down upon a roaring torrent now swollen by the rain. Without caring for his reception, Ned slowly ascended the rocky path and entered the village. To his astonishment he was met by a number of Arabs, instead of the natives to whom he had been accustomed. These people were engaged in storing elephants' tusks within a large shed that was constructed after a different fashion to the huts of the natives. Upon seeing Ned, they gathered around him; and he, tired, hungry, and dispirited, threw his two guns upon the ground, and then lay down exhausted at full length.

For some time Ned lay half asleep, but at length, having recovered sufficiently to speak, he endeavored to explain his situation. Although only a small portion of his narrative was understood, it was sufficient to arouse the sympathy of his hearers, who declared that Ned had brought good luck to the country, as the rain had arrived with him.

The Arabs were ivory and slave traders belonging to Zanzibar. Many of their slaves had been purchased from the country in which Ned had so long been a captive; thus, as he spoke their language, it was not difficult to procure an interpreter, and he shortly discovered several people who had served the Arabs for some years, and therefore had a knowledge of Arabic.

There was no further difficulty in describing the adventure. Ned, having arrived among them with the first storm of rain that had fallen for nearly twelve months, was regarded by the natives with a superstitious reverence that was also shared by the Arabs; the latter agreed that he should join their party and accompany them to Zanzibar on their return.

Some months passed away in the Arab camp, during which their parties made long excursions in the interior, and returned laden with ivory, together with many slaves. At length the long wished-for period arrived, and Ned, who sadly missed and mourned for his faithful companion Tim, hailed the day of departure with joy as the Arabs beat their drum and assembled a body of five hundred porters to transport the tusks to Zanzibar. Long strings of slaves of both sexes accompanied the march; many were fastened by ropes from neck to neck, while others were fettered by the forked stick similar to that in which Ned had been secured when first captured.

In six weeks' march they reached Zanzibar without any incident worthy of note, and having delivered the ivory, the captain of the party introduced Ned to his employer, who was a wealthy Parsee merchant from Bombay. This man not only received him kindly, but furnished him with clothes and money, and promised to send him to Egypt on board one of his own vessels that would shortly proceed to Cosseir, on the Red Sea. Ned presented the captain of the trading-party with his two guns as a return for the kindness he had received, and, when the day of departure arrived, he warmly thanked the Parsee merchant for his hospitality, and sailed on board a large Arab dhow loaded with ivory and slaves for Egypt.

Once more Ned's heart bounded with joy as he felt himself again upon the sea and steering toward home.

The wind was favorable throughout the voyage, and without an accident of any kind they reached Cosseir. There they disembarked, and the cargo was transported on camels, while the slaves marched on foot across the desert to the Nile. Ned was provided with a camel, as the Bombay merchant had ordered that he should be well cared for and be delivered to his agent at Alexandria.

Upon arrival at the Nile the slaves were divided among several large-decked vessels, upon one of which Ned was furnished with a cabin, and they sailed down the stream. They were detained at several large towns on the banks of the river, and especially at Cairo, at which place many of the slaves were disposed of at good prices; and, after a voyage of three weeks, the boats arrived at Alexandria, and Ned for the first time looked upon the blue waters of the Mediterranean. He felt almost at home; and having been kindly received by the agent of the Parsee merchant, he was provided with a passage on board an English vessel that was about to sail.

The sight of the union-jack flying at the mast-head that Ned had not seen for many years filled him with delight, and, as the boat took him alongside, he sprung up the ladder and found himself on the clean deck of a fine merchant vessel of about three hundred tons. The captain and crew were English, and Ned once more could speak his native tongue and associate with his own countrymen. The captain was a fine hearty fellow, who took a fancy to Ned at first sight, and sympathized warmly with the history of his adventures, which quickly made the round of the ship, and Ned was looked upon as a second Robinson Crusoe.

After a voyage of six weeks the vessel passed the Lizard Light and entered the Channel. They were within sight of the coast on the following day with a light but favorable breeze, when they met a large fishing-smack, which they spoke, being anxious to obtain the earliest news from England. To Ned's delight she hailed from Falmouth, which would be his most favorable landing-place; therefore he took leave of the captain and crew of the vessel, with whom he had shared a most agreeable voyage, and, going on board the smack, the sails filled, and the two ships parted on their different courses.

On the following day they sighted Falmouth, and once more Ned set his foot upon the soil of Old England.

CHAPTER XXI.

JEM STEVENS AND EDITH.

NED GREY happened to arrive at Falmouth a few days after Paul had been committed to prison by the magistrates on the original warrant for his apprehension; thus he was lying in jail at that town to await his trial at the Sessions at the very time that Ned unconsciously hurried through on his way home.

The committal of Paul to prison had been effected through the instrumentality of James Stevens, who had no sooner got rid of him from the rectory than he once more renewed his visits and pressed his suit with Edith. With consummate hypocrisy he had persuaded her, and also Polly Grey, that he was forced to commit Paul upon the warrant, but that, as the Sessions were drawing near, he would shortly be tried and acquitted, as there could be no doubt of his innocence.

Although Edith felt no love for Stevens, she had learned not to dislike him; she had been so constantly talked to by her mother and impressed with the idea that he was really a worthy object for her affection, that she regarded him as a person whom it was not impossible that she might some day learn to love. Nevertheless, she lingered fondly upon the recollections of the past, when her heart had first known the feelings of real love. It was by a pretended sympathy for her early affection for Ned Grey that Stevens had succeeded in winning her regard; and well aware of the influence thus obtained, he appeared to delight in frequent allusions to the time when Ned and he served together on board the "Sybille," during which he declared that he had been his greatest friend.

It was the morning after Ned's arrival at Falmouth that Stevens, having slept at the rectory, was at breakfast with Mrs. Jones, Polly Grey, and Edith. A fine young Newfoundland dog was sitting by her side watching her face intently, in the hope that some morsel would fall to his share. This dog had been given to her by Stevens on the previous day.

"I shall call him Nero," said Edith, "in memory of poor dear old Nero, who, you say, was drowned in the shipwreck."

"Yes," replied Stevens, with a hypocritical sigh; "on the day that I saw poor Ned sink when the 'Forte' was lost. Poor Ned," he continued, "I would have given the world to have saved him. Had I only had a boat-hook instead of an oar I think I could have caught him by his clothes. I shall never forget his last look as the water closed over him."

Stevens took out his handkerchief and wiped his eyes. At this moment the servant entered with the letters.

"Ha! a letter for me! I am so glad. I am so glad, for I seldom receive one!" said Edith. "I wonder who it's from," she continued, as she examined the seal that was simply the impression of a shilling.

"You had better open it, my dear," said her mother; "that's the quickest way of ascertaining the name of your correspondent."

Edith broke the seal and read the letter. She turned deathly pale; then a deep blush flushed across her face; it was only for a moment, when she again changed to the whiteness of marble.

"What's the matter, my child?" exclaimed her mother. "Are you ill? What are the contents of that mysterious letter that affect you so deeply?"

For a few minutes Edith was silent, and holding the letter in her hands, which rested in her lap, she seemed lost in reflection, and her lips quivered with emotion. Both her mother and Polly Grey regarded her with astonishment. At length, subduing her excitement, and entirely commanding her feelings, she fixed her large blue eyes upon Stevens, who sat opposite, and appeared to search him to the very heart. Her beautiful features gradually assumed a stern and determined expression as she calmly said, "Mother, shall I read this letter aloud?"

"By all means," said Mrs. Jones; "I'm quite curious to know the contents of this wonderful epistle."

Edith, in a clear voice that trembled slightly, read the following letter:

"FALMOUTH, *January* 8.

"Half mad with joy, and yet wilder with uncertainty, I am hurrying to the spot where my happiest days were spent, where last I parted from her whom I then called my own Edith. God grant that she and my dear parents are yet alive, and that she still remembers the love of her youthful days, and that her heart is as unchanged as mine.

"My story is short. The morning after I left you I was taken by a press-gang, together with Tim and Nero. I was carried on board the 'Sybille,' a frigate on her way to India. I could not write. On board I met Jem Stevens. God forgive him. In India we fought and captured the 'Forte.' We were both sent home in charge; she was wrecked. Stevens went off with the frigate's cutter, well manned, and hacked at my hands with a knife when I swam up and clung to the boat. I was forced to let go and swim to the wreck. Tim would not leave me. We saved ourselves with a raft, together with Nero, and at last reached the coast of Africa, where we were captives among the savages for many years. We at length endeavored to escape. Poor Tim, alas! is dead. Nero is also dead; and I am, thank God, alive and well, and hurrying on horseback, post-haste night and day, to see if Edith is still my own; if not, would that I had died with my devoted Tim and left my bones in Africa.

"If you are alive, Edith, dearest remembrance of my boyhood, I shall be with you almost as soon as you receive this letter, as I rush to meet my fate.

"Your own
"NED GREY."

Edith folded the letter carefully together and handed it to Polly Grey; at the same time she rose from her seat, and, with extraordinary calmness, she regarded Stevens fixedly. "Yes," she said, as her voice trembled and became hoarse with suppressed emotion, "his own Edith until death shall part us. An explanation, if you please, Mr. Stevens," continued Edith, as she gazed contemptuously at the miserable guilty object that sat before her, bowed down with shame and confusion.

Stevens rose hurriedly, and saying, "I will explain everything," was about to leave the room, when Edith, who was near the door, quickly turned the key, which she took from the lock and retained within her hand.

"You will have the kindness, sir, to amuse yourself with the newspaper until the arrival of your dear friend, Ned Grey, whom you endeavored to save from drowning; he will be rejoiced to return you his thanks, and to express his gratitude in person; he is expected every instant."

"Edith, for God's sake, let me depart, and I will shortly explain all!" exclaimed the terrified Stevens.

"You do not leave this room, sir, until Ned Grey arrives," replied Edith, with a disdainful calmness and determination before which Stevens quailed.

"What is all this? what is all this?" cried Mrs. Jones. "Edith, my dear, are you going mad?" continued the astonished mother; while Polly, having read the letter, now regarded Stevens with an expression of horror as though he had been some poisonous reptile.

At this moment the loud clattering of a horse's hoofs was heard upon the frosty road. Mrs. Jones looked from the window. "Dear me!" she exclaimed, "the horse has run away with somebody. Stop him!" she cried; but as nobody was there to hear her commands, the rider reined up his horse, and quickly dismounting, he rang the bell.

The bell continued ringing with such violence that the servant ran with more than his usual alacrity to the door.

Although Edith had, with wonderful self-possession, assumed a calm demeanor, she was in reality intensely excited. The suddenness of the shock that would have prostrated most of her sex had nerved her for the moment of trial, and perceiving at a glance the treachery and hypocrisy of Stevens, she was determined that the explanation should be made face to face with the long-lost Ned. At the same time that, insulted by Stevens's base deception, she resolved upon this course, Edith's mind was in a tumult of conflicting feelings. An intense disgust for Stevens was mingled with an overpowering ecstasy of delight at the knowledge that Ned not only had returned, but that his love for her was unaltered by years of absence. For the moment she felt independent of the whole world, and she was absorbed by a feeling of intense and perfect happiness that almost made her shudder as she imagined that it was too bright to last.

The servant attempted to enter the room, and Edith unlocked the door.

Almost as soon as he was announced, Ned Grey, who had thrown off his great-coat in the hall, entered.

For a few moments he stood confused as he looked at the various persons around him. Neither Polly nor Mrs. Jones were much changed, but he stared for some instants at the beautiful girl, who in her turn regarded his tall and handsome figure with an expression of surprise, mingled with the deepest affection.

Their eyes thus met, and in a few short seconds, without one word spoken, they explained their unchanged love.

"My Edith!" exclaimed Ned Grey. "Oh, Ned! dear Ned!" cried Edith, as they both instinctively rushed forward and were locked in each other's arms.

After a few moments of indescribable happiness the blushing girl released herself from Ned's embrace. Polly Grey was also hanging round his neck in a transport of delight; but Edith had a sterner task to perform, and drawing herself up to her full height, with an air of haughtiness that was entirely foreign to her usual character, she said:

"Mr. Stevens, you have now the pleasure of meeting your dear friend, Ned Grey, whom you so generously attempted to save from drowning in the wreck;" then turning to Ned, she continued: "Mr. Stevens has honored me by a proposal of marriage, as he declared that he saw you drowned after he had vainly endeavored to assist you."

For some moments Ned regarded Stevens with an expression of the lowest contempt. For one instant Stevens had attempted to meet his glance, but he quailed before it, and turned his eyes upon Mrs. Jones, who was in a state of utter confusion.

"Liar! and would-be murderer!" said Ned, as he grasped the unresisting Stevens by the collar with his powerful right hand and led him to the door, "leave this house, and never again cross the threshold, as you value your life!"

As the servant slammed the front door upon the disgraced Stevens, the wretch, pale and trembling, with a mixture of rage and despair, muttered, as he walked rapidly toward the stable for his horse, " There was a charge of willful murder, and a warrant for Ned Grey as well as for Paul."

It would be impossible to describe the happiness of Edith and Polly Grey. Ned had completed the long history of his adventures, during which Edith had shed tears at Tim's devoted martyrdom, and Mrs. Jones had on several occasions exclaimed, " Well, I never!" when he had described the base conduct of James Stevens. It was now Edith's turn to relate all that had happened since Ned's departure, and for the first time he learned that Paul was in custody, and that a warrant had also been issued for his own apprehension upon the suspicion that he had been concerned in the burglary and murder at the rectory. Although such a charge appeared ridiculous, Ned did not fail to perceive that the sudden disappearance of Paul, Tim, and himself on the day of the burglary was sufficient to justify the suspicion, combined with the discovery of the two hundred guineas at Paul's house, together with the jewels and articles of contraband. He now recalled to mind the fact of the two strange men having stealthily passed through the church-yard at the same time that Mother Lee had appeared, when he and Edith were sitting at dusk by the grave-stone of the unknown lady, and he had no doubt that the old hag was in some way connected with the robbery. The complexion of the affair caused him some uneasiness; for, although he had no fear of the ultimate result, the fact of so horrible a suspicion having fallen upon Paul and himself was sufficiently embarrassing.

Ned's life had been so full of adventure and difficulty that he quickly resolved to bear patiently with this dilemma. The daily prayer of many years past had been granted: he was once more at home with his Edith, who was changed only in appearance, from the girl he had left, to the beautiful woman whose heart had always been his own.

When the first shock of Stevens's disgrace had passed, Mrs. Jones regarded Ned with much curiosity and admira-

tion. "He certainly is handsome—very handsome; in
fact, extremely handsome," she said, as she sat alone with
Edith, as Polly Grey had retired with Ned to have a chat
with her boy alone for half an hour. "You see, my dear
child," continued Mrs. Jones, "that the ways of Providence are wonderful, and sailors are especially watched
over." Here Mrs. Jones thought of Captain Smart.
"Sailors are the finest class of the human race. St. Paul
was a sailor; or if he wasn't, he ought to have been; for he
was almost always at sea, and seemed to me to know much
more about it than the other people on board the ship when
she was wrecked; and all would have been lost if it had not
been for his knowledge of the profession when he was bit-
ten by the boa-constrictor, or the viper, or whatever the
snake was—which can't possibly be known, my dear, as the
name was never written—very likely because St. Paul had
no British Museum to refer to. However, that does not
alter the fact that Providence watches over sailors; thus we
must thank Heaven for Ned's safe return. A very handsome young man he is, indeed; so like his poor mother, as
I remember her beautiful body when she was brought on
shore, only she had no whiskers nor mustaches like Ned.
I think he is rather young to have such fine whiskers,"
continued the voluble and discursive Mrs. Jones; "only I
have heard that in hot climates the hair grows at a much
earlier age than in the temperate or the arctic zones. Ned
must have been born in a hot climate, as the vessel that
was lost was an Indiaman, therefore that may account in
some measure for his very early whiskers. I think he is
now about nineteen; is he not, my dear?"

"Twenty-one, mother," replied Edith; "but I think
he looks some years older."

"Well, my dear, it's all the same, and there's no doubt
that he is a gentleman born, for his appearance is most
noble; and, in fact, he might be a king, or even an arch-
bishop, for I never saw a more commanding figure; but as
there is no doubt about your affection for each other, it
would·be a comfort to know whether he ever had a father
—that is to say, of course he must have had one, but it's
of no use having one if you don't know who he is. You
see, my dear, it would look so very odd in the papers to
read the announcement of your marriage ' to Edward Grey,
son of blank—' Very odd, and not altogether proper.''

At this moment Ned re-entered the room, and Mrs. Jones, with much consideration, found an excuse for absenting herself, and left him alone with Edith.

An hour of intense happiness passed as though the interval had been but a few minutes, when a sudden ring was heard at the door-bell, and shortly after the door opened and several constables entered the room. A man approached Ned, and drawing a paper from his pocket, he presented a warrant for his apprehension, signed by James Stevens, upon the original charge for which Paul Grey had been committed.

Never had Edith known the terrible feeling of hatred that now for the first time seized upon her. Base as Stevens was, she had never expected this quick revenge; he had dashed the cup of happiness from her lips.

Pressing Edith to his heart, with a few words of comfort, as the Sessions were drawing near, when he was certain of an acquittal, Ned left the rectory in custody of the constables to be lodged in Falmouth jail.

CHAPTER XXII.

MESSAGE TO EDITH FROM A DYING MAN.

THE news of Ned Grey's return had spread throughout the neighborhood, and his almost instantaneous arrest had excited the sympathy of all the female portion of the population. The whole county was interested in the event, which became the current topic of the day, and James Stevens, of Heron Hall, was regarded with universal detestation as the story became widely known. In the meantime, full of revenge, he lost no opportunity of seeking for evidence that might lead to Ned's conviction.

It was about a fortnight after Ned's arrest, on a cold and stormy night, that a ring was heard at the back door of the rectory, and, shortly afterward, a servant entered the room in which Edith was sitting, with a message that a poor person from Sandy Cove wished to speak with her immediately. A woman was shown into the room, who, wet and cold with the journey, had been sent by a dying man at the cove to request the immediate attendance of Edith, as he had a most important communication to make that concerned her particularly. Regardless of the late hour and the stormy weather, Edith ordered the carriage without delay, and, accompanied by the messenger and Polly Grey, she at once drove to Sandy Cove, about five miles distant. Alighting at the cliff, they descended the zigzag path, and shortly arrived at the door of a hut formed of an inverted boat, from which a feeble light shone through a pane of glass fixed in the side. The messenger opened the door, and they entered.

Lying upon a miserable bed was the emaciated figure of a man who appeared to be in the last stage of his existence. One of the neighbors was sitting by his side, who retired when Edith appeared, and the messenger, having approached, informed him in a gentle voice that Edith was present.

"Where is she?" said the dying man; "it's very dark, bring her nearer to me. Yes!" he continued, as she drew near, "now leave me with her alone, as I have much to say, and little strength to say it."

The messenger withdrew, and Edith, with some hesitation, leaned her ear close to the mouth of the exhausted man.

He clasped his skinny hands together, and looking earnestly in her face, he exclaimed, "Pardon, pardon! give me pardon for my sins before I confess the whole!"

"What can I pardon, my good man?" said Edith. "God alone can grant forgiveness; but tell me, if it will relieve you, what weighs so heavily upon your mind?"

"Murder!" gasped the wretched man; "it was I that murdered your father!"

Startled with horror, Edith covered her eyes with her hand, and remained speechless.

"Yes," continued the man; "I will tell you all, for I shall not see another day, and I feel that hell awaits me if I die without your pardon. It was Mother Lee who planned the robbery, but I never intended murder. Jack Cain and I were always pals, and drink and dice led us to ruin. Mother Lee found out that the parson kept large sums of money in the house, and she put us up to the robbery. We hadn't had a wreck for a long time, and we were hard up for cash, so we took the job. I saw you and young Ned Grey sitting in the church-yard that evening as we went to lie in wait. It was a Sunday night, and we broke in at the kitchen window. We got the cash, and had packed up the plate, when we heard a noise. 'Don't let

us be nabbed,' said Cain. Just as he said this, the parson
came into the room, with a candle in one hand and a pistol
in the other. 'Shoot him!' said Cain, and I shot the poor
man down, and we escaped without the plate. We got off
through Mother Lee, who threw suspicion upon Paul and
Ned Grey to serve them a bad turn, for she hated them to
death.''

"Wretched man!" said Edith, bitterly; "why did you
not confess this earlier? Paul and Ned are now in prison
on this false charge. Where is your companion, Cain?"

"He was hanged two years ago for another murder, and
left his poor wife to die of starvation. Since that time I
took ill, and have never been well since. My lungs are
gone. I shall never see another sunrise. I feel my end is
close at hand. But I have still more to say," said the
dying man, as he was almost suffocated from exhaustion.

Having rested for a few minutes, he recovered sufficiently
to continue.

"I confessed all this two weeks ago to a magistrate," he
said; "but he's a bad 'un, and worse than I. I mean
Squire Stevens of the Hall," continued the man. "I told
him all, as I knew that I must die, and I didn't wish innocent blood to be shed for me. I knew that Paul and Ned
Grey had been arrested. The squire hates them both, and
he gave me five golden guineas to hold my tongue. There
they are, tied in the corner of that handkerchief beneath
the bed. I had them behind the pillow, but I couldn't get
a wink of sleep since I took them, so I threw them under
the bed. Give them to Paul, or to the poor. Give some
to the woman who looks after me; but beware of the squire,
for the devil isn't blacker than his heart, and he'll ruin
Paul and Ned if he can do it!"

Polly Grey had been a witness to this important confession.

"I'm lighter now," continued the sick man. "Say
that you forgive me, Miss Edith, for I can not die without
shuddering at the future; but if you pardon me, perhaps—
perhaps God may also; but I don't know how to ask him.
I never prayed to Him. I tried the other night, but I
couldn't do it. Pray for me, Miss Edith; for Heaven's
sake, pray! pray! pray quickly, for I'm sinking down,
down through the ground!"

In the fearful excitement of the last troubled hour, the man who had never prayed sought for his neglected God.

"May God forgive you as I do, poor miserable man," said Edith; "but," she continued, "there is much to be done before you die. Your confession is worth nothing unless it is in a proper form; it must be written down."

"Go!" said Edith to Polly Grey, "and tell the coachman to drive quickly to Captain Smart. Tell him to bring paper and ink, and to come himself without losing a moment."

Polly ran from the hut, and arrived breathless at the summit of the cliff. The rattle of the horses' hoofs quickly replied to her message.

A little more than an hour had passed, and Edith looked anxiously at her watch as the man appeared to be fast sinking, and she knew the importance of his dying deposition. At last hurried footsteps were heard without, succeeded by a quick and decided tap upon the door.

"Come in," said Edith, and Joe Smart entered, accompanied by one of the coast-guard.

In a few words, spoken in a whisper, Edith had explained all. Polly shook him affectionately by the hand as they had not met since Paul's return, and without loss of time he wrote down the statement which the dying man feebly but distinctly repeated. The handkerchief, with five guineas tied up in one corner, was found beneath the bed. With much difficulty the sick man, supported by Joe Smart, subscribed his name to the deposition, which was witnessed by Smart and the coast-guardsman, together with Edith and Polly Grey.

"This is all-important," said Captain Smart, "and it will checkmate that villain Stevens. We must be off to Falmouth by day-break to-morrow," he continued; "the Sessions open, you are witnesses, and Paul and Ned will be tried on the following day. This deposition will save them both, and be the ruin of Stevens."

That night Captain Smart accompanied Edith and Polly Grey to the rectory, while the woman who had brought the message attended to the sick man.

On the following morning Mrs. Jones, with Polly, Edith, and Captain Smart, started in the old family coach with four post-horses for Falmouth. As they had to pass Sandy Cove they took various comforts, in the shape of cordials, jellies, and good substantial food, in case the sick man should be still alive.

On arrival at the cliff, Edith- accompanied Joe Smart to the hut, and, to her delight, she found the man was not only not dead, but better than during the previous night; thus, leaving the wine and little luxuries with him, she returned to the carriage and posted rapidly toward Falmouth.

The town was crowded, as the Sessions had commenced, and some difficulty was found in procuring rooms at an hotel. Without a moment's delay Joe Smart went to the prison, accompanied by Polly Grey and Edith, to visit Paul and Ned, against whom a true bill had been found by the Grand Jury, upon which Stevens sat as a magistrate. The good news of the wrecker's confession relieved their minds from all uncertainty, and Joe Smart immediately intrusted the deposition to the counsel for their defense.

The day for the trial arrived, and Joe Smart having obtained seats, Edith and Polly Grey accompanied him to the court, which was much crowded. Paul and Ned were already standing at the bar. Two finer or more manly figures could hardly have been seen than those of the prisoners, who surveyed the crowded court with a simple curiosity and complete indifference until their eyes caught those of their own party. A murmur ran through the court as the people regarded Ned's handsome face and dignified bearing, and loud whispers were heard, "Impossible; he must be innocent!" until silence was enforced by order of the judge. They were both arraigned on the same charge, and in clear and decided tones they pleaded "Not guilty."

The counsel for the prosecution in a short speech explained to the jury the prominent features of the case, dwelling upon the salient facts that Paul and Ned, together with the negro Tim, now dead, had been missing in a mysterious manner on the day following the murder; that Mother Lee had sworn that she had seen them on their way to the village on the ʁ me night that the burglary was committed; and that the sum of two hundred guineas, which was the exact amount stolen from the rectory, had been discovered concealed, with valuable articles of jewelry, in a secret cave within the house of Paul Grey. Both the prisoners had been absent for years, and they had appeared in England within a few weeks of each other, with strange stories that required confirmation. The counsel then called as first witness the widow, Mrs. Jones. Having given her umbrella to Captain Smart until her examination should be concluded, she pushed her way with some difficulty to the witness box, and was duly sworn. She then proceeded to describe the event in the following words:

"I remember the night well. My sainted husband was in bed with me on the right side. He never liked to sleep on the left, poor man, as he said the world turned round from west to east, or from east to west, I'm sure I forget which, but it doesn't much signify. As I was saying he was on my right side, fast asleep. He was a very good sleeper, poor man, but was very quick at hearing a noise in his sleep. Presently he was disturbed, which, of course, awoke me, for I am a very light sleeper, and he said: ' Do you hear a noise, dear?' ' No, darling,' I said, ' I do not; unless it's the cat, that is always upsetting things under the pretense of catching mice ' (in fact I believe, taking them as a whole, that cats do much more damage themselves than the mice and rats); don't you think so, my lord?" continued Mrs. Jones, who now addressed the judge.

"Proceed with your description, madame, in as few words as possible," replied the judge; and Mrs. Jones continued:

"Well, my lord, and ladies, and gentlemen of the jury —I beg your pardon, gentlemen, I forgot there were no ladies on the jury; but why there should not be, I'm sure I can not understand, for ladies are just as—"

Here Mrs. Jones was stopped by the judge, and informed that she must confine herself to the actual description of what took place on the night of the murder.

"Well, my lord and gentlemen of the jury," she continued, "as I said to my dear husband, I think it's the cat; for you know how he broke my large china bowl the other night with his mouse-catching, which I dare say was an excuse for love-making or milk-stealing, for they're deceitful creatures. ' Well,' I said, ' my dear, there's nothing like seeing for one's self, so you had better get up and look if you can see in the dark; but perhaps it would be better to light a candle.' My dear husband then got out of bed and put on his dressing-gown for fear of catching cold, for he was very subject to sore throat; and then taking a pistol (which I was always afraid of, for I think fire-arms are dangerous things, and I think it's a pity that they were ever invented), he said to me, ' My darling, that's not a cat; I hear people in the house—they are thieves!' My dear husband was afraid of nothing, and he begged me to ring the alarm-bell, but I was too frightened to do anything but lie beneath the bed-clothes. Presently I heard a shot fired, and I got out of bed and fainted on the floor. That is all I knew of the affair, my lord, until I saw my poor husband's body." Here Mrs. Jones became deeply affected, and she sent to Captain Smart for her handkerchief, which she had intrusted to his keeping, with her umbrella.

During this rambling description, that was delivered with her usual volubility, the jury had been engaged in an examination of the various trinkets that had been discovered in Paul's house, together with the bag of two hundred guineas.

Edith having been called as a witness, gave her evidence in a plain straightforward manner that excited the admiration of the court. She concluded by declaring her conviction that when her dying father had mentioned the name of Ned Grey, to whom he was much attached, he had intended to give her some advice concerning their intimacy, as the subject that was nearest to his heart, and that he had no intention of connecting his name with the fearful tragedy.

At this stage of the proceedings the counsel for the defense rose suddenly, and holding in his hand the deposition of the sick man, he requested permission to make a few remarks, as, from respect to the court, he could no longer allow the case to proceed without laying this important document before the judge.

" My lord," he continued, " and gentlemen of the jury, I am prepared to prove that the charge against the prisoners is not only false, but that it originated in the conspiracy of a woman named Lee, now dead, which has, I am ashamed to declare, been supported by a man who not only occupies a high social position in this county, but who is himself a magistrate, and at the present moment is a member of the Grand Jury. The document that I hold in my hand, and which I am about to read to the court, to save valuable time and to stay further proceedings, is the actual confession of the true murderer! deposed by him when he imagined himself dying, and witnessed by four persons. It is as follows:

" ' I, Thomas Jackson, a dying man, do positively declare upon my oath, as I hope for pardon for my sins hereafter, that I am the murderer of the Rev. Henry Jones; and that, in company with one John Cain, since hanged for murder, I broke into the rectory of the said Henry Jones, and effected an entrance by forcing the kitchen window. Having stolen in cash a bag containing two hundred guineas, which we took from a writing-desk, we were disturbed while packing up the plate within a blanket by the appearance of the Rev. Henry Jones, who held a pistol in one hand and a lighted candle in the other. Cain cried " Shoot him!" and I fired the pistol which shot him down. We then escaped with the money. The burglary was planned by a woman of Sandy Cove, well known as Mother Lee, since dead. She swore falsely that she met Paul and Ned Grey, together with a negro named Tim, on the road from the rectory on the night of the murder. These persons are perfectly innocent, and knew nothing of the matter; but to save us, and to spite those whom she hated, Mother Lee conspired against them. I feared to die with this load upon my mind, and about fourteen days ago I sent to a magistrate to say that I wished to tell him all about the murder.

" ' Squire Stevens, of Heron Hall, was that magistrate. He came to me, and I told him all. He told me not to be such a fool as to inculpate myself, as I should be merely hanged, but to let the law take its course, as it would be better for me if I saved my neck and let Paul and Ned Grey be hanged instead. He gave me five golden guineas to hold my tongue. I took the guineas, but I couldn't sleep, and got frightened at night when I was alone. I knew the squire was a scoundrel, and I could not wrong Miss Edith by letting her marry such a man without some warning, after having killed her father; so I sent to her to make this confession, and to ask her forgiveness for my crime.—Signed Thomas Jackson, in the presence of Edith Jones, Mary Grey, Joseph Smart, and John Edwards.'

" My lord," continued the counsel, " and gentlemen of the jury, this confession terminates this extraordinary case, and, leaving the prisoners in your hands, I shall call no other witnesses but one. I charge James Stevens with fraudulent conspiracy, for which he shall answer to the laws of his country. Call Thomas Jackson," continued the counsel.

After some little delay, during which Stevens, who was pale as ashes, had endeavored to slip out of court, but had been recalled, a miserable-looking man, who appeared nearly dead, was brought in upon a stretcher, and Thomas Jackson, who had been secured for the occasion by Captain Smart, and conveyed in a carriage from Sandy Cove, repeated the substance of his deposition and pointed out Stevens, to whom he swore personally.

The court was amazed at the confession of the spectral murderer who thus declared his guilt. Paul and Ned Grey shared in the surprise occasioned by his unexpected and cadaverous appearance. The sick man was immediately taken possession of by the police, and the stretcher was raised by four men to be carried out of court. At this moment a violent convulsion seized upon the now really dying man, whose last energies had been expended in the struggle to deliver his confession. With drawn and contracted features he fell back upon the stretcher, and, after a few painful gasps for breath, his body remained in custody of the earthly authorities, but his soul was summoned before a higher judge.

Great excitement was caused in court by this distressing scene; it was hardly quieted when the judge addressed the jury previous to their dismissal. He was a calm, dignified-looking man, of about fifty-five years of age, tall, with handsome features, but shaded with a peculiar cast of sadness. He requested that the trinkets and the bag of guineas should be handed to him for inspection. The diamond necklace and locket, together with the rings, and also the parcel of hair that Polly Grey had saved from the drowned lady, were laid before him, while the counsel for the defense in a few words explained how they had come into the Greys' possession when Ned, as an infant, was washed ashore with the locket round his neck.

The judge examined the trinkets for a few minutes and turned deadly pale. He then touched a spring in the locket, of which Polly had been ignorant; it flew open, and exposed the portrait of an exceedingly handsome man of about thirty in a cavalry uniform: this strongly resembled the judge.

"What is the matter with his lordship? Bring water!" said several voices, as the judge, having opened the parcel that contained the long fair hair, fell back on his seat for the moment overpowered by faintness. Water was quickly brought, and recovering his calmness by a great effort, he looked fixedly at Ned Grey for some minutes in silence; "Edward Grey," he at length said, "retire with the usher to my private room." Ned Grey shortly found himself alone in the judge's private chamber.

Excusing himself for a few minutes on the plea of indisposition, the judge left the court, and entered the room where Ned remained alone. Advancing directly toward him, he seized both his hands, and as he stared intently in his face the tears rolled down his cheeks. Suddenly clasping him in his arms, the judge pressed him fervently to his breast, as he exclaimed in an agony of intense feeling: "My son! my child! cast up by the sea! At last I know your poor mother's fate! this is her own dear hair; the necklace, the rings, all were hers; the locket, with my portrait, I gave her on our wedding-day. She left for England, with you an infant, on the 'Calcutta,' Indiaman; the ship was never heard of; and until now I never knew her fate. You are Edward Neville—not Edward Grey. My own child! my son!"

Ned was bewildered with astonishment. He returned with affection his father's passionate embrace; he could hardly realize the situation. He had already been told that Polly was not his own mother, and he now discovered that the grave upon which he had often sat as a boy, and wondered at the melancholy epitaph, covered the bones of a parent whom he had never known.

CHAPTER XXIII.

STORY OF NED'S PARENTAGE.

CATHERINE NEVILLE, Ned's unfortunate and lovely mother, had been forced by ill-health to leave her husband in India after the birth of her first child, the hero of this story. At that time Sir Charles Neville was a cavalry officer in the East India Company's army, but after the mysterious disappearance of the vessel in which his young wife and child were lost, he had become melancholy, and had given up the army. Returned to England, he entered at the Bar, and distinguished himself by extraordinary ability until he at length became a judge. The early sorrow of his life had made a deep impression upon him from which he had never recovered. He was a man of large fortune, who had inherited the title and estates from his father, who was a baronet in the county of Devonshire; thus Ned, as we must still call him, suddenly found himself a man of both means and position.

The Sessions were over, and Sir Charles Neville now formed one of the party at the rectory of Stoke, as Ned had confided to him his affection for Edith, to whom he could have no possible objection; in fact, he was perfectly delighted with her good qualities, which, in addition to her beauty, brought her as near to perfection as any woman could attain.

Sir Charles Neville's first visit was to the church-yard of Stoke, where he found the simple inscription on the stone cross above his young wife's grave, which he shortly changed, as the mystery of the " lady unknown " had been dispelled. He accompanied Ned to Sandy Cove, where Paul and Polly Grey had already taken possession of the pretty old cottage on the cliff; there he sat upon the terrace wall and listened to the sad story of the wreck, as Polly described that fatal night, and pointed out the spot where she and Paul had discovered his lovely young wife floating drowned upon the surface, with her long fair hair that they had at first mistaken for yellow sea-weed.

Polly Grey then showed him the spot where Ned, as an infant, had been washed on shore, and she omitted nothing in her description of the boy's early life until the time when he had been taken on board the "Sybille."

A few days after he had visited Sandy Cove Paul Grey and Polly received a letter from Sir Charles Neville expressing his warm acknowledgments for all the parental kindness they had shown his son Ned, when friendless and destitute, and informing them that a sum of three thousand pounds was lodged to Paul Grey's credit at the bank in Falmouth, which he trusted would in some measure testify his admiration of their generosity, and render them independent for the remainder of their lives.

This sudden and unexpected wealth hardly compensated Polly Grey for the loss of Ned, whom she loved as her own son, and who now would most probably leave the neigh-

11

borhood of his old home.   Neither could Ned quite enjoy
his new position without a feeling of regret at the startling
change. He had received from Polly the care and affection
of a mother, which he returned as warmly; and he determined that no alteration in his social position should lessen
the filial gratitude that he owed to her.   Delighted that
his father had thus generously provided for his adopted
parents, Ned now longed to make Edith his own without
delay.

In the meantime James Stevens had been arrested on a
charge of conspiracy. He had been liberated upon bail to
appear at the next Sessions, but although freed from arrest,
he was scouted by all who knew him. When he rode
through the village the boys pelted him, and he was insulted continually in the streets; his life was a constant tor-
ment. In spite of his callous nature he had loved Edith
to desperation; he had been scorned by her; she was now
in the arms of his rival, who, no longer the foundling Ned
Grey, was heir to his father's title and estates.   Everything had turned against him.   Edith had returned to him
the horse and dog that he had presented to her. He shot
them both immediately.

But it was not only the world that was against him, it
was the law that he dreaded; he could hardly escape imprisonment for the conspiracy of which he had been guilty.
At all events, he would be forever disgraced.

Thus tormented in mind, Stevens was without a single
friend to whom he could turn for comfort or advice; he
had not even a dog that loved him.   Months passed away;
the day drew near when the Sessions would commence,
and Stevens's bail would expire; he would have to sur-
render himself for trial.

It was a lovely day in spring, as warm as midsummer;
the bright green leaves had clothed the trees with their
new-born foliage; the hawthorn was in full blossom; the
bluebells, and primroses on the banks, and the wild roses
in the hedges, gave a hopeful glow to the scene as Nature
seemed to rejoice that the icy fetters of winter were broken,
and she was once more free to revel in her beauties.   It
was a time when all should have been happy: there was a
peaceful calm in the soft air, broken only by the songs of
the skylark, and other birds that sung joyfully among the
tall trees.   The hens, proud of their young broods, busied

themselves in a search for insects for the newly hatched chickens; goslings, like balls of golden down. floated upon the ponds of the farm-yards; young foals gambooled in the fields, which resounded with the bleating of the now hardy lambs, and the earth had awakened to the command, "Increase and multiply." Could any one be unhappy in such a scene?

It was the morning, and James Stevens walked hastily to and fro on the broad terrace before his mansion that commanded a view of the sea, with the tall spire of the village of Stoke sheltered in the vale about three miles distant. All was beautiful and calm in nature, but there was no peace within his heart. His face was haggard with care, and deep lines already furrowed his features, while a gloomy frown had settled upon his brow. There was a mighty oak upon the lawn, whose gnarled branches cast a shadow far and wide: beneath this tree was a rustic seat. upon which Stevens presently sat for a few minutes, and then rose again in his restless humor.

He started. "Ha!" he said, "the bells! all happy but myself. Death and confusion seize them! They are the Stoke church-bells! He marries her this morning; and I am lost, despised, trampled down, disgraced, and my enemy triumphs!"

Stevens folded his arms, and biting his lips till the blood flowed, he slowly raised his head and looked steadfastly among the branches of the tree.

In the meantime, while his evil spirit held possession of him, and he brooded savagely over his defeat, all was joy and happiness at Stoke. It was the day of Edith's marriage. The church-bells were ringing merrily, and the village people were gayly dressed in their best clothes, while the approach from the rectory to the church was ornamented with triumphal arches of leaves and flowers; the pathway through the church-yard was carpeted and thickly strewn with sweet-scented blossoms, and lined on either side by rows of prettily dressed children, all of whom loved Edith and delighted in the happiness of the day.

Ned was already standing in the church, accompanied by Captain Smart, who acted as bridegroom's man. The noise of many wheels was heard, and the string of carriages approached, as Edith, having alighted, was received with cheers from the assembled throng of village children as she was led by Sir Charles Neville along the flowery pathway. Never had she looked so lovely, and as Ned received her at the altar, before which they knelt together, the blessings of the multitude were expressed in simple but earnest words, "God spare them to live happily together."

Once more the bells pealed merrily as Ned led his bride from the church door, and the children and women showered sweet nosegays before their feet, amid the loud hurrahs of many hundred voices.

"One cheer more," shouted Captain Smart, as with his only remaining hand he waved his cap above his head, and led the "Hip! hip! hip! hurrah!"

"What a nice dear man he is!" said Mrs. Jones to Polly Grey; "how I do love a sailor! What a pity that he does not marry; he would make such a perfect husband! although, by the bye, my dear, with only one arm he would be an *im*perfect husband, certainly, but it's all the same thing in the end. I do so wish Captain Smart would think of marriage."

The happy day was nearly over; the guests were gone, and only Mr. Banks, the clergyman who had officiated, remained. Ned called him on one side.

"My dear sir," said he, "to me this is a day of such true and perfect joy, after all the difficulties and dangers of my life, that I can not rest so long as I have an enemy whom I have not forgiven. There is one whom you know, James Stevens, the squire—who has through life, even from early boyhood, hated me with an uncalled-for intensity, although I would have made him my friend. Act for me as a peace-maker, I pray you. Go to him and tell him from me that I will forget every injury, and I trust that the past may be forgotten on both sides. Say to him that I stretch out my hand, and let him receive it in sincerity."

The good-natured clergyman would hear of no delay, but, happy in the office of peace-maker, he returned home, and mounting his pony, he rode at once to Heron Hall.

The moon was full when he started, and upon his strong black cob he trotted quickly forward.

On arrival at the entrance lodge he had to dismount to open the gate, as the porter and his family were enjoying themselves in the village, where a grand feast for all comers had been prepared by Mrs. Jones. Having passed

DISCOVERY OF THE BODY OF JEM STEVENS.

through, he rode up the long avenue of elm-trees until he arrived at the oak upon the lawn, the branches of which overhung the carriage-drive.

As the moon shone through the trees it cast a horrible shadow upon the ground before the horse's feet; the animal shied, and nearly gave the clergyman a fall. At this moment an owl upon the boughs gave a shrill and wild "too-hoo, too-hoo, too-hoo, too-hoo, too-hoo-o-o-o-o!" The pony startled, turned sharp round, and threw its rider heavily upon the lawn beneath the tree, while it galloped off in the direction of the village.

Mr. Banks, half-stunned and giddy with the fall, rose from the ground. He was not naturally superstitious, but he had an indescribable feeling of something terrible. There was an old swing upon the oak, and the creak of the iron hook now jarred on his ear as the wind swung it to and fro. He started at a shadow on the ground. It looked like a human being suspended by the neck to a naked and withered branch. He looked up, and the first object that met his view was the body of a man hanging from one of the ropes that had formed the swing. The feet were only a yard from the ground.

Without an instant's delay the terrified clergyman rushed frantically to the Hall and rang the door-bell loudly. It was quickly answered. "A ladder and a knife!" cried the clergyman. "Where is the squire?"

"The squire said he was going to Stoke, sir," replied the astonished servant.

"Quick with the knife and ladder! A man has hung himself on the oak-tree!" continued Mr. Banks.

In a few minutes several servants, with a knife and a ladder, had accompanied him to the oak, and the rope being quickly severed, the body was let down.

A cry of horror and surprise was uttered by all present as they recognized the swollen and discolored features of James Stevens.

*　　*　　*　　*　　*　　*　　*

Nearly two years had passed away since that fatal night. The rectory once more resounded with the shouts of merry boys, as Mr. Banks had married Mrs. Jones, and kept a school. She had comforted herself with the idea that "a minister of the Gospel was a more godly man than a sailor, not that sailors were ungodly, as St. Paul was a sailor, or very nearly one; it didn't matter which, so long as he went to sea; but the hearts of ministers of the Gospel were not so hard as those of sailors, as they were not so much exposed to the wind and weather. Captain Smart had been very much exposed. It was a very great pity, for he was a perfect specimen of a British sailor—that is to say, he would have been if he hadn't lost an arm; but a minister of the Gospel, with a tender heart and two arms, was certainly a more perfect husband than a British sailor with a tough heart and only one arm." Thus Mrs. Jones comforted herself with her own peculiar logic.

The cottage on the cliff at Sandy Cove had been much beautified and refurnished. There was a large porch, fitted with seats, and shaded with woodbine and sweet clematis; here Paul Grey delighted to sit with his still handsome wife, and smoke his pipe on a long summer evening, and talk over old times as he looked upon the sea. It was then that the well-known step was often heard, and Joe Smart appeared as in days of old; and the two friends, who loved each other like twin brothers, would chat over the adventurous deeds of their youth, while Polly knitted and listened untiringly to their oft-repeated tales. There was a pretty smart-looking lugger anchored in the bay, much resembling the old "Polly," and christened with her name. Now that Ned Grey was gone, this vessel was Paul's only child. Often would he cruise with his old friend Joe Smart (for he had long given up all dealings in contraband), and he delighted to point out to the revenue officer the places where he had run a cargo, and tell how the old "Polly" had dodged the government cruisers and laughed at their fastest cutters.

"Ah, those were good old times!" Paul would exclaim, as he laughed at his friend Smart. "The old 'Polly' was a saucy boat that was too sharp even for a certain Captain Smart of his majesty's coast-guard."

Whatever the good qualities and questionable virtues of the old "Polly" might have been, Paul's new lugger bore an unblemished reputation.

Ned and Edith lived happily with Sir Charles Neville at Elmley Court, his seat in Devon, whence they sometimes went to visit the cottage at Sandy Cove, to the great delight of Paul and Polly Grey.

It was a lovely day in August, the anniversary of that

when Ned as an infant had been washed on shore. He and Edith were expected at the cove. The carriage-wheels were heard upon the cliff, and Polly rushed out upon the terrace to meet her anxiously awaited guests.

Edith had a treasure that she longed to exhibit to her old friend Polly Grey. It was her first child, a boy about four months old; she had christened it Edward Grey Neville.

Descending the zigzag path with the child in her arms, wrapped in a warm shawl, Edith followed Ned, and then ascending from the little village by the steep footway, she arrived on the terrace in front of the old cottage.

After the first loving greeting, Polly, who considered herself the grandmother of Ned's child, hastily withdrew the shawl from the face of the lovely infant and took it in her arms. Gently kissing its sleeping face, she regarded it attentively for some moments, and exclaimed, " Three-and-twenty years have passed away this very day, and they seem but as yesterday! Here is the child! the same in face and age as that little Ned Grey that I pressed to my breast and nursed as my own—a blessing from God to my childless home—a son cast up by the sea!"

THE END.